**Praise for *New York Times*
bestselling author Linda Goodnight**

"*In the Spirit of…Christmas* joyfully portrays the
true spirit of the holiday season…. The ultimate
result is heartwarming."
—*RT Book Reviews*

"Linda Goodnight does her protagonists justice
with her sensitive writing in *A Season for Grace*."
—*RT Book Reviews*

"*The Heart of Grace*, by Linda Goodnight, is
a wonderfully poignant story with excellent
character development."
—*RT Book Reviews*

"From its sad, touching beginning to an equally
moving conclusion, *A Touch of Grace* will keep you
riveted."
—*RT Book Reviews*

New York Times Bestselling Author

LINDA GOODNIGHT

Sugarplum Homecoming

&

The Lawman's Honor

⬥ **HARLEQUIN®** LOVE INSPIRED®CLASSICS

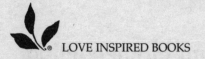

LOVE INSPIRED BOOKS

Recycling programs
for this product may
not exist in your area.

ISBN-13: 978-1-335-00672-1

Sugarplum Homecoming & The Lawman's Honor

Copyright © 2018 by Harlequin Books S.A.

The publisher acknowledges the copyright holders
of the individual works as follows:

Sugarplum Homecoming
Copyright © 2013 by Linda Goodnight

The Lawman's Honor
Copyright © 2014 by Linda Goodnight

CONTENTS

Linda Goodnight, a *New York Times* bestselling author and winner of a RITA® Award in inspirational fiction, has appeared on the Christian bestseller lists. Her novels have been translated into more than a dozen languages. Active in orphan ministry, Linda enjoys writing fiction that carries a message of hope in a sometimes dark world. She and her husband live in Oklahoma. Visit her website, lindagoodnight.com, for more information.

Books by Linda Goodnight

Love Inspired

The Buchanons

Cowboy Under the Mistletoe
The Christmas Family
Lone Star Dad
Lone Star Bachelor

Whisper Falls

Rancher's Refuge
Baby in His Arms
Sugarplum Homecoming
The Lawman's Honor

Redemption River

Finding Her Way Home
The Wedding Garden
A Place to Belong
The Christmas Child
The Last Bridge Home

Visit the Author Profile page at Harlequin.com for more titles.

SUGARPLUM HOMECOMING

Let he who is without sin cast the first stone.
—*John* 8:7

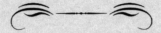

The Whisper Falls series is dedicated in memory of my brother, Stan Case. I miss you, bro.

Prologue

"Come *on,* Nathan," nine-year-old Paige whispered with urgency. "Hurry before Daddy wakes up."

Nathan cast a worried eye toward his father sprawled on a blanket beneath a tree, hands behind his head. The remnants of an early autumn picnic were strewn about the quiet glade deep in the Ozark Mountains. "We're going to get in trouble."

Paige fisted a hand on one slight hip. "Do you want a mom or not?"

Nathan's gray gaze went from his dad to the twenty-foot-high waterfall only yards away. "Well, yeah, but Whisper Falls is kind of big and scary."

Impatiently, Paige tugged on her little brother's arm. He could be such a baby sometimes. "You can do it, brother. God will help you."

Paige knew her brother well. Give him a challenge, tell him God was in it, and he would give everything he had. Which wasn't much considering how little he was.

As she expected, Nathan thrust out his dinosaur T-shirt and trotted toward the waterfall. The noise from the water tumbling over the mountainside *was* really loud but not that scary to Paige. Daddy had brought them here before. They loved Whisper Falls. They loved wading in the pool below, beyond the foam and current, where even now three teenagers splashed and yelled.

But fun wasn't Paige's mission today. She'd thought up the picnic as an excuse to get here, to do the one thing she was certain would bring her their heart's desire. To pray. Everybody said it was true. The story was in the brochures all over town. Anyone brave enough to reach the secret place behind the falls would get their prayer answered. And Paige had decided the time was now.

With her pointed chin as determined as her brother's, Paige jogged toward Whisper Falls. Nathan tagged along, a little reluctant but willing. Like her, he was ready to do anything to get a mom.

They reached the slippery gray rock face and started the climb. Natural cleaves in the mountainside offered a foothold but over the years so many people had made the climb that the path was well worn. If they clung tight, like the slugs Joel Snider brought to fourth grade for show-and-tell, they'd make it all the way up to God's special place.

"Why do we have to pray up *here?*" Nathan asked, his face wrinkled with worry as he crept along in front of her, small hands gripping the rocks. If Daddy caught them, they'd have to do more than pray to get out of trouble.

Paige grunted as she took another handhold and waited for her brother to inch forward. The waterfall grew louder by the second, so she raised her voice. "I told you already. We're on a mission. Like in the movies when that guy had to bring back the ring to save the world. We have to prove ourselves worthy of a new mom."

"Oh."

She hoped that satisfied him for now because she was getting out of breath trying to talk and climb. Climbing was harder than she'd imagined. Harder than the sixth graders said. Maybe none of them had really climbed the falls at all.

"We're almost there," she huffed.

Paige glanced down and wished she hadn't. Daddy looked tiny, like a Ken doll, and the pool looked huge and bubbly. Spray dampened her skin. The smells of trees and leaves and water swirled like the pool below. One of the teenagers saw her and pointed.

Please, please, don't let him tell.

She gave a casual nod, hoping the teen believed she wasn't nearly as scared as she was. When she turned back toward the climb, Nathan was gone!

Panic seized her. Her hands were cold and wet, but she climbed faster, praying that the stories were true, that a secret room existed behind the waterfall, that Nathan hadn't fallen to his death.

She stretched her leg as far as her muscles would go, felt a foothold with the toe of her tennis shoe and lunged…and found herself standing on a wide ledge behind a terrifying rush of water. There was Nathan grinning at her.

"This is way cool."

Paige heaved a shaky sigh. "Let's pray and get out of here fast."

"I like it up here." He stuck his fingers into the violent spray of water *whooshing* in front of them.

Paige grabbed his hand and pushed him back. She

had to get him out of here before he did something childish. Like fall off the mountain. "Never mind about that. Close your eyes and think about Jesus and a new mom."

"But—"

"Do it, Nathan. Dad might wake up any minute."

This was enough to get his attention. He nodded and clasped his hands beneath his chin. "Okay. Do we want a mom with blond hair or brown hair?"

"Silly, I don't care about that kind of stuff. I want a mom who reads to us and tucks us in and bakes cupcakes for school parties."

"Daddy does that. Well, except for the cupcakes. He gets those at the bakery."

"That's not the point. We need a mom. Dad can't even fix my hair." She slapped at the side of her super short cut, the only kind of hairstyle Daddy could manage. She was nearly ten, for goodness' sake. Most of all she longed for a mother to love. Sometimes her heart hurt so bad at night when she prayed that she thought it might burst right out of her chest.

"I want a mom with brown hair," Nathan said stubbornly. "Our other mom had brown hair."

Paige smothered a sigh. She loved her brother a great big lot but sometimes he didn't understand what was really important. Not the way she did. "Then pray for a mom with brown hair. I don't care. Just pray."

With all the reverence she'd been taught in Sunday school and children's church since the day she was born, Paige folded her hands beneath her chin.

"Dear God, we need a mom. Daddy needs a wife. He's been sad long enough and Aunt Jenny says it's time for him to move on. Please send us a mother. Before Christmas would be nice."

"With brown hair."

Paige opened one eye. Nathan didn't even remember their mother. He'd only seen pictures. Like the one at Daddy's bedside. A piece of her heart felt really sad for him about that. "Yes, God, if it's not too much to ask, send a great mom with brown hair. And make her pretty so Daddy will like her, too. Amen."

"Amen."

"Now, let's get out of here before Daddy wakes up."

"How do we get down?"

Oh, boy, she'd not considered that part.

"Nathan! Paige! Where are you?" Daddy's voice came as a faint but worried echo through the silver curtain of water.

Nathan turned accusing eyes on his sister. "We are in so much trouble."

Chapter One

Bad pennies always return. But what about bad people?

Lana Ross stepped up on the wooden porch of the weathered old two-story house. Her heart hammered painfully against her ribs. She'd not wanted to come to this place of bad memories. She'd had to.

A stern inner voice, the voice of hard-won peace, moved her forward, toward the door, toward the interior. A house couldn't hurt her. If she'd been alone perhaps she would have given in to the shaky knees and returned to the car. But she wasn't alone.

Lana aimed a wink at the child at her side. Sydney was her everything now and no memories were allowed to keep this nine-year-old darling from having her very first permanent home.

"Is this where you lived when you were my age?" Sydney asked, her vivid turquoise eyes alive with interest.

"Uh-huh, Tess and I grew up here." Grew up. Yanked up. Kicked out.

A tangle of a vanilla-scented vine, overgrown and

climbing upon the porch and around the paint-peeled pillar at one end, gave off a powerfully sweet smell. She didn't remember the bush being there before, especially this late in the fall. But then, she'd not seen this place in thirteen years. Not since she was eighteen and free to leave without looking over her shoulder for the long arm of the law.

With the sour taste of yesterday in her throat, Lana inserted the tarnished key into the front door, an old-time lock a person could peer through, and after a few tries felt the tumbler click. Breath held, she pushed the door open on its creaky hinges, but didn't step inside. Not yet. She needed a minute to be certain the house was empty, though she had the death certificate in her bag. Mama was dead. Had been for a couple of years. As far as she knew her entire family was dead. All except Lana and Tess and precious Sydney.

She couldn't make herself go inside. Everything was still and quiet in the dim living room, but inside her head Lana heard the yells, the fights, the horrible names she'd believed and mostly earned.

She and her twin sister, Tess, were no more and no less than what their mother had made them. Now, all these years later, Lana was determined to be more for Sydney's sake.

"We'll be happy here," Sydney declared with child-like confidence.

"Yes, we will." *If I have to fight the universe, you will have what you need and you will never, ever again live on the streets or inside a broken-down car.*

"Can we go in now? I want to see my room. You said I could have my own room, remember? And we'd fix it up fit for a princess? Remember?"

"I remember." The child's enthusiasm stirred Lana to action. Sydney had never had a room of her own. She'd never had a house. They'd lived here and there, in tiny one-room apartments and cheap hotels, all in pursuit of Lana's impossible dream. Most important of all, Sydney would be safe here. No one would ever expect Lana to return to the one place she'd tried so hard to escape. Especially Sydney's mother.

"Who's that?" Sydney asked from her spot half in and half out of what had once been the front parlor.

Across the street a man and two children stood in a neatly mowed yard watching them. Lana's stomach dropped into her resoled cowboy boots. It couldn't be. Surely not.

The thought had no more than crossed her mind than the sandy-brown haired man with the all-American good looks lifted a hand to wave and then started toward them. Two young children, close to Sydney's age, skipped along as if on an adventure.

Lana froze, one hand on the doorknob and the other gripping Sydney's as if Davis Turner would snatch her up and carry her away.

"Hello," he said when he reached the end of the cracked sidewalk leading to the two-story.

Yep. He was Davis Turner all right. Mr. Clean-cut and Righteous. He'd been a year ahead of her in school. No one in Whisper Falls had a smile as wide, as easy and as bright as Davis.

Please God, don't let him recognize me.

"Hi," she said, not bothering to smile.

"You moving into the old Ross place?" Davis slipped his hands into the back pocket of his jeans, relaxed and easy in his skin. The man was much like the boy she remembered.

"We are."

"Great." He flashed that smile again. White straight teeth, easy, flexible skin that had weathered nicely, leaving happy spokes around grayish-blue eyes and along his cheeks. "The house has been empty a long time. Houses need people to keep them young and healthy."

What an interesting thing to say. This house had never been healthy *because* of the people in it. "I suppose."

"We live across the street in the beige brick with the black shutters. I'm Davis Turner and these are my munchkins, Paige and Nathan."

Lana released a tiny inner sigh of relief. Davis didn't recognize her, though sooner or later he'd discover he lived too close to the town bad girl. Would the people of Whisper Falls still remember? Did she dare hope that time had erased her teenage indiscretions from inquiring minds?

Not a chance.

"I'm ten. Well, almost," the young girl at Davis's side announced. "Nathan's barely eight. I'm the oldest. What's your name?"

"This is Sydney," Lana said, purposely providing Sydney's name instead of hers. She couldn't avoid the introduction forever, but she wanted to buy some time before Davis's bright smile withered and he turned on his heels, dragging his children in a rush to lock his doors and keep them away. "She's also nine, just barely."

Sydney hung back, aqua eyes cautious. She was too shy, too hesitant with others, something Lana hoped would disappear once they were settled. Her niece needed friends badly and Lana prayed her prior reputation in this close-knit mountain community wouldn't interfere with Sydney's happiness.

"Say hello, Sydney."

Sydney ducked her head, displaying the precise part in her super curly brown hair. "Hello."

"Are you gonna live here?" the little boy, Nathan asked.

"We are."

"Just the two of you?" With the same blue-gray eyes, brown hair and square jaw of his father, Nathan was handsome. Unlike his father, he sported a dimple in one cheek.

"That's the plan," Lana answered.

"Are you married?"

Paige elbowed her brother. "Shh."

"But Paige, we have to know," Nathan protested. "She has brown hair!"

The adults exchanged glances and smiled. Davis appeared as clueless about the comment as Lana. What did her hair color have to do with anything, especially marriage?

Paige, an elfin beauty, simple and pure with pale brown freckles and ultrashort blond hair, attempted to explain. "What he means, ma'am, is that we're glad to meet you and we'd like to get better acquainted. Isn't that right, Daddy?"

Davis turned his twinkly smile on Lana again, clearly amused by his children. "Always glad to welcome new neighbors. I didn't get your name."

The jig was up. She'd prayed to get settled before her tainted past charged in with all guns blazing. Apparently, God, Who'd brought her this far, expected her to face her fears head-on.

It was now or never. Either Davis remembered or he didn't. Time to find out.

Chin up, eyes meeting his, she said, "I'm Lana Ross. You and I attended high school together."

Davis blinked rapidly, off balance. This was Lana Ross? The wild child from high school? The girl with the bad attitude and potty mouth who was rumored to do about anything with anyone?

"I thought you looked familiar." But different, too. The hard-eyed teenager who'd run off to seek fame and fortune in Nashville looked softer as an adult. Lana had always been pretty, but the softer look made her beautiful. Long, brown hair waving past her shoulders, dark mink eyebrows above clear eyes the color of the Tuscan blue tile he'd installed in a recent boutique remodel, cowboy boots over skinny jeans and an off-shoulder blouse on a petite form.

Pretty. Real pretty.

Davis was disturbed to feel a pull of interest.

Considering the welfare of his children, he wasn't even sure he wanted Lana Ross for a neighbor. He certainly didn't want to be attracted to her.

His conscience dinged, a sign the Lord was knocking on his door. *Let you without sin cast the first stone.*

Right. He agreed. He was no better than anyone else. But what about his kids? He was a firm believer in the old adage, "If you run with the wolves, you'll begin to howl." As a single father, he struggled to find exactly the right parenting balance, but he certainly didn't intend to have howling children.

"Daddy." Nathan tugged at his sleeve. "Can we go inside? Can we explore the haunted house?"

Lana arched an eyebrow at him. A little embarrassed, Davis said, "Sorry about that. You know how kids are. The house has been empty such a long time…."

"And it *is* spooky looking, Daddy," Paige said, eyes widening. "I looked in the windows before and didn't see no headless horsemen or creepy monsters, but Jaley says they only come out at night."

Jaley was Paige's best friend, a child with a vividly overactive imagination. He could, however, understand why the house had gained a reputation. Peeling paint, sagging doors and filthy dormer windows that looked out like empty eyes through faded black shutters were creepy enough, but the overgrown bushes and vines and the sheer loneliness lent an air of doom to the place. More than one shaky teenager had been caught climbing in through a window on a dare.

But Paige's comments had scared Lana's little girl. Small like Lana with kinky curly beige hair, Sydney had stiffened, growing paler with each spooky word. She clung to Lana as if she was now afraid to go inside the house.

Davis put a hand on his daughter's shoulder and squeezed, the signal he used in church to get her to stop talking. Paige hushed, shoulders slouching as her bottom lip protruded. She'd gotten the message.

"The house is not haunted," he said firmly. "I told you that. Houses get lonely. All this one needs is a family." And an enormous amount of work.

"Now it has one," Lana declared, relief in her husky voice, though she tugged Sydney closer to her jean-clad thigh and soothed the child with a pat on the back.

"She'll need some fixing up," Davis said. "You know how some teenagers are when they know a house sets empty."

He'd caught a few of them himself, usually on nights with a full moon or late in autumn just before Halloween when wind and dry, rustling leaves permeated the atmosphere.

Lana blanched, eyes widening as she swiveled her head toward the peeling paint and loose siding and then back to him. "The house has been vandalized?"

Hadn't the woman considered the possibility?

"I haven't been inside in a couple of years, since before your mother passed, but things had run down even then." He didn't say the obvious. Patricia Ross had two daughters and neither had come home to help their ailing mother. He couldn't imagine being that coldhearted against your own kin. But then, Lana and Tess Ross hadn't been the usual girls. Patricia's brother had come from Nevada to bury her.

"Vandals," Lana murmured, looking as if the weight of the house was on her shoulders. "Wonder what that will cost to repair?"

Regardless of his doubts about her, Davis's natural compassion kicked in. He could help her out. He had the expertise. He *was* her neighbor. He fought the urge, but kindness won out in the end. Might as well give in to it now and save wrestling with his conscience later.

"I could take a look around the place if you want and give you a rough estimate." That was all he planned. Just a quick walk-through.

"You do that sort of thing?"

The warm autumn wind lifted a lock of her hair and swirled it around until she had a spiderweb of brown matted on top of her head. She brushed at the nest, making it worse. He found the look charming and vulnerable. Davis was a sucker for vulnerable.

Tough-as-nails Lana Ross, vulnerable?

"I can," he said. "Mostly, I lay tile but I've flipped a house or two. I can do a little of everything when the situation calls for it." His face relaxed in a self-mocking grin. "In tile work, especially around here, the situation almost always calls for it. If I redo a shower, the floor beneath is inevitably rotten. Tile a floor? Bad joists."

For the first time since his arrival, Lana's pretty mouth curved. Just a little. "A true renaissance man?"

"Nowhere near that interesting, but I do know my way around a construction site."

Renaissance man. Huh. Funny. Except when he had a trowel or a hammer in hand, he was as boring as vanilla pudding. Didn't his sister remind him of that fact at least once a month? Jenny was forever trying to get him out into the world again. The dating world.

"Thanks for the offer, Davis," Lana was saying, "but I guess we need to get settled in first and then figure out where to go from there."

"Got it. Good plan." She was blowing him off, rejecting his offer. Even though disappointment made his smile droop, Davis knew he should be glad about her refusal. He'd have no obligation now, no guilty conscience for not being neighborly to a woman and her daughter living alone.

Which brought him to another subject: Where was Sydney's father?

As soon as the question settled in like good grouting mud, another followed. She'd never addressed Nathan's oddball question about being married, and she and Sydney were moving in without any sign of a man. Recalling Lana's teenage years, Davis thought the chances were very good the two were alone.

Chapter Two

"He was nice," Sydney said.

Lana absently stroked a hand over Sydney's frizzy hair as they stood on the top porch step—the only porch step—and watched Davis Turner and his kids recross the quiet residential street. A vanilla breeze danced around their feet, tossing leaves and dirt over their shoes and into a growing pile against the siding.

Davis *was* nice, but she'd seen the shock in his eyes and felt the temperature drop when she'd told him her name. He remembered.

Nothing she hadn't expected but still the reaction stung. She'd changed, thank God, the day she'd stumbled into a Nashville street mission drunk as a skunk after getting turned down for an important gig at the Opry. She hadn't known it then, but both had been her last chance. She'd never sung in public again, but she'd found the Lord and started on a new path.

Lana looked at Sydney, her throat aching with love and guilt. "Maybe you can be friends with Paige and Nathan."

Dear Lord, don't make Sydney pay any more for

Tess's or my mistakes. Let this work. *Make* it work for her sake.

"Will Paige be in my class at school?"

"Probably. Maybe. I don't know. We'll have to ask. Come on, let's get the car unloaded." She thumped the flat of her palm against the center pillar in a show of energy she didn't feel. They still hadn't worked up the nerve to go inside the forlorn two-story, but they were here and they would stay. Regardless. Somehow she and Sydney would turn this dreary old relic into a real home, clearing out one room and one old ghost at a time.

"Nathan was nice, too," Sydney said. She reached her skinny arms into the backseat of the old Ford and dragged out a cardboard box. "He said I could swing on his swing set sometime."

"He did?" Lana had not even noticed the children talking, probably because she'd been too focused on their handsome father. Boy, did she ever remember *him!*

"Uh-huh. He did. So, can I?"

"We'll see."

"Paige said they have a dog. Can we get a dog?"

"I don't think so." When she saw Sydney's expression, Lana hurried to say, "Maybe later after we're well settled."

Sydney shoved the box onto the grass with a grunt. "Am I staying at this school forever?"

"Poor baby." Lana squatted for a hug. Sydney had changed schools frequently enough to develop reading difficulties. Lana was determined to remedy that problem this year. Stability was the answer, even if it meant living in this awful house. "We're going to try."

Sydney rested her hands on Lana's shoulders, face

close. She had the most beautiful olive skin and turquoise eyes.

"You're not going to sing no more? Never?"

The loss was still as sharp as a hot stick in the eye. Music was the only thing Lana had ever been good at, though like everything else, not good enough. "No, baby. I have a real job now."

"Oh, yeah. I forgot." Sydney screwed up her face, feathery dark eyebrows drawing together over her nose. "What was it?"

"I'll be working for the Whisper Falls newspaper." She popped the lid on the trunk. Their pitiful possessions were stuffed into two cardboard boxes and a couple of battered suitcases. "I'll have press passes which means we'll get to go to lots of fun events for free. Football games, carnivals, plays, all kinds of things."

"Cool."

Actually, she was a stringer covering local events for the small paper. The pay was minimal but it was money. Along with the amount her mother left behind—unintentionally, Lana was certain—they should be all right for a while. That is if she could figure out how to write an acceptable article. School hadn't exactly been her thing, but like singing she could always write. She'd written lots of songs, none of which had been picked up, of course.

Joshua Kendle, the newspaperman on the other end of the telephone, had promised on-the-job training and hired her sight unseen, so how hard could the reporter job be?

Desperate times meant desperate measures. She would personally hand deliver every paper in town—or live in this house—to give Sydney a normal, stable life.

Sydney, slender back bent in half, began pushing a cardboard box across the grass.

"Hold on and I'll help you." Lana slammed the trunk of the dependable old Focus with one hand while balancing yet another box on her hip. Though she mourned the loss of her pickup truck, the Focus had been more economical and more sensible.

"I can do it by myself."

Box on one hip, Lana grabbed the smaller of the suitcases and rolled it, bumping along behind Sydney as she crossed the dry brown grassy distance from the cracked driveway to the porch. Times like these she could use a man around to help out.

Her thoughts shifted again to Davis Turner. She'd had a mild crush on him in high school though he'd never known it. He was an upperclassman, the boy everyone liked because, unlike his sister Jenny, he didn't have a snarky bone in his body. She wondered if he was still that way.

Time hadn't damaged his appeal. That was for certain. If anything, maturity had made him more attractive. Very Matt Damon-ish, and hadn't she always had a crush on the fresh-faced actor?

Lana shook her head in disgust. Men had been her downfall one too many times. Now that she had Sydney to consider and she no longer drank, she wasn't going down that road again.

Arms full and Sydney nowhere in sight, she kicked the storm door with her boot toe and caught it on the first bounce, thrusting it open with the rolling luggage. The door swung out and back quicker than she'd expected, catching her in the backside and knocking her off balance. The cardboard box tumbled from her arms, spilling its contents. In a juggle to stop her fall, Lana caught her boot on a loose piece of threshold and hit her knee against the suitcase. The rollers spun the bag in front of her, entangled her feet, and down she went.

Dusty carpet came up to kiss her. The musty odor of disuse and grime tickled her nostrils. Inside her childhood home for the first time in thirteen years and here she was sprawled flat on her face. With her underwear spread all over the floor.

Lips twisting wryly, Lana lifted her head and looked around. Crude red graffiti scrawled across the wall directly in front of her. She glanced to the right and then to the left. More graffiti. She shuddered and buried her face in the crook of her arm, breathing deep the lonely, musty smells. The buoyant hope that had propelled her four hundred miles scuttled away with the sound of whatever vermin roamed her childhood home. For the first time since the idea struck, Lana questioned her decision to bring Sydney to this house.

Maybe she should have let Davis have a look around after all.

Davis slid a pan of lasagna from the oven with a fat maroon oven mitt. The warm oregano scent filled his modern kitchen. He set the casserole dish on an iron trivet, careful to protect the gleaming black granite countertops he'd installed himself. If there was anything Davis enjoyed, it was transforming the looks of a room with tile and granite.

"Come and eat!" he called and was gratified to hear the scramble for the remote as one of the kids shut off the Wii game. "Red velvet cake for dessert."

Thank the good Lord for a sister who occasionally

took pity on him and sent over dessert. He'd learned the basics of cooking but baking was out of his league. Jenny said a trained monkey could learn to follow instructions on the back of a cake box. Which Davis figured disproved the theory of evolution once and for all since he, a human, couldn't successfully manage the task.

"Did you wash your hands?" he asked when Nathan, forehead sweaty from the active boxing game, plopped into his chair at one side of the polished ash table.

Fingers stretched wide, Nathan held his palms up for inspection. "See? All clean. They smell good, too. Want to sniff?"

Davis scuffed his son's hair, affection welling in his chest." Good enough for me, bud. Who wants to pray?"

"I will," Paige said, her face suddenly radiant as if transfigured by the idea of talking to God.

That was his daughter. She had an ethereal faith, disconcerting at times when she offered to pray for total strangers. "All right. Go for it."

They bowed their heads. Davis kept one eye open, trained on Nathan who had a habit of sneaking food into his mouth during prayer. Today, he was as pious as his sister.

"And Jesus, thank you for sending us new neighbors," Paige was saying. "Bless them and I hope they have plenty to eat, too, just like we do. Do you think they like red velvet cake? Amen."

Frowning, Davis turned his gaze on his daughter. Her sweet prayers never failed to move and impress him, but today he suspected an ulterior motive. "What was that about?"

"Well." With studied innocence that he didn't buy for

one second, she took a slice of buttery garlic bread from
the offered plate. "The Bible says to love our neighbor. Right?"

Davis looked down at the lasagna dish, suddenly
uncomfortable. He suspected where this was headed.
"Right."

"Lana and Sydney are moving in that old haunted
house. They might not have any groceries in the fridge
yet. They might not even have peanut butter and jelly
sandwiches!"

"Or Popsicles," Nathan said. To Nathan, a Popsicle
was one of life's necessities.

"A house without a Popsicle is a sad house indeed,"
Davis said, amused. He dolloped ranch dressing onto
his salad and forked a bite.

"Anyway, Daddy," Paige said. "I was thinking. We
want to love our neighbors and invite them to church
and everything, right?" She jammed a glob of lasagna
into her mouth while awaiting his reply.

Davis skirted the issue momentarily. "Nathan, put
some salad on your plate."

Nathan's square shoulders slumped, a picture of de-
jection. "Aw, Daddy."

"Nonnegotiable. No salad, no cake."

Nathan reached for the salad.

Paige put down her fork. "Daddy, are you listening
to me?"

"Sure, princess. What is it?"

"Are we going to take some lasagna and cake over
to Lana and Sydney?"

Davis eyed the long casserole. They'd barely made
a dent in the cheesy dish.

"I don't know, Paige. They might be busy getting settled." Lana had said those very words. They needed time.

"Everybody has to eat."

"She's pretty, isn't she, Daddy?" This from Nathan who was clearly avoiding the three tomatoes lined up like British redcoats on the edge of his plate.

"Who?"

"Lana. I think she's real pretty. Her hair is pretty, too. I like brown hair."

Davis swallowed. The forkful of noodles stuck in his throat. He grabbed for his water and swigged.

Yes, Lana was pretty. She and her sassy boots had been prancing around in his head the entire time he was cooking supper. He was curious about her, wondered why she'd left her life in Nashville and what secrets lurked behind her cool blue eyes. He wasn't sure he wanted answers, but he wondered.

He'd taught his kids to do the right thing, to treat people the way they would want to be treated, and that included greeting new neighbors. He was head of the neighborhood welcome community and co-chair of block parties and summer cookouts. Might as well find out early if Lana Ross and her child were people he wanted his children associating with.

"After dinner, if you kids will help clean the kitchen without grumbling, we'll take a couple of plates down the block. How does that sound?"

"You are the best daddy ever," Paige said.

"Yeah," Nathan added, nodding sagely. "Everything is going exactly like we planned."

"Nathan!" Paige shot him a paralyzing look and

shook her head. Nathan clapped both hands over his mouth.

Davis looked from one child to the other, puzzled. What was that all about?

Chapter Three

Beware of really handsome men bearing gifts.

These random thoughts ran through Lana's head as she tried to find a clean place in her filthy, run-down, pathetic kitchen to put two foil-covered plates.

Davis Turner was every bit as nice as she remembered. He'd brought food. Something she had not yet bothered to think about. Her stomach rumbled at the spicy, warm smells coming from the dishes. When was the last time she'd eaten anything healthy, much less homemade lasagna? She'd fed Sydney burgers and breakfast burritos on the road but had been too uptight to eat since yesterday.

"Sorry everything is a mess. The house is worse than I'd expected." A lot, *lot* worse. Apparently, Mother had let the place go and the years of sitting empty had taken a worse toll.

"You've got your work cut out."

"Don't I know it? I didn't expect it to be this bad." She grimaced. "Or to have graffiti on the living room walls."

"Is the living room the only place that bad?"

"Seems to be. I guess vandals haven't gotten much farther than the front of the house. Hopefully, a good cleaning will make a big difference."

"What about the holes?"

"Not sure yet. Put something over them, I guess. Sydney and I decided sleeping quarters were number one, so we started on her bedroom first. We can camp there for a while." She didn't add that she'd camped in worse.

The three kids bumped around inside the small kitchen. Pixielike Paige, the oldest and clearly the leader, said, "Sydney wants to show us the upstairs. Can we go?"

"Lana may not want a bunch of kids traipsing through her house."

Lana gave a wry laugh. "Nothing they can hurt. Let them go."

At a wave of Davis's hand, the three kids took off in a rush, pounding up the wooden steps. Sydney was eager to share her room, such as it was, and Lana suspected the other two wanted to explore the "haunted house." She didn't hold it against them. She'd have done the same thing as a kid.

"Are the stairs secure?" Davis glanced toward the front of the house, though the entry stairwell was invisible from here. The kitchen was an add-on to the 1910 dwelling and as such, ran lengthwise across the back of the house where it met with the back porch. Long, narrow and inconveniently arranged, the kitchen could use some serious modernizing. Someday.

"We've been up and down quite a few times and I've not noticed any loose boards or weak areas."

"Good. Stairs can be an issue in older homes."

"These are sturdy oak, I think. Anyway, that's what I remember." Not that she'd paid much attention to the house other than her attempts to get out of it as often as possible.

"The place appears to have good bones. Old houses usually have better construction materials than newer ones unless there's dry rot."

"I hope that's true in this case." She shoved a bundle of old newspapers, yellowed with age, off a bar stool and onto the floor. "Have a seat?" she asked, not altogether sure he'd want to.

"Sure." To her relief he didn't seem all that bothered by the dirt and grime. Truth was she'd lived in worse. So had Sydney, bless her sweet, accepting soul. At least here in Whisper Falls they had a roof over their heads that no one could take away. Eventually, things under that roof would be clean and tidy and hopefully, free of the past.

"I'm glad you came over. Really glad," she started, twisting her hands on the back rung of a wooden chair. She was still amazed he'd returned after learning her identity. "I've been thinking about you." Her face heated. "I meant I was reconsidering your offer."

During the past few hours of bagging trash and scrubbing, she'd thought about Davis Turner. Beyond the fact that her skin sizzled when he'd smiled and her blood had hummed when she'd opened the door and found him standing there again. She wasn't too happy about *noticing* him so much, but she did need his help.

"I could use your expertise. I have a little money put aside. Not a lot but enough to address the most important needs of the house." She bunched her shoulders, aware of the knot forming at the base of her neck. She'd have a doozy of a muscle spasm if she wasn't careful. "Other than covering the holes in some of the walls, I don't know what those are."

"I can look around, make a list, give you some advice if you think that would help."

"Would you?"

"Sure. No problem. Got a pencil and paper handy?"

"Now?"

"No time like the present. That is, if now works for you."

"Of course. Thank you. Now is perfect." If she could find a piece of paper.

Feet pounded on the floor above their heads. Both adults raised their eyes toward the ceiling.

Lana was poignantly aware of the oddity of having Davis Turner in her house. He wouldn't have been caught dead here as a teenager. He'd been a Christian, raised in church, the boy teachers and parents put on a pedestal as the way all teens should behave.

Lana Ross had been his antithesis.

"What are they doing?" Lana asked.

"Don't know but that floor is solid or we'd be covered in ceiling plaster." He flashed that smile, lighting up the dim room.

The man had a killer smile. And two kids. It suddenly occurred to her that he'd never mentioned a wife. But then, half the world was divorced. She supposed he was, too, or his wife would have accompanied him on this neighborly expedition.

Lana rummaged around in the kitchen drawers, not surprised to find a dusty pad and a scattering of stubby, round-point pencils. Mother had always kept them there.

Davis took the writing materials and rose. He was

considerably taller than her, even in her high-heeled boots, and filled the narrow kitchen with his masculine presence. Her awareness factor elevated. Above the kitchen's dust and must, he smelled of men's spice— just the faintest whiff but enough for her foolish female nose to enjoy.

Focus on the mission. Think of Sydney.

Even if she hadn't had a date in two years, Davis Turner was way out of her league.

They started through the house talking about the structure and basic needs, as well as noting cosmetic needs. After a bit, the kids came thundering down the stairs, a breathless chattering group that made Lana's heart glad. Sydney's happy face said it all. She'd made friends. Being back in this awful house just got easier.

"Can we go out in the backyard?" Paige asked. "Sydney said there was a cellar."

The cellar. Like a giant vacuum, the word sucked the pleasure from the room. "Stay out of that cellar."

Her sharp tone stopped the children in their happy tracks. "Why?" Nathan's eyes widened. "Is it haunted?"

Lana rubbed her suddenly cold arms. She hated that cellar, hated the darkness, the damp musty odor and the creepy crawlies inside. "I haven't cleaned it yet. Spiders, snakes, who knows what could be in there?"

"Eww. I don't like spiders." Paige shivered. "Can we go outside and play in the yard? Sydney said there's an apple tree."

Lana nodded. "Go on. Have fun but watch out for anything broken or dangerous. I haven't explored out there yet."

"Okay."

With youthful energy, voices excited, the trio zipped

out the back door, leaving it standing open, spilling the sunshine and cool, clean air of Indian summer inside. Lana didn't bother to close it. She wanted to keep a watch on Sydney. Airing the house while the weather was favorable wasn't a bad thing either.

"Your children are really sweet."

"Thanks, so is yours. They're great kids, though they can be a handful at times. Paige has, shall we say, ideas that sometimes lead her and her brother into trouble."

Lana didn't bother to correct his mistake. It was better for everyone if he and the town assumed Sydney was her child. "But Paige seems like such a nice little girl."

"She is. I don't mean that." He hunkered down to look up into the fireplace. "Don't light this until it's been inspected and cleaned."

"Okay. I heard noises up there. Probably birds."

"Or bats," he said with male matter-of-factness.

Lana crossed her arms as she gave the fireplace an uncertain look. "You would have to mention bats."

"Bats won't hurt you."

"Remind me you said that when I'm in traction with a broken leg from running out of the room."

He laughed at her, the corners of his eyes crinkling upward. "Tough Lana Ross afraid of a bat?"

He had no idea what he was talking about. She'd never been tough. She'd only pretended to be. "Don't tell Sydney, okay? She thinks I'm fearless."

He dusted his hands together. Dust motes danced in the sunlight streaming in from the window next to the big, old-fashioned brick fireplace. "My kids are the same. Nathan told one of his buddies I could pick up a house."

"So what happened? Did the kid come over and ask for proof?"

"Naturally."

"What did you do?"

"What else could I do?" His hands thrust out to each side. "I picked up the house."

The silliness made her laugh. This was the Davis she remembered. Self-effacing, warm, kind to anyone. Even her. "Be glad he didn't go for the 'my dad can beat up your dad scenario.'"

"I remember saying that when I was in elementary school."

"Like father like son?"

"Absolutely. But Paige is the same. Between the two of them, they slay me sometimes." He leaned the note-pad against the fireplace brick and scribbled something on the paper. "A few weeks ago, the kids and I went up to Whisper Falls on a picnic. I made the mistake of falling asleep."

"What happened? Did they tie you to a tree? Douse you with water? Cover you with mayo?"

"Nothing that simple for those two. They climbed Whisper Falls."

"No way!" Lana glanced out the grimy window at the two Turner children running across the thick brown grass. Whisper Falls was a long, slippery climb, especially for two small children. She should know. She'd climbed it plenty, usually on some stupid dare or when she'd had too much beer to be walking, much less climbing. "Why would they do that?"

"Paige says they went up there to pray. I suppose you've heard the rumor about praying behind the falls."

"The moment I hit town, but it must be a new thing. No one said that when I lived here before. What started it?"

"I'm not sure. Some say Digger and Evelyn Parsons made up the story. Others say they've actually had prayers answered after going up there. Someone got the city council on board and they changed the name of the town to match the waterfall. Next thing we knew, tourists started making pilgrimages up the mountain."

"Do you believe it's true?" Because if it was, she was climbing those falls again. This time without a party— and stone cold sober.

"A rumor of that caliber is good PR, but I don't think God needs a waterfall to answer prayers, do you?"

So, he was still a Christian.

"I agree, but maybe your daughter doesn't."

"Paige." He huffed out a sound that was half frustration and half affection. "My daughter's faith is kind of hard to explain. Sometimes she's scary in the mature things she says about God. Other times she's a goofy kid, like that day. My heart stopped when I looked up and saw Nathan clinging like a spider monkey to the side of the mountain."

"What did you do?"

"What else could I do? I climbed up after them. Once we were on the ground, I hugged them, told them how scared I was and how much I loved them. Then I grounded them both from TV for a full week."

Lana laughed. "You are a cruel father."

"They thought so." He stuck the stubby pencil in his shirt pocket and started across the room. His long legs ate up the floor, even though the parlor was large. "All the while, Nathan kept saying the oddest things."

Lana followed his lead, taking a left down a dim hallway. "Such as?"

"Nothing specific. Random things about brown hair." He tapped on the paneling, made a note of loose trim and a cracked light fixture.

"Sydney once asked me to dye her hair green, but that was for a costume party." Lana opened the door to the downstairs bathroom, a small space with an old claw-foot tub.

"Nice." Davis ran a hand along the rounded edge. He didn't seem to mind that it was filthy. "Do you know what these sell for in today's market?"

"If it's more than a new one, this one is for sale."

"Seriously?"

"I've had old stuff all my life, Davis. All these antique fixtures can go for all I care."

"I'll check around. You might be able to make some money. Lots of people like authentic vintage."

The idea heartened her. She and Sydney would make it here. She would find a way to turn this house into a home.

"Tell me about yourself, Lana," he said, tapping the wall above the bathroom sink with his knuckles. "What happened to your singing career in Nashville?"

"You knew I lived there?"

"This is Whisper Falls. We hear everything. Usually, about five minutes after it happens."

He was right, and the memory of a small, gossipy town was not a comfort. People would remember her teen years. People would gossip. All she could do was pray the talk didn't harm Sydney. There would be enough speculation about her as it was.

"So what about Nashville?" He leaned forward to

inspect the hot water tank. Other than being coated in dust and cobwebs, it worked. She knew that already.

"The usual, I guess. I thought I was a better singer than I am. But I had some great experiences." Some lousy ones, too. "I sang for my supper, met some famous stars." Usually at the hotel where she'd cleaned rooms, though she'd once encountered Faith Hill and Tim McGraw coming out of Banana Republic with their kids.

"I remember when you and your sister used to sing the national anthem at the football games. You were good. Where's Tess living now?"

That was anyone's guess. Under a bridge. In a crack house. But hopefully, in the same mission that had brought Lana to Christ. "She's still in Nashville."

The conversation was beginning to take an uncomfortable turn. Lana didn't want to discuss Tess or Nashville for that matter.

"You've lived a glamorous life. Why come back to Whisper Falls?"

Glamorous? "Time to settle down. Sydney needs to be settled in one place, one school, and the music industry is not always a stable lifestyle. Anyway, it wasn't for me."

"I get that. My kids are everything. I'd walk on fire for them."

"Or climb Whisper Falls?" Lana asked, surprised at the easy joke.

"Exactly."

He opened the vanity cabinet. A dead mouse smell rushed out.

"Eww." Lana grabbed her nose and backed out of the small space into the hallway. Davis, more resourceful, leaned over the tub to shove open a tiny window. Fresh air, spurred by the breeze, swirled inside, but the stench remained. Outside, an overgrown pine scraped against the screen, dropping pine needles without enough scent to matter.

Davis followed her out into the hall, pulling the door behind him. "Let that air a while."

"Good idea. Maybe for a year."

"If you've got a plastic bag, I'll see if I can find and remove the source."

In the narrow hallway, they were crowded. If either moved more than a few inches they would be touching. Rather, she'd be touching that work-muscled chest of his. A man who carried boxes of tile and grouting mud had to be strong.

"You'd do that?"

Davis didn't seem to notice her discomfiture. He tilted his head, looking down at her while she looked up. "I work in remodels. You wouldn't believe some of the things I find behind walls and under old cabinets."

She squeezed her eyes shut and shivered in pretend horror, though the ploy was more to get her mind off him than true repugnance. "I don't think I want to know."

After he had dispatched the mouse carcass, for which she would forever be grateful, they made their way on through the house. Lana watched in dismay as his list of repairs grew longer and longer.

By the time they'd worked the way back to the kitchen, the kids came flying through the back door, faces red and sweaty.

"We're thirsty," Sydney said. "I wish we had some pop."

"Sorry, peanut. Water will have to do. It's all we have."

None of the trio looked all that thrilled with ordinary water but Lana scrubbed three glasses and filled them. They gulped it down and wiped hands across their faces.

Nathan, who was too cute for words, plunked his empty glass on the counter. Cheeks as red as a slap, he looked from Lana to Davis and said, "This is nice."

Paige grabbed his arm. "Let's go, Nathan."

"Why? I want to see if Daddy and Lana are having fun, too."

The little boy's comment amused and touched her, too. He was having fun. He wanted his daddy to have a good time, too.

"Nathan," Paige said urgently. "Let God do the work." She put her fingers to her lips and twisted in the classic gesture of turning a key in a lock. Whatever the boy was about to say, his sister wanted him to be quiet.

Nathan opened his mouth as if to protest but then closed it again. "Okay."

"Last one to the apple tree is a monkey's uncle," Paige said. And away they flew.

Lana cocked her head. "I wonder what that was all about."

"With those two, don't even ask."

"I think they're enjoying themselves," she said. *Thank you, Lord.* Seeing Sydney carefree made the sacrifice of coming back to this town worth it.

"I wouldn't mind a glass of that water myself." Davis stuck his hands beneath the faucet and scrubbed. "I can wash my own glass."

"I'll do it."

"Too late." He stuck a glass beneath the spray and scrubbed. Then he filled and drank. With his hips leaning against the sink, he faced her. She could see he had something on his mind.

"Am I crazy for trying to live in this run-down old house?" she asked. "Is that what you're about to say?"

"What? No. Most of this is cosmetic." He waved a hand around in the air. "Structure is sound, plumbing is old but sturdy. Electrical box looks fairly new. Lots of work and a fair expenditure of money but livable."

Lana drew a deep breath through her nose. The knot in her neck eased. As much as she wanted to do this on her own, she couldn't. If she was alone, she wouldn't care where she lived. But Sydney mattered. "You're hired."

"Don't rush into anything. I'm pretty booked up right now with the holidays on the horizon, but I'll run some figures for you, work up an estimate, talk to other contractors. Then we'll need to talk budget."

"Small." She eased into a chair. "I want to do most of the work myself, but some of these things…" She shrugged.

"There you go, then. Start there. Take this list." He handed her the tablet. "Figure out what you want to do yourself. Then sub out the rest to the experts. I can give you a list of those, too."

"You've been a lot of help."

"That's what neighbors do."

Neighbors? Really? Then where had they been years ago when she and Tess had needed them?

Chapter Four

The next evening after a long, fruitful day of work, Davis hurried up the sidewalk to his sister's home to collect his children. Jenny had been, quite literally, a godsend after Cheryl's death. A homeschooling, stay-at-home mom married to an accountant, she lived on the opposite side of town from Davis, which in Whisper Falls wasn't that far. Located in a newer addition along the bluff overlooking the Blackberry River, the speckled brick house had an aboveground pool in the backyard, closed now for the season, and a massive play fort that kept his kids enthralled for hours.

He let himself inside his sister's house which always smelled of candle scents and looked freshly polished. Every piece of furniture, every flower arrangement and picture was pristine. He marveled at how well Jenny managed with his kids and hers, including a son with health challenges, and two cocker spaniels.

"Anybody home?" he called, his usual announcement, and one that started the dogs barking.

"Daddy!" a joyful voice squealed. In seconds, Nathan came racing into the living room, a red superhero cape flying out behind him. He leaped into Davis's arms and wrapped his legs around his daddy's waist.

The weary workday melted away in the warm, exuberant little-boy hug from his son. His baby. The child he'd made with a woman he loved. He thanked God every day for his kids. They'd kept him sane when he'd wanted to curl into a ball and let go of life.

Though sometimes he still ached from the lonely spot Cheryl had left behind, he was a content man. Breathing deep, he held his son close to his chest, not caring that he was dirty and stained with grout. Life didn't get any better than the love of his sweet little boy and girl.

Jenny came around the dining room divider, smiling as she wiped her hands on a dish towel. Blonde and almost as tall as he, his sister had continued to gain weight after twin boys were born seven years ago. He thought she looked okay, but Jenny worried about being fat and was on some kind of crazy diet more often than not.

"You look bushed," she said. "Want to sit a while and have some tea?"

Davis shook his head. "Thanks, but no. Laundry to do tonight."

"You got a minute then? I want to ask you about something."

"Sure." He shifted, repositioning Nathan onto his hip. The boy's legs were starting to dangle like octopus tentacles, a sign he would soon be too big to leap into his daddy's embrace. Davis wasn't ready for that. "What's up?"

"The kids told me Lana Ross has moved back into her family's old house."

"True."

"They also said you'd been over to see her. Twice."

He could see his sister was not happy about his friendliness. Never one to keep her opinions to herself, if Jenny had something to say, she'd say it. Sometimes that propensity was a good thing, but not always.

"True, as well. Being neighborly." He unwound Nathan's arms and let him slide to the floor. "Go get your sister, bud. We gotta go."

Jenny waited until Nathan skidded around the corner, spaniels in nail-tapping pursuit, before continuing. "Is Lana planning to stay in Whisper Falls?"

"I didn't ask her, but she's remodeling the Ross house. I figure that's a sign she's here for good."

"You're not going to get involved with *that,* are you?"

Her tone raised bristles on the back of his neck. "I might. Why?"

"Davis, don't you remember Lana Ross at all? What she was? How she was always in trouble, always doing the worst possible things? Surely, you aren't going to let your children associate with a woman like her."

Davis sucked in a chest full of air and tilted back on his boot heels. Jenny was protective of him and his kids, especially since Cheryl's death. Besides, hadn't he thought the same things about Lana?

"Come on, Jen, that was years ago. Teenagers do crazy things but they grow up."

"Maybe. But where has she been all this time? What has she been doing? Why would she come back here where everyone knows about her?"

"Maybe because she owns a house here?" he said with a hint of sarcasm, hands up and out. "I don't know."

"Don't risk your children to find out. Stay clear of her, Davis. She's a bad influence."

"Sis. Come on. Chill out. This is not like you. Lana

is new in town. Even though she was born here, she's been gone for years. She's in my neighborhood."

"Which does not mean you have to associate with her. You have plenty of friends." She put a hand on his arm in a gesture of concern, her eyes worried. "Keep a nice, safe distance. That's all I'm asking."

"Too late for that. Nathan and Paige like her and her little girl. They're already begging to have Sydney to the house for a sleepover."

Jenny's head dropped backward as she gave an exasperated sigh. "That's another thing. Lana has a child. I'll bet you anything she isn't married. If she's like she was in high school, she probably doesn't even know who the father is."

Davis's jaw tightened. He loved his sister and appreciated her help, but she was taking this too far. In a deceptively quiet voice, he said, "Passing judgment, are we, sis?"

Jenny's chin went up. Her nostrils flared below pale eyes that arced fire. "Not in the least. Protecting our loved ones from harm is a Christian responsibility. Remember what Dad used to tell us about running with the wrong people? The Bible even warns against 'casting your pearls before swine.'"

"Wait a minute. Stop right there." She was starting to get under his skin. "Are you calling Lana a swine? You don't even know her."

"But I *remember* her. We had more than one run-in during high school." Jenny twisted the towel as if wringing Lana's neck. Or his. "I love your kids. I don't want them exposed to alcohol and drugs and Lord only knows what else. Do you want them to have a reputation like those awful Ross sisters?"

"They're in grade school, for crying out loud! Come on, Jenny. You're being ridiculous."

And she was making him uncomfortable. Hadn't he struggled with these same, ugly thoughts yesterday? Yet, Lana and her little girl gave no sign of being anything but decent people. Even if they weren't, didn't God expect him to show grace and charity?

But he wanted to protect his children, too.

While brother and sister stared each other down and Davis wrestled with his thoughts, Nathan and Paige entered the room, followed by seven-year-old twins Charlie and Kent. The boys were apple-cheeked replicas of their dark-skinned father, though Charlie was smaller and wore a pallor lacking in his healthier sibling. Born with a heart defect, he'd had surgery soon after birth but he still took medication and had never been quite as vigorous as Kent. His condition was the main reason Jenny homeschooled. A valve replacement was in his near future, a fact that stressed the whole family, especially Jenny. Because of Charlie's uncertain health, Davis felt for his sister, but she could make him crazy, too.

"Ready?" Davis asked, grateful for the interruption to the contentious conversation. He was a peacemaker. Arguments made him miserable. Besides, his sister had enough on her plate. He didn't want to add to her worries by fighting over a woman neither of them knew that well.

But he was also a grown man, capable of making his own decisions and caring for his children. He didn't need his baby sister's dire warnings.

"Can we go see Sydney when we get home?" Nathan asked, presenting a cupcake smashed inside a Ziploc bag. "I saved her half of my cupcake."

Jenny hissed, her glare burning a hole into her brother. "See?"

Davis ignored her. "That was really thoughtful of you, son."

"Paige saved *all* of hers for Lana." Nathan nodded sagely. "She has brown hair."

"My cupcake! I almost forgot." Paige clapped a hand against her forehead. "Wait a minute, Daddy, while I go get it."

His little girl hurried out of the room.

Jenny rolled her eyes at Davis. "Nathan has mentioned brown hair several times today. He even drew a picture of a woman with brown hair. What is *that* about?"

Davis shrugged. "Couldn't say. Why don't you ask him?" He dropped a hand on his son's shoulder. "What's the deal, Lucille? Why are you suddenly obsessed with brown hair?"

"Because," Nathan said, his voice exasperated as if Davis should understand. "Me and Paige prayed. God is going to send us a new mom with brown hair."

"What?" Davis exchanged stunned glances with his sister. This did not sound good.

"Don't you see, Daddy?" Nathan stretched his small arms wide, the smashed cupcake dangling in its bag. "After we prayed, Lana moved into the haunted house. Get it?"

A slow dawning broke through Davis's thoughts. "Was that why you climbed up Whisper Falls? To pray for a new mom with brown hair?"

Nathan slapped a hand over his mouth. "I wasn't supposed to tell. Paige says we have to let God do the work. We're just His helpers."

Davis squeezed the small shoulder in a gesture of comfort.

The kids had prayed. Lana Ross had moved in. She was single—and she had brown hair.

Naturally, their wild imaginations would take over and assume Lana was God's answer.

He raised his eyes from his son's dejected body to his sister's face.

"This is already getting out of hand, Davis."

He dragged a hand down his face and felt the rough dryness of tile glue still stuck to his fingers. "No kidding."

Jenny touched his arm. "Promise me you'll be careful, okay? You know what she is even if they don't. These kids have been hurt enough."

Davis's belly took a nosedive.

How could he argue with that?

Lana drove through the quiet, lazy town of Whisper Falls—past the train depot in the center town circle, past the Tress and Tan Salon, Jessup's Pharmacy, Aunt Annie's Antiques, and nearly drooled at the delights in the window of the Sweets and Eats candy store. The town didn't look as tired and run-down as it had when she'd left, when it had been Millerville.

"Look, Lana." Sydney, on the passenger side of the car, whipped her head toward Lana, eyes widened. "Sorry. I meant Mom."

Though Lana had been Sydney's primary caregiver most of her life, she'd never usurped Tess's title as Mom. Until now.

"You understand why it's important that everyone believe you're my daughter, don't you, peanut?"

Sydney nodded. "So I don't have to go to foster care."

"That's the gist of the matter. But if you slip up and say my name instead, we'll just pretend that's the way we do things. Okay?"

Pretending—or more accurately, lying—bothered Lana. She'd promised the Lord to change her bad habits but shading the truth was for Sydney's protection. Surely, God would agree the end justified the means when a child's well-being was on the line. Wouldn't He?

Sydney nodded though her expression was worried. "I remember what happened in Nashville when that woman came to school and asked me all those questions about you and Mama and where we lived. I was real scared. I thought I might never see you again."

Lana reached across the console to pat her niece's knee, taking note that Sydney didn't worry about the loss of her birth mother. She worried about losing the aunt who'd raised her. "I know, baby. That's why we're here now. Nobody is going to take you away. Not ever."

"You won't let them, will you?"

"No." *Not as long as I have breath in my body and legs that can run.*

Because of Tess's constant run-ins with the law, the child protective agency had investigated Sydney's living situation. The interview at school had been a warning to Lana that she might lose Sydney if she didn't take action. So she had. With her own less-than-stellar background, she feared social services would reject her as well as Tess—the reasons she and Sydney had come to Whisper Falls, the one place Lana had never wanted to see again.

"I didn't mean to tell my teacher about living in the

car. It just kind of slipped out when she asked about making a fire escape plan for our house."

"It's okay. You're safe. We're going to have a good, good life in Whisper Falls." No matter what it takes.

"Are we having Christmas here?"

"Christmas?" Lana said, laughing softly. "We're barely into November."

"But look." Sydney's nail-gnawed fingertip pecked against the passenger window.

City workers high on the "cherry picker" lifts normally used to change streetlights, strung Christmas decorations across the short five-block main street. Christmas. She was always amazed how quickly the holiday arrived once October slipped away. With Thanksgiving on the horizon, Christmas, and winter, would be upon them before she could get the house in shape.

Unless she enlisted considerable assistance.

Her thoughts flashed to Davis Turner. He'd actually made her feel welcome as if her ugly reputation wasn't dancing around inside his head. As if she would be accepted in her old hometown.

He'd given her hope.

With Sydney jabbering about Christmas and wondering if Paige would be in her class at school, Lana drove through town, turning down a side street and into a residential area that led to the school. A long, low, red-brick complex of buildings and facilities, the school had grown considerably since her days of skipping class to smoke in the gym locker room.

But Jesus had wiped her slate clean. All she had to do was convince the rest of the world she'd changed.

Tall order.

She parked the car and went inside the elementary school, holding Sydney's hand. Lana's own palm sweated, though the temperature wasn't overly warm as they stepped through the door marked Principal. Memories flashed. Detentions, threats, suspensions. Her own smirks and bad attitude. Not in this particular office, but in others like it.

Lord, she'd been a nightmare.

"May I help you?"

The woman behind the reception desk looked familiar. Lana glanced at the nameplate. *Wendy Begley.*

Choosing her words carefully, Lana said, "My little girl needs to enroll in third grade."

Wendy turned her attention to Sydney with a smile. "What's your name, honey?"

"Sydney Ross, ma'am. Are you the principal?"

"No, honey. The principal is up in the high school right now. I'm the secretary." Her eyes lifted to Lana. "I thought I recognized you. Lana Ross, right? Or is it Tess?"

"Lana."

"I don't know if you remember me. I was a few years behind you in school but I remember you and your sister, the infamous Ross girls." She gave a soft chuckle that held no rancor. "I used to be Wendy Westerfeld. Married Doug Begley. You remember him, don't you? His daddy owned the car wash. We have it now that Gordon retired."

"Oh, yes, of course." Lana did her best to appear bland and polite but inwardly she cringed. She remembered Doug all right. He'd been a party to a few of her self-destructive moments. "Do we need to fill out some paperwork to get Sydney enrolled?"

"Do you have her records from the other school?"

"Uh, no. We, uh, I—homeschooled her. We moved around a lot with my job." *Liar, liar. Forgive me, God.* "I have her shot record and birth certificate, though."

Before the other woman could inquire more deeply, Lana handed over the records.

Wendy took the documents to a file cabinet where she extracted a folder and a packet of papers. "Here is the enrollment packet. The paperwork is lengthy so you can take the whole packet home if you'd like and send it back with Sydney tomorrow."

Lana accepted the thick stack, thankful for the re-laxed manner of a small-town school. Trusting and nice, and oh, she wanted to be worthy of both those things. "Sounds good. Thank you."

"All I need today is this top form of contact info, emergency numbers, that kind of thing. Will she be riding the bus?"

"We live in town. I'll drive her."

Wendy made a notation on the form. "Cafeteria or bringing her lunch?"

"Cafeteria for now. How much money does she need?"

Wendy named the amount and Lana paid for the week, relieved that the enrollment was going so well. She held her breath while the secretary made a copy of Sydney's birth certificate without so much as a glance at the parent's name and slid the copy into a folder.

One hurdle down.

Afterward, Wendy walked them down a long hallway decorated in happy primary colors and motivational bulletin boards to one of the third-grade classrooms to meet Sydney's new teacher.

With a final hug, Sydney hitched her Hello Kitty backpack and disappeared into the classroom. As the frosty-haired teacher closed the door, Wendy said, "Mrs. Pierce is a wonderful veteran teacher. Sydney will love her class."

"She's kind of shy."

"She'll be fine."

Lana's boot heels tapped against the white tile floor as they headed back toward the office. "You have children?"

"Four of the little boogers. Two, six, eight and ten." Wendy laughed. "That adorable two-year-old snuck up on us."

Lana laughed, too, relieved and grateful to Wendy Begley for her easy, welcoming demeanor. The school had chosen their secretary well.

She was beginning to think her return to Whisper Falls would not be as difficult as she'd imagined when another woman stepped into the office.

"Here's our principal now," Wendy said as she regained her desk chair. "Ms. Chester, do you remember Lana Ross? She just enrolled her daughter in third grade."

"Lana," the woman said coolly, slowly turning on black, shiny pumps, her suit the color of eggplant and her eyes as frosty as January. "How…interesting to see you again. What brings you back to this dull little mountain town?"

Lana's confidence, buoyed first by Davis's kindness and then Wendy's, now wilted like a daisy in the snow. She barely remembered this woman but clearly she'd been judged and found wanting.

The trouble was, she couldn't argue. She was as guilty as charged.

Lana left the school feeling lower than a snake's belly. Her fingers itched for her guitar and a chance to let the music melt away the disquiet in her chest. But she couldn't today. Today she had her first face-to-face meeting with her new boss, Joshua Kendle.

She drove to the newspaper office, past more of the quaint, picturesque mountain town she'd once wanted to escape. Even now, the need to run pressed in. Sometimes she was ashamed because the desire to get dog drunk and escape her problems almost overwhelmed her. Only the thought of how far she'd come, of how much God had done for her, and of Sydney, kept her straight and sober.

As she parked at an angle in front of the newspaper office, her hands trembled against the steering wheel. She took out her phone and punched in the speed dial number to Amber, her counselor at the mission in Nashville. After a brief conversation and prayer, she stepped out of the car with renewed courage. She'd come too far to turn back now.

Assailed by the scent of bacon, she spotted Marvin's diner, a familiar old haunt tucked in between the dry cleaners and an antique shop across the street from the *Gazette,* and smiled. Not everything in Whisper Falls had been bad. She could do this.

Head up, shoulders back, she marched through the half-windowed door into the *Gazette.* Immediately, the wonderful bacon smell gave way to printer's ink and old-fashioned type set that harkened to days gone by. The *Gazette,* it seemed, had yet to enter the full digital age.

"Morning. May I help you?" A short, potbellied man with sleeves rolled back on thick arms and wearing a backward baseball cap rounded a counter. He was probably in his early forties.

"I have an appointment with Joshua Kendle."

"You must be Lana." He scraped a hand down the leg of his faded jeans. "I'm Joshua. Welcome. You ready to get to work?"

Her shoulders relaxed at his affable warmth. "Ready. What do I do first?"

"Come meet the rest of the staff and then I'll show you the ropes." He took her through the back where several cubicles were set up with computers and introduced her to the small group of employees, including his wife, a heavyset blonde with big hair and a gold print scarf. "Hannah is the brains of the outfit. She handles the classifieds and subscriptions."

As Lana met the others, she relaxed more. No one here seemed to remember the awful Ross girls, or if they did, they didn't care.

After the introductions, Joshua led the way to his desk crammed inside a tiny, messy office and got down to business, explaining Lana's duties and her pay-per-article salary. "Hannah gathers an events list from the schools, churches, civic groups, and posts it on the computer and out front on the bulletin board. You can access it yourself from home if you want. Attend as many of them as you can, write up a report, email it to me. I'll edit and proof and let you know if I have questions. Pick up your check every other Friday."

"That sounds too easy." Even if she hadn't written a full page of anything other than songs in years.

"You grew up in Whisper Falls, right?"

How did he know that? He wasn't a native. "Except it was Millerville back then."

"Your local knowledge should come in handy." Joshua didn't appear to be in a rush, but he moved and spoke quickly as if always on a deadline. Which in fact, he probably was. "This job will put you in contact with practically everyone in town at some point. It is a great way for you to get reacquainted."

She'd considered that, although she hadn't seen it as an advantage. Joshua might know she was a Whisper Falls native but apparently he knew little else. Thank goodness.

"You got a camera?"

"Only an old used one. The pictures are pretty good."

"That'll work. Simon is our staff photographer but he can't be everywhere. I use photos from anyone who'll send them in, so if you see something picture-worthy, take a shot, add a caption and email it to me. I'll go from there. If I use it, you get paid."

Awesome. "Okay."

"Good." He dug around in the mess of papers on his desk and pulled out a sheet. "Here you go. Friday night. Football play-offs. Give the kids a good write-up, mention lots of names so we can keep the mamas and daddies buying newspapers."

She wanted to ask how she was supposed to know who was who but held back. She needed this job. Any show of uncertainty on her part could kill the deal before she had a chance.

"I need the article by Saturday morning to make the Sunday edition. Can you do it?"

The offer, like the man, came fast and immediate. She hadn't been as ready as she'd let on. She'd planned to take some time and study back editions of the *Gazette,* to check out library books on writing.

But Joshua was waiting for her answer now.

She stuck her phone in her back pocket and tossed

her hair with a fake smile. "Sure. First thing Saturday morning."

She'd write that article if she had to sit up all Friday night to do it.

Chapter Five

As Davis stood in the tool aisle at the Whisper Falls Hardware Store, he faced a dilemma. He was there buying a blade for his tile saw, a frequent expense, but he'd noticed Lana Ross leaving the store with two buckets of paint right after he'd arrived. Since the day he'd made a repair list inside her old two-story, he'd been thinking of his promise to help. He'd also been troubled by his sister's warning against getting too friendly with his new neighbor, especially since Nathan and Paige had some wild idea about matchmaking between him and Lana.

Brown hair. Good grief.

"That you, Turner?"

Davis swiveled to look at the newcomer, Pete Abernathy, a burly frame carpenter. They'd played football together in high school and frequently crossed paths in the construction business. "How you doing, Pete?"

"Good. Did you just see what I saw?"

"What was that?"

"Lana Ross. I heard she was back, but who would guess she'd look that good. Man! Eye candy." Pete smacked his tongue against his teeth, tsking. "You live close to the old Ross place, don't you? Did she move back in there?"

Irritation, like a gnat around the nose, buzzed along Davis's nerves endings. "Yep."

"I bet things are hopping around your neighborhood now."

"Not that I've noticed. She's a quiet neighbor."

"No way. Luscious Lana and her twin quiet? They were party central."

"That was a long time ago, Pete." His defense of Lana was starting to sound like an instant replay. And he wasn't even sure he was right. "So far, no parties. Just a lot of work on that run-down house."

"I heard she's single. No boyfriend. No husband. That true?"

"As far as I know."

"A shame. A woman like that alone. Figure she could use some *expert advice* from a willing man?" His tone indicated he wasn't discussing the Ross house.

Davis turned a cool gaze on the man. "Does your wife know you talk that way about other women?"

"Loosen up, dude. I didn't mean nothing by it. People talk. She's got a kid. I figured she's still a party girl." Flushing red, Pete yanked a saw blade from the rack and stalked away.

Davis watched him storm off, saw him muttering to the checker and suspected either he or Lana was the likely topic of conversation. With a sigh, he reached for an extra blade and headed to the checkout himself.

It didn't seem right that people would assume the worst about anyone, especially a woman they hadn't seen since the teen years. Sure, she'd been wild and crazy, but so had a lot of kids back then. Lana and Tess were known as the ringleaders, the party girls, always looking for trouble, but they never had to look far. There were plenty ready to run with them. Davis leaned toward a different crowd and had kept his nose clean for a couple of reasons. He'd been a Christian or had tried to be. He sure hadn't been perfect, but he'd wanted a scholarship. He hadn't gotten it and after a semester of barely making ends meet at college, he had ended up joining his dad's tile business. Much as the rejection had hurt when he was eighteen, he was content with his life today. For the most part.

On the drive to Jenny's to pick up the kids and then all the way home, he fumed over the conversation with Pete. For all he knew, Pete was right about Lana, and if people were already talking, her reintroduction to Whisper Falls might prove bumpy.

None of which was Sydney's fault. The little girl had crossed the street yesterday and invited his kids to play. She was a pretty thing, with bright eyes the color of the Hawaiian ocean and a sweet, gentle smile. He'd refused her request, using homework as an excuse.

He stole a glance in the rearview mirror at the kids in the backseat, heads together, focused on a handheld video game. Electronic zings and zaps mingled with their happy giggles. How would he feel if the neighbors snubbed them?

He was letting the opinions of others determine his actions when, in truth, Lana and Sydney had given him no reason to avoid them.

He was as big a jerk as Pete Abernathy.

As he turned down Dogwood Street into his neighborhood, he spotted the woman occupying his thoughts.

His chest clenched. He ran a hand down the front of his T-shirt, pushing at the uncomfortable feeling.

In a pair of old jeans with one knee torn out and the hems frayed above white tennis shoes, Lana was standing on a ladder sweeping leaves from the gutters. One end of the gutter hung loose. A mishmash of building supplies was scattered on the porch.

Instead of turning toward his house, he pulled into Lana's driveway and got out. Both his kids hopped out, chattering like chipmunks.

When the car doors slammed, Lana turned her head. The brown hair that mesmerized his son was pulled back in a tail and held with a skinny red headband.

"Looks like you've got gutter problems," he called. Not exactly scintillating conversation but an easy opening.

"I hope not." She frowned and glanced back to the roofline. "You think so?"

"Maybe not. If you'll come down I'll take a look."

"Would you?"

"Sure."

She was already backing down the ladder.

As he took her place, she said, "I'm trying to learn as much as I can about this remodeling business, but it's a sharp learning curve."

He squinted down at her. "YouTube?"

Her mouth curved. "How did you guess?"

"I've gone there myself a few times. There's some good advice and some really bad advice. Be careful." He tugged at the loose strip of gutter.

"What do you think?"

"The hangers need to be replaced but the fascia wood is in good shape."

"Are they expensive?"

"Under ten bucks apiece. An easy fix."

"Whew." Her face was tilted upward, so he was staring down at dark mink eyelashes that reached all the way up to equally dark eyebrows, the smooth, pretty curve of her neck and her full lips. "That's a relief. So far, it's the only thing less expensive than I'd hoped."

"What have you gotten done so far?"

"If you have a minute, I'll show you."

Davis twitched a shoulder. "Okay." He turned to tell the kids, but they'd heard and were already on the porch, ready to barge in. "Hey, you two. Slow down," he said coming down from the ladder.

"Is Sydney home? Can she play?"

"She's inside doing homework."

"Which is where you two munchkins should be," Davis said, grabbing them both in a headlock from the back.

"Da-ad!"

"Please, Daddy, can we play for a minute while you talk to Lana?" She measured with her thumb and finger. "One teeny-weeny minute?"

"We can't stay long," he warned.

Taking that as a yes, they barreled inside and up the staircase, thundering like prairie buffalo.

"Sydney!" he heard Paige yell.

Lana laughed as they, too, went inside. "I'm beat from battling this house all day and they still have energy to run."

"Remodeling is a big job." He looked around the living room. "Nice. I didn't expect you to have the walls covered already."

She'd not only painted the ugly green walls and ceilings, she'd scrubbed the windows and fireplace and tossed sheets over the old furniture. The room was, at least, now livable.

Next to the fireplace, an acoustic guitar leaned against the wall, classic Lana. He remembered how good her voice had been. Anyway, she'd impressed their small town.

"I couldn't stand the graffiti," she was saying. "Some of the writing wasn't exactly family fare. I didn't want Sydney to read it."

"I hear that." And he liked it, too. If she didn't approve of rough language, she *had* changed. "The color is nice. Sort of a pale chocolate milk."

"I still have to paint the wood trim. What do you think of white enamel all around?"

"White's always nice. A good accent to the soft brown."

"That's what I was thinking, but the trim will have to wait until the true basics are done. Time has taken a toll on a lot of things, and the vandals didn't improve matters."

"Yeah, we should have done a better job of keeping watch after your mother passed."

"It wasn't your responsibility."

"Maybe not, but it was fun to catch those kids." He chuckled at the memory. "One night I saw a couple of shadowy figures sneaking around up here and decided to give them a scare."

"Did you really?" Her eyes sparkled with amusement. "What did you do?"

"There was this pair of teenage boys, probably 13 or 14. One was crawling through the kitchen window, the other hoisting from below." He pumped his upturned palms in a lifting motion. "I must have flashed back to my teenage days that night because I couldn't stop myself from what came next. It was too good an opportunity."

She cocked a hip, amused. "All right, spill it. I'm dying of suspense."

"Well, you see, it was dark. Barely a moon, and I had this chain saw." When she sucked in a knowing gasp, he grinned. "So, I carried it with me and hid behind a tree on the south side of the house. At the perfect moment, I jumped out screaming like a banshee and revved that chain saw for all I was worth."

Lana slapped both hands over her face and laughed. "You're kidding me? *You* did *that?*"

"Yep. Sure did. The kid in the window nearly knocked his brains out in his rush to escape. The one below took off in a screaming run and left his buddy hanging." The vision was as fresh in his head as yesterday and still cracked him up. "There he hung, with his legs dangling from the window and no way down except toward the chain saw."

"Oh, my goodness. That's priceless." She pointed her finger at him. "And exactly what they deserved for breaking into my house!"

"I laughed for days. Every time I thought about those big, brave, macho boys squealing like scared rabbits." He rubbed his hands together like an old-time villain. The tile glue made sandpaper sounds. "For a long time afterward no one bothered the spooky house on Dogwood Street."

"Davis Turner, you bad man. I had no idea you had it in you."

"You might be surprised at what I have in me," he

said, and then wondered where that had come from and what he was talking about. Suddenly aware of how much he was enjoying her reaction to his tale, he grew self-conscious. "Well, okay then. Where were we?" He fisted his hands on his hips and stared around. "Oh, yeah, right. Working on the basics. Winterizing should be your priority this time of year."

She gave him a funny look, but followed along. "I bought caulk and weather stripping. Any other suggestions?"

"Pipes."

Her face fell. "You said the plumbing was solid."

"It is. I meant winterize the pipes."

"Oh. What does that entail?" Her top teeth gnawed at her bottom lip. He watched until it occurred to him that he was staring at her mouth. This was getting ridiculous. Instead of scaring him away, Jenny's pushiness had made him more interested.

"Any exposed plumbing needs to be wrapped or insulated in some way. The attic, crawl space, outside faucets." He saw her consternation at this latest addition to her growing list of repairs. "Not expensive. Just more work."

She blew out a breath. "Okay. Good. Work I can handle."

"Have you ever crawled under a house? That's the worst part."

She gave a little shiver. "Small, dark spaces don't rank at the top of my list."

"I don't think they're on anyone's list, but some people are bothered less than others. I don't mind too much. I'll have a look under there for you."

"You will?"

"It won't take that long." He hoped. A man had no idea what he'd encounter under an old house like this.

"I don't expect you to work for nothing. I'll pay you."

He waved off the suggestion. "We'll worry about that later."

"Speaking of lists, I've made mine."

He arched an eyebrow. "What list is that?"

"The things I can do myself. You offered to suggest subcontractors to do the rest."

"Oh, right, I did." His thoughts flashed to the frame carpenter in the hardware store. That was one subcontractor he would not recommend. "Got your list handy?"

"Always. It's on the kitchen counter, along with a general budget. Maybe you can tell me if I'm way off on the numbers."

She led the way into the kitchen. Little had been accomplished here other than a thorough cleaning. That in itself was a vast improvement.

"Let's see what you've got."

She handed over the list. "Do I have any hope of getting the house in decent shape before the colder weather arrives?"

"Hard to know. Could stay warm or could turn bad." He leaned back against the counter to peruse the tidy hand-printed list. She'd used purple ink. "The lasting cold can't be far away though."

"I remember once when we were snowed in for two weeks. I thought I'd go crazy." She gave a soft, reminiscent laugh. "Tess and I finally bundled up in boots and coats, called a bunch of friends and trekked all the way up to Whisper Falls to go sledding on cardboard boxes."

"In the ice and snow? That's five miles." But it was the kind of thing the Ross girls would do.

"I've never been so cold in my life. One of the guys who came along finally built a campfire. We thought the smoke signals would bring out the fire department so we wouldn't have to walk back, but no such luck."

Davis nodded. "Remember that ice storm back in high school? Now that was cold."

"I remember. They called off school because the buses couldn't run, but those of us who lived in town were already there. Jack Macabee slid his VW off in a ditch and all of us piled out and lifted it back onto the road."

"I heard about that. You were in that car?"

She laughed again, stronger this time, and he could tell it was a good memory. "We must have had ten kids in that little Bug. All the boys thought they were strong enough to lift it out and Jack feared his dad would take his keys if anything happened to his car, so we got him going again. We slipped and fell, pushed and lifted, and laughed so hard." She leaned an elbow on the faded old countertop. "Whatever happened to Jack anyway? Did he take over his dad's car dealership?"

"No, Harvey closed the dealership when business disappeared to the bigger cities, but he still sells used cars on the side. Jack's a pumpkin farmer. You missed the Pumpkin Fest by only a couple of weeks. He was there in full force."

"Really? Pumpkins? I can't imagine preppy Jack in the agriculture business."

"It's kind of interesting to look at who we were then and where we are now. Life has a way of changing us."

"Isn't that the truth?" She'd gone pensive on him, bottom lip between her teeth, gaze somewhere in the distance. "I wouldn't want Sydney to be anything like I was."

"Aw, come on. Teenagers are goofy. You weren't so bad."

This time her laugh was harsh and disbelieving. "You always were the nicest guy. With an apparently faulty memory." She motioned toward the paper in his hand. "So what do you think? Any ideas for me?"

She was shutting off the conversation, unwilling to talk about herself anymore, but for a moment he'd glimpsed the young girl. He'd seen some things in her expression that surprised him. Hurt. Regret. Sadness.

Lana intrigued him. She also attracted him. He hadn't quite figured out why, other than his natural propensity toward the underdog and his sister's nosiness.

Troubled, he turned his attention to the list, though he was more aware of Lana Ross than he wanted to be. Her soft perfume played hide-and-seek in the narrow space. One minute, he caught the scent. The next it was gone.

He swallowed, bothered to be thinking about her, not as a neighbor in need as he'd told his sister but as a beautiful, interesting woman an arm's length away.

He cleared his throat. "You'll be putting in a lot of hours to do all this by yourself."

"I don't mind work as long as I can squeeze it in between my job."

The comment caught him off guard. He hadn't realized she had a job already. "Where are you working?"

"The *Gazette*." She glanced to one side, self-conscious and hitched a shoulder. "It's nothing big. A stringer position writing up local events. I get paid per article beginning tomorrow night."

"The football play-offs?"

Lana tilted her head. "How did you know?"

"Woman, the state play-offs are the biggest thing to hit the Whisper Falls Warriors in five years. Didn't you notice the signs plastered in all the businesses and the cars with Take State written on their back windows with shoe polish?"

"I guess you're right. Football fever has taken over and I don't even have a Warrior sweatshirt anymore."

"You'll have to remedy that."

"I will, but I've got bigger problems to worry about tomorrow night."

"What's that?"

"My boss, Mr. Kendle, wants an article filled with names. I don't know any of those kids. I might remember their parents, but not the kids."

"Easy fix. Get a spotter."

"A spotter?"

"That's what the announcers in the press box do. Someone sits up there with them and spots the numbers. They match the number to the program list and the problem is solved. The player gets recognized and everyone is happy."

"Perfect idea, but who? I'm still getting reacquainted."

"Well, let's see." He rubbed his chin, holding back the easy answer for two beats before saying, "How about me?"

Lana blinked, incredulous. "You?"

"Why not me?"

"Well, I, uh, I—" Rosy-red crested her cheekbones.

Davis lifted both hands. The paper crinkled, so he put it on the table. "Hey, if that doesn't work for you, I'm okay with it."

"No, no, I would love for you to be the one." The blush deepened, a pretty sight on pale pink cheeks. "What I meant is, I don't want to impose. You've been so nice already."

"I haven't done anything, Lana. I'm going to the game anyway. If you want help, I'm in. If you'd prefer someone else, fine."

"I want you. There is no one else."

He didn't want to like the sound of that. "I'm expensive. You'll have to buy the popcorn."

"Deal. I might even throw in a bowl of chili."

Davis tossed the list onto the table and rubbed his hands together. "Chili, popcorn and the state play-offs right here in my own backyard. Gotta love it."

"I remember when you played."

"You do?"

"I sang the national anthem at every game from the time I was twelve. I was always there." She pulled the headband from her hair and smoothed the stray wisps, reminding him of Nathan's fixation on brown hair. "What was your number?"

"Twenty-eight. Running back."

Lana twirled the stretchy band in her fingers, playing with it. "You were awesome."

"So were you."

"Thanks."

Before he could pursue the titillating line of conversation, footsteps sounded on the stairs. Exchanging smiles, they both turned toward the doorway as three breathless, beaming children came running.

"How are things going, Dad?" Nathan's bright eyes moved back and forth between Davis and Lana. "Do you like her yet?"

Paige grabbed her brother's arm. "Nathan!" To Davis, she said, "Sorry, Dad. He's such a kid sometimes."

Davis exchanged a half chagrined, half amused glance with Lana. Her face was pink again, but her eyes gleamed as though she was holding back a laugh.

To the kids, he said, "Head for the truck, you two. We've got to go."

As soon as they disappeared, with Sydney trailing along, he said, "I apologize for my irrepressible son. I'll have a talk with him. As you might have guessed, he likes you."

Davis didn't add the rest—that her brown hair had made her the target of his children's Christmas matchmaking prayer. He wasn't sure he could handle the embarrassment or the uncomfortable yearning they'd ignited in him. A yearning he'd thought would never return after Cheryl's death. A desire he was, this moment, battling down like a bad cold.

If his sister could read his mind, she'd have him committed. He wondered what she'd say Friday night when she spotted him in the stands with Lana and Sydney at his side?

Chapter Six

Lana was sure she felt stares and caught a few double takes as she and Sydney passed through the gate at Warrior Field and stood behind the blue-and-gold streamer-laden goalposts soaking up the ambience of small-town football. She took a minute to look around, identifying familiar faces, scoping out the changes as well as the things that had remained the same.

Already in the stands, an overzealous drummer pounded a rhythm while the band warmed up. Flutes squeaked and tubas oomphed. On the grassy field, fresh-faced boys in shoulder pads went through their pregame warm-up ritual. Number seventeen called out drills that had the players falling to the ground and popping up to high-step in place a few seconds and then start the drill all over again. They counted out in a raspy chorus of adolescent male voices.

The stands were filling rapidly. Dozens of people filed through the gate while buttery popcorn permeated the air with its alluring scent.

Lana shaded her eyes from the glare of the tall bright

lights, searching for Davis. "Do you see Paige and Nathan yet?"

Sydney, giddy with excitement but clueless about football, shook her head. "Not yet."

"Hello, Lana."

Lana turned to see a familiar face. "Jack?"

Jack Macabee hadn't changed much other than some lines around his eyes. He still wore his golden-blond hair a little long and his eyes were still as green as grass. Tall, thin and lanky, he'd been a good basketball player. Tonight, he wore his high school letter jacket, as did many alumni, and it still fit him as well as it had thirteen years ago.

"I heard you were back," he said. "How's it going?"

"So far so good." Lana felt her shoulders relaxing. Just having a friendly face to talk to helped ease the strain of being in a new situation. She and Jack had gotten along pretty well way back when. "Davis Turner and I were talking about you the other day. He said you're a farmer now."

"Chief supplier to the pumpkin cannery," he said.

"That's great."

After that she wasn't sure what to say so they stood in silence until he asked, "Is this your little girl?"

"This is Sydney," she answered with a smile of agreement. "Do you have kids?"

"One. Ryan. He's ten. Since the divorce he lives with his mother in Fayetteville so I don't see him as much as I'd like. I get him every other weekend."

"That must be tough."

A look of resignation flashed. "You adjust to what you have to."

She certainly understood that and was about to say
so when a hand wrapped around her upper arm.

A masculine voice muttered, "You got here first."

"Davis!"

The two men exchanged handshakes and began to
talk about the Warriors' chances against their mighty
rivals, the Longview Lions. After a brief conversation,
Davis motioned toward the stands. "If we want a good
spot, we'd better get up there. Want to join us, Jack?"

"Sounds good." He stuck his hands in his jacket
pockets, an action that made him look like the youthful athlete she remembered. "Sure you don't mind?"

"Not a bit. Right, Lana?"

"Absolutely." She turned a genuine smile on Jack.
Having another person along besides Davis's matchmaking kids provided more buffer and made her life
easier. "The more the merrier as far as I'm concerned.
It will be great to catch up again."

"I appreciate it. Since the divorce, I feel like the odd
man out."

"I'm with you there," Davis said. "Being single again
is awkward at times."

As they started forward, lost in manly conversation
about offenses and defenses, Lana held back for a moment, thinking. The men were similar in many ways,
though Jack's hair was more blond than sandy brown
and he was much taller and thinner than Davis. It occurred to Lana that they had their bachelor status in
common, as well. She'd never considered that a man
who'd lost his wife, whether through death or divorce,
might feel as much an outsider as she did.

Pondering this, she hoisted her writing tablet and
shoulder bag and hurried to catch up. As the group

moved down the sidelines and up the stairs into the bleachers, Lana occasionally heard her name in murmurs and whispers. Heat crept up the back of her neck, but she tried not to react. She'd expected gossip. This was, after all, a very small town. Everyone was fodder for gossip, especially the returned bad egg.

Suddenly, an older woman with a tight, salt-and-pepper corkscrew perm and a warm, bustling personality pushed up from a blue portable seat cushion boldly marked with a Warrior emblem.

"Lana Ross. Honey, is that you?" Clad in an oversize blue-and-gold Warriors jacket with matching earmuffs, Miss Evelyn Parsons waved a pom-pom on a stick directly at Lana. Of all the people in Whisper Falls, Miss Evelyn was one of the handful who never confused Lana with her sister. Though the twins were not identical, most folks didn't pay close enough attention to "those Ross girls" to notice the subtle differences.

"Miss Evelyn." Delighted, Lana stopped and accepted the hug, warmed by the best greeting she'd received so far. The Parsonses had always been kind, even after Tess had shoplifted from their snack shop.

"They tell me you're back and that you have the most adorable little girl." Miss Evelyn's gaze landed on the curious-faced child next to Lana. "This must be Sydney."

No surprise that Miss Evelyn, who made it her business to know everything possible about Whisper Falls and its citizens, had been informed not only of Lana's return but of her status as a parent.

"This is my darling girl." Lana touched Sydney's shoulder. "Say hello to Miss Evelyn, the matriarch of Whisper Falls. She practically runs the whole town."

"Especially me," said a portly man with white hair and handlebar mustache and a jolly chuckle. In his striped overalls and engineer's cap, Miss Evelyn's husband was a throwback to an earlier time, and he hadn't changed a bit since Lana had last seen him.

Lana smiled. "This gentleman is Uncle Digger. And before you ask, no, he's not your blood uncle."

"But he's everyone's uncle just the same," Miss Evelyn said, patting her round, Santa-looking husband on the shoulder.

Sydney smiled her shy hello at both adults. "Hi," she said in a tiny, breathy voice.

"Lana, she is a *darling*." Miss Evelyn beamed at Sydney. "You come by the Iron Horse sometime soon and see me, okay? Do you like ice cream?"

"Yes, ma'am."

"Oh, doesn't she have lovely manners!" Miss Evelyn wiggled the pom-pom over Sydney's head like a wand, making Sydney hunch her shoulders in a cute giggle. "I think Uncle Digger and I have a special treat with your name on it."

"Thank you, Miss Evelyn," Lana said, touched by more than the gesture to Sydney. It felt good to be greeted as an old friend. Even if she wasn't one.

Miss Evelyn winked. "You come see me, too. We'll catch up."

A male voice came over the PA then to make announcements, and Miss Evelyn shook her pom-pom again and yelled, "Go Warriors!"

Smiling, feeling positive and not really caring that others around them in the crowded stands had been watching with interest, she nodded and started the climb toward a spot in the third row where Davis and his kids had already settled with Jack.

Davis patted the space he'd saved. "Sit fast before someone grabs it."

A tap on the shoulder turned her around. She recognized the dark-skinned man immediately. "Creed Carter. Hello."

"I thought that was you, Lana. How's it going? When are we going to hear you on the radio?"

She figured she'd hear that question for a long time. "Never, I'm afraid. Nashville didn't work out."

"Their loss. Our gain." Rather than pursue the topic, he motioned to the woman and child beside him. "This is my wife, Haley, and our baby, Rose. Haley, meet Lana Ross. We attended high school together."

Easy as that, he introduced them. No references to her wilder side or any crazy stories from her past.

The two women exchanged greetings. Haley had an artsy, natural quality about her that Lana found interesting. Fair-skinned with no makeup, she wore her shoulder-length auburn hair loose with a silk flower pinned above one ear. The bouncy, apple-cheeked baby had olive skin and dark hair like her father with bright button eyes and a happy, alert expression. Lana liked them both instantly.

With an inward sigh of relief, Lana thought things were going very well. Maybe she'd misjudged Whisper Falls. Sure, a few people whispered and stared, but maybe the adjustment wouldn't be so difficult after all.

The PA announcer asked everyone to stand for the national anthem and the capacity crowd grew quiet. Ball caps were ripped from heads and held over hearts. Mothers shushed their children. Football players stood at attention, sweat already gleaming on their young faces.

Lana was always amazed at how, even in a large stadium, silence could shimmer through the autumn air like a cold front while the band played the dignified, rousing tune. As the music reached the crescendo, cymbals crashed. Goose bumps prickled Lana's arms. An undeniable longing to sing rose up to clog her throat. A longing she would never again see fulfilled.

By the end of the first quarter, Davis had memorized the main players and numbers, and he suspected Lana had too—at least on the Warriors' team. She was smart, jotting notes in her spiral notebook, noting specific plays, asking astute questions about the game as she scribbled away.

She was also smart enough to know she had drawn plenty of stares and whispers since their arrival. Only a handful of people had greeted her but plenty had stared outright as they'd passed. Maybe he was being oversensitive after Jenny's remarks, but their behavior put him on the defensive. He thought they were being ridiculous. Time passed. People changed. Get over it. Maybe they were just curious about the newcomer, the woman who'd gone to Nashville to be a star and come home again with a daughter.

Whichever, he was glad they'd sat together. She'd made him and Jack laugh more than once and she was kind to his kids—Nathan, in particular, who repeatedly found reasons to stand in front of her and ask eight-year-old questions. She'd been patient to the extreme even when she'd missed seeing a quarterback sack and worse, when she'd missed a touchdown.

"Nathan," he said. "Sit next to me." He patted the side opposite Lana.

"That's okay, Daddy. I don't mind standing up."

"You're blocking Lana's view."

Nathan flashed worried eyes to Lana. "I am?"

Lana opened her mouth to speak but appeared to reconsider before saying, "I like your company, Nathan."

"See, Daddy? Lana likes me. She's pretty. Don't you think she's pretty?"

He was not touching that with a ten-foot-pole. Instead, Davis leaned in to Lana's ear and whispered, "Pushover."

She shrugged and pulled Nathan close to her knees.

Just then, the Warriors scored on a long breakaway run and the crowd erupted. Davis leaped to his feet, anxious to get his son's attachment to Lana out of his head. This was a football game, not a date.

When the buzzer announced halftime, the score was tied fourteen to fourteen. Lana made a note in her book before turning to him. "I owe you some chili and popcorn."

"Sounds good to me. My lunch is long gone."

"You didn't have dinner?"

"Not yet." He grinned down at her, feeling that unwanted tug of attraction. He had a feeling there was a lot more to Lana Ross than her rough teenage years and a stab at stardom. The troubling thing was, he liked being around her. He liked *her*. Was he out of his mind?

Nathan pushed against Davis's legs, drawing his attention away from Lana and the uncomfortable thoughts. "I'm cold, Daddy."

"Want some chili?" Lana asked, smiling down at his

son, who had taken Sydney's spot at Lana's side when Sydney had moved down to sit next to Paige.

"Uh-uh. Can I have hot cocoa instead?" Nathan asked, hopefully.

"Yes, you can. But aren't you hungry?"

"I don't like chili."

"Maybe a hot dog?"

"Yeah!"

Davis stooped to pull up the boy's hood and tie it under his chin. His cheeks and nose had reddened. "There's a blanket in the truck if you need it."

"I'm not a baby, Dad. I'll be okay after Lana gets me a hot dog and some cocoa." Nathan beamed a gap-toothed grin at the object of his affections, his gray eyes shining under the stadium lights. "You sure look pretty, Lana. Are you having fun with my daddy?"

Lana exchanged an amused glance with Davis. "Yes, I'm having a good time, Nathan. Your dad is a great spotter."

Nathan was right. Lana looked pretty in her skinny jeans tucked into high-heeled boots and wearing a fitted leather jacket over a white shirt, her dark hair swooped up on the sides and large hoops dangling in her ears. A cheetah print scarf cozied up against her throat.

"Yeah. He's the best daddy in the whole world. He's nice, too. Don't you think my daddy's nice?"

"Very nice," Lana obliged, tapping Nathan's up-turned chin with a fingertip.

Exasperating as it was, the boy's innocent matchmaking touched Davis down deep. Nathan didn't remember Cheryl. But he apparently longed for a brown-haired woman in his life, for a mother. As hard as he'd tried to be everything to his kids, Davis couldn't be a mother.

The group tromped down the wooden stadium bleachers through the crowd of spectators and across the end zone to the concession area. The line was long and the smell of nachos and popcorn strong enough to make them worth the wait.

"I gotta *go,* Daddy," Nathan said, hopping up and down in the classic stance.

"I'll hold our place in line with the girls," Lana said to Davis, "if you want to go with Nathan."

"Thanks." Taking Nathan's hand, Davis made his way toward the men's room.

He returned to find the females still in line, talking to Retta Jeffers, a woman from their high school days. From the stiff set of Lana's shoulders and the red blotches on her cheeks, the conversation wasn't particularly comfortable. As he approached, Retta took her husband's arm and walked away.

Unsure of what to say, Davis looked at Lana in question. She met his gaze and then looked away.

Something was not right.

"You okay? You seem upset."

"Fine."

"That lady wasn't nice to Lana, Daddy."

"How so?"

Lana put a hand on Paige's shoulders. "It's all right, Paige. Let's not talk about it anymore. We won't let her spoil our fun, okay?"

Paige looked from Lana to Davis. The longing to tattle was clear and Davis wanted to know what Retta had done, but he didn't push.

"Okay." Paige took a deep breath. "But I'm gonna pray for that lady."

Lana's closed face softened. She pulled his little girl

close to her side in a gentle hug. "That's exactly the right thing to do, Paige. Thank you."

Lana's response encouraged Davis. Though he was a Christian, he didn't push his faith on other people and he normally didn't pry into their business. But he wanted to know if the woman up the street was a good influence on his children. Not that being a Christian made her perfect. Lord knows he had his share of negatives. But if she was a woman of faith, perhaps Jenny would stop nagging him. Or not. Jenny had her own way of looking at things.

The line shifted and they moved closer to the concession counter. With an effort at keeping the conversation flowing, he said, "Do we have our orders ready? This place is a madhouse tonight."

"We do." She patted her notebook. "Jotted them down so I wouldn't forget. Chili, popcorn and Coke for you, right?"

"Right." He pulled his wallet from his pocket.

Lana pushed his arm away. "My treat, remember?"

"Hey, I was joking. I never let a lady pay."

"I invited you. I pay."

After a bit of haggling, she agreed to let him pay for his children, but not the rest. She paid for his, as she'd promised. The idea felt a little awkward. Call him prideful, but he preferred to buy.

With a mountain of junk food and drinks in hand, they started back through the crowd to their seats. A Latin-themed halftime show was going on in a dazzling display of gold and blue. The uniformed marching band strutted around the empty field behind somersaulting cheerleaders and a flag-waving drill team.

Lana froze in the end zone. "Oh, my goodness, I should be getting pictures of the band!"

She juggled popcorn, coffee and the notebook, finally bending to place them on the ground while she snapped some photos. "I'm never going to be good at this reporter stuff."

She seemed genuinely upset and Davis had a feeling her distress had little to do with missed photos and a lot to do with Retta Jeffers.

"You want to tell me what happened earlier with Retta?" He knew she didn't but he was asking anyway.

"Not particularly."

"Will you?"

She slid the camera into her back pocket and retrieved her belongings from the grassy field. Steam rose from her coffee cup and a few kernels of popcorn fluttered to the ground like snow against the green grass.

"Let's just say she brought up some unpleasant things from our high school days. I was on her hate list."

"That's what I figured." He moved closer, bothered by her downcast eyes and tight mouth. "They should let it go. High school is ancient history."

"Yeah." She sighed and looked down, biting her lip. "But I can't blame someone else for the way I was."

"Hey." Hands full but wanting to comfort her, he nudged his shoulder against hers.

To his chagrin, she took a step away and said, "Better get back to our seats before the game resumes."

Lana's head hurt. After the encounter with Retta, she wanted to go home. A dozen people in the line had heard Retta's snide remarks and innuendoes about Lana and her sister. Worse, she'd insulted Davis, asking how Lana had gotten her hooks into the grieving widower.

She straightened her shoulders, determined not to let one hateful person push her out. She'd known this would happen, known she would encounter people who didn't like the person she'd been thirteen years ago. Even *she* didn't like the person she'd been in high school. She'd hurt some people, especially the girls, and she'd made her share of enemies.

Now, the last thing she wanted to do was cause gossip about a nice man like Davis Turner. So, she walked a step away, putting distance between them, protecting him and his adorable kids from her reputation.

The inner voice that said she wasn't good enough started talking. She'd worked hard to keep it quiet. Those kinds of thoughts had pushed her to drink, and she wasn't going back there again.

Swallowing hard, she prayed an inner prayer for strength and peace and walked past the now silent Davis.

Such a nice, nice man. What was he doing here with her?

On the way back to their seats, they encountered more familiar faces. Most expressions seemed curious but not malicious like Retta. Lana began to relax again, though her good mood had soured. She understood their curiosity. She'd told the town she was going to be a star. Naturally, they would wonder what had happened.

She stopped occasionally to field the Nashville questions, avoiding the dark side, and simply repeated the limited truth. Things had not worked out in Nashville the way she and Tess had hoped, but they'd learned a lot and met a few stars. The last always turned the conversation away from her and toward the handful of famous people she'd encountered.

When the football game resumed, she breathed a word of thanks. She could do this. She would do this. She had a job to do and, for Sydney's sake, she would not let Retta or the past take away this opportunity.

By the end of the third quarter, Lana was so focused on the game, her notes and the photos that her headache ebbed. As the players trotted off the field and the band struck up a fight song, Paige and Sydney required a trip to the ladies' room. Haley Carter, sitting behind them, asked to tag along, leaving the baby with Creed.

"How long have you and Creed been married?" Lana asked as they walked, jostling shoulders in the crowd, voices raised above the pounding drums and chanting cheerleaders.

"About a year."

Their baby was older than a year, but Lana was certainly not one to comment on that. "Creed was always a good guy. You look happy. So does he."

"He's amazing. The best husband. The best dad. My best friend. Can you tell I adore the man?" Haley laughed softly, her face aglow with a love Lana could only imagine. "Did you know he has a scenic helicopter service?"

"I'm not surprised. He always wanted to fly. That's what I remember most about him."

Creed was also one of the guys too focused on his goals to hang out much with girls, especially girls like her. He'd treated her with respect...and plenty of distance. Except for when they'd been lab partners in biology.

Haley tossed her auburn hair behind the shoulder of

her wrap-style coat. "Can you imagine Creed marrying a woman who is afraid of flying?"

"Seriously?"

"Seriously, and he loves me anyway." Haley pushed her hair back, nose wrinkling in amusement. "Which proves he's either a wonderful man or a little crazy. Probably both." They chuckled together before Haley continued. "Davis is a nice guy, too. We attend the same church. Have you been dating him long?"

Lana stopped so fast Sydney slammed into the back of her. "We're not together."

"Oh?"

"I mean, we're together. For tonight. He's my spotter. The football players. For the newspaper. I work there." She was rambling. She clapped her lips shut.

Haley placed a hand on her arm. Her fingers were short-nailed and stained with paint. Lana found the look comfortable. Haley was real. "I assumed and shouldn't have. Never mind. I'm sorry."

"Don't be sorry." She didn't want to lose this budding friendship. "He's only my neighbor. Really."

Davis Turner was so far out of her league, she'd never considered that people might think they were together, as in a date. Given his children's charming matchmaking attempts, she should have. Well, let them assume. As long as it didn't hurt Davis or his kids.

She was *so* not the right kind of woman for Davis. Even if she wanted to be.

Chapter Seven

At 4:00 a.m. Lana leaned her forehead on the laptop keyboard and closed her eyes for a tenth of a second. Exhausted but too worried about the newspaper article to do anything but work, she'd written and rewritten until her eyes were dry and gritty.

"This is harder than it looks," she murmured to the quiet. "A lot harder."

After reading dozens of online posts about writing a newspaper article, she'd hoped to get her thoughts organized. At this late hour, they'd become jumbled and skewed. She had names, positions and plays but what did she do with them? And how did she decide which were most important?

"Aunt Lana?"

She jerked her head up, stunned not to have heard Sydney's footsteps on the wooden stairs. "What are you doing up?"

The little girl's hair was a tousled, curly mess, her aqua eyes droopy with sleep. One leg of her pink princess pajamas rolled back on itself to display a shin bruised from a fall against the school merry-go-round. "I missed you."

Lana's heart constricted with a love she could never put into words, no matter how hard she tried.

Both she and Sydney had been sleeping in Sydney's pink-and-purple room, the first to be redone while working on the rest of the house. For now, Lana knew the arrangement was a comfort to her niece. The old house's squeaks and groans would take some getting used to.

"I'm still working."

Sydney rubbed at her eyes and yawned. "Do you know what time it is?"

The adult question made Lana smile, though her mouth felt too weary to move more than a fraction. "Too late to be working, huh?"

"Will you come to bed now?"

Lana stared at the computer for two beats, sighed and hit Save before closing the lid. "I'll get up early."

Sydney's giggle was drowsy. "You already did."

Wearily, Lana traipsed up the stairs behind her niece. Maybe things would look better after a couple of hours of sleep. They had to. The article was due before ten.

Someone was breaking down the door.

Lana shot up in bed, heart banging wildly against her rib cage. Next to her, Sydney stirred and mumbled something unintelligible but didn't wake.

Lana tossed back the covers, grabbed her trusty base-ball bat and tiptoed down the stairs, the wood cold on the bottoms of her warm feet.

The pounding came again, along with voices.

She paused on the bottom step to listen. A man's

voice. Then something scraped across the porch. And a dog barked.

She frowned, more curious now than afraid. A burglar didn't bring his dog.

At the door, she peered through the tall glass side pane and spotted three familiar figures. One of them wore a tool belt.

Lana blew out a relieved sigh and yanked the door open. The sun nearly blinded her. "You're up early."

Davis Turner stood on a ladder repairing her gutters. On the porch Paige played tug-of-war with a small, shaggy white dog and a knotted doggy rope.

Davis grinned down from his high perch. He looked really good this morning. Too good. "I said I'd be here by eight. Remember?"

Shock made her jerk. "Is it after eight?"

He glanced at his watch. "Eight-thirty-five. I take it we woke you up? You gonna hit me with that thing?"

Lana looked down at the bat in her hand. "I forgot."

"I can see that. Sorry. Want us to leave?"

She propped the bat against the wall of the house, trying to get the cobwebs out of her head. She must look a sight. Barefooted. Ancient gray sleep sweats. Hair everywhere.

"What time did you say it is?"

"Eight-thirty-seven now." He backed down the ladder. "Want me to make some coffee?"

Dismay filled her. "I was supposed to turn in the article by ten."

"You've got time."

"No, I don't. It's not finished." But she was. Finished. Kaput. Out of a job.

"How long could it take to write up a football game?"

She glared at him and reconsidered the ball bat. "You have no idea what you're talking about."

He dropped his hammer and fittings into a toolbox. The metallic clatter gave her a headache. The glare gave her a headache. Her utter failure gave her a headache.

"Oooh," she groaned, backing into the house. She was awake now, fully aware of her disheveled state, the unfinished article and one very appealing neighbor standing in her living area in a tool belt and a gray plaid shirt.

"Have you started on it?"

"Worked until four this morning but it still doesn't seem right."

"Maybe I can help?" he asked, sounding every bit as uncertain as she felt. "I'm not a writer but I know football."

Desperate as she was, that was enough. "Would you?"

"Go," he said, flicking his hand. "Get your computer or whatever. Let me see what you've got. I'll make coffee."

She was up the stairs, dressed and had her hair yanked back in a headband in minutes. Sydney awakened and upon hearing that Paige and Nathan and a dog were on the porch, threw her clothes on and rushed outside.

Laptop in hand, Lana made her way into the kitchen, bolstered by the scent of strong coffee.

"There you go. No sugar. A spoon of milk. Hot and strong." Davis slid a faded Snoopy mug onto the chipped and equally faded counter before pouring himself a cup.

Lana blinked down at the mug in puzzlement. He

knew how she liked coffee? "Remind me to pay you a bonus."

As she settled on the stool and sipped, Davis joined her. He smelled good, like a fresh shower, a little outdoors and just the right amount of woodsy sandalwood aftershave. Having once done a three-week stint as a sales clerk at a Dillard's cosmetic counter, she could probably name his cologne. Not designer but not cheap either. Something she liked. A lot.

He reached for the laptop, turning the screen in his direction. A nice waft of the fragrance came with him. "Let me see."

She blew across the top of her coffee, waiting while he did a quick read-through. Once he said, "hmm," which told her nothing. She took a sip of the brew. Stronger than she made it but not bad.

Finished reading, he tilted away from the computer in a contemplative mood.

"What do you think?"

"Not terrible. You're a good writer."

"But?"

"Some of the football language is missing and a few places you could summarize the number of tackles, the run and pass yards, other stats for each of the top players of the game instead of that long list of everyone."

"Oh. Makes sense." She pulled the screen back to her and set her coffee mug aside. As she read through, she saw what he meant and made changes here and there, trimming the extraneous words and getting to the point.

For the next forty-five minutes, they talked last night's game and Lana rewrote. She was distracted at times, especially when Davis leaned in close to the small screen so they were practically cheek to cheek and that tantalizing scent she couldn't quite name tick-led her nose. But at fifteen minutes until ten, she had no choice other than to send the document to Joshua Kendle's email address and hope it was good enough.

Breath held, she hesitated two beats and then hit Send.

"Do you think Joshua will like it?" she asked, rub-bing the back of her neck, stiff now from tension and bending over the screen.

"He's an easygoing guy. He'll edit it for you."

That wasn't too encouraging. "I'll do better next time."

"The library might have some journalism books."

"That's a good idea. Online articles are helpful, but they're all mostly the same. After who, what, where and when, I'm pretty much lost."

He poured himself another cup of coffee and strad-dled a chair, arms folded across the back, mug cupped in both hands. "Do you remember Meg Banning?"

"No, I don't think so. Should I?"

"Probably not. She's in charge of the library."

Lana snorted. "A place I once avoided like the flu. No wonder I don't remember her."

"Nice woman. She'll help you out."

Lana angled her chair in his direction and then wished she hadn't. Having him in her space was…both-ersome. "I take it you're a big reader?"

"I've been known to pick up a James Patterson novel, but the kids are the main reason I go to the library. Meg is great with kids. She does a reading program and a lot of other activities, especially in the summer, and Paige is a certified bookworm." He flashed that wide-open smile that told of his affection for his daughter.

"And Nathan?"

"Nathan likes the cookies Miss Banning hands out during story hour."

A smile bloomed inside Lana and spread from her chest to her lips. "He's the cutest little boy, Davis. Such a charmer."

"Don't let him hear you say that. He's already half in love with you."

Lana squelched the uncomfortable wish poking at the back of her mind and came up with a joke of her own. "There is no accounting for taste but he's young. He'll learn."

"Hey! What is that supposed to mean?"

Lana felt the heat rush over face. "Nothing. A joke."

Davis *had* to know exactly what she meant. He'd heard the gossip, most of which was true, at least back then.

"You're still bothered by whatever Retta Jenner said last night, aren't you?" He took her coffee cup and re-filled it. As he set the cup in front of her, he placed a hand on her shoulder.

Comfort. Friendship. Mr. Nicest-guy-on-the-planet doing what came naturally.

Don't read anything into it.

She shrugged him off. "A little, I suppose. People in a small town have long memories, Davis. I don't care about me. But I want them to give Sydney a chance. She's a great kid with the sweetest little spirit."

"How's she adjusting to the new school?"

"She likes her teacher but school is hard for her." She didn't relate the reasons for Sydney's struggles. She took the blame for the problem. If she'd been more stable, more unselfish, more sober, Sydney wouldn't have missed out on important learning. "Do you know if Miss Banning tutors in reading? Sydney could use some help."

"I can't say for sure, but you should ask. If she doesn't, she'll know someone."

At that moment, her cell phone chimed with a text. One glance at the message and her heart fell.

Her editor, Joshua Kendle, wanted to see her.

Davis hoisted one end of the claw-foot tub while the middle-aged buyer hoisted the other. "Cast iron weighs a ton."

"No lie, but my wife has wanted one of these things ever since we started building the new house." The bulky man's face darkened with effort. "Even if it costs me a visit to the chiropractor, it will be worth the money to see her expression on Christmas morning."

"Great Christmas gift idea."

"That's what I thought. I hope her mom doesn't let the secret slip. She's hiding the tub in her garage until then."

"Sorry you have to hold on to it so long but I'm hoping to get as much of Lana's major work done as possible before the holidays. I need this out of the way."

"No problem, man. You're still on schedule to finish my tile work by Christmas, aren't you?"

"Plan on it."

The truth was, Davis was snowed under with work and adding Lana's to the list was overload, but he couldn't seem to say no. She had asked him to recommend subs, but why should he when he could pop up the street a few hours at a time and do the work for half the price? Lana didn't seem to be rolling in extra money so why not help out where he could? Being neighborly and all. He couldn't wait to see her amazement when he told her how much money he'd gotten for the old tub.

As he and the buyer started down the narrow hall, bumping walls and straining, Lana suddenly appeared in the opening. "Guys! Wait a minute. Let me help."

An hour ago, she had lit out of here a bundle of nerves. She was so worried about losing her job that he'd started worrying, too. She'd been on his mind for the entire time she'd been gone to the newspaper office, but from her behavior now the meeting must have gone all right.

"We've got it." Besides, what good could she do? She probably didn't weigh a buck twenty.

"Let me add my muscle."

Before he could laugh, she grabbed onto the side next to Davis and lifted. Davis felt the shift in weight instantly and, impressed with the strength in such a small woman, was glad he'd had the good sense to keep his mouth shut.

"You balance," he said, admiring her effort. "I'll work the dolly."

With plenty of grunts and maneuvering they managed to get the old tub out of the house and loaded into the back of Ted's truck.

After Ted drove off, Lana opened the folded check and gasped. "Davis! He paid *this much* for that old tub and the fittings?"

Davis couldn't stop the smile that pulled at his mouth. "Happy?"

She turned those sparkling blue eyes on him at full wattage. "I can't believe it. This is enough to buy all new bathroom fixtures with a little money left over for Christmas."

Just as he'd imagined, she was thrilled. Beyond happy. Impressed.

Davis resisted the most powerful urge to toss an arm over her shoulders and hug her against his side. Last night's football game coupled with this morning's session at the computer must have rattled his brain. Not the game or the article exactly. The woman.

He shrugged, pretending a nonchalance he didn't feel. "Sydney needs to have an extra good Christmas this year. Moving to a new place is tough on kids."

Lana pocketed the check as she bumped his shoulder with hers, teasing. "How would you know? You've lived in the same town all your life."

Davis liked when she teased. The meeting with Joshua Kendle must have gone really well.

He thought she looked great in a red sweater thing that came to her thighs and a pair of dark navy jeans tucked into her boots, her mink hair shining around her shoulders and her eyes happy. She was standing incredibly close, there in her front yard on that cloudy, gray November morning. A chill was in the air. Winter was breathing down their necks.

He gave in to the urge and dropped a casual arm over her shoulders. He felt her stiffen, just for a second, and then relax. But the reaction was enough to make him remove his arm. That was the second time today she'd pushed him away.

Get a clue, Turner.

"Where are the kids?" She stared around as if she'd lost them.

"Out in the backyard chasing Ruffles. Or being chased."

"Your poor dog must be worn out."

"Don't worry about Ruffles. He's in his element. Kids and more kids." Davis started up the steps. "Thanks for letting us bring him over."

Lana followed, hands stuck in her back pockets. "Sydney wants a dog so badly. It's nice of your kids to share Ruffles."

"Puppies make good Christmas presents. Cheap and easy. Adopt one from the pound."

She paused on the steps, head tilted. "Is that where you found Ruffles?"

"Yep. She was this bundle of white, matted fur, probably the ugliest little dog in the place." He cupped his hands in a gesture indicating her size and shape. "Both my kids went directly to her. She curled up in Paige's lap with this kind of sad, beleaguered sigh, and that was that. Puppy love at first sight."

"What a great story. I've never had a dog."

"Seriously?" He stopped. "You've never owned a dog? Don't you like dogs?"

"Yes, of course, I like dogs. I always wanted one but my mother said she was allergic, and since then…" She shrugged. "A dog wouldn't have fit my lifestyle. We moved too much."

"You should get one. I'm sure I could find a couple of eager young volunteers to go with you to the pound."

He held the door open for her, trying not to enjoy the sway of her hair and the smell of her flowery perfume as she moved past him. They were doing construction work. Dirty, nasty construction. Ripping out the old. Loading trash. Cleaning. Granted she hadn't helped all that much, but still, she smelled better than a flower garden. Looked better, too.

"I don't know," she said. "What if something happens and I have to move again?"

He paused in the living room to stare at her. "Why would you have to move again?"

She shrugged. "You never know how things will work out."

He wished he didn't understand her concerns but he did. Last night while she'd taken the girls to the ladies' room, his sister had made a point to corner him. As he'd expected, Jenny had been none too happy to see him sitting by Lana Ross. In fact, she'd insinuated he was damaging his children, subjecting himself and the entire Turner family to unnecessary gossip. Regardless of his plea that he was only helping out as spotter, Jenny had pleaded with him not to associate with Lana for the sake of his kids.

Yet, here he was. His kids were having a grand time, safe and sound. So was he. He felt good about helping Lana get the old house in shape. And yes, he liked her as a person. She wasn't the tough girl of old, though a thread of strength ran through her, a determination that, even if he didn't quite understand, he could admire. He didn't know where she'd been or what she'd been doing all these years, but Lana Ross was no longer a troubled teenager.

Yet, if his sister, a good woman who gave to charities and headed the benevolence committee at church couldn't see past Lana's youthful indiscretions, how would the rest of Whisper Falls treat her?

"You should make up your mind to stay, for Sydney's sake, no matter what. This is your home."

"For the most part I have made up my mind. Sydney's never really had permanence. I want that for her." Her boots tapped on worn and faded linoleum as they entered the kitchen.

"But you're holding back a reserve."

"I'm avoiding a puppy," she insisted with a pointed finger. "That's my only reserve. I don't have time for an animal right now." She opened the fridge and handed him a bottle of water. "I'll just borrow yours. Okay?"

"Deal. For now." He unscrewed the cap and swigged. "You gonna tell me what happened at the newspaper office?"

She took a water bottle for herself but didn't open it. The refrigerator shut with a soft whoosh of cold air. "He said the article was okay for a first-timer."

"That's it? That's the only reason he called you in?"

"He gave me some pointers and advice, showed me how he expected future articles to look, things like that. He was very kind." She widened her eyes in a grimace. "I was relieved not to get fired."

"See? Told you." He was ridiculously glad for her.

"Yeah, you did. Thanks for the boost of confidence and the help. I couldn't have done it without you."

He liked that more than he should.

"Speaking of getting fired," he said. "I'd better start that tile work or the boss will not be happy."

"She's a real slave driver." Her quick, easy smile warmed him. "A willing helper, too. Let's get to it."

He started to protest, to remind her that he could handle the job alone while she did something else. But the truth was he wanted her company. He wanted to know more about the woman his children wouldn't stop talking about.

Inside the old bathroom, a tedious job awaited. Over the years, home owners had layered linoleum over the original wood. Subsequent owners had added additional layers. He had removed all those layers before installing the backer board. He'd started on the open areas while awaiting the tub buyer's arrival and fortunately the bathroom was small.

Conversation was comfortable and mostly centered around the remodeling work, but Davis found Lana an easy person to talk to. She was witty, in a self-critical way that made him even more curious about what made her tick. Regardless, he liked her company.

Jenny would have an attack if she could read his mind.

But Jenny didn't run his life. She might be his sister and she might have his best interest at heart, but he was a grown man. He'd been making his own decisions for a long time. Granted, they all hadn't turned out well, but he was responsible.

His wife's untimely death flashed into memory. Prayer had absolved him of guilt, but he still wondered sometimes if he'd done the right thing. If Cheryl would still be alive…

He shoved the trowel under a chunk of ancient linoleum and pried it loose. On his knees, with Lana not three feet away also scraping at old, well-stuck glue, Davis let the rhythm of his work soothe his troubled thoughts.

The trio of children trooped to the entry and stayed a while to watch the adults sweat and work. Sydney, curly hair frizzing around her head like a halo, cradled Ruffles as she would a baby doll. The happy dog lay with eyes closed, head back, legs sticking straight up, being her usual rag-doll self. The little girl needed a puppy. He'd have to work on Lana about that.

"Whatcha doing, Daddy?" Nathan asked. He had dirt on his elbows and knees.

"Getting ready to lay out Lana's tile design."

"How long does that take?"

Davis sat back to look at the trio. "Why? Are you getting hungry?"

"A little," Paige said. "We were thinking maybe the five of us could go to the Iron Horse for hot dogs."

"Oh, you were, were you?" Davis shot an amused glance at Lana.

She was already shaking her head. "I don't think I can make it today, kids. Too much work to do."

Davis scooted a box of tile into place and ripped open the cardboard top. Dust motes flew from the movement, sending the dank smell of old wood into his senses. "Tell you what? How about I order a pizza from the Pizza Pan?"

The children looked at each other and grinned. "Yes! Pizza!"

"You mind, Lana?" he asked.

Lana, sweeping bits of old vinyl and other trash into a dustpan, paused and leaned against the broom. "Sounds good to me. I skipped breakfast."

To prove the point, her stomach growled. The kids cracked up laughing.

"Okay, pizza it is." Davis took out his cell phone, a little embarrassed that the Pizza Pan was in his list of contacts. But what could he say? He was a single father. Pizza emergencies happened. Often.

"Daddy?" Nathan said again after the food and drink was ordered.

"What?" He removed several pieces of tile from the box and began arranging them in a pattern in one corner. Lana had chosen a marbled tan and sand with waves of off-white. The soothing, classic color had been a surprise. He'd expected something more flamboyant from someone who'd hobnobbed with famous entertainers.

"Can Sydney come to church with us tomorrow?"

Davis's head shot up. "Church? Sure, if Lana doesn't mind."

"Can Lana come, too?" Paige asked.

"If she wants to." He found Lana's eyes and held on.

She paused in her clean-up to say, "We need to find a church."

His heart jumped with gladness. Lana wanted to go to church. "Great. You can ride with us if you want."

Her smile did funny things to his stomach. Or was that hunger?

"Perfect. We'd love to, wouldn't we, Sydney?"

The little girl shifted Ruffles to her shoulder and nodded. Ruffles slouched forward with a sigh and settled her nose in Sydney's neck.

"And afterward," Paige announced with a clap, "we can all go out to Grandma's for Sunday dinner."

The unexpected comment not only surprised him, it put him on the spot. Davis didn't know what to say. Jenny would be there. Worse, he had no idea how Mom and Dad would react to him bringing any woman besides Cheryl to Sunday dinner, much less Lana Ross.

Little Miss Paige needed a good talking to.

He chanced a quick glance at Lana. She was busy loading a wheelbarrow nearly jammed full of trash and old flooring.

"Sydney and I have plans after church, Paige, but

thank you for asking," Lana said as she shoved a long piece of red vinyl into the wheelbarrow. Did he detect stiffness in the answer? Had she noticed his consternation?

"Rain check?" he asked. Clearing the way with his family was a necessity before he could invite Lana—or anyone—to a family gathering.

Lana glanced up. He put all the sincerity he could muster into his expression. He'd never wanted to be a hypocrite, one of those in-name-only Christians who talked a good talk but treated people shabbily.

"We'll see," she answered. He knew then, from the quiet hurt in her eyes, that she'd guessed. And he felt like a total jerk.

"I'll go empty the wheelbarrow," she said.

He had to give her credit. Other than short breaks, she'd stayed with him, working every bit as hard as he.

"Thanks." Troubled by his confusion and the voice of his sister in his head, he didn't watch Lana leave though he heard the rumble of the wheelbarrow.

The kids remained, observing with the curiosity of children and asking too many questions.

After a bit Davis sat back on his haunches and waved at the corner where he'd laid the first pieces of tile. He'd planned out a design pattern with diamond accents, already visible. Cutting each piece took extra time but Lana had especially liked the look in his portfolio of photos. "What do you think?"

The trio studied the tile as if they were experts, making him smile.

"Pretty, Daddy," Paige said. "You're the best tile putter-downer in the world."

"How about you, Sydney?" he asked. "This is your house. What do you think? Like it?"

Sydney's head bobbed. She wasn't a big talker but her expressive blue-green eyes said plenty. At the moment, they sparkled. "Yes."

"Ever had a fancy diamond pattern in your house before?"

Her small, oval face grew serious. "We never had a real house before."

The admission struck him in the heart. "Where did you live before moving here?"

He knew he was prying, but Lana was about as forthcoming as the Sphinx about her years away from Whisper Falls.

Sydney bunched narrow shoulders. "Sometimes in motels or other places. Sometimes in the car."

Whoa. What kind of other places? And what was a child doing living in a car?

Stomach rolling, Davis wanted to press for details but Lana chose that moment to return, wheelbarrow clattering against the hall floor.

As he looked up into Lana's pretty face, Jenny's voice echoed in his head. What kind of mother was Lana Ross?

Chapter Eight

Monday morning Lana dropped Sydney at school, and then stopped at the newspaper office, relieved to pick up another assignment. Afterward, with a renewed determination to learn more about this writing stuff, she drove straight to the Whisper Falls Public Library.

Unfamiliar with libraries in general, she was glad to see a row of computers, a desk manned by two women and more books than she'd known existed. Nothing weird or confusing. Surely, she could find help in here.

She approached a thirtyish redhead with stunning posture and a face that belonged on magazines.

"May I help you?" the gorgeous woman asked.

"I'm looking for Meg Banning."

Absolutely perfect teeth smiled at her across the desk. "I'm Meg. What can I do for you?"

This was Meg? No wonder Davis hung out at the library!

Somehow she managed to stutter around her surprise. True to reputation, Meg led her to a section of books and offered to order others through inter-library loan.

"Do you have a library card with us?" Meg asked.

"Do I need one?" She hated feeling this stupid but libraries had never been on her list of hangouts.

"The application is short and easy."

"Will I be able to check out a book today?"

"Sure, though we limit you to two books per visit for the first three trial months." Meg led the way back to the desk where she withdrew an application from beneath the counter. "Here you go. Fill out all the contact information, add two references, preferably local, sign the bottom and you're good to go."

With a sinking feeling Lana worked her way through the easy part. Name, address, phone, employment. But at the reference lines she was stuck. Who in this town would vouch for her?

Finally, she scribbled two names.

"I moved here recently," she said as she handed the application back to Meg. "I'm not that acquainted yet but I think these two references will be okay."

Meg glanced at the names. Her beautiful face lit up. "You know Davis Turner?"

"He's my neighbor."

"Great guy and a terrific dad. You're lucky."

Was Meg the Beautiful interested in Davis? The notion gave Lana a funny feeling under her rib cage. Was Davis interested in Meg, too? Why should she be surprised that other women found him attractive? Any sensible woman would be thrilled to call Davis Turner her man.

Another patron approached the desk and Lana moved away to the stacks and shelves of books, shaking off the odd sensation. She wasn't jealous. She couldn't be. She and Davis were just friendly neighbors.

As she perused one volume Meg had recommended,

several people moved past her, scanning titles. She shifted her position and, focused on the book, was paying no attention to the other browsers when a whispered conversation caught her ear. The speakers, hidden on the opposite side of the wall of books, were unknown.

"Did you see her at the football game? She was all over Davis Turner."

"Just like in high school. She probably slept her way around Nashville."

"I wonder what happened to her big singing career?"

"Singing? Is that what they call it these days?"

A giggle. "Retta, you're awful."

Lana's stomach churned. To her consternation, tears stung at the back of her eyelids. She spun away from the whispers and started down the aisle to escape the ugly gossip. One of the speakers was Retta Jennings, who had never liked her, but the talk still hurt. She wanted to scream, "I've changed. I'm not that girl anymore." Instead, she pressed a hand to her mouth, closed her eyes and took several deep breaths through her nose, trying to recall her counselor's wise words, "You're a new creation in Christ. *You* know. *He* knows. But the rest of the world will need some time to catch up."

"Lana?"

She jumped at the sudden hand on her forearm. "Haley!"

Haley Carter, in a fleece-lined jean jacket and long corduroy jumper, stood in front of her, toddler in arms, compassion in her expression.

A hot flush of embarrassment rose on Lana's neck and spread over her face. "You heard?"

Haley nodded. "Don't let them get to you."

She let out a long breath. "I'm trying. No one seems to believe I've changed."

"No one?"

"Well…some don't."

"Only a few, Lana, and they don't matter. Don't let them matter." Haley shifted the baby to her hip. The pretty little girl grinned at Lana. "Want to go get some coffee and talk?"

Not that talking would help but she liked Haley and the Lord knew she could use a friend. "Let me check out this book first. Okay?"

"I have one, too." Haley hoisted a large volume of photographed artwork. Baby Rose grabbed the edge and tried to gnaw it. The young mother gently eased the book away.

They checked out at the desk and left the library, walking the few blocks down Easy Street to the Iron Horse Snack Shop. They took their time, letting Rose toddle along in her tiny baby steps. She was dressed warmly, a knit cap over her dark hair, and a soft fleece coat zipped to her chin. A beautiful child, Rose was happy, too, and clearly adored by her mother.

Lana stifled a regretful sigh. Haley was a blessed woman to have a child and a husband who loved her. In Lana's teen years, her thoughts about marriage and family had mostly been negative, impacted by her parents' constant battles. Today…well, today she didn't know. With her background, what worthwhile man would want her?

The day was cold and clear, the streets quiet. In the five-block swath that made up most of the town, they passed the Tress and Tan Salon where Cassie Blackwell pecked on the glass and waved a hairbrush. That simple act of friendliness made Lana feel better. Haley was right. Not everyone in Whisper Falls bore her ill feelings.

She waved back. "I met Cassie at church yesterday," she told Haley. "She and her brother and sister-in-law."

"The Blackwells are great people, not like some I could name."

"Yeah." The negative feeling returned.

"I know how you feel." Haley's voice was quiet as she stooped to lift Rose into her arms. Her skirt pooled around her boots.

"Oh, Haley, I don't think so. You're so sweet. I can't believe you ever did anything bad in your life that would make people hate you."

"I had an…unorthodox upbringing. Some people looked down their noses at me." Haley tossed her hair back and laughed. "And let's face it, I'm a little different. Creed calls it 'artistic' but those who don't love me have used terms such as 'weirdo' or 'flaky'. In fact, Creed called me Flaky Haley for a long time."

"He did not!" Lana couldn't help laughing.

"Yes, he did. I know what it's like to be…well, different. Kind of an outcast. Things have changed since I married Creed, but now I don't really care. I like who I am. Creed likes who I am. Most importantly, God likes me."

"My counselor keeps telling me that."

"Your counselor?"

Lana flinched. She hadn't intended to say that. The less anyone knew about her time in Nashville, the better chance Sydney would have for a normal life. "A mentor, really. Amber took me under her wing after I met Jesus and turned my life around."

"Things were bumpy in Nashville?"

"You could say so." And that's really all she wanted to say on the subject.

"Do you miss it? Your music, I mean?"

Like I'd miss my right arm. "That part of my life is behind me now. Sydney is my focus."

"Rose and Creed are my focus, too, Lana, but there's room for my art, as well. Having one doesn't mean I can't enjoy the other."

Haley had no idea what she was saying. Painting and sculpting were private art forms. Make a mistake and simply start over. Singing was make-or-break every single time she went on stage. Failure was one wrong note away.

Now, the only time she could sing was at night with only her guitar and her pen and pad for company. Alone, where no one would know the fraud she'd been.

But she was a long way from telling anyone what had happened to her singing career. A very long way.

Thankfully, they reached the Iron Horse, a snack shop connected to the historic train depot and museum run by Digger and Evelyn Parsons. Inside, the smell of cinnamon and apples filled the air, a result, she knew, of Miss Evelyn's almost-famous apple pie. A handful of small, square tables, unchanged in all these years, scattered around the small space while a counter with bar stools lined one end. A few customers sat here and there. Haley spoke to a couple of them, introducing Lana.

Along one wall of the room were an office door and an exit leading out to the train. The depot, which harkened back to the early days of the railroad, still displayed the rustic wood, antique green lanterns and other train paraphernalia.

Miss Evelyn came bustling toward them, her cheeks rosy in a round face. "Got some apple pie fresh from the oven."

Lana and Haley exchanged glances.

"Pie and coffee?" Haley asked.

"Sounds good. I'm chilled."

"Do you have a banana for Rose?" Haley said to Miss Evelyn.

"With a cup of milk?" the older woman asked.

Haley smiled. "Perfect."

"Coming right up." Miss Evelyn moved away in her characteristic rush, a sharp contrast to her amiable husband who never hurried. She returned with the order, lingering briefly to chat until another customer lifted his coffee cup.

"Awk. I'll be glad when Annalisa feels better. I don't know how we ever managed this shop without her. She runs the place now so I can do my work with the town council. When she's not here, I'm in a dither. With Thanksgiving just around the corner and the Christmas bazaar to plan, I really need her."

"Is Annalisa sick?" Haley asked. "She looked fine at church yesterday."

"Fine one minute, sick as a dog whenever she smells food cooking." Miss Evelyn pumped her eyebrows and grinned. "In a few months, she'll feel right as a summer rain."

With that pronouncement, she hurried away to the coffeemaker.

Haley's eyes widened. She peeled the skin from

Rose's banana and broke the fruit into bite-size pieces. "The Blackwells are having a baby?"

A twinge of longing surprised Lana. "Sounds that way."

"I'm so happy for them. There is nothing in the world better than your own precious child." Haley bent to the high chair and kissed her baby on the forehead, receiving a banana-coated pat on the check in return. "Didn't you feel that way when Sydney was born?"

Lana dropped her gaze to the steaming apple pie. Guilt pressed at her conscience. Even though the deception was for Sydney's sake, she felt guilty for lying about the relationship, especially to someone like Haley who'd befriended her. "She was a wonderful baby."

She cut a bite of the pie and blew on it before tasting. Her answer wasn't a lie. It just wasn't the whole truth.

She chewed, expecting the pie to be delicious but it tasted like ashes on her tongue. Even a half-truth had a way of sucking the joy out of a situation.

"I never dreamed I would ever have a child of my own," Haley was saying.

"Why not?"

"I was afraid of getting too attached, of loving too much, of getting hurt."

"You? But you're such a great mother."

"It was only when I thought I was going to lose her that I woke up. Even though she wasn't mine by birth, I loved her. She was worth anything, even risking a broken heart."

"Rose isn't yours?"

Haley paused in wiping her daughter's face to give Lana a stern look. "Adopted means she's as much my daughter as Sydney is yours."

More so.

Again, the opportunity to tell the truth arose but the friendship was too new, so Lana kept quiet.

"I'm sorry. I didn't mean it that way."

"No offense taken. Creed is adopted, too, so he thinks adoption is the way to go. I'd like to be pregnant some day, but if it doesn't happen, I have the daughter I want, the child God intended me to have."

"And a pretty great husband, too."

"Absolutely." She pointed a fork at Lana. "So what gives with you and Davis Turner?"

"Nothing. I told you that at the game."

"I don't believe you. Neither does Creed. He said Davis couldn't take his eyes off you even when you and I went to the concession stand."

"Stop." Lana gave a short, embarrassed laugh. "He's a nice neighbor, taking pity on me. That's all."

Haley rolled her eyes. "Uh-huh. Whatever."

"Really, Haley. Even if I was interested, I wouldn't stand a chance. He is so out of my league." And it hurt to admit the truth. Davis Turner occupied her time and her thoughts way more than was prudent.

"Is he dating anyone else?"

The question gave her pause. Hadn't she wondered the same thing? Davis had been working on her house nearly every evening after dinner. Some nights they ate together, usually a pizza delivered from the Pizza Pan, while planning strategies for the old house or talking about town events and football play-offs. If Whisper Falls won another game, they'd play for the state championship. Exciting stuff in a small town and especially for a stringer reporter who only made money when she wrote a story.

"Is he?" Haley pressed, hoisting her coffee cup.

"Not that I know of. But he's really busy with work and his kids. It doesn't mean he's interested in me!"

"But it doesn't mean he's not either."

Oh boy. Just what she needed. Another misguided matchmaker.

"Davis, you will *love* her. Tara is the sweetest girl ever. She's only been working for Chuck a short time, but he's mad about her."

After a hard, extra long day on the job, Davis was worn slick, grimy and ready to head home to the shower and a little time in front of a televised basketball game. The last thing he wanted was to be nagged about his single status. Again.

"Maybe Chuck should date her."

Jenny whacked Davis on the arm and growled like a bear. "Only if he has a death wish." She bared her teeth in mock anger. "My hubby is as faithful as that old dog we had when we were kids."

"Patches? Not flattering to compare your successful CPA husband to a Heinz 57 mutt." He gave up expecting to grab his kids and head home. Jenny was on a mission and he might as well sit down on her couch and endure her good intentions.

"Loyalty, Davis. Loyalty." She perched on the edge of the couch a couple of feet down from him, her back straight as an arrow, her dark blond hair fresh from the beauty parlor. "Now stop changing the subject. Tara Brewster is perfect for you. She's pretty and funny and smart as a whip. And she's new in town. Act now before some other smart man discovers her."

"I don't know if I'm ready for the whole dating thing,

sis." Hadn't they had this conversation at least five times lately?

Jenny put her hand on his knee, her face filled with love and concern. She loved him, worried about him, even if he didn't want her to. "You know I loved Cheryl, but she's been gone a long time, Davis. You are young and good-looking—" When he flexed an arm, she pursed her lips and swatted him again. "Don't get the big head."

"Look, sis. I know you mean well, but I'd prefer to find my own dates."

"You aren't doing a very good job of it."

"I can't risk choosing wrong and messing up my kids."

"Which is exactly what you seem to be doing."

Her tone got his back up. "Are you talking about Lana?"

"I admire you for being a good neighbor. Even for bringing her to church. Lord knows, she needs it, but you can't let her get the wrong idea."

A cold feeling settled into his tired bones. Was this blind date Jenny's way of short-circuiting any interest he might have in Lana?

"What idea would that be?"

"You know what I mean."

Actually he didn't.

"Tara is more your type. And it would be a favor to me and Chuck if you'd go out with her. I know you're going to like her. You have so much in common."

He suppressed a sigh. Might as well listen and get it over with. "What makes you think so?"

"Tara's a widow. Car accident, I think."

He felt an instant, undesirable connection to the unknown Tara. "Any kids?"

"No. Which makes her perfect. Don't you see? She will adore Paige and Nathan."

At the mention of his children, a ridiculous, random thought penetrated Davis's mind. "What color is her hair?"

Jenny looked at him as if he was crazy. "What?"

"Remember Nathan's prayer?" A brown-haired mother. Preferably for Christmas.

"Oh, good cow." Jenny made a snorting noise. "Anyone can get brown hair if they want it. Tara's a blonde. A beautiful, green-eyed knockout. Nathan will fall in love with her. So will you."

Davis held up a hand. "Hold on now. It's only a date. I'm not marrying her, Jenny."

"So you'll go?" Jenny hopped up and hugged him. "Oh, I knew you would. You're the best brother. You won't be sorry, I promise."

Snared by his own words, he nodded, resigned. What would it hurt? If taking Chuck's new office assistant out for dinner would get his sister off his back for a while and Lana out of his head, he'd do it. Once.

"How did I get into this?" Davis muttered as he stood in front of his bathroom mirror and retied his tie for the fourth time. Anxious as a teenager dressing for the prom, he was not ready for this dating thing.

"Daddy?" Nathan appeared in the mirror behind him.

"What, buddy?"

"Can I go with you?"

"Not this time. You're spending the night with Aunt

Jenny and the twins. Remember?" He flipped one end of the blue striped tie over the other and poked the pointed fabric through the knot. The result was one tail shorter than the other. He pulled it apart again.

"I don't want to go to Aunt Jenny's. I want to go with you."

Davis dropped the ends of the tie, leaving them to dangle around his neck, and turned to crouch before his son. "What's the deal? You love spending the night with the twins."

"I don't like her."

"Jenny?"

"That girl. Paige says you're going on a date with a girl."

"That's right. I am. Her name is Tara. She seems very nice. I met her at Uncle Chuck's office this afternoon." Blonde, bubbly and sweet just like his sister had promised.

"What about Lana? She's real nice, too."

An arrow to the heart. But nice had different meanings to different people. As much as he liked Lana, some of the things he knew troubled him. Not for himself but for his children. He couldn't stop picturing little Sydney living in a car.

"Aunt Jenny is going to let you make Rice Krispie treats."

Nathan had a one-track mind. "Are you going to marry her?"

"We're going to dinner and a basketball game. That's all."

"I think I should go with you, Dad. I'm a good judge of character."

Davis hid a smile as he pulled his son into the *V* between his knees. "Not this time, buddy."

He hugged his boy close, enjoying the puppy-dog smell and tender love of his child. Paige had him wrapped around her finger. Nathan was wrapped around his heart. Both were too young to understand his dilemma. Being a single father, wanting to do the right things for his kids as well as address his needs as a man, was a difficult balance and part of the reason he'd avoided the dating game for so long.

Thanks a lot, Jenny.

"Dad?" Paige entered the room. Pixielike, with fairy-dusted freckles, she looked too serious this evening. "I'm worried about something."

"What's that, pumpkin?" He reached out to bring her into the family huddle.

"If you marry Uncle Chuck's assistant, what happens to Lana? Will that mean God doesn't answer prayers of little kids?"

Davis blew out a huffed breath. Good grief. This was getting crazy. "God always answers prayers, especially of little kids, Paige. But He doesn't always answer them the way we want."

"You mean Nathan might not get a brown-haired mom?"

"I can't answer that. I'm only going on a date. I'm not getting married."

Nathan raised his face so they were nose to nose. "Never?"

He shifted the children so that one sat on each raised knee, facing him. "Going on a date isn't the same as getting married, kids. Getting married means falling in love with someone very special, taking time to get to know her and then deciding if she's God's choice for our family. For all three of us. If I ever get married again, we'll all be getting married. Not just me."

Paige's gray eyes sought his. "You won't marry someone we don't like?"

"Not a chance."

"Promise?"

"Yes. I promise."

The children exchanged long looks before Nathan said, "Good. We like Lana."

Lana saw them come into the gymnasium. From her seat behind the clock keeper where she could take notes and see every play of the season opener, she'd spotted Davis and a pretty blonde the moment Davis had purchased tickets at the window box. He'd taken the woman's elbow, gentleman that he was, and guided her up into the stands where they'd sat down beside Mayor Rusty Fairchild, an Opie look-alike.

Davis had a date.

She tried to turn her attention to the pregame warm-up.

Sydney saw him too and leaned forward, gaze intent. "Davis is here but he's with a lady. Where are Paige and Nathan?"

"I have no idea. Sit up and don't stare." She pushed Sydney upright with a little more energy than usual.

She wanted to stare, too. Davis looked great, more dressed up than she'd ever seen him, as accustomed as she was to seeing him in work clothes covered with grouting mud or wall plaster. In a pale blue dress shirt with a darker blue striped tie and black slacks, he was killer handsome. When he smiled at the woman at his side, Lana expected the gym lights to dim in comparison.

The fluffy blonde woman was no slouch either. Dressed in a demure black dress with white pearls and trendy little heels, she was pretty as a picture. Davis couldn't seem to take his eyes off her. She was definitely his type. As sweet and wholesome-looking as a sugar cookie.

So, this was the woman Jenny had told her about at church, the woman Davis was dating. With all the flowery gushing of a mother, she'd discussed Tara Brewster, extolling her virtues, her Christian education, her classy lifestyle. With every gushy sentence, Lana had felt smaller and dirtier.

Now she got it. Jenny was warning her off, reminding her that Lana wasn't good enough for her brother. As if she didn't already know that.

With a heavy heart, she focused on her job and refused to look to the right again. The players, bouncing basketballs in staccato rhythm, moved off the floor, taking their places along the sidelines, to await the national anthem and their introduction.

"Can we get some popcorn?" Sydney asked.

"Not now." Though the buttery smell had her salivating, there was no way she was walking past Davis and his date to get to the concession stand.

The PA system squeaked and crackled. "Ladies and gentlemen, please stand for the singing of the national anthem."

The PA crackled again and Lana could both see and hear the conversation going on below her between the announcer and the high school principal. The crowd was standing, restless but waiting, but the music didn't start.

She watched as a note was passed to the announcer. He cleared his throat.

"Bear with us a moment," he said. "Our singer has taken ill."

After a momentary pause, an unseen person shouted into the quiet. "Lana Ross is here. She can sing."

The blood in Lana's veins froze as people nearby began to turn and stare.

"Go on, Lana," the woman behind her urged with a smile. "Just like old times."

The woman had no way of knowing what she asked.

Lana shook her head but by now, the announcer had heard the comments and turned in her direction.

Her heart stuttered in her chest. She met his gaze, frowning as she mouthed, "No. Don't ask."

To her horror, the idea picked up momentum and the announcer said, "Some of you may remember home-town girl, Lana Ross, formerly of Nashville, Tennessee. How about it, Lana? Would you do the honor of singing our national anthem the way you used to?"

A sea of smiling, expectant faces stared at her. Her body went hot and then cold and then hot again. Her stomach rolled. Her knees and hands started to shake.

She shook her head vigorously. "No."

"Ah, come on, Lana. We remember your pretty voice."

"I don't sing anymore. I'm sorry."

He turned to the spectators. "Come on, folks. Give Lana a little encouragement."

The crowd started clapping. She stared around at the faces, some familiar, some not, but all expecting something she couldn't give.

Her chest tightened. Her heart pounded. The air grew thin. She couldn't breathe.

She leaped from the seat, climbing over laps and legs, stumbling blindly out of the stands, face aflame. Her body shook so hard she thought she might fall.

She hit the bathroom door with the palm of her hand and made it to the stall right in time to be sick.

Chapter Nine

Her light was still on.

Standing on his front porch, Davis slid the tie from his neck as he stared down the block at Lana's two-story. Something had happened tonight at the ball game that bothered him. He wasn't sure why she wouldn't sing the national anthem but her reaction had been over the top. Did she dislike Whisper Falls that much? Or as some had murmured, did she think she was too good to sing for such a small-time gig? Or was there another reason? Whatever, he was curious, bothered.

Now, as the cold, clear night closed around him and only the corner streetlight illuminated the neighborhood in dark shadows, he was very tempted to jog across the street and up the block. The kids were at Jenny's until tomorrow. Ruffles had gone with them. No reason to go inside the lonely house yet.

Before he could overthink the moment, Davis stuffed the tie in his jacket pocket and jogged across the street to Lana's house. The neighbor's dog barked, a deep German shepherd *woof* intended to scare away prowlers.

Yellow light streamed out from a front window that

opened into Lana's parlor. As he neared her porch, he thought he heard music, but the moment he knocked, the sound ceased. The porch light came on. He squinted, blinking as she opened the door.

"Davis?" Her throaty voice sent a shiver over him.

Sparkling conversationalist that he was, he said, "Hey."

She fumbled with the latch before pushing open the screen. "Come in."

"Is it too late?"

"Never."

He liked the sound of that. As he stepped inside, the warmth of the fireplace met him. She'd wisely had the chimney cleaned and serviced and now a snapping fire sent off a pleasant heat. A colorful, lopsided Thanksgiving turkey, similar to one Paige had made in art class, graced the mantel next to a cross and a photo of Sydney. Beside the hearth leaned the same acoustic guitar he'd noticed before.

"Nice."

She tilted her head to one side, lifting a shoulder. "A little early for a fire, maybe, but the heat felt good tonight."

She was dressed as she'd been at the ball game. Skinny black pants, a lacy white, off-shoulder sweater thing draped over a red long-sleeved shirt. The only change was on her feet. Instead of her usual high-heeled boots, she wore fuzzy socks. The cozy sight made him smile a little. That was Lana. All country-singer trendy but real and comfortable to be with.

"You okay?" He shed his jacket without waiting to be asked.

"Great. Want some coffee?"

"Too late. I'd be up all night."

"The very reason I drink it." She smiled.

"In that case, why not live dangerously? The kids are spending the night with Jenny."

"Sydney's asleep, too. I usually work after she goes to bed. Sit. I'll get the coffee." She motioned toward the sheet-covered couch, but he followed her into the kitchen.

"I was worried about you."

At the counter, she glanced over one shoulder. "How so?"

"Tonight at the basketball game."

"Oh." She shook her head and turned back to the cabinets. "I'm fine."

Just that. She was fine. No explanation.

She loaded the coffeemaker and pushed On. "I'm working on the article about the basketball game. I think I'm starting to get the hang of this newspaper gig."

"Didn't you leave before the tip-off?"

"I didn't miss a second. Warriors went down 78 to 60."

Hmm. Interesting. She hadn't returned to the stands. He knew because he'd looked for her. He'd even been tempted to explore the lobby but with Tara at his side he couldn't. "Tough loss but the season's young."

She was standing with the upper cabinet open, her back to him, taking down cups and a container of powdered creamer. "How was your date?"

So she'd seen them. "A bust."

Lana head jerked toward him. "Really? She's so pretty."

"Can't argue that. Pretty, pleasant, good conversationalist."

By now, the coffee scented the room and warmed the end of his cold nose. Lana poured two cups. He reached around her and took one, brushing against her left arm. She looked up, met his gaze and went right on stirring creamer into her coffee. They were a whisper apart. In fact, he could feel the rise and fall of her breathing, detect the faint scent of mint on her breath and his heart seemed to swell in his chest.

"So what's the problem?" she asked.

Davis swallowed.

She wasn't you.

That's when the realization hit him. Jenny was right. He felt more than neighborly toward Lana Ross. In fact, if he didn't step away right now, he might kiss her. From the distant expression on her face, it was the last thing in the world she had on her mind.

He stepped back, taking his mug. "I don't think I'm ready."

She gave him a long, thoughtful look. "I understand."

Then, coffee in hand, she snapped off the light above the sink and headed back into the living room.

Lana settled at one end of the couch and curled her feet under her. Davis took the other end, cradling his coffee in both hands. He was comfortable here with Lana, in ways he hadn't been with Tara Brewster.

"Is she the first girl you've dated?" Lana asked, her husky voice sliding over his skin, warmer than the coffee.

He nodded. "Since Cheryl died, yes. Tara works for my brother-in-law."

"Jenny thought the two of you would be a perfect match."

Davis blinked, surprised that she'd known. "She told you?"

A momentary pause and then, "She might have mentioned something about it at church."

Jenny was talking to Lana about him? About his date? Why? As much as she disapproved of Lana why would his sister confide in her about anything? He had an idea and he didn't much like it.

"My sister doesn't run my life."

"That's good to know."

"Did she say something…?" He stopped. How did he ask if Jenny had insulted her without insinuating she had reason?

"I know Jenny doesn't like me, Davis. Don't worry about it. It's not as if you're interested in me."

But what if he was?

"It must be hard for you." She sipped the strong brew and watched him over the cup rim. "I mean, dating again after being settled and married."

"Really hard. Awkward. I loved my wife."

"She was a lucky woman."

"We had a good life."

"What happened? Or does it bother you to talk about her?"

"Not anymore. In fact, I wish people would talk about her more. My family is afraid of upsetting me or the kids."

"Paige has told me a lot about her."

"She has?" He'd had no idea his daughter was discussing something this important with the neighbor.

"She seemed to need that outlet. I hope you don't mind."

Did he? "I'm surprised. That's all."

"When I listen to Paige, to her wonderful common sense, her values, even her ideas about life and God, I know that Cheryl was a wonderful woman and a great mom."

Her compliment heartened him. "She was."

"Tell me about her."

Easy as that, she drew him out, listened, wanted to know, and he wanted to tell her. Everything.

"We met in college in Fayetteville in our freshmen year, first semester. Bam!" He whacked his chest with his fist. "Love at first sight. Married at Christmas, dropped out of school and came home to Whisper Falls. I went to work with Dad, using the skills he'd taught me since I was small. We never looked back. Cheryl worked at the bank until Nathan was born. By then, my business was going strong and she wanted to stay home with the kids. Really, that's all she ever wanted. Me, the kids, our life together as a family." He smiled, remembering the dark-haired woman who'd filled his life with love.

"I'm sorry. Really sorry for all you've lost." She unwound her legs from beneath her and shifted toward him. "Bad things shouldn't happen to such good people."

"I had a lot of questions, let me tell you. Questions that have no answers. That's the way this life is. If I believe God is in charge of the big things—and I do—I have to trust Him even in this."

"I admire that."

"Don't. I didn't get there overnight, but the bit about time being the great healer is true. Time and a couple of growing kids who needed me to be Daddy, not a grieving ball of mush lying across the bed." He huffed softly at the apt description, surprised he was telling her this.

"What happened? An accident?"

"No, but almost as sudden and every bit as unexpected. Sometimes I think if we'd done things differently, if I'd acted sooner, maybe she would still be here."

"You feel guilty?"

"Not guilty exactly." He shrugged, admitting the existence of that tiny niggle. "Maybe a little. Cheryl didn't like going to doctors. Of any kind. Once she had a toothache for a week before I could convince her to see a dentist. So when she got sick with what she considered the flu, we thought she'd be okay in a few days. She took over-the-counter medicines, stayed in bed. At her insistence I left the kids with Jenny, so they wouldn't get sick, too. But she didn't get better."

"She died of the flu?"

He shook his head, remembering the terrible moment when he'd known something much worse than flu infected his wife. "That last day, I'd taken off work at noon to come home. She scolded me, told me to stop worrying, and get back to work. It was the last time we ever spoke. When I arrived home that evening, she was unconscious." He drew in a ragged breath. "I couldn't wake her up."

"Oh, Davis, I can't imagine. You must have been scared out of your mind."

"I was." He dragged a hand down his face. "I carried her to the car and drove like a madman to the clinic. Dr. Ron took one look at her and called Creed Carter to fly her to a hospital in Little Rock. She died en route. Cardiac arrest."

"But she was so young."

"She had some kind of heart defect we didn't even know about. Probably had it all her life."

The terror and shock followed by an ice-cold numbness came back to Davis. He'd been zombielike for a while, with no emotions.

Lana set her mug on a scarred end table and scooted closer to him. "How awful."

"It was." He'd gone through the motions of life, of death, of a funeral. He'd accepted the flowers and sympathies, the fried chicken and prayers, feeling the love and compassion of a small town. The real grief struck later after everyone had gone back to their normal lives, but his life would never be the same again. "I know it's foolish to dwell on, but I can't help wondering now and then. What if I'd insisted she see a doctor, if I'd acted sooner when she didn't get better?"

Her hand closed over his. "God is in charge of things, even the big picture, right?" She gave his words back to him.

"Wise woman." Before he could think better of it, he put his arm around her and pulled her next to him. He knew he shouldn't have. It was a bad idea considering the late hour and the fact that they were completely alone without the worry of a kid interruption. Add the emotion of discussing Cheryl, the dinner date that had made him feel more awkward than anything and the nearness of this particular woman. Touching her might not be a smart move.

She laid her head on his shoulder and sighed. His pulse kicked up. This was nice, actually. Harmless and nice. Sitting together on the couch with the fireplace snapping and the old house creaking around them was a pleasant end to the evening. They were simply neighbors having a conversation.

Then why did he have this overpowering desire to kiss her?

He was going to kiss her.

Lana's heart thudded wildly against her rib cage, a captive bird begging to be released.

Davis's fingertips, calloused and rough from work, brushed her hair away from her cheek. The rough tenderness sent a shiver through her body. She wanted to reciprocate, to stroke his strong, clean-shaven jaw, to snuggle closer.

They were alone. Sydney was asleep. The fireplace lulled with its golden glow and warm, crackling flame. No one would know the nicest guy in Whisper Falls had kissed the town's bad girl.

Was the man completely out of his mind? Was she?

Reluctantly, she broke contact and scooted away, thrusting about in her head for something to say. Automatically, she went to the one thing that had always been her answer, her solace, her conversation when she had no words. She went to the fireside, picked up the guitar and strummed a quiet chord.

She dared a glance at Davis. He'd sat forward on the sofa, leaning toward her, puzzled.

She was puzzled, too. Puzzled by the sweet yearning to be something that she wasn't for his sake.

"You must wonder," she started, perching on the brick hearth, knees crossed to balance the instrument.

The caged bird beat harder, fluttering up to her throat. What would he think if she told him? Would he

walk away and never return? And if he did, wouldn't that
be the best thing for him and his beautiful little kids?

She searched his face, her chin high and cool as if
she didn't know she'd rejected him. He watched her,
eyes a stormy color.

"I wonder about a lot of things."

Lana thought she understood. He wondered why
she'd hustled away, a woman like her with nothing left
to lose. Certainly no reputation that mattered. He could
stay here in her house all night and no one would be
surprised that she'd allowed it. There might be a titter of
conversation and Davis's reputation would be smirched
but not hers. It was too late for her.

"That's not what I meant," she said.

He cocked his head, sandy brown eyebrows dipping
to a *V.* "I think I'm lost."

So am I.

"At the ball game. I refused to sing tonight even
though I've sung that song dozens of times." Her fingers found the strings and strummed again, restless,
needing the comfort music could bring. "Do you want
to know why?"

He shook his head. "I admit I was curious, but you
have a right not to sing if you don't want to. It's your
voice, your God-given talent. You can share it or not.
Your choice."

"But you think I'm being selfish?" She could see
the hint of accusation in his eyes, hear it in the slightly
tense comments.

His gaze slid away from hers. "They shouldn't have
pounced on you without asking first."

"What did they say?" She pressed, a glutton for pun-
ishment, wanting him to say something cruel so she

wouldn't like him so much. The basketball crowd had complained. She was sure of it. This town disliked her and tonight she'd added to their long list of reasons. "Go on. I'm tough. You have to grow thick skin in the music business." Though she'd learned most of her toughness in Whisper Falls.

"Forget tonight. Like I said, your voice, your choice."

"I don't think I'm too good to sing in Whisper Falls, Davis, if that's what you think. And it's not about money. I've sung for nothing a lot more often than I've sung for pay." The whisper of a song pushed up in her throat. She let it loose, humming.

He rose from the sofa and came toward her. Her stomach fluttered. She fought down the quiver of emotion, one part of her wanting him closer, the other willing him to keep his distance.

"So, if singing tonight wasn't about money or prestige, what was the problem?" He stood too close, one hand on the brick surrounding the fireplace, his scent mixing with the wood smoke. He'd carried the night in with him and she could smell the stars and moon. Man and moon, a heady combination.

"Some things happened in Nashville. I lost my..." Telling him about the fear was easy. But what about the rest?

"Voice?"

"In a manner of speaking. I lost my confidence." Truth was, her confidence had been artificial, taken from a gin glass. But she couldn't tell him that.

"No way. Even your humming sounds incredible to me." He tugged at his pant leg and settled next to her on the hearth. "Rough honey. Isn't that what the *Music City News* said about your voice?"

She recalled the wild thrill of reading her name in the prestigious publication. "You saw that?"

His eyes twinkled into hers. "Everyone in Whisper Falls saw it. We thought you were on your way to the top. Small-town girl making it big."

Such a good man. Such a sweet, all-American face. Good to the soul.

"All I made was a mess," she admitted, the words tumbling out before she could stop them. But that was as much as she dared say. She couldn't bear for him to know the rest, the debauchery, the nights spent too drunk to remember. Before he could press for details, she said, "Somewhere along the way, I developed a powerful case of stage fright. I can't get in front of an audience anymore."

"Stage fright?" He blinked, head tilted as if he couldn't quite take in her admission. "That's why you wouldn't sing tonight? You were afraid?"

"More than afraid, Davis. Terrified. Panicked. I can't really even describe how bad it is." She found the strings again, this time finger-picking a soft tune she'd composed. "I get so scared I think I'm going to die. I can't breathe. My heart races out of my chest."

"Did you see a doctor?"

"Doctors cost money, and they can't cure what ails me."

"You're too good to let fear stand in the way."

"Thank you for that." The melody from her guitar floated in the space between them. A love song. "But I'm okay with letting it go. My career was over before it started."

"I don't believe you." He placed his hard fingers across hers, stopping the music. "God doesn't take back

His gifts, and your gift is music. Look at you. The guitar is as much as a part of you as your beautiful hair."

He thought her hair was pretty? "I gave up singing, not music."

"Do you want to perform again?" He pulled his hand away, but hers remained on the strings, the feel of him vibrating through her skin.

"I—" She opened her mouth to deny the desire, but the words wouldn't come. She didn't want to sing the way she'd done before but oh, if she could sing unfettered by fear. If the songbird in her soul could fly free of its captivity. "Maybe," she ended.

He pulled her right hand from the guitar and into his, turning it palm up where he traced the line from thumb to pinky. Then he found the fingertip calluses, made deep by the frequent rub against the strings, and stroked them over and over. A tiny, raspy sound whispered from his skin to hers. A shiver, pure and lovely, ran along her arm.

"Do you believe in prayer?" he murmured.

"Absolutely." Prayer had literally saved her life. "Why?"

"The Bible says God has not given us the spirit of fear. He can take away that stage fright."

"You pray for me, then," she said.

"Count on it."

The thought of Davis calling out her name to God was a balm to her bruised spirit. God would listen to a good man like Davis.

They sat in silence for a bit, the fire warming their backs and Davis's skin warming hers. She thought she should pull away but she couldn't. She'd always been weak.

After a few tender moments, he squeezed her fingers and turned her loose. "What about Tess? Did she stop singing too?"

"She still works the clubs." Some. When she's not too strung out to show up.

"You still write?"

He remembered that? "I tried selling some of my songs. No takers."

"Play one for me. You don't have to sing it. Just play."

"I don't mind singing at home." And even if she did, she'd play for him.

Her fingers coaxed a melody from the guitar, and this time she sang along, softly at first and then louder until the room filled with music.

"On wings of the wind, through the clouds and the rain, your love carries me, carries me."

She closed her eyes and let the music take her as it always could, letting the emotion flow. The words and the melody rose from somewhere deep inside, an underground cavern of diamonds and gold, hidden from the world but always there, rich and beautiful. Only when the music took her did she feel this way, as if she was elevated to another plane where nothing could hurt her.

She looked toward Davis. Was he feeling it too? Yes, she thought he was, and she was mesmerized by his expression. Rapt. Impressed. Entertained.

The pleasure of sharing her music thickened in her chest. She hadn't felt that buzz of connection in a long time and it was good. Really good.

As the song ended and her voice faded away, the lilting melody hummed in the cozy quiet for several seconds.

Davis shook his head back and forth in a slow pendulum. "Wow."

Self-consciousness rushed in. "Does that mean, wow, it was good or wow, you're glad it's over?"

"That means, wow, I'd like to have a copy."

"Really?" Complimented, she pulled a sheet from a folder on the hearth. "Take it. I have more."

With a near reverence she found both touching and amusing, he accepted the simple sheet music. "You know this is amazing, don't you? *You're* amazing. Talented, gifted, whatever word you want to use. Not that I know a thing about writing music, but that was beautiful. And your voice is stunning. I don't understand why you'd be afraid to share it."

"You haven't been to Music City. I'm not too impressive there."

"Must be a really tough business or else you didn't meet the right people."

"You have no idea. Definitely not for the weak." Which she had been. She set her guitar against the wall and stood.

Davis followed her up where he stretched his hands out toward the fireplace. He couldn't be cold but the heat was nice. She joined him, stretching out her hands as he had done.

He rolled his head her direction. "There's nothing weak about you, Lana."

"Oh, but I am. I was." She tossed her hair back, eyeing the ceiling with its fresh coat of paint. "That's why I'm here, in the house I swore I would never again lay eyes on. After I found Jesus, I had to make some changes for Sydney's sake as well as my own."

"Why did you hate this place so much?" He backed

away from the fire, his cheeks rosy. "Why didn't you ever visit?"

She heard the accusation and knew he asked why she'd never visited her mother, why she'd missed the funeral attended only by an uncle and a few townspeople. She drew a deep breath and let it seep out, contemplating. What difference did it make if she told him?

"My family was about as dysfunctional as you can find. Or it seemed that way to me as a kid."

"I never knew that."

Why would he? They'd never hung out. "My dad kept up a good front but my mother was a nightmare. Looking back, I think she might have suffered from mental illness, but to a child, she was just plain mean. Tess and I stayed as far away from her as we could."

"Was she that bad?"

"Oh, yeah. That bad and worse. She did some things to us...." Her voice trailed off. "Mostly words but not always. She locked us in the cellar a couple of times overnight."

She tried to say it as if the abuse didn't matter, as if she wasn't bothered by her mother's cruelty but she knew she failed.

Davis, always Mr. Nice Guy, rubbed her back. She didn't read anything into it. He was a friend, offering comfort. "I'm sorry, Lana. Stuff like that shouldn't happen."

"We survived. It was just spooky and cold." She tossed her head and tried for bravado. "Gosh, I was mad at her."

So mad she hadn't gone home for three days. But mostly, she'd been heartsick that her own mother could hate her that much. And that her father could care so little that he'd leave and never even call. She'd found him once on the internet but hadn't made contact. What was the point?

"No wonder you didn't want to come back to this house."

"No, I didn't. That's for sure. But Sydney deserved more than I could give her on the road. At least here she has stability. This house may not be much, but it's ours." And Mama was gone. Lana felt guilty for being glad about that, but no matter how much she prayed, she was still glad.

"By next fall you won't recognize this place."

Which was exactly what she wanted. Wipe out all the ugly memories and replace them with Sydney's laughter and her music. Even now, the living room felt cozy and friendly in a way that it had never been when she was young.

"If the money holds out."

"What about Sydney's father? Doesn't he help with expenses?"

The words were cold water in the face. She'd known he would ask, sooner or later. She also knew he wouldn't like the answer, but for Sydney's safety, the partial truth was all she was willing to give. Even if it meant he would walk away and never look back. For his sake, that's exactly what he should do. He and his children needed a woman like blonde Tara or one of Jenny's church friends, not a has-been, former drunk singer with the reputation of an alley cat.

"That isn't possible."

"Why not?"

A beat passed. A log fell and shot sparks. Neither of them moved.

Lana cleared her throat. Confident she was doing the right thing, she said, "I have no idea who Sydney's father is."

Davis lay awake a long time after he left Lana's house. Thoughts shot through his head like fiery arrows, sharp and burning. Tonight Lana had opened up to him as never before and he wasn't sure what to do with the information.

Her childhood had been horrible. He couldn't imagine a parent locking her child in the cellar, and he didn't doubt Patricia Ross had been abusive in other ways.

Despite her confession about Sydney's parentage, he was still attracted to her. He'd wanted to be with her, to kiss her, as badly afterward as before. Maybe more. Her strange mix of invincible warrior and vulnerability had touched him. She seemed so bravely alone, as if she expected him to pass judgment and kick her out.

Was the woman intentionally trying to push him away? Was that it?

He tossed onto his side, pummeled his pillow. She liked him. At least, he thought she did. Or was she using him, as Jenny had suggested, as a means to get her house remodeled?

No, that wasn't Lana. She'd never asked him for anything. Not once. He'd offered. She was the workaholic, stripping wood and scrubbing floors at all hours of the day and night.

No one had asked her to be kind to his kids either. She'd fluffed Paige's too-short hair for church, obviously feeling sorry for his little girl and her inept dad. Paige had been so proud of the curls and bows she'd pranced around like a princess.

A couple of nights ago, Lana sat on her couch next to Nathan and read the same story four times in a row. And time after time, she'd tolerated three children tearing wildly through her house or perching at her table for PB and J sandwiches. No, she wasn't trying to take advantage of his neighborly kindness.

The more he knew about Lana Ross, the less he understood. She was a contradiction, a mystery. A beautiful, gifted, complicated mystery. He was both muddled and mesmerized.

He recalled the power and beauty of her voice, and he wanted to hear it again. Just a hum from that smoky throat captivated him. So what had happened in Nashville to bring on stage fright so bad that she couldn't get on stage? She'd sung for him. Why not on a stage? She was twice the singer Tess was and yet, Tess was still in Nashville while she was here, writing articles for the *Gazette*.

The song she'd shared lingered in his mind even now. She should do something with it. Not that he knew anything about the music world. The lyrics and melody were a hauntingly beautiful combination, better than anything he'd heard on the radio in a while. Why hadn't it been published? Had she tried? Or was this one something new?

He flopped onto his back and stared up at the faint shadows on his ceiling. The house felt lonely. *He* was lonely. For more than his children.

Tossing the covers back, he padded to the window and pushed the curtains to one side. Curtains Cheryl had ordered from J.C. Penney years ago. Not unusual for him to think about those days when he and Lana had talked about Cheryl tonight. Another thing he liked about Lana Ross.

Fumbling in the dark, he found the lamp and snapped it on. Cheryl's photo sat on the bedside table where he'd placed it the day after she died.

"Hi," he said, as he'd done dozens of times over the years. Her brown eyes twinkled in response. At least in his imagination. "What am I doing up at this hour? Good question. You see, there's this neighbor. Yeah, a woman. Lana. What do you think about her? Should I run for the hills?" He chuckled quietly. "Oh, right, we live in the hills."

He studied the simple face of his first love, the crooked smile that they'd never had the money to get straightened, the sweeping length of brown hair he'd loved to touch.

That, of course, brought him back to Lana. Lana, of the brown hair.

Carrying the silver frame, he returned his gaze to the window and beyond. From this spot, he could see the old house down the street and across the way. Lana's light remained on. Probably working on her article for the *Gazette*. Or was she, like him, too restless to sleep? Too bothered by feelings neither of them seemed to want?

His breath fogged the cold pane. He placed his late wife's photo back on the table.

"I like her, Cheryl," he said, admitting the truth to the emptiness, but mostly to himself. "I'm not sure that's smart. She's carrying a lot of baggage, but there's something special about her, too. A lot special. She's a good person, a Christian, but she wasn't always. I know, I know." He puffed out a gusty breath. "It's the kids. I have to be sure. I have to do what's best for our kids."

Davis rubbed a hand down his T-shirt, kissed his fingertips and touched them to the photo.

Then he snapped off the light and climbed back into bed, no closer to answers than he'd been before.

Chapter Ten

Thanksgiving Day arrived cold and rainy, the skies weeping down the windowpanes of the Ross house. A blustery wind whipped the barren crepe myrtle trees against the needed-to-be-replaced siding.

Inside the house all was snug while the Macy's Thanksgiving Day Parade boomed from a nineteen-inch TV Lana had found at a garage sale. A vigorous marching band pounded out a cheerful, familiar rhythm. Surrounded by autumn color, a pair of talking heads blabbed over the music. Bundled against the cold, their breaths puffed white fog.

Lana stood over the gas range where warm moisture from boiling potatoes dampened her face. Sydney chopped lettuce for a salad. The ancient oven hadn't worked since Lana was fourteen, so she'd bought a pre-cooked rotisserie chicken from the IGA for their main course. A turkey was too much for the two of them anyway.

Cooking wasn't Lana's game but as with her newspaper job, she could read and she could learn. Sydney learned along with her, probably more natural in the kitchen than Lana would ever be. Store-bought chicken, canned gravy, packaged stuffing was as close as she could come to a traditional meal. At least she and Sydney were together.

Times like these she wished for a big, noisy family, especially for her niece. A mother who baked for days and a sister with the perfect recipe for sweet potato casserole and pecan pie. A dad to carve the turkey and maybe a few brothers to horse around and yell at televised football games. Sydney deserved better than one single aunt and an AWOL mother she barely knew.

"Can I smash the potatoes?" Sydney asked. She'd pulled her fuzzy hair into a ponytail and tied it with a purple ribbon, a match for her purple monkey sweatshirt. Loose beige curls corkscrewed along her hairline.

"Smash 'em, mash 'em, stomp 'em. Whatever works."

Sydney's aqua eyes laughed before her mouth did. Lana smacked a kiss on her forehead, then handed her Mama's metal potato masher, tossed some butter in the bowl and let Sydney pound away while she put the food on the table.

Today was the day they started their own holiday customs, something Sydney hadn't had heretofore. Lana had shared family traditions once, and the memories were some of her happiest. Daddy had made a fuss over the fine brown bird, which had made Mama smile. Usually by day's end, Mama found something to be angry about but the meal was usually peaceful, thanks to her father.

She wanted that for Sydney. Good memories, good times to block out the bad.

"Here you go, Miss Ross," she said, pulling the chair

out for Sydney. "Please be seated for this luscious, marvelous Thanksgiving feast."

"Just like the Pilgrims," Sydney said as she minced into the seat like a pampered princess. "But who's going to hold your chair?"

Lana winked. "Good ol' me." She wiggled all ten fingers. "I'm so handy."

The silliness made Sydney giggle again. "This smells yummy."

"It should. I've slaved over that boxed stuffing for a full five minutes." She fanned her face and grinned, then took her place kitty-corner from the little girl who held her heart. "Would you like to ask the blessing?"

They bowed their heads and Lana listened, throat full, as Sydney prayed a litany of thank-yous and blessings.

Finally, she said, "And bless Paige and Nathan and their dad. I hope you give them a real good dinner like ours. Thank you for sending me a friend. And please take care of my mom. I hope she's okay. Amen."

Unexpected tears spurted behind Lana's eyelids. *Tess. Oh, Tess. Where are you?*

She pressed her fingertips hard into her eyelids to gain control. A small hand patted her arm.

"It's okay, Lana. God's taking care of my mom."

Most times she tried not to worry about her twin but she'd heard from her only once since the return to Whisper Falls. Tess had called, full of over-the-top excitement, an endless spiel of chatter and wild promises that told Lana immediately she was high. She'd tried to talk to her sister, urging her again to go to the mission for help. Tess had hung up on her.

"I wish I knew where she was." Lana scooped mashed potatoes onto her plate.

"You miss her," Sydney said, adultlike. "Maybe we can call some of her old friends?"

Most of Tess's friends had long since abandoned her but it was worth a try. Though Tess had never been much of a mother, she'd once been a good sister, and Lana *did* miss her. Terribly. "That's actually a very good idea, Sydney. After dinner, we'll give it a try. Now, do you want some of these fluffy, creamy, Sydney-awesome mashed potatoes or not?"

Sydney grinned and took the bowl. "And some of that Lana-awesome gravy and stuffing, too!"

They both laughed heartily at that comment, considering the foods were packaged.

"Paige said her grandma cooks everything in the universe for Thanksgiving dinner. They even have corn on the cob and chocolate pie."

"Wow. Wish I'd thought of that."

"It must be fun to have a grandma." Sydney drizzled brown gravy over the potatoes and stuffing as well as the chicken. A sea of gravy. "She lets Paige and Nathan and their cousins decorate cookies, and they play games with her, too. Did you ever have a grandma?"

"I did. My Grandmother Packard lived right here in Whisper Falls."

"Was she nice?"

"Really great. She sewed Tess and me matching dresses every year for Easter." Losing Grandma Packard at age nine had been a turning point in her young life and in her mother's, too. Mama's anger and moods had spun out of control once Grandma was gone.

"That's cool. I wish I had a grandma." Sydney's

matter-of-fact comment hurt worse than if she'd whined
in self-pity.

"Next time we're in Walmart, we'll buy you one."
Lana pointed a hot roll. "Nine ninety-five plus tax."

Sydney put a hand over her full mouth and giggled.
"Will you buy me a sister and brother too?"

"Tall order but why not? As long as they are on sale."

Smiling, feeling good, they continued their feast. The
day was going great, better than she'd expected. *Thank
you, Lord. Really. Thank you.*

"Lana?" Sydney said, putting down her roll and looking suddenly serious.

"Mmm-hmm," Lana managed to answer while chewing a succulent piece of chicken breast.

"You know what I'd really like to have more than
anything?"

Lana swallowed and reached for her coffee cup.
"More than a grandma or a brother or a sister?"

"Yes, even more than that."

A puppy, Lana was certain. She was going to have
to give this pet thing more serious thought. "What?"

"A daddy. A real good daddy. Just like Davis."

The kids were bouncing off the walls.

Davis, his belly full, flopped into his recliner and
pointed the remote. Mom had outdone herself this year.
He couldn't think of a single Thanksgiving food she
hadn't produced at some point during the rainy day.
They'd stayed even longer than usual playing board
games and snacking while the Cowboys and Lions battled on the gridiron.

He snagged Paige as she romped through with Nathan in hot pursuit. "Good day, huh, pumpkin?"

"Yep, except I felt bad for Charlie. He didn't even feel like eating Grandma's magic cookie bars."

Jenny's son, always frail, had seemed worse today. He'd slept most of the afternoon, worrying his parents.

"Me, too." He hugged his child, thankful for her robust health. "Aunt Jenny is taking him to the doctor in Little Rock tomorrow."

"I hope he's better. He said he was going to have to get an operation."

"That's true."

"I prayed for him."

Of course she did. That was Paige. Freckles and faith.

Nathan, who stood beside Davis's chair, head cocked as if he was listening, clearly wasn't. He said, "I'm hungry."

"Hungry?" Davis burst out laughing. "You can't be hungry."

Nathan pooched out his belly, rubbing the tiny mound beneath his camo T-shirt. "Can I have some pie?"

"Grandma sent home enough leftovers to last a week. Go for it."

Paige, still draped across Davis's lap like a blanket, patted Davis's neck. "Daddy, why doesn't Aunt Jenny like Lana and Sydney?"

Whoa. Where had that come from? He grasped Paige's hand and sat her up. "Did she say that?"

"She said Lana was a bad person and she might hurt us. I heard her tell Grandma."

Heat rose on the back of his neck. Where did Jenny get off saying such a thing? "Lana's *not* a bad person. Aunt Jenny's upset because Charlie's sick. She says things she doesn't mean."

"That's what Grandma said. She said you have to be

careful about judging people. She said Lana might have problems we don't know about."

Thanks, Mom. "Grandma's right."

"Does Lana have problems, Daddy? She's really nice to me and Nathan. I'm sure she would never, ever do anything to hurt us. Never. We love her. I don't think she has problems. I think she's wonderful, like Mommy was."

"Everyone has problems, pumpkin. Lana is no different than Aunt Jenny or you or me."

Davis felt like a hypocrite, considering how he'd wrestled with Lana's admission about Sydney's father. How did a woman not know who fathered her child?

But all day today he'd thought about her. Not just today but every day. Even though he'd avoided her house all week, he thought about her. Missed her.

When they'd pulled into their driveway after the wonderful day at Mom's and Dad's, he'd noticed her car was home. His conscience had twinged then and it twinged now. Today was Thanksgiving, a family day, a day he and his children had basked in all the noise and pleasure that was family. Yet, he was fairly certain Lana and Sydney had spent the holiday alone.

He should have invited her to the Turner Thanksgiving madness, regardless of Jenny. He didn't appreciate the seed of gossip his sister had placed in his daughter's head. That was wrong, no matter how upset or how protective Jenny might be.

He popped his chair upright. "I have an idea. Let's take one of Grandma's pies over to Lana and Sydney."

Ten minutes later, he and his kids stood on the Ross porch, each of them holding containers of food. The rain continued to drip like a leaky shower from a cold, slate sky.

Lana opened the door. As soon as she saw him, her smile bloomed. His stomach, full as it was, went south. He smiled back, staring long enough that Paige said, "Dad! It's cold out here."

Lana blushed a pretty pink and opened the door. They flooded inside, all talking at once. Sydney exclaimed over the pecan pie while Nathan hugged Lana's waist and told her she was pretty. She hugged him back and told him he was the handsomest little boy she'd ever seen. Then the trio of kids headed to the kitchen to eat pie as if they hadn't eaten all day long.

"How was your Thanksgiving?" Lana asked once the kids had disappeared.

"Great. The whole clan was there. Even my aunts and uncles from out of town." *Everyone I wanted to see except you.* "So how did the Rosses celebrate?"

"We made dinner together and watched a Christmas movie. The oven doesn't work so we had Oreos for dessert. And ice cream."

He laughed. "Works for me. Ice cream on top of pecan pie sounds pretty good."

"Want some?"

No. I want you. I want to hold you and smell your hair and touch your creamy-looking skin.

Davis shook the flash of forbidden thought out of his head. "I'm still stuffed. You?"

"Later, but I should probably look in on the kids now."

"Good plan."

"Sit down and relax. I'll put on some fresh coffee while I'm in there." Lana disappeared through the

French doors leading through the dining room and beyond to the kitchen. Davis watched her until she disappeared from sight, unnervingly glad to see her again.

The ever-present work list—the one he and she had made together weeks ago—lay on a side table. Restless, he picked it up and ran a finger down the check marks. She had a long way to go on a complete remodel but the house was ready for winter. He was glad about that. He didn't like to think of her and Sydney in a draughty, cold house with frozen pipes.

The French door clicked open and Lana came to where he stood. His belly dipped again and he didn't deny his attraction. She smelled like flowers. Gardenias, he thought. In her heeled boots she reached his ear. Her reputation from long ago didn't matter to him at all, and he wondered if he should worry about that fact. Lana Ross had him by the heart.

"You've been busy," he said to her tilted face, gripping the notepad to keep his hands off her.

"Mostly I've painted and cleaned and ripped out old flooring."

"And put weather stripping around the doors and windows."

"Some of the doors and windows need replacing but there's no time for that now." She made a face. "Or money yet."

He laid aside the notepad and stuck his hands behind his back. "How's the *Gazette* job going?"

"Better. I think I'm getting the hang of this article-writing business. Saturday morning, I'm covering the Christmas Bazaar committee meeting. Saturday evening is the Cheerleaders' chili supper. Sunday, the Baptist Church is having its one hundredth birthday homecoming with a special speaker and a dedication of the new family center. I'm covering all those."

"I'm impressed."

"Me, too." She widened her eyes, laughing at herself. "So what have you been up to lately?"

"Thinking about you too much." The reply shocked her as much as it shocked him.

"Really?"

"I missed you."

"I'm right down the street."

The words flailed him, though her tone held no accusation. He was the one who'd withdrawn, not her. "If I had invited you to the Turner Thanksgiving feast, would you have come?"

"And given your sister a heart attack?" Lana smiled but her bottom lip trembled. Jenny's attitude hurt her, no matter how tough she tried to be.

Davis moved closer, finding her fingers. They felt cold. "Jenny's had some stuff going on, Lana. Not just with you. Her son is really sick."

Lana's chin came up, her eyes searching. "I didn't know that."

"He has a heart condition. I don't know the details. I just know he's been sickly all his life and is going to need another surgery real soon."

"I am so sorry." The cold fingers laced into his.

"Yeah. Me, too, but that's no excuse for her weird animosity against you."

"It's not exactly weird, Davis." She dropped her head. "I wasn't nice to her in high school."

He studied the top of her head, that pale strip of scalp where the dark brown hair parted. "Ancient history. Time to get over it."

"I guess."

"No guessing needed." He tilted her chin and gazed into her troubled eyes. "The rest of my family likes you. Especially me."

And then he didn't resist what he'd wanted to do for days. He kissed her.

Lana gripped the sides of Davis's jacket and gave herself to the kiss. His mouth was warm and tender like the man and tasted vaguely sweet like whipped topping. His chest, honed by work, was firm and strong, the perfect refuge for her personal storms. She wanted to sail into his safe harbor and stay. And oh, the way he kissed. The way his calloused hand cupped her cheek and threaded into her hair. She dropped her hands to his waist and around his back, snuggling closer.

She was dimly aware of the children's voices and a coffee smell drifting from the kitchen. But most of her senses were attuned to Davis, this man who didn't seem to have the good sense to stay away.

For two years, she'd steered clear of men, not trusting herself or them. Then along came Davis Turner to shatter her resolve.

A giggle broke through her fog. She jerked away from the warmth of Davis to find three children standing inside the French doors, eyes dancing, smiles a mile wide.

Oh, boy.

She shot a glance at Davis. Though his face was flushed, he allowed a sheepish grin and shrugged.

He cleared his throat and asked, "How was the pie?"

Paige and Sydney exchanged looks and giggled again. Then the three of them exchanged high fives and nearly fell over themselves as they ran out of the living room.

Lana started after them.

Davis caught her arm and pulled her back.

"But I need to explain...."

"Explain what, Lana? That we like each other? That I kissed you? I think they've figured that much out." He tugged her closer. "Now where were we?"

Lana was already shaking her head. This could not happen. She'd promised not to let it happen. Davis's sister was right about her whether Davis believed it or not. Lana knew too many things he didn't, especially about why his sister hated her.

"This is a bad idea, Davis." She stepped back, putting several feet between them though Davis didn't let go of her hand.

"I disagree. I wanted to kiss you a week ago."

"Why?"

He ran a frustrated hand through the top of his hair, sending it up into a wild spike. "Because I'm attracted to you. Is that so hard to imagine? Look at you. You're gorgeous and kind and we get along great. Come on. Give us a chance."

Lana's stomach churned. Her heart thundered louder than Digger Parsons's antique locomotive. She wanted to be with Davis more than he could ever know. Kissing him, being with him, was not like anything she'd experienced in her sordid past. With a man like Davis she almost felt clean. Almost.

With all her heart, she wished she could be the woman he needed, but he didn't know the real Lana Ross. The girl who'd drunk too much and slept around, who'd shoplifted and spent a few nights in jail, who'd

basically kidnapped her niece and even now was hiding
her out in Whisper Falls. Sure, he knew a little about her
wild teen years, but his ardor would vanish like vapor
if he learned everything.

She reached out and squeezed his fingers. "Let's go
have a piece of your mother's pie. Okay?"

"No." He yanked his hand away and loomed over
her. The hurt and confusion in his eyes clawed at her.
"We're not ignoring this, Lana. I kissed you. You kissed
me back. But it's not just about kissing." He grinned a
small grin. "Though I have to admit kissing you was
awesome. I want a relationship with you. We have something." When she stood there, unresponsive, he touched
her face and said softly, "Cut me some slack here. Am
I making a total fool of myself? Are you interested or
not?"

His rough fingers were tender against her skin, melt-
ing her, muddling her conviction. "Yes, but—"

He put his hand over her mouth. "You said yes. That's
good enough for now. No buts. Okay?"

Wanting to erase the hurt in his eyes, she nodded.
How did she get out of this situation without hurting
the most incredible man in her life?

She closed her eyes against the misgivings hammering at her conscience.

She needed time. Like a million years.

Chapter Eleven

The meeting of the Whisper Falls Christmas Bazaar Committee commenced Saturday morning in the conference room of the library, Miss Evelyn Parsons presiding. Lana arrived early, notebook and telephone recorder in hand to find others already there before her. She took a seat in back, heartened by the welcoming smiles of several familiar faces. Haley left her spot on the front row to sit next to Lana. She'd come alone.

"Where's your baby?" Lana asked.

"Daddy's play day." Haley smiled. "Creed loves having Rose to himself once in a while, and we already know his part in the bazaar. He works at my table and donates helicopter rides." She gave a little shiver. "Which I will never bid on."

Lana laughed at her friend's aversion. "You're so lucky."

"I know and I'm really thankful." Haley set a huge, lime-green tote bag on the floor. "How are things going with you and Mr. Looks-great-in-a-tool-belt?"

Lana rolled her eyes at the description though she had to agree. Davis in work clothes was every bit as attractive as Davis in church attire. She was still reeling from Thanksgiving Day and the feelings he'd stirred up inside her. For two days now she'd done nothing but wish for the impossible. "I think he likes me, Haley, and it won't work."

"Why?"

"You know why. We're all wrong for each other." When Haley only stared at her, head tilted, as if she was crazy, Lana admitted, "I stupidly let him kiss me."

"And?"

A slow grin pulled at Lana's cheeks. "It was amazing. *He's* amazing. And his kids are adorable but…"

"But you think you're not good enough because of all that junk from your past. That's it, isn't it?"

At that moment, several more people entered the room, among them Tara Brewster and Jenny Cranton. When Jenny saw Lana, she stiffened, grabbed Tara's elbow, leaned in and whispered something. Tara glanced at Lana, curiosity in her expression.

Shame rose in Lana.

"Who is that?" Haley asked.

"Davis's sister."

"Oh. Not good. Not good at all."

That was putting it mildly.

Others arrived, among them Annalisa and Cassie and a few other familiar faces in addition to some new ones. Head high, determined not to let Jenny's slight get to her, Lana introduced herself to the newcomers as a reporter for the *Gazette*.

Then the meeting commenced with Miss Evelyn in charge, efficiently setting up committees for everything from donations and advertising to volunteers and decorations. The bazaar, it seemed, was a very big event in Whisper Falls.

After a while, Miss Evelyn switched on some background Christmas music and the attendees split into groups to brainstorm and organize. Lana ventured from group to group, listening in, taking notes, gaining a buzz of excitement from the creativity flowing in the room. Had it not been for Jenny's coolness, Lana would have felt a part of the group. This was fun and fulfilling.

Kind of like kissing Davis Turner.

She shook her head at the random thought. The man gave her no rest at all. She knew she'd hurt his feelings on Thanksgiving, a truth that made her ache. She didn't want to hurt him. That was the whole point. But Davis, kind and wonderful Davis, had stayed another hour to eat pie and talk as if nothing had happened. When he'd left he'd kissed her on the cheek. That one little act— slow, sweet and powerful in its simple tenderness—had rocked her world.

Then, as if she hadn't felt like a big enough loser, he'd called her yesterday. He'd found a Black Friday deal on bicycles for his kids and asked if she wanted one for Sydney's Christmas.

No wonder she couldn't stop thinking about him.

She shot a glance at Jenny's table. Davis's sister was busily writing something on a notepad but Tara Brewster glanced up, caught Lana's eye and smiled. Pleasantly surprised, Lana smiled back at the pretty blonde. The warm buzz increased and she moved on to the committee in charge of arts and crafts, Haley's group. As she listened in, she wished she had something to offer but creative arts were not her gift.

When they returned to full session, ideas fairly sizzled through the air to Miss Evelyn who fielded them all with alacrity. When no one volunteered for a task, Miss Evelyn appointed. And no one refused.

"Lana." The older woman peered over a pair of reading glasses. "I expect you to help with advertising."

Lana blinked a couple of times. "All right."

"Joshua Kendle isn't here but you ask him. He'll give us free space. Make us a pretty ad. Nice and big and run it often. Ted Beggs and I will take care of social media and the radio stations."

Now she understood how Miss Evelyn accomplished so much. With humor and strength, she delegated. Refusal was not an option. "Okay."

"Think about the music, too. The high school chorus is singing and the Methodist Choir. Maybe the Boggy Boys Band. But we could use you. Something modern and fresh and a little bit country."

Lana felt the stares turning in her direction. Haley gave her a thumbs-up. Thankfully, Miss Evelyn didn't push for a response, but simply said, "You think on it," and moved on to Edie, the owner of Sweets and Eats, who co-chaired the food and concessions.

Think on it? Her heart was pounding so hard, Lana couldn't think at all.

She bent to her notepad and pretended to write, missing several minutes of the meeting to calm her anxiety. Miss Evelyn surely must have heard about the incident at the basketball game and yet, she'd casually urged Lana to sing as if she hadn't made a fool of herself in front of several hundred people.

What was that about?

Ears buzzing, Lana scribbled madly, doodling little nothings.

Why couldn't she simply tell them the truth? Why couldn't she admit the reasons she wouldn't sing? But she knew the answer. They thought badly enough of her as it was. No way she'd admit that she couldn't sing sober.

After a bit, she shook off her dark thoughts to hear Miss Evelyn say, "This year we're reaching out, going for more tourist trade. Work your Facebook and Twitter." She tapped a pen against her lip. "Now if we could somehow promise them a white Christmas."

Titters of laughter trickled around the room. If anyone could wrangle snow from the sky for the sake of Whisper Falls tourism, Miss Evelyn would figure out a way.

A white-haired woman on the third row—Reverend Schmidt's wife—raised her hand. "Miss Evelyn? What is this year's charity?"

"Good question, Phoebe. Let me explain to the newcomers. Each year the town council chooses a charity to receive a portion of the money raised by the Christmas Bazaar. Townspeople may nominate an individual, a service group, or an outright charity such as missions. This year one of our own is in need."

Heads swiveled in the direction of Jenny's table. Curious, Lana watched as Jenny's face changed from puzzled to a slow dawning.

"Oh, my goodness," she said. "Oh, my. You didn't?"

Miss Evelyn's smile was benevolent. "We certainly did. You and Chuck put time and energy and love into this town. We want Charlie to have that operation ASAP."

"How did you know?" Jenny glanced left and right, expression incredulous, palms lifted. "We only found out ourselves yesterday."

"Don't you worry about that, hon, or anything else for that matter. God's taking care of that precious little boy of yours, and Whisper Falls will help with the rest."

Jenny covered her face with her hands and burst into tears. The women around her hugged her shoulders and patted her back. Tears glistened in more than one pair of eyes.

Lana was stunned. Davis had told her about Charlie's illness and the stress it had put on his sister, but she had never viewed Jenny as anything but a mean-spirited woman. Like Lana's mother. Whisper Falls apparently didn't see her that way.

The revelation shook her. Just as Jenny had judged her, she'd judged Jenny.

She still had a lot of growing to do.

As the meeting broke up, and Lana started to leave, mind reeling with this new information, Miss Evelyn called her name. "Lana, wait up, please."

Braced for more unwanted conversation about music, Lana nonetheless waited while other women huddled around Miss Evelyn like chicks around a hen. During the wait, she made a lunch date with Haley and chatted with Cassie and Annalisa and Pastor Ed. When a tear-streaked Jenny exited, surrounded by supportive friends, Lana felt the stirrings of compassion. In an odd kind of way, Lana understood the desire of a mother to do everything possible for the welfare of her child.

Soon the committee members cleared out, leaving only Lana, Haley and Miss Evelyn. Haley hitched her green tote and said, "Gotta run, ladies. See you at church tomorrow."

Church. Lana's heart thumped. Davis would be there. After this revelation about Jenny, she was more flustered than ever. She lifted a hand and waved but Haley was already gone.

"I have a story idea for you," Miss Evelyn said without fanfare.

Some of the tension went out of Lana. No questions about the music. No pushy request for her to sing. Just a story idea. "Great. What is it?"

"The Christmas Express." Palm open, Miss Evelyn dramatically waved the word across the sky in a rainbow. "How's that sound?"

"Enticing. What is it?"

"Uncle Digger and I renamed the train for the holidays but we came up with this great idea kind of late, so we need you to write up a Jim-dandy article and spread the word."

Lana had stuffed the notebook in her tote but pulled it out again. "Tell me all about it."

"I have a better idea. We've gotten all the particulars in order for the inaugural ride which takes place tomorrow afternoon. Just a handful of invited people, mostly news folks. I even called the radio station down in Moreburg."

"You're inviting me along on the ride?"

"I sure am, though we could use more kiddies. You see, it's a family ride with lots of fun things for the children. You gather up that darling girl of yours and ask Davis to bring his children, too. Take lots of photos and write this up from the children's perspective."

Lana got stuck on the part about asking Davis. Would that be wise? Or would she be an even worse loser to let his children miss an opportunity to experience the brand-new Christmas Express?

"So what do you think? Isn't this a grand idea?"

Lana looped her bag over her shoulder.

Oh, yeah. Just grand.

An Arctic front moved through the state late on Saturday night, chilling Sunday to freezing temperatures. Snow was in the forecast, much to the kids' delight. A sheen of lacy frost formed on windows and wood smoke puffed from atop houses, scenting the air as Davis stepped out of his truck. Car doors slammed and voices echoed over the parking spaces outside the train depot and museum. Below the town but visible from the depot, a handful of boats puttered along the shiny Blackberry River.

"Looks like a good turnout." Davis motioned with his chin toward the Channel Six news van.

"I saw some others pulling in, as well." Lana's lips puffed vapor. "Miss Evelyn mentioned a 'handful' of people but I think there might be a few more than that."

Davis shook his head, amused. Miss Evelyn had a way about her. "Any idea exactly what she has in mind?"

"Only what I told you on the phone. A *Polar Express* experience."

"You mean, like the movie?"

"We'll soon find out. Knowing Miss Evelyn and Uncle Digger, our evening will be way more than a train ride into the mountains." When they'd gotten out of the truck, Lana had taken Nathan's hand. Now she paused to tug his sock cap down over his ears, smiling. "Don't want your ears to freeze off."

Nathan giggled, eating up the attention.

The scene touched Davis in a way that had him wondering. Did Lana know the effect she had on his son? On him?

"It feels like Christmas," Paige said, hopping up and down in her thick, hooded parka. "This is going to be fun."

"A great way to start the Christmas season," Davis agreed.

The train depot sat in the center of town, a salute to the glory days of the railroad that had built Whisper Falls and other small Ozark towns round about. The 1920's passenger train, used for tourist excursions year-round, waited beyond the boardwalk steps. The engine's green-and-red paint had been transformed to Christmas colors by the addition of tiny lights and a giant wreath on the cow-catcher.

"Look," Sydney said, fairly bursting with excitement. Bundled in a bright blue coat that turned her eyes to gleaming jewels, Lana's little girl pointed to two red-clad characters standing in the train's open doorway. "Santa and Mrs. Claus!"

Sure enough Uncle Digger Parsons had traded his usual striped overalls in favor of a red Santa suit and a snowy beard attached beneath his horseshoe mustache. On his head, though, was his engineer cap decorated with a sprig of holly. No doubt about it. Uncle Santa was driving this train. Miss Evelyn, cheeks rosy and eyes twinkling, wore a long red velvet dress, white apron and white hair covered by a ruffled red mobcap, a perfect Mrs. Claus.

Nathan stopped dead in his tracks. "Wow. Dad," he said in breathless awe. "This is so cool. An almost-real Santa."

The adults exchanged amused looks. Davis had always been truthful with his children about Santa Claus, not wanting them to confuse Santa and Jesus, but he'd never been militant about it.

"Sometimes pretending is fun," Lana said, kindly.

Nathan's earnest, innocent eyes raised to hers. "Can I pretend you're my mommy?"

Davis thought his heart would stop beating. Ever since some kid at school had asked him why his mother left, Nathan had craved the one thing Davis could not be. But his innocent blunder was both embarrassing and unanswerable. He'd put Lana in a tough spot and Davis didn't know how to help, especially after Thanksgiving. He still wondered why she'd invited them on today's outing. Surprised but glad.

Sorry, he mouthed over Nathan's head. Inside he was praying she wouldn't break his son's heart, that she'd somehow let the little guy down easy.

In her snug jeans and brown fitted coat with glossy hair around her shoulders, Lana bent to cup Nathan's chin. "You are such a fine boy. Any woman would be honored."

Nathan looked from Lana to Davis, face twisted into a question mark. "Does that mean okay?"

His cute response broke the tension and both adults chuckled. A sudden lightness filled Davis's chest, and he felt relieved and grateful to the woman. Lana had done more than let Nathan down easy. She'd let him in.

He placed a hand on Nathan's shoulder and squeezed.

"Just like Santa Claus. We'll pretend for today." He wanted Nathan to have good memories of Christmas. The boy would learn soon enough that life—and love— were more complicated than a game of pretend.

With excited whoops, the children rushed ahead,

climbing onto the train platform, not waiting for the adults. Miss Evelyn—aka Mrs. Santa—welcomed them. Uncle Digger disappeared inside but his ho-ho-ho echoed out into the late afternoon.

"Up you go." Davis put his hand beneath Lana's elbow as she took the first step, more because he wanted to touch her than because she needed help. "Thanks for the way you handled that," he said. "I'll have a talk with Nathan."

"He's just a little boy, Davis. He doesn't understand there is more to getting a mother than brown hair."

Davis gave a short huff. That was an understatement. Still, he was grateful to her. "Missed you at church this morning."

"It's nice to be missed." She didn't offer an explanation and before he could ask, she gasped. "Look at this place."

He did. The interior of the old train had been turned into a Christmas spectacular. Bright red stars and huge snowflakes dangled from a rounded ceiling festooned with lighted garland. The side posts looked like red-and-white peppermint sticks. Swags of shiny tinsel dipped from one side of the car to the other. More silver tinsel had been roped along the backs of the seats and topped with bright red bows. Christmas music seeped through the speakers, quiet but cheery. It was an over-the-top wonderland of Christmas, missing only the snow and presents.

"I've ridden the train before during the fall foliage tours, but this is something."

Lana lifted her nose and looked around. "Do you smell cinnamon?"

He took a long sniff, filling his lungs with a smell

that reminded him of Mom's Christmas cookies. "I think it's coming through the vents. Nice touch."

"It's making me hungry for a cinnamon roll!" Lana said with a laugh, her eyes sparkling. She looked fresh and pretty and full of joy today. He liked the look. In fact, he liked a lot of things about Lana Ross and unless his male radar had gone completely bust, she liked him, too. They got along great, could talk about anything and they liked each other's kids. So why did she push him away every time he ventured near?

The cars were filling rapidly and the same gush of excited pleasure escaped from many of the riders as they found their seats. Miss Evelyn and Uncle Digger had outdone themselves and the trip hadn't even begun.

Davis and Lana followed the children, coming to rest in the center of the car with the kids in a front seat and the two adults behind. Davis was certain the three munchkins had intentionally maneuvered him and Lana into sharing a seat. He had to admit sitting next to Lana in a seat built for the smaller bodies of 1920's riders was pretty cozy. Their shoulders brushed and Lana's flowery fragrance messed with his head. And when she turned her head the tiniest bit, they were as close as a whisper.

While he was enjoying the attraction, Uncle Digger's voice came over the intercom calling, "All aboard for the Christmas Express!" The train lurched once before slowly chugging out of the depot. "Settle back and enjoy the ride, folks. We're on our way to the North Pole!"

"North Pole!" A wide-eyed Paige squealed and grabbed Sydney in a mutual little-girl hug. "North Pole!"

Nathan, crammed against the window, whipped around. "Dad, guess what? We're going to the North Pole. Right now!"

Davis's mouth lifted. "So I heard. I'm sure glad we brought our coats."

"Yeah." His boy looked from Davis to Lana. "You can snuggle up if you get too cold."

Davis laughed. "I'll keep that in mind." Snuggling with Lana sounded pretty good, if he thought about it. Which he did. "Look out the window, buddy."

Easily distracted, the excited boy whipped around and pressed his face into the window. Rings of vapor clouded the pane. He swiped at them with his coat sleeve and watched the town slip away.

Miss Evelyn and her helpers, all appropriately dressed in elf attire, moved through the cars handing out candy canes and programs.

Lana took out her camera and said, "I should get some photos. Will you excuse me?"

"What? No snuggling?" he teased.

She stuck a finger in his face. "You have to wait until we reach the North Pole. Remember?"

Her lighthearted reply tickled him. He stood to let her out of the seat, grinning when she leaned around to face the kids, camera at the ready. "All right, you three, say cheese."

The children hammed it up, giggling, crossing their eyes and poking out pink tongues. Laughing, too, Lana snapped and snapped before moving on to other children in their car, taking the time to gather names and permission. He watched her, interested in the genuinely nice way she had about her. Lana had changed a lot in her years away. The name was the same but the woman wasn't.

The classic song, "Rockin' Around the Christmas

Tree" came through the speakers. Lana began to bebop toward him, mouthing the words.

He thought about her music and knew she missed it. On Thanksgiving she'd played the guitar and sang with the children in her rich mezzo-soprano voice. Her gift was meant to be shared whether she was a big star or not. Though she claimed stage fright, he couldn't stop thinking there was more, something she hadn't told him.

Lana had secrets.

Suddenly, she stuck the camera in his face and before he could recover from the shock, she pressed the shutter button.

"Hey!"

"My boss likes lots of photos and so do the readers."

"The only person who will like that one is my mother."

"There you go then. One happy reader." Full of energy and Christmas cheer, she scootched him with her shoulder and hip, pushing him to the inside of the seat. The mountains outside the window were brown and bare except for the glades of deep green pines and cedar. Occasionally a vivid red cardinal flitted through the trees.

"I want to sit with you, Daddy," Nathan said after a while. Davis wasn't surprised. His boy had never been good at long-distance rides.

Lana patted the tiny space between them. "Come on back. We'll make room."

Crawling over the girls, he came, crowding into the narrow spot.

"Tired of riding, little man?" Lana asked.

"Yeah." Candy cane in his mouth, he leaned against her, slowly inching down as if to put his head in her lap.

Davis considered stopping him but Lana didn't seem to mind.

She gathered Nathan close as if holding Davis's growing eight-year-old was the natural thing for her to do. When Nathan grew too warm, she helped him with his coat, murmuring something in his ear that made him smile around the peppermint stick.

Davis's insides clenched. His children adored Lana and she treated them with such tender consideration it took his breath. She was good for them. There was nothing sweeter to a dad than knowing a woman cared about his children.

They'd ridden a while when Miss Evelyn announced a sing-along and familiar Christmas songs filtered through the speakers. Nathan sat up then, candy cane still in his mouth to sing "Jingle Bells." The elves came through the car handing out bell bracelets for the children to shake. And shake them, they did!

Paige whipped around in her seat and, above the noise said, "Sing, Dad. Sing, Lana."

Davis obliged, pleased when Lana's husky voice joined in. The sound really was rough honey, flowing over him sweet and thick with a touch of gravel that raised goose bumps on his arms.

When the song ended, he leaned toward her. "Your voice knocks me out. You still love to sing, don't you?"

"I do. I shouldn't. I promised God I'd lay it down if He'd—" She stopped again and shook her head. "Never mind."

"If He would do what?"

A beat passed and he could see the wheels turning in her head. Would she lie to him or share a little glimpse of herself?

"If He would change my life. And He did."

"Do you really think God doesn't want you to use your talent?"

"It was the only thing I had to trade." She dropped her gaze to Nathan's shirt collar. Davis caught her hand, pulled her around to face him. "You think the stage fright came from God?"

"No. Maybe." She heaved a heavy sigh and moved her hand back to Nathan. "I don't know where it came from, Davis, but my life is better now. Sharing my music with strangers is behind me. I'm happy."

If that was true Davis had made a mistake that could come back to bite him.

"Deck the Halls" broke out over the gathering, led by a slightly off-key but no less enthusiastic Miss Evelyn. Davis dropped a friendly arm around Lana's shoulders and hugged. "Then make me happy, too. Sing. Sing like nobody's listening."

So she did. As the music fell from their lips, Paige looked over one shoulder to listen. Seeing Davis with his arm around Lana, she punched Sydney. Both girls turned to grin. Above the music, Sydney pumped her fist and proclaimed, "Now that's what I'm talking about!"

Chapter Twelve

The North Pole proved to be every bit as exciting as the train ride.

Though enjoying the pleasure of Davis's company too much, Lana let herself go with the moment for the sake of the children. They were having such a grand time. Hadn't she told Nathan that today they could pretend all they wanted? She could pretend she wasn't the town party girl and that she deserved the attention of a good man like Davis. She could even pretend that Sydney was her daughter and neither would ever again have to worry about the authorities taking her away.

By the time the train stopped in what she knew was another small town over the mountains, the sun had set. They disembarked beneath a giant sign proclaiming The North Pole, where a wonderland of light displays circled a small man-made lake. Halfway around the walking track, on the opposite side of the glistening water, a warming hut painted in bright colors was labeled Santa's Workshop.

"Oh, this is perfect," she murmured and started toward the winding trail. "Look, kids, you can write letters to Santa."

"Wait!" Nathan's urgent voice stopped her in midstride. He grabbed Lana, tugging her back to Davis's side. Then, he pulled them closer until they'd clasped gloved hands.

"There. That's better." The little guy was persistent. She'd give him that.

She glanced at Davis who shrugged, his eyes twinkling as with merriment. "Can't argue with pretend."

Right. Pretend. She could do that. She let herself enjoy the strength of Davis's gloved hand.

Nathan insisted on holding Lana's other hand and Davis reached out to Sydney, an act that made the child light up brighter than the light displays. On the far end, Paige grabbed onto her new best friend, and all five of them were connected by a bridge of fingers.

"This is nice," she said, meaning it.

They looked like a family, strolling through the displays, exclaiming over the animations. A happy family.

Waving elves and a blinking Rudolph gave way to whimsical displays by businesses. Nathan giggled at an animated toothbrush sponsored by a dentist and at the Elvis-Santa driving a car from the local dealership.

With their cheeks and noses rosy cold, they stopped at a nativity set up by a local church. There they were serenaded by a group of carolers, bundled against the cold to sing along to a portable stereo. Lana snapped more photos, committing the scene to memory. How would she ever put all this into one article? When she replaced the camera in her tote, Davis took her hand again. She let him.

The evening was beautiful, cold and clear, the kind

she'd dreamed of where a mother and father took their children out to make Christmas memories.

A silly dream but as sweet as the peppermint on her tongue.

When their toes began to tingle, they stopped inside Santa's Workshop to warm up. Here the children scribbled letters to Santa before sliding them into a big red mailbox marked *S. Claus.*

All too soon, the train whistle announced the time of departure. The children groaned. Lana felt like doing the same. Like Cinderella at the ball, her time with Prince Charming was drawing to a close.

"Too much fun," Davis said, smiling at the dejected trio of children.

"Can we come back again?" Even Paige's snazzy freckles lost their cheer.

Davis's gaze found Lana's. "Maybe," he said, sending a wild root of hope shooting through her heart.

She was being ridiculous and she knew it. When she got home, she'd remind herself of all the reasons she was not good for Davis and his kids. But not now, not when the evening had become nothing short of a fairy tale.

With light hearts and more protests from the children, they moved with the crowd back onto the train. The kids were tired. The excitement had taken a toll. They crowded into their seat, quieter but still talking about the wonders of the light displays.

After the train rolled on again, chugging smoothly through the deep forest and over Blackberry Mountain toward Whisper Falls, a pair of elves passed out foam cups of hot chocolate loaded with mini-marshmallows. The overhead lights dimmed, bathing everyone in shadows. Toward the front of the car, Miss Evelyn sat under a spotlight on a high stool and read a Christmas story. Lana suspected the elves read similar stories in the remaining cars.

The rocking of the train and Miss Evelyn's story lulled the passengers, including herself. More than one woman leaned her head on the shoulder of the man beside her. Lana was tempted to do the same.

The semilit car created an air of privacy as though dozens of other people weren't sitting nearby. She felt cocooned between the cool window and the warm, masculine man.

Mellowed by the thoughts, she sipped at her cocoa, the taste sweet on her tongue.

"Mustache," Davis murmured, leaning close enough to make her pulse misbehave.

"Hmm?" she asked, head tilted toward him.

In the shadows he leaned closer, grinning. He touched her upper lip. "Marshmallow mustache."

"Oh." Before she could raise her hand to clear it away, Davis touched his lips to hers. Tender, sweet and over too quickly.

"I think I got it for you." His grin had become a gentle, quizzical smile. His eyes held questions though Lana had no adequate answers.

"Great." She touched her mouth, breathless. One very innocent, friendly kiss and she could hardly think straight.

"Let me know if I didn't." He winked. "Or better yet, have another drink."

Have another drink. The old familiar phrase meant something different in Lana's world than marshmallow-laden cocoa.

She'd had too many drinks too many times with too

many different men. Though she'd not touched alcohol for nearly two years, she couldn't forget what it had done to her.

She squeezed Davis's arm in an apology he would never understand and turned to stare out at the passing night.

"Hey."

Not this time. This time she talked to him. If she was going to shut him down, she was going to give him a reason.

Davis took Lana by the shoulder and gently tugged.

She turned her head, her hair swishing against her sweater, her eyebrows lifted in question. "Hmm?"

"What's going on? You invited me on this trip. We've had a terrific time. At least I have. I thought you were enjoying yourself, too."

"I am."

"Then what's the deal? Why do you disappear like that?"

Her head tilted. "Did I?"

He gave an annoyed sigh. "Are you intentionally trying to frustrate me?"

"Why would I do that?"

"I don't know. That's why I'm asking. I like you, Lana. You know I do. I'm a guy. You're a girl. It's only natural that I'd want to kiss you."

She closed her eyes as if his words were too hard to hear. Her rusty voice sounded small and tired. "I like you, too."

"Good." He pulled her unresisting hand into his. "Let's start over then. I like you. You like me. Life is good."

"It's not that simple."

"Then explain it to me because I must be slow. Maybe I'm too dumb or out of practice to get the message when a woman is giving me the brush-off." He sounded testy, even to himself. So, okay, he *was* testy. She was making him crazy.

"I'm not trying to… Today has been—" she searched for the words, staring around the darkened train "—a beautiful dream."

His anger dissolved, fizzled, died. "For me, too. You, me, these kids. Pretty special stuff."

"Yes." The affirmation was a mere breath but he heard it.

He heard something else. too, a yearning that was answered deep in his heart. At that moment, he thought he understood. "You're scared."

She offered a small smile. "Terrified."

His protective gene activated. "Don't be. It's just me, your friendly neighborhood handyman, and you, the most amazing woman I've met in a long time. We can handle anything together."

And I think I'm in love with you.

He didn't say that, of course, but the words coursed through his veins, like a steady beat of his heart.

"Oh, Davis." Lana turned completely away from the window to lay her head on his shoulder.

Now they were getting somewhere. He didn't know what dragons she battled, but he wanted to slay them all.

He found her cheek and caressed the soft, smooth skin. "Give us a chance. Okay?"

She sighed, a warm, breathy, marshmallow sigh against his jaw. After a painfully long moment, she nodded. "I'd like that."

Her admission slammed into him with g-force. Finally.

Davis figured he might as well test the waters. See if she meant it. He touched her cheek, her eyelids, her mouth. And then he kissed her again.

Mr. Kendle loved the Christmas Express article. So much so that he gave Lana a byline and a small raise in pay.

Feeling happier than she could remember, Lana walked with a purposeful stride down Easy Street, the chilly breeze in her hair and the smell of the river in her nose. Her boot heels tapped music on the sidewalk. Her red scarf lifted on the breeze, bouncing against her faux-leather coat, as if to keep the beat.

Yesterday had been wonderful. The ending had been even better. For a few minutes guilt had tried to ruin the day, but Davis had pushed his way past her shame and given her hope.

Maybe she could be different. Maybe she could let go of the past. Maybe she could love and be loved by a good man.

Did she dare believe?

Her years in music had made her a night owl and last night, long after Sydney was asleep, she'd stayed up so buoyed by hope and happiness that she'd written another new song from start to finish. A love song.

This morning the music poured through her mind and soul. She hummed as she did errands and gathered ideas for future articles, enjoying the blast of holiday music coming from a bullhorn speaker above Classy Girls Boutique.

A short time later she drove to Haley Carter's home for the promised lunch date. The Carters lived on the edge of town on a small acreage surrounded by trees and an enormous garden. Various garden plots lay all around the house, though they were mostly sleeping under mulch for the winter months.

Everything about the white frame cottage screamed, "artsy." Haley's folk art was visible on the porch, in the yard and gardens and inside the house.

"Come on in," Haley called before Lana could knock. "I have my hands in dough."

Having visited before, Lana knew the way and passed through the living room to the kitchen. Baby Rose sat on the floor banging a spoon against a plastic bowl. Haley stood at the counter mixing a fragrant dough. Flour powdered the front of her green blouse.

"Bread?" Lana asked. "Smells great."

Haley scratched her chin against her shoulder, hands deep in the dough. "The fabulous tree ornaments we're making for the bazaar."

"You really think you can teach me well enough that people will buy them?"

Haley hitched her chin toward Lana's coat. "Take off your coat, roll up your sleeves and we'll find out. Lesson one in progress while lunch bakes."

Lana did as she was told and soon had her hands in the soft, elastic dough.

"I hear you had a date with Davis last night."

"How did you hear—" Lana shook her head. "Never mind. This is Whisper Falls." She told Haley a little about the Christmas Express. "You and Creed should go."

"It sounds fun. We will. But that's not the part I wanted to know. Tell me about you and Davis. Did you have fun together?"

"We did." Lana smiled down in the dough. "We really did."

Haley had her back turned but she spun around, eyes wide with sudden comprehension. "I think you're falling in love with him."

Lana tweaked a shoulder. "Maybe."

"Oh, you are. I know the symptoms. Just look at the way you sparkle and the energy pouring out of you. I bet you wrote another song."

Lana's mouth dropped open. "How did you know that?"

"Because falling in love made me more creative. It's what artists do. If we're sad, we create. If we're happy, we create. But love is the best motivator of all."

"Davis invited Sydney and me to go with them to the Blackwell's Ranch. He and his kids cut their own Christmas tree from the woods. Apparently, it's a tradition he started after his wife died. And he asked us to go along."

"You're going, of course."

"Well, yeah. Sydney and I need a Christmas tree, too."

They both laughed and Haley bumped Lana's side with hers.

Lana needed more than a Christmas tree. She needed to have her head examined. Sooner or later, she and Davis must have a long, open conversation about some very painful subjects. If their budding relationship was to have a chance, he'd have to know everything, even the worst. He deserved to know.

But today she was too happy, too hopeful to worry about the ugly darkness in her past.

"We're going on horseback?"

The surprise on Lana's face was exactly what Davis had expected.

The five of them had arrived at the Blackwell Ranch on a cold Saturday, eager to cut fresh Christmas trees, and now, they were walking toward a large, dirt corral. A light dusting of snow covered the ground like powdered sugar on cake.

Davis allowed a small, teasing grin. "Did I forget to mention the horses?"

Lana squinted her eyes at him in pretend anger. "Yes, you did."

"Is that a problem? You're not scared of horses or anything, are you?"

"No. Well, maybe a little. They are awfully big. But it sounds…adventurous. I *am* dressed for it." She glanced down at her jeans and cowboy boots, the latter older and lower-heeled than he'd seen her wear before. "But Sydney's wearing tennies."

"So is Paige. We aren't going far and Austin's horses are used to kids. They don't care what's on your feet."

"And how would you know that?" she asked. "Do the horses speak to you? Do they tell you all their secrets?"

He liked when she joked around. Today she was light and easy and sparkling. "Nothing as mysterious as that. Nathan went through a horse obsession last year. Austin gave him lessons for a while on old Tinker. All three of us got to do some riding."

"All my animals are gentle as overgrown dogs." Austin came out of the barn, leading a pair of horses, a large bay and a buckskin. Austin was a tall man, taller than Davis by several inches though the boots added a couple more. Broad and well-muscled in a rough-hewn leather coat and white cowboy hat, Austin was a quiet man with a big presence. Davis was proud to call him friend. "Ever ridden before?"

"I actually have." Lana eased toward the bay, gloved hand extended. "A friend of mine owned a ranch outside Nashville. But I haven't in a long time."

It was one of the few times she'd mentioned her life in Tennessee. Davis was curious to know more, to know everything about the woman who was rapidly invading his heart and life.

The ride on the Christmas Express had done him in. Since that night, he thought about her all the time, smelled her gardenia perfume in his sleep and spent every free moment at her house. Most of the time the two of them worked on the house while the three kids romped like cubs or did homework. Sometimes they just hung out. They watched TV together, played checkers—always a formidable match—or listened to music. Often Lana would sing for him—spurts and starts of whatever composition she was working on, slightly self-conscious because the song wasn't finished, but wistful and dreamy. He wondered if she'd eventually return to Nashville. If she even wanted that. He didn't know much about music, but he knew what he liked to hear. If Lana wanted another shot at the stars, he wanted it for her.

Davis caught her elbow. "Are you sure you're okay with the horses? If you're not, we can walk. It's no big deal."

Her smile convinced him. But then that smile of hers could turn his brain to vanilla pudding. "The kids will love going by horseback, Davis. A memory to treasure forever."

"That's what I thought." The five of them looked like a family making memories together.

"Come over here, Sydney." Lana reached back to where the kids hopped and danced and ran in circles like animations. Smoky vapor exited their noses, three fire-breathing dragons. Sydney stopped immediately to obey. "Put your hand out. Let the horse smell you."

"Like dogs do?"

"Exactly."

The little girl, her curly brown hair poking from beneath a hooded coat, eagerly offered her palm. Both horses leaned in, naturally curious, for a sniff. Sydney giggled, a sound that touched Davis for some reason. She was a shy, sweet little girl with a great giggle. He wondered if she'd ever wanted a dad the way Nathan wanted a mom.

Not to be left out, Nathan and Paige let the horses sniff, and then rubbed their gloved hands down the noble necks.

"If you'll hold on to these," Austin said, "I'll see if Annalisa has the other two saddled."

"Is she going with us?"

"She wouldn't miss it, but Cassie will. She's working." Cassie was his single sister. She lived on the ranch, too. "Saturday is a big day at the shop."

"I thought Annalisa was expecting a baby?" Lana said.

This was news to Davis, but Austin's chest expanded at the mention. A grin spread across Davis's face. He remembered that feeling, the pride and joy.

"Doc says the exercise is good for her. For both of them." Still grinning like a new daddy, Austin pivoted toward the barn.

Davis followed, willing to help with the animals.

"We still on to get that bathroom retiled?" the cowboy asked.

"Next week maybe." Davis narrowed his eyes to

think through his schedule. He knew Austin wanted the work done before Christmas, as a gift to his wife. "Is that soon enough?"

"Yup."

The large barn smelled of hay and leather and horse flesh. Annalisa, a saddle blanket in her hands, smiled at her husband. The big rancher visibly melted, a teddy bear where his wife was concerned. It was a beautiful thing, Davis thought, the love between a man and a woman. A very beautiful thing.

Soon the horses were saddled, and the party mounted. Austin's big bay, a horse he called Cisco, was loaded with gear. He and Annalisa led the way. Davis and Lana brought up the rear. With the children sandwiched between the adults, they headed up a well-traveled trail into the mountainous forest spreading around and beyond the Blackwell Ranch.

Lana rode at Davis's flank. He thought she handled a horse pretty well, if a little stiffly. Sydney bounced up and down on Tinker, the old gelding with the gentle spirit.

To reassure both Lana and the little girl, Davis said, "He'll take care of her. Don't worry."

The horses trudged with practiced ease, heads down and bobbing up the incline through hickory and oak. As the trail steepened, conical evergreens began to dot the landscape. They'd journeyed only a short distance, less than a mile, when Austin raised a leather-clad hand to stop.

Lana sucked in a breath as a doe and fawn bolted from the brush, crossed the trail in front of them and then leaped into the trees on the opposite side. Not one of the horses reacted other than an ear flicker.

"Beautiful," Lana breathed.

Davis stared at the side of her face. "Sure is."

"Dad, Dad, did you see that?" In wide-eyed wonder, Paige drew his attention. "A mama and a baby deer."

He understood the thrill. Even as an adult, he found the grace and beauty of white-tailed deer a sight to behold. His kids would talk about it for days.

Austin dropped his hand and the journey continued, ending in a thick stand of evergreen.

"Here we are," Austin announced as he dismounted and walked back to lift his wife tenderly from the horse. When Annalisa's feet touched the ground, the big cowboy lowered his head and kissed her.

Davis couldn't help looking at Lana. What would she think if he did the same? But before he could act on the impulse, she was off the buckskin, helping the children dismount.

Once the horses were secured, Annalisa swept her arms in a wide arc around the glade. "Pick your Christmas tree. There are plenty."

"Too many," Austin said with a frown. "Can't graze cattle on juniper."

Annalisa laughed, her blond beauty enhanced by her early pregnancy. Not that Davis could even tell she was expecting other than the happy glow.

Nathan, Paige and Sydney made a beeline through the trees, exclaiming over first one evergreen and then another. The adults trudged along, grinning at the childish excitement.

"I want a giant one. Tall as the ceiling," Nathan exclaimed, stretching his arms as high as possible. "Big as the sky."

"How about you, Lana?" Davis asked. "Want one big as the sky?"

"Bigger." Her blue eyes sparkled in the winter sunlight. She slipped her hand into the crook of his elbow.

Blood humming with pleasure, Davis put a hand over her fingers and squeezed gently. His heart was doing funny things, happy things, inside his chest. "Whatever the lady wants."

She turned her head to look at him and he leaned in to kiss the corner of her mouth. Her smile widened and she returned the favor, her lips warm against his cold cheek.

This was good. Really good.

He could imagine himself with Lana, searching for the perfect tree, year after year. Could she imagine it, too?

"How about this one?" Nathan shouted, drawing their focus, though Davis's heart continued to dance to music no one could hear but him.

Up ahead, Paige and Sydney were slowly circling a tall, stately cedar while Nathan, nose red, ran back to Austin for the ax.

"This is it. This is it!" he called.

"Remember, we need two."

"Make that three," Annalisa said. "I think you've picked a good one, though." She circled the tree with the children, hands on hips. "No gaps. Nice and cone shaped. Very green."

"It's beautiful." Sydney had removed a glove and was testing the branches as she talked to Paige. "And it smells really good. I think it's kind of perfect. You and Nathan can have this one."

Her generosity touched a tender spot in Davis. Truth

was Sydney got to him as much as her mother did. He'd
seen her let Nathan have the first turn or the last cookie.
Generous, caring. Like Lana.

Why had he ever wondered about Lana's mothering
skills? She'd done an amazing job with Sydney.

"It *is* kind of perfect," he said, taking the ax from
Nathan as Austin and Annalisa moved deeper into the
woods in search of their own perfect Christmas tree.
"Who gets the first whack?"

"You chop it, Daddy." Paige grabbed Sydney's coat
sleeve and dragged her backward from the tree.

"I want to help." Nathan stuck close to his dad. "I'll
hold the tree so it won't fall down. Huh, Dad?"

Before Davis could give the warning, Nathan stuck
his bare hand into the prickly limbs of the cedar. He let
out a yowling cry and jerked back.

Davis dropped the ax and reached for his son. To
his surprise, Nathan threw himself into Lana's waiting
arms, tears falling.

"Shh. Let me see. Let me see, sugar." Lana knelt on
the cold ground to look at Nathan's hand. "There now.
It's only a sticker."

Nathan stopped crying and blinked dark, wet lashes.
His lip quivered but he was trying to be brave. "Can
you get it out? It hurts me."

"I think I can," Lana said, "Will you hold real still
while I try? I promise to be careful."

Trusting, Nathan nodded. He sniffed one long sniff
and said, "Okay."

By now, Davis was on his knees next to the pair
and Sydney and Paige hovered as though Nathan had
lost a limb.

Using her fingernails, Lana carefully extracted a

half-inch splinter from Nathan's palm. Then, while Davis watched with his heart in his throat, she placed a kiss on the dirty spot.

"How's that feel? Better?"

Nathan, his face inches from hers, nodded. With a long sniffing shudder, he said, "I love you, Lana."

Lana's eyelids dropped shut. She pulled his baby into her arms and murmured, "I love you, too, sugar."

Davis put his arms around the pair of them, heart bursting, the scent of cedar in his nose and wild hope in his chest.

Chapter Thirteen

Who knew decorating a Christmas tree could be both romantic and hilarious?

Lana smiled up at Davis as she dug through a plastic shopping bag of brand-new decorations. There had been a box of old ones in the attic but she was starting fresh. No need to drag out bad memories. Especially of the Christmas Mama had slapped Tess for sneaking a present and her parents had fought far into the night. That was the year Daddy went to work one day and never came home again.

She shook her head, abolishing dark thoughts from the perfect evening. The fireplace crackled. They'd made popcorn and put on a Christmas CD of kids' songs. Most importantly, people she cared about were present.

"Thank you for this," she said. "Decorating this tree means a lot to Sydney."

They'd left Davis's tree propped against the side of the side of his garage in a bucket of water, agreeing to decorate Sydney's lopsided wonder first.

"What about her mom?"

Her conscience tweaked. She should tell him Sydney was not her child, but now didn't seem the right time. Soon, though, she promised. Soon.

She simply said, "It means a lot to her, too." Wherever she is. "Decorating yours tomorrow gives us another good excuse to get together and have fun."

Davis, a strand of glittery tinsel in his calloused hands, moved closer. He jacked a sandy eyebrow. "Do we need an excuse?"

Lana's pulse jumped. She studied his eyes, saw the affection in their depths and marveled. "No," she answered. "I don't think we do."

At moments like this, Lana wanted to pinch herself. Davis Turner, the nicest guy on the planet, wanted to be with her. Plenty of men had been attracted to her, but not like this. When Davis touched or kissed her, she felt clean, unused. She felt new again.

He draped a length of tinsel around her neck and slowly drew her to him. When she laughed, he rubbed her nose with his and laughed, too.

From her peripheral vision, she saw the children approach and tried to pull away. But Davis held her fast.

"Too late," he said. "You can't escape the inevitable."

She glanced around, not understanding. The three matchmakers grinned from ear to ear as Paige stretched tall to hold a branch of plastic mistletoe over their heads.

"You're right," she answered, moving back into his space. "Far too late."

Davis was standing at his kitchen sink scrubbing paint from beneath his fingernails when his front door burst open. Expecting Jenny with his kids, he didn't bother to turn around until Paige rushed to his side and burst into great heaving sobs.

"Oh, Daddy!"

Davis jerked his hands from beneath the flow of warm water, splashing the cabinets and floor. "Hey! What's going on here?"

Paige was not one to wail and cry, but before she could pull herself together, an agitated Jenny plowed through the doorway with Nathan and Kent in tow, their eyes wide and worried. Charlie was nowhere to be seen.

The noise in the room was worse than a jackhammer on concrete. Paige crying. Jenny talking. Davis asking what was going on. Nathan grabbed onto his daddy's leg and clung like a spider monkey.

Fear snaked up Davis's spine.

"What's wrong? Where's Charlie? Has something happened?"

The noise grew louder as everyone started talking at once. Finally, he stuck his fingers in his mouth and whistled like a referee. The noise ceased.

"Will someone tell me what's going on before I call 9-1-1?"

"That woman is a kidnapper."

This statement from Jenny started the sobs in Paige again.

"I didn't mean to tell, Daddy. Sydney made me promise. It was an accident."

"Who's a kidnapper? You didn't mean to tell what?" The hysteria was starting to scare him.

Jenny put a hand on Paige's shoulder. "Honey, you did the right thing. Now, go wash your face and calm down while I speak to your daddy. None of this is your fault."

Paige looked from Jenny to Davis. When Davis nodded reassuringly, she trudged out of the kitchen, shoulders drooping.

"You boys go in the living room and watch TV while Aunt Jenny and I talk," Davis said. Hands still dripping on the floor, he grabbed a dish towel. Whatever was going on, he didn't need crying, clinging children involved.

Once the boys were dispatched, he wiped his hands and said, "All right. What's going on? Is Charlie all right?"

"He's in the car. No worse than usual. That's not why I'm here."

"Is anyone hurt?"

"Not physically." When he hitched a hip in a get-on-with-it stance, his sister said, "Paige told me something about Sydney and Lana today that I think you should know before you get any more involved with them."

He straightened, suddenly wary. Any more involved and they'd be standing before a preacher.

A bad feeling snaked up the back of his neck. "I won't listen to gossip about her, Jenny. She's changed."

"I'm not repeating gossip. Paige let something slip today that Sydney wasn't supposed to tell. It's crucial you know or I wouldn't be here." She looked toward the ceiling and back as if searching for the right words. "I'm your sister. I want what's best for you. I know things about Lana Ross that I won't bring up because as you said, they happened in high school. But this is happening now, and it's too important to brush aside just because you have the hots for her."

He clenched his fists, mouth going from dry to tight. "I think I resent your implication."

"If I'm speaking out of turn, I'm sorry. Nathan told me about all the kissing and snuggling that's been going on lately."

"Which does not translate to anything inappropriate, if that's what you're implying. You've nagged me for a year about dating. I like Lana. A lot." He sucked in a breath. "I might even be in love with her."

That silenced her for all of five seconds.

"Oh, Davis. It breaks my heart to see you hurt again. Lana has misled you. She's lied to you. She's used you to get her house remodeled."

"Gee, thanks, sis." He laid on the sarcasm. "A man likes to know what his sister thinks about his ability to attract women."

"I didn't mean that. You could have had a nice woman in Tara, but you're like a moth to the flame."

"I'm not a moth. I'm a man. Now, either spit it out or go home. Paige needs me."

Jenny brushed a tired hand over her forehead. "Lana Ross may be a criminal."

His brow lowered in disbelief. Lana, a criminal? Not a chance. "What did she do, forget to return a library book? Double-park on Easy Street?"

As if she truly did not want to tell him, Jenny swallowed and looked away, shaking her head in regret. "Oh, Davis. Oh, my brother. Sydney is not Lana's child. She brought her here under false pretenses."

The revelation was like being hit in the face with a bucket of ice water. He went cold all over.

"What are you talking about? Of course, Sydney's her child. Why would Lana lie about a thing like that?" Particularly since he'd asked about Sydney's father and she'd told him an uncomfortable truth.

"I don't know, Davis. Perhaps you should ask Lana outright. Or better yet, call the authorities in Nashville."

His head buzzed with the information. It couldn't be true. Could it? "Paige told you this?"

"Don't blame the child. She didn't mean to let the cat out of the bag. She was devastated, as you could see, to have betrayed a confidence." Jenny reached in the pocket of her slacks and withdrew a tissue. "Apparently, child welfare was threatening to put Sydney into foster care because of her mother's lifestyle so Lana ran away with her. Drugs, I gather."

"Lana? Drugs?" He dropped his chin and wagged his head back and forth. "Not even close to being true." He was sure, wasn't he?

"No, Lana wasn't the one doing drugs. It was Sydney's *real* mother."

"Sydney's real mother?" He grabbed the back of his head with one hand, his nerves fraying. "Who *is* Sydney's real mother? And what does Lana have to do with any of it?"

"She brought Sydney here to escape the authorities. That's all I know. Paige was fuzzy on the particulars. I suggest you speak to Lana, although if she lied once, she'll lie again." Tears glistened in her eyes. "I'm sorry, Davis. You and the kids have been through so much. I didn't want you to be hurt by that woman. Please don't be angry at me for telling you. You have a right to know."

Yes, he did. He had a right to honesty.

Jenny was his sister, a good woman with a lot on her plate. He trusted her. She wouldn't tell him something unless she believed it was true. She might not like Lana but she cared about him and his kids.

He tossed the dishtowel on the counter. His whole body trembled. His heart raced like a juiced thoroughbred's. He didn't know what was going on up the street, but he intended to find out. Now.

Lana strummed her guitar, softly singing the newly composed tune. Funny how the house she'd hated had become a house of hope. When her work was done for the day, she loved sitting on the wide hearth with the fire at her back as she wrote articles or music or prayed, full of gratitude for the changes in her life.

With joy blooming inside, the music flooded out, filling an unexplainable void. Haley was right. Creativity flowed when an artist was happy. Because of Davis and his two adorable children, Lana was happy for the first time in years. She felt accepted, cared for, appreciated for who she was now instead of being despised for who she used to be.

Above the melody, she heard footsteps on the wooden porch and stopped playing.

The door burst open and there was her heart's desire.

"Davis," she said, elated, leaning her guitar against the hearth as she stood to greet him.

He stalked toward her, his normal smile hidden behind a serious face. "We need to talk."

"Something is wrong." Her good mood disappeared faster than dandelion dust. "What's happened?"

He paced to the hearth, back turned.

"Davis? Tell me. What's wrong? What is it?" She could hear the rising panic in her voice. A few days ago, before she'd let down her guard, she couldn't imagine being this vulnerable. But now, Davis Turner had the power to shatter her into pieces.

"Is it true?" His voice was low, urgent, wounded. "Sydney is not your child?"

The world fell out from under her. She stared at his broad, anvil-shaped back, his sandy hair, the twisted collar of his plaid work shirt and knew in that moment that the dream had ended before it really ever started. She should have told him. She should never have waited.

"Is it?" He spoke softly, still not facing her. The notion hurt like a cinder in the eye. Davis couldn't stand to look at her now.

"I planned to tell you. I wanted to. A thousand times I tried."

He whirled then, the suppressed anger rising to the surface. More devastating than the anger, she saw the hurt. "When? When were you going to tell me that you stole someone else's child and brought her to Whisper Falls where you convinced everyone she was your daughter?"

"I didn't steal her. Sydney is my niece."

That stopped him for several painful heartbeats. "Tess's?"

"Yes." Her insides quivered. Davis knew she'd lied to him, to everyone, and he was furious. "How did you find out?"

"Does it matter?"

"No, no, I suppose it doesn't." She rubbed a hand over her face. "Yes, it does. No one can know. Please, don't say a word to anyone. I don't want Sydney hurt. She's safe here."

"Haven't you already hurt her by taking her away from her mother, from her home?"

She almost laughed, though nothing was funny. They'd had no home.

"I'm protecting her. You have no right to judge my actions when you know nothing about the situation."

"I know you lied to me. You had every chance to tell me about Sydney, but you didn't." He barked a bitter laugh. "You even made up some story about not knowing who the father is. You let me think the worst."

"I told the truth."

"Yeah? Then why not tell me the whole truth? That's what I don't get."

"I was going to."

"When?"

"Soon. When I was sure—"

"Of what? That your house repairs were finished? That I wouldn't turn you in to the police?"

The remark about the house jabbed but she was accustomed to dealing with personal attacks. It was Sydney she worried about.

She held out her hands, pleading. Her fingers shook. "Please, Davis, promise me you won't tell anyone about this. Sydney belongs with me. They'll put her in foster care. I'm her mother in every way but one."

"What about Tess? Doesn't she deserve a say in her daughter's life?"

"She can't take care of Sydney. Never could. Sydney has been with me for years." Even through the ugly times, Sydney had been better off with Lana than Tess. But not a lot.

"Does Tess even know where her daughter is?"

Lana shook her head, knowing how this looked. Her chest tightened, mouth drier than sand. "Telling Tess was too risky."

His mouth twisted sadly. "I can only imagine."

"Tess wasn't a good mother. She had—" She swallowed, ashamed of outing her sister. "Tess has a drug problem."

He didn't seem surprised. "Why not tell the authorities the situation? Why leave Nashville? Why not tell the truth? They'd much rather give custody to a family member than to put in a child in foster care with strangers."

"It wasn't that simple. They would never have let me have custody."

"Why not?"

Lana opened her mouth to admit the ugly reality, but the words wouldn't come. It was bad enough that he believed her a liar and a law-breaker. "I just couldn't risk it."

His jaw tightened. A muscle flexed. Mild-mannered Davis spoke between clenched teeth. "In other words, you won't tell me the truth even now when you have a chance to come clean. What's wrong with you that you can't be honest?"

She gestured absently at the couch, buying time, praying wild prayers for a miracle. "Sit down, Davis. Please. Let's talk."

But he was past listening.

"Talk? So you can tell more lies? So I can be an even bigger fool? What else have you lied about, Lana? Do I dare ask?"

She turned away, afraid. The lid was open to her Pandora's box and she was terribly aware of what could spew forth.

Davis spun her around, holding her by the shoulders. "What are you hiding, Lana? What other things have you kept from me?"

Lana wrapped her arms around her waist and held

on tight, shivering. "I don't want you to know. You'll be…disgusted."

He stared down at her, looking her over as if he saw what she was, what she'd been, what she'd always be. His beloved face was close enough to touch and oh, how she wanted to touch him, to plead with him not to hate her. She dropped her head, too ashamed to meet his stormy eyes.

"Tell me, Lana. You owe me that much. What are you hiding?"

She swallowed a thick wad of despair. Nothing mattered now. Whether she told him or not, he was gone. She could hear it in his voice. They were over.

She threw her head back and blurted the words to the ceiling. "I'm a drunk, Davis. An alcoholic. I spent time in jail, in back alleys and a lot of other places I can't remember. I'd do anything to get blitzed. Anything." She glared at him, sick with fury at having to remember. "Don't you get it? I couldn't even sing unless I was stoned out of my mind. Even after I gave my life to Jesus, with a record like that, no one was going to let me raise a child."

His face had paled as she spoke. He dropped his hands to his sides and stood, like a defeated boxer, spent.

His terrible, dark silence broke her. A tear seeped and slowly slid down her face. Tension vibrated in the room, thick enough to make her shudder.

In a low and wounded voice, Davis said, "You should have told me."

"Would you have understood if I had?"

"I don't know. I would have tried. You never gave me the chance." He paced to the window, a pane he'd put in himself and looked outside on the yard he'd helped her clean. "Tell me this much, Lana." His voice was soft, wounded. "Were you using me, the way Jenny said, to get your house remodeled?"

"No!" An aching chasm widened in her chest, dark and bottomless. If she fell into that black hole again, she'd be lost forever. "You can't believe that—"

"People tried to warn me, but you had me fooled. I thought you'd changed. I believed you were the pious woman you claimed to be. I believed you cared about me and my kids."

"I do. I do." She moved toward him, hands outstretched.

He backed away, shaking his head. "I cared about you, Lana. For the first time since Cheryl died, I thought I'd found a woman who matched me, someone I could love and build a life with. But you're not who I thought you were. Not even close."

With that searing judgment, he spun on the heel of his work boots and stormed out of her house. She followed him to the door, one hand on her mouth to stop the cries of despair, the other holding her churning stomach.

She watched him jog across the street and down the block. She watched until he disappeared into the pretty, buff brick house. A few hundred feet might as well be a million miles.

"Lana?"

Lana lay on the couch, one arm thrown across her eyes when she heard Sydney's footsteps on the stairs.

"What?" she mumbled, wishing she didn't have to talk to anyone right this minute, not even the child she would sacrifice anything for. As much as Lana anguished over losing Davis, she'd lie again to protect this precious little girl.

"Davis was really mad, wasn't he?"

Her heart sank. Sydney had been upstairs doing a school project on the laptop. Lana had prayed the child hadn't heard the argument. Lately, she was batting zero on answered prayers.

"I'm sorry you heard that."

"Why is he so mad? Is it because of me? He's mad because I'm not your real daughter."

Hearing the anxiety and hurt in Sydney's voice, Lana sat up. "No, sugar. Davis is not mad at you."

"I thought he liked me."

"He does. He adores you." She pulled Sydney onto her lap with a heavy sigh. "What's not to like? One smart, beautiful, well-behaved girl with the prettiest eyes and the brightest smile in the world. Anyone would love you, Sydney."

"Not my mom."

The load was impossible. No one should have to explain to a nine-year-old the facts of a drug-addicted life. "Tess loves you, baby. She's too sick to take care of you."

"She's not sick. She takes drugs. We learned at school about bad drugs, Lana. My mom takes them. The kind with the spoons and the needles. I saw her. And then she'd be all weird and scary."

"I know. I know." Lana buried her face in Sydney's hair. "That's why she gave you to me. She knew she wasn't good for you and she loved you enough to let you go. That took courage on her part." And Lana threatening to turn her in.

"Really?"

"Yes." She folded Sydney into her lap and rocked,

humming softly the way she'd done so many times when the girl was small.

"Lana?"

Lana stopped humming. "What, baby?"

"Davis isn't going to be my daddy, is he?"

The question crushed her. This is the way it would always be. She and Sydney against the world, alone and wishing for the impossible. No one in Whisper Falls would ever believe Lana was a new creature in Christ. She didn't even believe it herself. She'd always be one of those "awful Ross girls."

Maybe they should move again. Somewhere.

Chapter Fourteen

Davis finally found time to do the remodel work for Austin and Annalisa, but it wasn't going well. Not well at all.

With a grunt, he jammed a freshly cut diamond of tile into place above the sink. Frustrated that it was a fraction too large, he pushed harder. The expensive tile snapped.

He grabbed the fragments and threw them as hard as he could. The sound banged against the wall and clattered to the floor.

"Rough day?" Austin Blackwell's voice turned him around.

He felt as Nathan must have when Davis caught him drawing happy faces on his bedroom wall. "I thought you were moving cattle."

"Moved 'em." The big cowboy leaned a shoulder against the doorjamb. "Everything all right with you?"

"Yeah." Davis stacked his hands on his hips and dropped his head. Pieces of tile sparkled in the artificial light at his feet. He'd never done that before. Not even in the frustrating days of training. "No."

"That's what I figured. You're not yourself the past couple of days." Austin jerked his head toward the hallway. "Coffee's on."

"Thanks." Davis followed the other man down the hall and into the kitchen, feeling awkward but wanting to explain. Somehow. "Look, Austin, I apologize for what just happened. I don't want you to think this has anything to do with your tile job. I'll get this fixed up nice for Annalisa before Christmas the way you want. I want to. It's just that…I've got…stuff on my mind."

"I figured. You're not a person to throw things and have fits." The tall cowboy pointed a coffee mug and grinned. "That would be my sister."

Davis returned the grin as he scraped back a chair and sat down at the wooden table. Austin put the cup of coffee in front him and sat down with his own.

"I don't make a habit of sticking my face in another man's business but if you want to talk…"

The statement almost made Davis laugh. Austin was about as private as a man could get, a man who didn't carry tales, a man to trust.

"I'm a mess."

"Must be a woman."

Davis huffed out a frustrated breath. "Yeah."

"Been there."

Yes, he had, though Davis didn't know all the details. Right now, he hurt so bad, he couldn't sleep, couldn't think straight and, apparently, couldn't even do his job well—the work he loved, the work Lana referred to as his art.

He felt torn between what he wanted and what he thought was the right thing to do. His first priority was his children, but all Nathan and Paige had done since the big reveal was mope around or ask to go to Lana's house. Even the coming Christmas parade and bazaar didn't excite them. They wanted Lana and Sydney to come along, and even his best explanation wasn't good enough. As disappointed as he was with Lana, he'd never tell his kids about her lifestyle.

"Lana," he said.

"Figured as much. You two seemed pretty tight. Annalisa predicted wedding bells."

The comment shot a knife through his gut. "Not hardly." And then, like a compressed volcano, the words flowed out. There in the Blackwells' kitchen with an old black dog at his feet and a coffee cup in hand, he opened his soul to a good friend. Austin reacted as expected. He sipped his coffee and listened.

When the words ran out, the room grew silent except for the occasional tick of a digital clock and the soft snore of the old dog.

Austin pushed back from the table to refill the coffee cups. Davis shook his head. He'd barely touched his. A fuzzy poodle with red painted toenails tapped into the kitchen and laid her head on the lab. The old dog sighed as if he'd been expecting the interruption.

"What are you going to do?"

"I don't know." Davis stuck his elbows on the table and clasped his hands. "Nothing, I suppose, though I worry about Sydney, Lana's little—" He caught himself. "The little girl."

"Why? Does Lana mistreat her?"

"Lana? No way! Lana's a great mother. She's crazy about that kid. She sacrificed everything to bring Sydney here and give her a good home."

Austin studied him for a long, silent moment. "Sounds like you still care. Are you going to turn her in?"

"No. No." The idea of pulling Sydney away from the woman she considered her mother was impossible. "I can't. Maybe I should but I can't. I'm not sure what to do. I wish Lana had been straight with me from the beginning."

"Secrets hurt."

"Tell me about it. I thought we had something. I knew she hadn't led a perfect life and she knew that I knew. So why couldn't she trust me with the rest?"

Austin was quiet again for a few seconds. Then, he set his coffee aside and leaned forward. "When my first wife died, I was accused of her murder. You probably know that."

Davis nodded. He'd heard. He also knew the cowboy was found innocent.

"You can't imagine the pain and shame that comes with a charge of that magnitude. And the grief. I was out of my mind with it. I moved here, kept to myself, afraid my secret would get out." Austin huffed softly. "Afraid of what people would think and of how they'd stare at me and wonder if I'd kill them, too. That's a hard thing to bear, Davis."

"But you were innocent." Lana wasn't, and Davis didn't see how the two situations compared.

"Yes. But keeping that secret almost cost me a chance at a life with Annalisa." Austin swigged his coffee and stood. "Only got one other thing to say, Davis. A man knows his own heart and you gotta do what's right for you and your family. But remember this, too. It's carried me through some tough times. *Whom the Son has set free is free indeed.*"

While Davis pondered the Bible verse, Austin jammed his hat on his dark head. "I gotta get back to work. I suspect you do, too. Don't bother to lock up when you leave. I'll be in the barn."

He nodded once and went out the back door.

The poodle hopped up to follow, then changed her mind and tagged along with Davis. He went back to the broken tile, his mind trying to unravel the conversation with Austin. What exactly was his friend getting at?

After another frustrating hour of mismeasuring, broken tile and questioning looks from a prissy poodle, Davis tossed his tools into his truck and headed toward Jenny's house. Getting over Lana was going to take more than a conversation and a cup of hot coffee.

As he drove through town, he spotted her coming out of the newspaper office. His heart leaped and then sank like the *Titanic*. She looked great, her mink hair flowing over her shoulders, a bright blue scarf around her neck. Sydney was with her. The little girl pointed at something and smiled her shy smile. Davis suffered an undeniable pull toward the woman and child. Would she even speak to him if he stopped? He tapped the brake and then thought better of it.

Leave it alone. Let her go. Trust is crucial in a relationship.

He wished she'd told him. He liked to think he would have been man enough to weather the storm.

Even after he drove on, he watched Lana and Sydney in the rearview mirror until, holding hands they went inside the dollar store.

Tomorrow was the Christmas bazaar, a massive event that took place inside the community center. She'd be there, gathering the news for the paper. He'd be there, too, as promised, helping with setup, teardown and anything else Miss Evelyn needed. Along with most other business people, he'd donated to the cause. This year, he'd upped his donation, hoping for larger bids that would help Jenny and Chuck gather the finances they needed for Charlie's surgery. Not that they didn't have insurance, but insurance didn't cover everything. Not even close. For people from remote areas, just the cost of staying away from home for long stretches of time was burdensome. Add transportation, co-pays, deductibles and all the extras, and average folk were strapped.

At Jenny's house, he said hello to Charlie before collecting his children. The boy was on oxygen now most of the time, his lips blue and his energy low. He'd gone downhill rapidly.

"The cardiologist thinks we can wait until after the New Year to have the surgery." Jenny twisted her hands, a perpetual stress line between her eyes. "Chuck isn't sure that's the right thing to do."

"He's scared, sis."

"I know. I am, too. But the doctor gave me his personal number in case something goes wrong. I trust him."

"That's good." He shifted, worried, wanting to help and not knowing how. "Are Nathan and Paige too much right now? I can ask Mom to watch them."

"Of course not. Unless you don't want them staying with me anymore." She put a hand to her mouth. "You're still mad at me, aren't you?"

"No." He wasn't mad, he was broken.

"I can't bear it if you are. With all of this—" Her hand fluttered but he understood. She was on overload, afraid for her child, working on town and church events, preparing for Christmas while caring for a husband and kids, including his.

"You did what you did out of love. I get that." Davis pulled her into a hug, heavy-hearted. When he released her, he said, "See you tomorrow?"

"Wouldn't miss it. Charlie's excited about going."

"Come on, munchkins," he called to his kids and led the way to the truck.

On the short drive home, Paige and Nathan were unusually subdued. They weren't even playing a video game. He knew something was up.

"Daddy," Paige said, as they drove past the glistening river. "Is Charlie going to die?"

Davis flinched. He didn't normally balk at discussing anything with his kids, but this was a tough one. He made his voice sound especially chipper. "Charlie is going to get an operation. If all goes well, he'll be jumping on the trampoline pretty soon and by summer, you can all go swimming together."

"But he could die. Like Mommy."

Davis gripped the steering wheel tighter. So much for being chipper. "No one can answer that for sure, pumpkin, but we will pray every day that Charlie gets well."

"Can we pray for Lana, too? She's sad that you're mad at her."

"I'm not mad—" He shot a look in the mirror. "How do you know she's sad?"

"Sydney told me at school. She said they might move away again and she's scared she'll have to go to foster care."

Move away? Where?

"That's not going to happen." As if he had any say in either matter.

"Can we go see them after dinner?" Nathan asked. "I made Lana a present in art class."

"That's not a good idea, buddy."

"Why? Sydney said they bought us a present. She said they miss us something awful. I miss them something awful, too. Can't you kiss and make up?"

"I don't think so, pal."

"Don't you love her anymore?"

There was the crux. He did. His kids did. Nothing she'd told him had changed that.

He stopped the truck in the driveway and sat at the wheel looking up the street at the Ross house. He had no words to explain the complicated issue to his children. He couldn't even explain it to himself. Even if he could, their thinking was different. They saw with their hearts. They lived in the here and now, heedless of past mistakes, believing in the person Lana appeared to be. She'd been good to them. She'd loved them and they'd loved her in return. That's all they understood.

Why couldn't adulthood could be that simple?

The Whisper Falls Community Center was packed. An all-purpose building, the floor had been covered and now boasted long tables and booths laden with Christmas arts and crafts, silent auction items and tons of beautiful food and colorful gift baskets. At one end, a stage had been set up for entertainment and announcements.

Lana moved around the large open area, Sydney at her side, admiring the handiwork of many artists and crafters. Even her best attempts at making Christmas ornaments with Haley were laughable compared to the blown glass, the leatherwork, the gorgeous woodworking. She was glad she'd left her childish attempts at home. Haley's art, on the other hand, was proving popular. Her auburn-haired friend's table was surrounded by customers snatching up whimsical birdhouses and elegantly carved vases. All the while, Haley painted, personalizing the artwork on request. She was in her element with a proud husband at her side, talking to customers in his charming way.

"Donations are off the charts this year," Miss Evelyn said as she bustled past, an iPad in hand. "Look at all these out-of-towners. You're going to sing for us later, aren't you?"

Lana's heart jumped into her throat. They'd hired a band. They didn't need her. Someone called Evelyn's name and she rushed away, leaving Lana to wonder why the older woman kept pushing.

Across the gym she saw Davis and the children arrive along with Jenny and Chuck. Chuck pushed a wan, listless Charlie in a wheelchair, a heartbreaking sight. Little boys were supposed to be full of energy like Nathan. Her gaze went to the dimple-cheeked boy who'd stolen her heart. She missed his hugs, his sweetness, his funny, little-boy view of the world.

Davis caught her looking and leveled a steady, heart-thudding stare in return. She glanced away.

Apparently, he'd kept her secret, though he'd never promised. She'd worried about that, afraid she'd have to take Sydney and run again. She'd do it if she had to, just as any mother would do what was right for her child. But Sydney was happy here. She was doing better in school. She'd made friends. Even though she missed the Davis children, Sydney was excited about Christmas. Lana was determined to give her the best one of her life.

"There's a lot to see," she said as the Boggy Boys Band struck up a bluegrass tune. "Do you want your face painted?"

"Can I ask Paige to come with me?"

"I don't think so, sugar." She'd known they would run into the Davis trio, but she couldn't let that stop her from doing her part for the event. In a town as small as Whisper Falls, seeing the Turner family was inevitable. They'd have to cope and move on. Somehow.

"I signed up to help with the concession. Want some barbecue?"

"I guess."

Lana poked a finger in Sydney's ribs. "Don't be so enthusiastic."

They made their way through a sea of people to the concession area, drawn by the smell of donated barbecued ribs and all the fixings. Lana got busy filling foam plates with baked beans while Cassie Blackwell added the potato salad. Uninterested in food, Sydney moped for a few minutes until a girl from her class whisked her off to the face painting.

"Great crowd," Cassie said. "I'm really glad. The more money we make, the more we can donate to Charlie's fund."

Cassie was one of those irrepressible personalities that everyone liked. Pretty in a long, sparkly Christmas sweater, black tights and very high heels, her white skin was accented by straight black hair and bright red lipstick. She loved to talk and was even better at listening.

"Here girls, put on your Santa hats." The speaker, an older woman she recognized as Creed Carter's mother, handed out the red-and-white caps. Lana tried to get into the festive mood though her heart wasn't in it. How could it be, when her heart was across the room? Try as she might, she couldn't stop watching for him. He was working, too, carrying boxes to the various tables to keep the merchants stocked.

For the thousandth time she wished she'd trusted him from the beginning. He'd always been a stand-up guy—a fact that brought her full circle. Davis deserved better. The breakup was for the best.

But he'd said he cared for her, and dreams die hard.

She missed him something awful, missed the evenings with him and his children, missed the conversations, the laughter, the kisses.

"Hi, Lana."

The small voice pulled her focus away from Davis to his children standing on the opposite side of the serving counter. Paige and Nathan, money in hand, had joined the line of diners.

"Hi, you two. Want some barbecue?" She tried to be as casual as possible, but she wanted to run around the end of the counter and scoop them up.

"Three rib dinners, please," Paige said. "But I don't want any potato salad."

"No potato salad. Coming right up."

She fixed the plates and handed them over, adding an extra couple of ribs to Davis's order. A meat and potato man, he loved barbecue, as she'd learned the day they'd ripped out the kitchen's ancient, decayed paneling. He'd purposely ordered enough barbecue ribs to last the weekend. They'd giggled like kids over the messy sauce, the pile of red-stained paper towels and the hot, hot sauce he'd convinced her to try. Her tongue still burned at the memory.

Paige leaned in closer. "Daddy said to tell you hi."

She doubted that very much. "That's really nice of him."

"Should I tell him hi for you?" The child's face was so eager, Lana couldn't let her down.

"That would be nice."

The pair exchanged a conspiratorial glance as they left. Lana shook her head. Such good kids. As they walked away, Lana saw that Paige's red hair bow matched Sydney's, a purchase they'd made together. "Like sisters," they'd said proudly.

I love you. You love me. Let's be sisters. If only life was that simple.

"Why don't you knock off a while and eat with them?" Cassie pointed a ladle at the pair weaving their way through the crowd and toward their father.

"Better not. Davis is not speaking to me at the moment."

"Could have fooled me. I'm watching you watch him. And he's watching you when you aren't watching him."

Lana snorted. "Can you repeat that?"

Cassie laughed and stuck out her tongue. "Not a chance. Just go. Make both of you happy."

But Lana didn't. The community center grew more crowded by the moment and her line was long and getting longer. Bluegrass music shifted to country and she found herself humming to the familiar tunes as she dipped the steaming beans. No one seemed to mind that their server was one of those Ross girls.

After a while, the band took a break and Miss Evelyn made announcements, reminding everyone to sign up for the silent auction. A man Lana didn't recognize moved close to the stage and handed Miss Evelyn a note. She read it silently and then stuck the paper in her pocket. Then she completed her announcements and left the stage with her usual bustling energy. Lana didn't see her again until she appeared at the concession.

"Lana, honey, we need to talk." Miss Evelyn motioned to a bald man in the line. "Cecil, take Lana's spot for a few minutes, will you? As a favor to me? Come see me on Monday for a slice of hot apple pie. On the house."

Cecil looked a little surprised but good-naturedly did as she requested. That was the power of Evelyn Parsons.

Lana was surprised, too. What could Miss Evelyn possibly want to say that couldn't wait?

She followed the bustling, curly haired dynamo to a quiet corner—the quietest place they could find in the jam-packed building.

"Is something wrong?" Lana glanced around for Sydney. Spotting her with a friend, she relaxed.

Miss Evelyn pulled a rumpled piece of paper from her skirt pocket. "A man has offered a large sum of money to Charlie's fund."

"That's fantastic!"

"I thought so, too. All he wants in exchange is to hear you sing."

Lana blinked. Her brain went numb. "What?"

"He requested this specific song." Evelyn pushed the paper into Lana's hands. "Do you know it?"

With trembling fingers, Lana smoothed the note and read the song title. In a shocked whisper, she said, "Yes, I do. I wrote this song."

"Well, how about that!" Miss Evelyn exclaimed, clearly more pleased than Lana. "This could not be more perfect. The town can enjoy your fabulous gift and Charlie's fund gets a fat boost."

"No, I can't, Miss Evelyn, I can't. Don't ask me to sing. I'll do anything else, but not that."

The older woman took both of Lana's hands in hers, crumpling the paper between them. "Lana, I've known you since you were a sad little girl trying to deal with that troubled mother of yours. Every time you came into the Iron Horse with your sister, I'd think, 'That child is special.'"

"You were always kind to us." Emotion pushed up inside Lana's chest. Evelyn and Digger had let the twins hang out at the Iron Horse many days when going home was too hard. Free food and a kind word had made a difference. "I remember when you tried to help Mama."

"Actually I was trying to help you girls. Your mama didn't want help. Called me an old biddy and told me to mind my own business." Miss Evelyn chuckled as if the insult was funny. "But you girls—well, I regret not doing more. I knew things were bad after your daddy left and Patricia was so bitter."

"Daddy couldn't take it anymore."

"He shouldn't have left you girls to deal with her. Looking back I think she might have been sick. But that didn't help you and Tess. You had it rough, but look at you now. Doing great, raising that precious Sydney. And writing songs like this. God gave you a magnificent gift."

Lana shook her head. "Not so magnificent, Miss Evelyn. I can't sing in public anymore."

"Not even for a sick child?" The disappointment on Evelyn's face hurt. "Why, honey?"

Lana wanted to sing, but she couldn't. She'd freeze up and fall apart. She'd make a fool of herself.

"Something happened. I had to stop." Evelyn's questioning eyes bore into her until she finally whispered, "I gave my life to Christ. I stopped drinking."

"That's a good thing, Lana, but I don't see what it has to do with singing that song." She dropped her hold on Lana's hands and tapped the paper.

Quietly, painfully, Lana told her. Hiding the truth had already cost her one friend. "A bottle of gin was my courage. I can't go on stage without it."

Evelyn's eyes searched hers, piercing as if she could see inside. She took Lana's face between her soft, lotion-scented hands and leaned close. "Lana, honey. Don't you know who you are?"

Lana shook her head. Of course, she knew. She was one of those awful Ross girls. She was a loser, a failure.

But Miss Evelyn held her in a fast grip, forcing her to listen. "You are a child of the Most High God. You can do anything He says you can do. God is your strength. You don't need gin or anything else." Evelyn pointed toward Charlie. "But that little boy over there in the wheelchair needs something and you can help him get it."

All she had to do was go on stage and fall apart in front of the entire town. If she wasn't already the least liked person in Whisper Falls, she would be then.

But there was Charlie, Davis's nephew.

Torn, struggling, longing to help but afraid, Lana looked again at the sheet of paper. As she read the song title, Lana was suddenly aware of a startling fact. She'd never submitted that song anywhere. "How does this man know me? Where did he get this?"

Miss Evelyn looked baffled. "He didn't say. I suppose wherever songwriters send their music to be published."

"I didn't. No one has a copy of this except—" Davis. A shock ran through her like electricity. Davis didn't have this kind of money. "Is Davis Turner the donor?"

"Davis? No. The man's name is on the back. Perry Grider."

Lana turned the paper over and read the dark scrawl. Who was this guy? "I don't know him."

"Neither do I, but he had cash in hand, Lana. This is for real."

Cash in hand. A large donation for Charlie's fund. All in exchange for a three-minute song.

"Let me think a minute, okay?" Think and pray and throw up a while.

"Don't take too long. We got a live one. We don't want him to get away." Evelyn chortled at her own joke before growing serious again. "Remember, honey, your gift is your music. God gave you that. If your gift can help someone, He expects you to use it. He'll carry you through. Remember who you are."

Already starting to hyperventilate, Lana nodded numbly. "Okay. Okay."

Then she rushed to the restroom and locked herself inside a stall. This was crazy. Weird and incomprehensible. A thousand thoughts ran through her head. Fear of getting on that stage. Evelyn's strange comments. Charlie's need for surgery. Curiosity about the stranger. Who was he and why would he pay to hear her sing her own song?

She closed her eyes tight. She couldn't get on that stage.

What if it was Sydney? The thought flashed through her head like a Las Vegas marquee. What if her precious girl needed an expensive operation?

She took a deep, shaky breath and prayed. Miss Evelyn's words came back to her. *Don't you know who you are?* You're not Lana Ross, the drunk party girl. You're Lana Ross, child of the Most High, cleansed by a sacrifice far greater than singing in front of hundreds of people.

Her strength was in God. Not a bottle of gin. Her gift was her music. A God gift. Hadn't Davis said the same thing? If she could use her gift to help a child, shouldn't she try?

So what if she failed? She'd been humiliated before. She had to make the effort.

Knees shaking, she straightened her shoulders and headed out of the restroom and across the floor. She passed Davis and Jenny and Chuck and with more courage than she thought she had, she stopped to say hello to Charlie whose sick, little-boy smile encouraged her to keep going. He reminded her so much of Nathan.

Davis's gaze snagged hers, and he started to say something. She touched his arm and went on. Her heart hammered louder than the drums.

When she approached the stage Miss Evelyn saw her and lifted her eyebrows in question.

"I need to borrow a guitar." Jitters raced up her spine and quivered in her voice.

Evelyn did a mini fist pump. "That's our girl. I knew you wouldn't let us down."

Don't be so sure. I still might run like a rabbit on amphetamines.

Fighting down the butterflies, swallowing the threat of sickness, Lana moved to the edge of the stage while Miss Evelyn approached the microphone. The band stopped playing. The noise in the building continued, the voices and the shuffling feet. Doors opened, paper crinkled.

Help me, Lord Jesus. I can't do this by myself. I don't know if I can do it at all. I am Your child. I am Your child.

She'd no more than whispered the prayer than she spotted Davis, slowly pushing Charlie's wheelchair closer to the stage. His eyes were on her, questioning, though she didn't know the reason.

She looked at the little boy in the chair, focused on him instead of the violent shaking inside. "Not for me. For Charlie."

She heard Miss Evelyn's voice making the announcement, but her ears roared so loud she comprehended nothing other than her name. A gasp rose from the audience and then applause. All eyes, not just Davis's, were on her.

A band member held out an electric acoustic.

What if she bolted? What if she couldn't do this? What if she failed?

The old need for a drink roared in, vicious and clawing. One drink. Just one to stop the shakes. To loosen up the dry vocal cords.

Don't you know who you are?

Lana gripped the neck of the guitar and nodded her thanks. Slipping the strap over her shoulder felt natural, second nature. She tested the strings, found them well-tuned, though her fingers felt numb and cold.

Throat drier than Arizona, breath short, she stepped to the mike. She cleared her throat, buying time, wondering if her heart was going to fly out of her chest or if her knees would buckle.

The audience waited, quieter now.

She strummed the strings, found the melody in her head and began to fingerpick the intro. She played it once, twice, praying the words would come.

The wild urge to run made her legs wobbly.

Her eyes found Charlie and the man behind him. Davis smiled at her. Like a drowning soul, she clung to the life raft in his eyes. He gave one encouraging nod and mouthed something.

What did he say? She frowned at him in question, aware that her fingers were moving and the audience waited in expectation.

As his mouth moved again, Davis tapped a fist over his heart, and then he pointed at Lana with a nod.

And Lana began to sing.

Goose bumps raced up and down Davis's spine. He recognized that song. His song. The one she'd given him. The one he'd— Unfettered delight exploded in his chest. He jerked his head right and left, quickly scanning the packed crowd for Joshua Kendle. Did he know? Was he here?

"On wings of the wind, through clouds and the rain, your love carries me, carries me."

The lyrics drew him back to Lana. The other would take care of itself. For now, he wanted nothing more than to watch a miracle unfold.

She was as pale as a sheet, but the rough honey vocals were perfection. Like a tile mosaic of intricate design, emotion flowed from her lips and fingers. At first her eyes were closed but she'd opened them and found him. He held on, willing her to stand strong. She could do this. He knew she could.

He saw her knees shake, her fingers tremble and once

in a while her lips quivered. He knew how scared she was. But while her body quaked, beauty and emotion flowed from her throat.

"You got this," he murmured, encouraging her in every way possible from ten feet away. "I'm sorry. Thank you. You're awesome."

He muttered a litany of apologies and random thoughts, more grateful than he could ever say for her sacrifice.

Miss Evelyn's announcement had nearly taken him to his knees. Even Jenny had begun to weep. Though Lana had not sung in public for a long time, someone was donating to Charlie's fund in exchange for a song. So she had agreed.

He knew the fear that haunted her. He knew how hard this was. She was terrified and yet, she had agreed for Charlie. His nephew. For the child of a woman who'd given her nothing but grief.

Why had he been such a coldhearted, selfish idiot? Lana would always put a child's needs before her own. Sydney's and now Charlie's.

Suddenly he understood what Austin had been trying to tell him. Lana's mistakes, like his and everyone else's, had been nailed to a cross. The moment she accepted Him, she was free of her past. She might still be working through some areas, trying to find her way, but who wasn't?

She was a good and decent person. And he loved her. He'd been miserable without her. He'd known all along she made him better, that she was the missing piece of his life, but he had allowed pride and opinion to rob them both.

She had every reason not to forgive him, but he prayed she would.

As Lana kicked into the final chorus, Davis turned to Jenny. "She did this for Charlie. Lana has paralyzing stage fright but she went up there for *your son*."

Tears gathered in his sister's eyes. "I don't know what to say."

"Say you were wrong. I was, too. I love her, Jenny, and I'm going to tell her even if she kicks me to the curb." Leaving his weeping sister, he excused his way through the crowd that now pressed against the stage. He approached the steps at one end, counting on her to exit the direction she'd entered.

The song ended and the building erupted in applause and cheers. Lana remained at the microphone, guitar against her body, with a bewildered expression as if she couldn't believe the applause was for her. Someone whistled a loud *whoot*. On the opposite side of the stage, Miss Evelyn practically levitated with excitement.

Davis started up the steps, not wanting to steal Lana's moment but eager to hold her in his arms, to apologize. If she'd let him.

Then Lana smiled—a wide, relieved smile—handed the guitar to its owner and took a quick bow. As she turned to exit the stage she saw him and froze.

Davis paused, adrenaline jacked, feeling a bit trembly himself. "You were phenomenal."

She took a step toward him. "I was scared to death."

"That's what made it phenomenal. You were afraid, but you sang. For Charlie."

She took another step. And then another.

The crowd of people faded into the background.

Sound ceased. Davis saw and heard nothing but the special woman he'd almost thrown away.

"I've been an idiot," he said. "Forgive me? *Please* forgive me."

She didn't hesitate. Faster than he could breathe, Lana was in his embrace.

"I was wrong not to tell you," she said. "You had every right to despise me. I've made too many mistakes."

He stroked her soft hair. "Shh. Shh. I don't despise you. I never could. You're amazing. I was the one out of line."

The calloused tips of her fingers rubbed lovingly across his jaw. "I missed you so much."

"I was such a jerk. You should make this harder on me. Make me grovel." He looped a lock of hair behind her ear. "Do you know how many times I've had to stop myself from coming to your house?"

"Me, too. I'd look out the window and see you or the kids coming or going and I wanted to run to you."

"Can we start fresh? Start new? Try again?"

"Are you sure you can forget what I've done and where I've been? I don't want to hold you back or make you or the kids ashamed to know me."

"You could never do that. I'm proud of you, Lana. *Proud.*" He cupped her face, more grateful than he could ever express. She'd forgiven him. Just like that. "Can you forget the ugly things I said?"

"I already have."

"There we are then. Forgotten. Forgiven." *Whom the Son has set free is free indeed.* Austin Blackwell was a wise man. "Lana Ross," he said. "You are an amazing, gifted child of God, a loving mother, a good friend, the woman who holds my heart. I want you in my life. Say you want me, too."

"Oh, I do. So much." Lana pressed her cheek against Davis's chest. "I feel like I'm dreaming."

He cupped the back of her head, aware of her warm breath seeping through his shirt. "If you are, don't wake up. I like it here."

"Daddy?" a small voice said.

Davis let his head drop against her hair. "Uh-oh. The dream is over."

Lana laughed softly and took a step away. Her absence left a cold spot. He caught her hand and tugged her back, sliding a possessive arm around her. No matter what anyone thought or said, he wasn't letting go this time. Let the whole world know for all he cared.

"Daddy." Nathan squinted up at them, expression intense. "Does this mean you and Lana are in love again?"

The adults exchanged looks. What Davis saw in Lana's eyes was all the answer he needed.

"Yes, son. I think it does."

Chapter Fifteen

The Christmas Bazaar was in a word, bizarre. Good bizarre.

Too astonished and happy to do anything but grin, Lana held Davis's hand in a near death grip as they walked through the exhibits in search of the man who'd paid such a high price for a song. Her knees still shook but for a different reason now. It was as if the earth had moved and the world had suddenly righted itself. A world that had never made sense finally did.

Love was a powerful thing. She prayed with all her heart that this would last. That Davis wouldn't change his mind again and that she would have the courage to keep believing.

In front of them, Sydney, Paige and Nathan hopped and giggled and whirled in circles like wind-up Christmas toys, making a path through the well-wishers. With each step, someone stopped her to compliment her music, to ask when she would sing again, to invite her to events.

The terror had come, but she'd won. She and God. With the help of a very special man.

"I didn't fall down," she whispered as they walked past a display of wood-carved clocks.

Davis smiled his thousand-watt smile. "I would never let you fall."

That was part of the wonder, the knowledge that somehow the finest man on earth had seen past her faults and loved her anyway.

The same way Jesus had.

"Lana." A female voice turned her around. Jenny stood there, a determined expression on her face.

Lana stiffened, sucked in a breath and waited for the subtle digs or outright hostility. Coming off the high of singing again, she didn't want this confrontation, but she wouldn't run away from it either. Jenny had reason to dislike her but it was time for both of them to grow up and move on.

Not wanting to put Davis in the middle, Lana removed her hand from his.

Wonder of wonders, Davis shifted closer and put his strong workman's arm around her waist, securing her to his side, supporting her.

"Hi, sis," he said to Jenny.

Twisting her fingers, Jenny barely nodded to her brother. Her focus was on Lana. Instead of the expected hostility, Lana saw sadness.

"Your song...Miss Evelyn said..." Jenny's eyes dropped shut. Tears slid from beneath each lid. "Thank you for what you did."

"I hope Charlie's operation makes him well. That's all that matters."

Jenny smiled a wobbly, watery smile and walked away.

"You let her off easy," Davis said. "I love you for

that. She's my sister, a good woman, but lately—" He shook his head, palms up in a gesture of helplessness.

"She's a scared mother. No matter what happened before, Charlie's situation takes center stage. I feel sorry for what Jenny's going through."

"See? Amazing. Generous. Good to the core." He snagged her hand again and looked around. "Now where is that Perry guy?"

"I can't imagine what that was all about. He knew about my song, Davis, the one I shared with you."

"We'll find out, don't worry," Davis said with an odd twinkle in his eyes.

But they didn't. Regardless of their search and even after speaking with Miss Evelyn, they never found him. For some baffling reasons, a stranger named Perry Grider had come in, requested the song, left a large chunk of money and disappeared without another word.

Finally, Lana said, "I have to get back to the serving line." She didn't want to. She wanted to stay right beside Davis and enjoy the pure freedom the night had brought. "I promised."

"I hear you. I have some things to do, too." He leaned in to kiss her forehead. "You smell really good."

Lana wrinkled her nose. "Like barbecue?"

"Hey, nothing wrong with that. Love that smell. Very romantic."

She laughed. "I'll remember that."

They stood smiling at each other like two lunatics, knowing they had to separate but reluctant.

"Later?" Davis asked.

"Absolutely."

The rest of the evening flew by in a happy blur of dishing up beans while catching glimpses of Davis.

She saw him everywhere helping out. He even talked to Joshua Kendle for a while, apparently about something that made them both happy. They exchanged high fives and slapped each other on the back. During the exchange he glanced her way and grinned. Her silly pulse had gone off the charts.

The three little matchmakers popped by a couple of times to be sure the five of them would have some togetherness before the day ended.

"Daddy says come to our house after," Nathan insisted. "We have mistletoe."

Chuckling at the pure cuteness, Lana stopped serving long enough to grab a hug. "How can I turn that down?"

Back with the baked beans, she watched them skip away, giggling and excited. They were such loves, all three of them.

"Great event, huh?" Cassie asked suggestively as she twitched her perfectly arched eyebrows.

"Can't argue with that." The only imperfection was the mystery she hadn't solved. Who was Perry Grider and how did he know about her song?

The days leading up to Christmas were the happiest of Lana's life. She was loved by a wonderful man and the association with Davis brought her a new respectability. At least, she assumed that was the reason she no longer felt like an outcast in Whisper Falls.

She and Sydney, usually with Davis, Nathan and Paige along, attended a whirlwind of Christmas events—everything from church plays, caroling and cantatas to the adorable musical program at Sydney's school. As her writing skills improved, the articles came faster and easier, and she found more time for her music and for working on the house with Davis. The latter, when they could talk and unwind together, was the best part of her day.

With Davis's support, she'd gathered the courage to file for Sydney's guardianship. Guided by Haley and Creed, who had gone through a similar situation with Rose and knew the ropes, the process wasn't nearly as bad as Lana had expected. Even with her past, the social worker had been confident that two years of sobriety and a town filled with references would do the trick. Lana's eyes filled with grateful tears every time she thought about all the good things that had happened to her in Whisper Falls.

Yesterday with enthusiastic help from the three children, she'd created "gifts in a jar" for teachers and friends, the pastor, her boss and others. Then, today, Christmas Eve, the trio made the rounds, ho-ho-hoing and singing "Jingle Bells" at the top of their lungs as they delivered the goodies while Davis put the final touches on Annalisa Blackwell's tile work.

Davis was picking up something afterward, though the children had no idea she and Davis had found exactly the right puppy to put under Sydney's tree. Why not? They were here for good. Whisper Falls was finally home.

Steps light, she guided the children across the street, listening to their excited chatter. Her Sydney seemed so much happier and more secure these days. Lana giggled inside, anticipating the child's joy when she met the fat ball of love.

At the newspaper office, Joshua Kendle gave her a "little something" in an envelope, her first bonus ever, and requested all the articles she had time to write.

She threw her arms around his neck and hugged him. Then embarrassed, she stepped away only to find him laughing at her.

"You folks have a merry Christmas," he said. "And tell Davis not to worry. I'll be happy whatever you decide."

Lana stopped in the doorway. "What?"

"Never mind. You'll know soon enough. And you don't even have to thank me." When she frowned in bewilderment, he waved her off. "Merry Christmas, now."

Then he turned back to his computer and left her to wonder.

"I'm a little nervous," Lana said that evening as the five of them drove toward Davis's parents' home.

Davis was nervous for a completely different reason. His palms were sweating against the steering wheel. "No need to be. After what you did for Charlie and the way my kids go on about you, my parents already think you're terrific."

Traditionally, the entire Davis clan gathered at Mom and Dad's house on Christmas Eve for a light meal before heading to candlelight service at church. Christmas morning was reserved for the kids to open gifts and a return to Grandma's for dinner Christmas afternoon. This year, Davis no longer felt at loose ends. He had Lana, and being with her filled him with contentment.

"I don't want to embarrass you." Fingers spread, she jiggled her hands up and down in front of her body. "Is this outfit okay?"

He glanced at her, there in the passenger seat of his truck, full of gratitude that he'd had the good sense to see her value in time to salvage what neither had intended to start. He was also amused. Did women always worry about their clothes being right? "You're perfect. Makes me want to drop off the kids and run away with you."

She laughed, flushing. "Maybe someday."

After tonight he'd know for sure if she really meant those words. Lana had choices she didn't know about. Davis wanted all her dreams to come true. He hoped he was one of them.

"Any word from Tess?" he asked, keeping his voice low.

Lana shook her head. "Not yet."

"Don't give up. It's Christmas."

He knew how badly she wanted to get her sister into rehab, but all their efforts so far were in vain. Tess had Lana's cell number. Davis prayed she'd someday make that call and ask for help.

"I'll never stop praying," Lana said. "If God can change my life, He can change hers, too."

As they pulled into his parents' driveway, Duncan, Dad's Great Dane, lumbered toward them, backlit by the red lights glowing around the roofline. Though they were dressed in Sunday best, the three kids tumbled out to roughhouse with the giant, friendly dog. The sharp air was spiced with wood smoke and, as soon as Mom opened the front door, all smiles, Davis smelled his favorite chicken gumbo.

Amidst introductions, kids whooping it up and the background of television blaring *It's a Wonderful Life,* they were sucked into the warmth of family. He knew Lana was nervous, especially around Jenny, but she offered her help and disappeared into the kitchen with the other women. Mom would love her for chipping in.

In the living room, the men, including little Charlie, watched the familiar DVD. They'd watched it every Christmas Eve for as long as he could remember. Davis really wanted to talk to his dad in private, but the opportunity never presented itself. Tonight would be a surprise for him, as well.

One of the kids, Nathan he suspected, let Duncan in the house. The Great Dane went straight for the Christmas tree and snatched a candy cane before he could be wrestled back outside by the three guilty parties. Charlie laughed himself breathless which brought Jenny rushing into the living room.

After they'd stuffed themselves on gumbo and pecan pie, Davis glanced at his watch. Plenty of time before church. Lana sat at his side, the perfect spot and exactly where he'd planned for her to be. Where he always wanted her. But the choice was hers, starting now.

He waited for a pause in the conversation and when it finally came, he cleared his throat. A sudden fit of nerves danced in his belly. He reached for Lana's hand beneath the table and squeezed. She squeezed back.

"Everyone," he said, "I have something to say."

All eyes jerked to him and then to Lana. Speculative grins appeared on his parents' faces as they exchanged quick glances.

"Go ahead, son." Behind black-rimmed glasses, his dad's gaze was warm and encouraging. "If this is about you and Lana, I don't think any of us will be surprised."

His heart staccatoed. "It is. In a way." He shifted his chair to angle toward Lana. She'd turned a pretty shade of pink. Doing this in front of his family was harder than he'd expected. But absolutely right, too. He wanted

Lana to know how proud he was of her. Here on Christmas Eve in front of the people he loved the most.

"Lana," he said and swallowed again. "I love you. My kids love you. We want you in our lives. You and Sydney. I never thought I'd feel this way about a woman again, but I do."

"I love you, too," she whispered, face red as Christmas but her blue eyes glowing with happiness. "I want—"

"Hear me out." He touched her lips with one finger, silencing her. "Before this goes any further, I have a Christmas present for you to open tonight."

Expression puzzled, she took the envelope from his hands and turned it over. "What is this?"

"It's one of your dreams. I want you to have it even if it means losing you."

"You won't—"

"I found Perry Grider."

"What?"

"Open the envelope, Lana."

He waited with a blood rush in his brain and his ears roaring while Lana read the letter.

"Someone wants to publish my song. For money." Astonishment quickly changed to excitement. "Is this legit? Is he for real? How did this happen?"

Though scared of losing her, Davis couldn't help the smile in his chest. He'd given her this and she was thrilled.

"Remember when you gave me the song? I told Joshua Kendle about it and asked if he knew anyone in the music business."

"I'd forgotten he once lived in Nashville."

"Yeah, well, he called around and this is the result.

They not only want to buy this song, they want to see what else you have. They're interested in putting you under contract to write exclusively for GT Music."

"GT? No way. They're big-time."

He grinned, both proud and scared. "Merry Christmas."

"Is this for real?" She pressed the sheet of paper to her face and laughed in awe. "This can't be real."

He watched her delight and reveled in it, all the while wondering if he'd just given her a reason to leave Whisper Falls. His family began to talk all at once, excited for her.

Suddenly, a dimple cheeked boy pushed between them, expression stricken as he faced Lana. "Does this mean you're not gonna be my mom?"

The conversations quieted. Davis put a hand on Nathan's shoulder, waiting for the answer, too. Slowly, Lana lowered the contract to her lap.

"Is that what you think?" she asked, incredulous. "That this would change the way I feel about you?"

"This is a game changer, Lana. You can move back to Nashville, write your songs, maybe even get another shot at a singing contract. This is your big chance."

"Yes, it *is* my big chance. To do the one thing I really want to do with my music…write songs. I don't want to live in Nashville. Been there, done that and have the scars to show. I don't want a singing contract. That life nearly destroyed me and Sydney. I want to write…but most of all, I want to be with you."

As if someone had turned on a vacuum and sucked out the anxiety, the tightness in Davis's chest eased.

"Positive?"

"More sure than I've ever been of anything."

"Nathan, son," he said as he gently moved his son

to one side. "You'll have to excuse your old dad. I have a proposal to make."

Lana's hands flew to her mouth. "I'm going to pass out."

"Don't even think about it. I only want to do this once." Laughing at her a little and so thrilled, he thought *he* might pass out, Davis awkwardly maneuvered between the chairs and slipped to one knee in front of Lana.

"Lana Ross, I want to marry you and raise these kids together and if you want more, I'm good with that. I want to grow old with you, to share our lives and loves, to share your music. Will you give me the best Christmas gift a man could ever have? Will you be my wife?"

By the time he ended what he considered the longest speech of his life, Lana wept. No sound, but a waterfall of tears that touched him. His throat filled.

"Oh, yes." Her honeyed voice was thick with emotion as she whispered, "I would be honored."

They reached for each other, but before they connected, three small bodies barreled into the fray. The rest of the family was up, too, talking and pounding backs and grabbing hugs. Davis found Lana's gaze through the melee and winked.

"Meet you later," he said. "Under Nathan's mistletoe."

Through tears, she laughed and nodded.

And of course, they did.

* * * * *

THE LAWMAN'S HONOR

Immediately Jesus made His disciples get into the boat and go before Him to the other side, while He sent the multitudes away. And when He had sent the multitudes away, He went up on the mountain by Himself to pray. Now when evening came, He was alone there. But the boat was now in the middle of the sea, tossed by the waves, for the wind was contrary…. And they cried out for fear. But immediately Jesus spoke to them, saying, "Be of good cheer! It is I; do not be afraid."
—*Matthew* 14:22–27

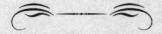

The entire Whisper Falls series is dedicated to the memory of my brother, Stan Case.

Rumor says that if a prayer is murmured beneath Whisper Falls, God will hear and answer. Some folks think it's superstitious nonsense. Some think it's a clever ploy to attract tourists. Others believe that God works in mysterious ways, and prayers, no matter where whispered, are always heard.

Prologue

She was probably crazy for doing this. As a local, she should know better. Climbing Whisper Falls to pray was a rumor, a myth, a publicity stunt. But for reasons she couldn't explain or deny, Cassie Blackwell felt the need to do it anyway. Her sister-in-law had prayed here and look how well that had turned out.

Sticking one boot against the wall of slippery rocks, Cassie started the ascent. Whisper Falls sprayed water against the side of her face as it tumbled to the pool below. Spring was here and with it the Blackberry River rushing wildly to embrace the sea like a long lost love.

Feeling self-conscious, Cassie glanced below—and promptly wished she hadn't. Her stomach rose into her throat, shortening her breath. The top was a long way from the bottom, the roar of the falls a deafening threat to safety.

With a firm admonishment not to look down again, she turned her gaze to the cliff top. No one else was here in the remote wooded area. Thank goodness. No one would ever know the ridiculous thing she'd done. Clinging now to the dampness, digging in with her fingers and toes, she clambered up and, with heart banging against her rib cage, Cassie catapulted onto the narrow ledge behind the cascade of magnificent white foam.

The inner sanctum behind the falls was stunningly quiet. She took a minute to catch her breath and soak up the atmosphere. It was beautiful, peaceful and private as though the world below was another universe.

"Will Heaven be like this, Lord?" she asked, awed, for she knew in that moment what others before her had discovered. God was here. Oh, sure, she believed He was everywhere, but something about this place seemed spiritual.

So she lifted her face to the astounding sight above her and prayed.

"Father God, it's me, Cassie. Since the funeral, I've been numb, like I'm frozen inside. I don't know how to fix it. I don't know how to make the emptiness go away. I want to feel again."

There was a certain fear in admitting such a thing. It was as if she was throwing away what she and Darrell had shared. But she would never do that. And yet, she wanted something. No, she *needed* something. The problem? She didn't know what that something was. But with all her heart, she prayed that God would know and answer.

Chapter One

The rain had started a few miles back. On a moonless black night on an unfamiliar rural road, a man could easily get lost. Heath Monroe had a feeling he might have done exactly that.

He cast a cautious eye at the sky, at jagged streaks of lightning in approaching clouds. This section of the Ozarks was in for a storm. Hopefully, he could find the little town of Whisper Falls before the worst of it struck.

Heath was weary from the long drive, and his GPS had long ago stopped telling the truth. When he'd pulled off for gasoline at a tiny whistle-stop community no bigger than a convenience store and a handful of houses, he'd grabbed some junk food to hold him over. He'd eaten worse and certainly gone longer without healthy food. The friendly woman at the store assured him he was headed in the right direction.

"Keep going until you see the turnoff," she'd said. "It's kind of hard to see at night but there's a little green sign."

A muscle in his left shoulder had tightened and the

pain now ran up the side of his neck. Heath exhaled through his lips, eager to find that road sign.

But it wasn't only the drive making him weary. He was soul weary, the only reason he could think of for his sudden decision to exchange a job he'd loved for work in a small Ozark town. He was tired of the constant travel, the short-circuited relationships that were over before they had a chance, and worst of all, the feeling that he was trying to empty the ocean with a teaspoon.

And yet, he was driven to keep fighting. His father had taught him that. Never give up. Right the wrongs. Fight the fight. He was an army of one. One man could change the world.

Heath took a hand from the wheel to touch the badge in his pants pocket. His father's life mattered and Heath aimed to carry the torch. *Had* carried it for a lot of years. The new assignment was different but the overriding mission remained the same.

Thunder rumbled in the distance.

"Couldn't be too much farther." He'd give Mom and Holt a call as soon as he hit town. They'd both be worried, his brother as much as his mother. After all the places he'd been, the training he'd received and all his successful missions, Mom still feared he'd end up like his father.

He hoped she was wrong, but he couldn't count on it.

Cassie Blackwell hunched over the steering wheel and squinted through the rain-lashed windshield. Wind buffeted the dependable little Nissan as a clap of thunder vibrated through Cassie's bones. She shivered, though the heater pumped out plenty of clammy warmth. Her eyes burned from staring into the pitch-black night lit only by the pale wash of headlights and the frequent, unpredictable lightning.

In the last ten minutes, the storm had gotten progressively worse. Scary bad.

Like blue laser fingers, lightning suddenly splayed across the ominous clouds. As if the skies had opened, rain fell in sheets, loud and unnerving. The lightning was quickly sucked back into the swirling masses overhead, into a blackness so deep Cassie couldn't tell for sure where she was.

This looked bad. Real bad. Tornado season was upon them and though she was no meteorologist, she understood tornadic thunderstorms. Texans cut their teeth on tornados, and a half dozen years in the Ozarks couldn't erase a lifetime of experience.

Through the deluge, she spotted the car ahead. One lone vehicle other than hers crawled through the night, clinging to the curvy mountain roadway. It reminded Cassie of a commercial in which the tires had grown tiger claws to grip the pavement. Tonight her Nissan needed claws.

If a tornado fell out of those ominous clouds, she didn't know what she'd do. There was no ditch, no storm shelter, no houses for miles, other than her own still a dozen miles ahead.

Her eyes had started to burn from the strain of peering into the astonishing blackness. The air was sticky, a harbinger. Small hail ping-ponged off the hood and bounced in the headlights like popcorn on the blacktop. Her windshield wipers kept up a rhythmic *whap-whap* to battle the sluicing rain, a battle they couldn't win tonight.

She punched on the radio, hoping for weather reports. Static, intensified by sizzles of lightning, filled the car. She turned off the useless noise. Whatever the weather, she would have to ride it out.

Normally, Cassie loved thunderstorms. The clean smell, the invigorating wind, the sudden burst of cold wetness. Most of all she enjoyed the wild, showy side of nature, the power of an awesome God. She liked to sit on the ranch's front porch and watch the storms move over the mountains, to wrap in a blanket and sip a cup of hot tea and dream of the one and only time she and Darrell had gotten to do that very thing together. Before they married. Before he was gone.

Lightning flared in the sky for scant seconds. Cassie noticed the car again, its watery red taillights barely discernible through the deep black curtain of heavy rain. She watched the lights waver and then fishtail crazily as the driver lost control.

"Jesus!" Cassie cried, a prayer for the driver. The lightning disappeared as quickly as it had come. In the blackness, she didn't know if the car had righted itself or if even now, the driver plunged down an incline into the thick woods...or worse, into one of the canyons.

She dared not speed up, lest she, too, lose control. The road curved sharply ahead where she'd last seen the other vehicle. She crept forward, a prayer on her lips, her eyes wide and scratchy as she tried to make out the exact spot where she'd seen the driver lose control.

There. Cassie decelerated and tapped her brake. To her right and fifty feet down into a deep ravine she spotted the faint impression of light. Dread in her gut, heart racing, she pulled as far to the side of the road as possible and stopped. The rain still came in drenching torrents. Storm or not, she had to do something. Someone could be hurt.

Cell phones were great when they worked, which was rarely the case in remote areas like this one. In this storm she had serious doubts, but she quickly pressed 911 anyway. When nothing happened, she fired a text to her brother and another to Police Chief JoEtta Farnsworth in the nearest town, Whisper Falls. Maybe, just maybe, the text could get through the storm.

Then, she did what she had to do. Flashlight in hand, she leaped out into the wild, raging night and plunged down the brushy incline toward the accident.

In seconds she was drenched. Brush grabbed at her naked legs, ripping flesh. Of all the crummy times to wear a skirt. Slipping and sliding, Cassie stumbled once on a fallen tree her light hadn't picked up. A bolt of lightning, blue with fire, had her up and scurrying faster. Old leaves mushy with rain squished beneath her pretty new heels, a gift from her mother from only yesterday.

Through the noisy storm, she heard the rumble of a motor. The vehicle, which she now saw was a smaller SUV, was still running, the headlights eerie in the deep, tangled woods.

Cassie ran to the driver's side and pounded on the window. "Hello. Are you all right? Hello!"

A dark form slumped over the steering wheel. Shaking now, from both cold and anxiety, Cassie pulled at the back door. Locked. Frustrated, she banged on the driver's window.

"Wake up. Wake up." She prayed he wasn't dead. The last dead person she'd seen had been her husband.

Darrell's lifeless face flashed in her mental viewer. She shook her head to dispel the image.

Shivering, face dripping rain, hair plastered against her skull and vision skewed by the torrent, she shined the flashlight toward the ground, searching for anything to break out a window. Finding a thick branch, she heaved it against the back passenger glass. Nothing other than a jarred wrist for her efforts.

She hurried to the front of the car. The windshield had spider-webbed in the crash but hadn't given way. It was weak. She could possibly break through the glass, much as she disliked the idea of exposing the injured driver to a flood of rain. She started around the car to the passenger's side. Better to break the windshield out on the side farthest from the driver.

Behind her, the driver's door popped. In a burst of adrenaline, Cassie whirled toward the sound. The dark woods were eerie and she was alone. Her flashlight picked out a man's hand and wrist on the armrest. A watch glowed green in the darkness right before the arm fell, limp.

Cassie hurried to the door and pulled, but the door had opened as far as it could. Only a few inches. Her fingers fumbled around inside the door and found the locks, popping them.

"Thank You, Lord."

She yanked the back door open and crawled inside, shivering at the interior warmth and the sudden, wonderful cessation of rain. Rain dripped all over the nice leather interior, but that was the least of her worries.

She shook the broad shoulder in front of her. "Can you hear me?"

He mumbled something.

Cassie shined the flashlight at the side of his face and scrambled over the seat, leaving a trail of water.

The man's face turned slightly toward her. "What—?"

"Where are you hurt?"

"Hurt?"

He must be addled, concussed or…something. She owned a beauty salon. What did she know about injuries other than sunburn from too much time in the tanning beds?

"Do you think you can walk? I have my car up on the road. I can take you to a doctor." Dr. Ron, the only physician in Whisper Falls, was accustomed to being awakened in the night for emergencies.

He shook his head. "My leg."

What about his leg? Was it broken? Crushed? Were bones sticking out? The last, grizzly thought rattled her nerves but bones or not, she was his only help.

Using the flashlight, Cassie started at the top of his head and began a slow perusal of the driver. "I can't see that well, but let me check you over. I texted for help. I don't know if I had reception though. The storm."

He nodded, his jaw tight and lines of pain radiating from his lips all the way into the stretched cords of his neck. His was a manly face with wide, chiseled jawbones and deep-set eyes. She couldn't tell the color but she could see the pain and confusion. He was addled, no doubt about it.

She'd never been much for facial hair but his suited. A wisp of whiskers above his lip and on his chin. Just a little, just enough to make a woman notice. Not that she was noticing in a situation like this.

"Forgive the intrusion," she murmured, not sure if he heard or understood, but her vision was limited. His medium-length dark hair could easily conceal a wound. She had no choice but to touch him. "Are you bleeding anywhere?"

Her fingers scanned the back of his head, up and over to the forehead. There. A knot the size of a softball along his left temple. "You've hit your head."

She pulled her fingers back and shined the light on them. No blood. She breathed a sigh of relief. No blood suited her fine.

"My leg," he said again and attempted a slight shift in the seat.

Cassie aimed the light lower, searching in the dimness. "I can't see."

He reached above his head and snapped on the dome light. He wasn't as addled as she'd thought. *She* hadn't thought of that.

Cassie blinked against the brightness. "Thanks."

"What happened?"

Or maybe he was. "You missed the curve and hit a tree."

That was the short version.

"My leg. What happened?"

"I can't tell. I think it might be stuck. Can you move it at all?" Beneath the dash was a crumpled mess of metal and wires. She didn't want to think about his leg underneath that weight.

"No."

"Does it hurt?"

He paused as if having to think about the question. "I don't think so."

Strange answer. Either it did or it didn't.

She shined the light in his face. Glazed eyes barely blinked.

Okay, this was not good. The man had a head injury and couldn't get out of the car. And it was likely her text hadn't gone through.

Thunder rumbled. Rain kept up a steady swoosh. Flashes of lightning radiated through the night sky.

She did not want to make that trip back up to the road.

"Will you be all right while I go to my car and try to call again? I left my cell up there." Stupid decision but water and cell phones didn't mix. She should know. She'd knocked one into the shampoo bowl before and that had cost a pretty penny to replace. "With the storm moving on, I might be able to get through."

"Yeah."

As Cassie pulled at the passenger door, an iron grip manacled her wrist. She whipped around.

"What's your name?"

She stared down at his fingers. For a wounded man, he was strong! "I'm Cassie. What's yours?"

"What happened?"

There again the hint that he was more injured than he let on.

"You've had an accident." Gently she wiggled her wrist but he held fast. "What's your name?"

Not a bad idea to know in case he went unconscious again before emergency help arrived. You could never tell about head injuries.

"Monroe." Did his voice sound slurred? "Heath Monroe."

It fit him. Masculine. Strong. She tugged against his powerful grip. "You can turn loose now."

Slowly, he shook his head.

"Cassie." The way he said it sent a little tremor

down her spine. He moistened his lips and swallowed. "Don't go."

His fingers went slack. Definitely addled.

"Hang tight, Heath, I'll be right back. Promise."

As good as her word, she was back in minutes. This time she'd tucked her cell phone inside a plastic shopping bag and brought it along. Just in case.

By the time she returned, he'd removed his seat belt and was rummaging in the console. The deployed air bag draped over his lap like an enormous melted marshmallow. Maybe that explained his confusion. An air bag packed a wallop.

She slammed the door, grateful to be inside again. The wet cold seeped into her bones.

"I made contact with my brother. He knows the area. He'll get help and bring them here."

The man's head dropped back against the headrest, eyes drifting closed. Whatever he'd been rummaging for was forgotten. He was still as pale as toothpaste. "Good."

"It could take a while. We're deep in the woods."

He rolled his head toward her. Beneath the dome light, his eyes were green like hers, though darker and more intense. The knowledge gave Cassie a funny feeling, as if they were connected somehow. "How far to Whisper Falls?"

Talking seemed to take more effort than it should.

"The town or the waterfall?"

"What?"

He was either addled or a total stranger to the area. "Whisper Falls is both a waterfall and a small town up here in the Ozarks. It's a long story but basically the town council decided to rename the town for the waterfall to attract tourists."

"And other things," he murmured, a statement which made her wonder all over again about his mental acuity.

"The falls is north of town, not far from where I live. The town itself is another six miles east. If you're headed to town, you missed the turn." Which made her wonder—why would a stranger be driving into Whisper Falls at this hour of the night?

Though the heater pumped out a warm hiss, it wasn't enough to penetrate the wet chill that had settled over her skin. Cassie shivered.

"You're cold."

"I'll live." She hugged herself, rubbing her hands up and down on her goose-bumped arms. She had a sudden memory of accident victims needing a blanket to keep from going into shock. Or something like that. There was no blanket available, but she had a suitcase full of clothes in the car. She could cover him with a sweater or two. "Are you warm enough?"

He didn't answer. He'd closed his eyes again and gotten quiet. Cassie fretted. Had his pallor increased? Was he asleep or unconscious? Remembering all the movies in which sleep was bad for a head injury, Cassie thought she should keep him talking. If there was one thing other than haircuts Cassie was good at, it was talking. "How's the leg?"

His eyelids fluttered but he didn't move otherwise. "Numb. Stuck. Frustrating."

"That's an understatement." She'd always been a talker, but years as a hairdresser had honed the skill. As her brother, Austin, often said, she could talk to a fence post. He should know. She talked to him, a man who'd rather have a stick in the eye as to carry on a conversation. "Do you hurt anywhere? Any other injuries you can determine?"

"A little headache."

"Little? Or one of those headaches where a burly construction worker is slamming your brains with a hammer?"

"Yeah. Rattled my brains." He drew in a shuddering breath, wincing at the effort. Something else hurt whether he acknowledged it or not. "Careless. I'm a better driver than that."

Now they were getting somewhere. An entire coherent thought.

Encouraged, Cassie pushed on. "Male pride. You sound like my brother when a horse throws him."

One corner of Heath's mouth moved the slightest bit as if he wanted to engage but didn't quite have the energy. "Cowboy?"

"Austin's a rancher. His place is a few more miles up this road and then back down a gravel road another mile and a half. Or did I tell you that already?"

"Boonies."

The comment was both apt and revealing. "Where are you from, Heath? Are you a city boy?"

He went silent again though Cassie was pretty sure he was conscious. It was as if he had to think about his answers. Either he'd had his memory knocked sideways or he was avoiding the question, something that made no sense. The headache must be taking a toll on his thought processes.

Finally, as though his mouth was parched, he moistened his lips again and muttered, "Houston."

"Texas?"

He managed a wry glance, one eyebrow arched the tiniest bit. "Is there any other?"

Good. He was sounding better. Texans were a proud lot.

"Surprised, because I'm from Texas, too. Austin and I moved here from outside of Dallas. We've been here a long time, but Mom and Dad still live there. That's where I've been this week. A friend got married and I was in the wedding." She smiled a little at the memory of her old friend so much in love. She'd suffered a bite of the green-eyed monster, too, normal she supposed even though she never expected to fall in love again. "I did some shopping, ate Mama's cooking. Gained weight. Fun times."

That brought about as much response as kissing a mirror. She glanced at the clock on the dash, fretting again. Where was Austin? He should have been here by now. She was growing weary of trying to carry on a one-sided conversation with a disturbingly attractive, head-injured man during a pretty scary thunderstorm. But keeping him alert, or at least awake, was imperative. Wasn't it?

She should have paid more attention in first aid classes.

"I do hair," she said. Okay, that was lame, but what was she supposed to talk about to a total stranger who didn't give her much to work with? "I'm good at it, too."

Not that you could tell right now, with her straight black layers plastered flat against her head and dripping all over his leather interior.

"'Scuse me?" His eyelids lifted to half-staff. He had noticeably long lashes, thick and spiky, that shadowed his cheekbones. Thick eyebrows slashed above his eyes.

No wax. She would know. She did plenty of wax jobs, even on men, though some of them swore her to secrecy.

"I'm a hairstylist. I do nails, too. My partner, Louise, and I run the Tress and Tan Salon in Whisper Falls." She wiggled her fingers at him. Her nails were acrylic, a tidy length but decorated with tiny tuxedoes in honor of the wedding. "Need a mani-pedi?"

His face was still too pale, but he managed a faint smile. More of a grimace, really, but an attempt to stay awake. "If I have any toes left."

Ouch. "My brother should be here soon. Don't worry. We'll get you out of here and that pedicure will be on the house. All ten toes."

"Optimist." The word had weakened, tapering off at the end so that it sounded more like 'optimisss.' Not good. *Come on, Austin.*

"Do you always drive off into strange places during raging thunderstorms? And why Whisper Falls? Visiting relatives?" When he didn't answer, she touched his arm. "Come on, Heath, stay awake."

"Late start." He was trying. She'd give him that much. "GPS…not too dependable."

"You got lost. Figures. Anyone can get lost out here." And he probably had been too proud and stubborn to stop and ask directions. Darrell had been like that, confident the location was right around the corner. "Mountains and trees are not impressed by modern technology."

He closed his eyes again, worrying Cassie. The car engine was still engaged, and a quick glance at the dash indicated plenty of gas. At least he'd had the presence of mind to fill up sometime in the recent past. They were warm and secure, the thunderstorm subsiding somewhat as it moved toward the east, though the rumbles continued and lightning flickered.

"Thunderstorms here are pretty spectacular. The noise echoes for miles." His cheek twitched but he didn't answer. Cassie reached for his pulse. "Are you still with me?"

"Yeah." The word was barely a whisper.

Was he bleeding internally? Going into shock? Cassie's mind raced, but all she could come up with were scenes from *General Hospital* and crazy words like *subdural hematoma*. Whatever that was.

The car grew silent. Cassie thought she should be doing something proactive but didn't know what. So she sat beside the injured man and chatted away about Whisper Falls and every single head of hair she'd ever groomed, praying that Austin and an emergency crew would get here soon. The man would know more about Whisper Falls than she did—if he could remember.

"Heath?" she said, shaking his shoulder.

His eyes fluttered up. Did they look more glazed now than before?

"You're pretty," he mumbled. "Got a boyfriend?"

Yes, he was delusional. Delirious. Poor man.

"No. My husband died."

"Sorry."

Not wanting to discuss Darrell's death, she shifted the topic to him. "What about you? Any significant other I should call? Girlfriend? Wife?"

"No more."

Okay, so he was either divorced or had recently broken it off with a girlfriend or worse, like her, his spouse had died. A curl of empathy circled through her. Being alone hurt. No matter how she'd tried to fill her life with activities, she missed the closeness of being a couple. She missed Darrell. In fact, she'd been missing him the day she'd climbed Whisper Falls. And guess what? Her prayer hadn't been answered. She was still laughing at herself over that silly episode.

"Who are you visiting in Whisper Falls?"

"Police chief."

"JoEtta Farnsworth?"

"Know her?"

His words were definitely slurring.

"Everyone in Whisper Falls knows Chief Farnsworth. Tough, fair and…eccentric to say the least. Are you related?"

The chief had kids somewhere but Cassie couldn't recall whether they were male or female or where they lived. One thing for certain, they didn't come around Whisper Falls too often. Heath's last name was different but that didn't mean much these days, and if Heath was the chief's son, he was a jerk of the first order for never coming to see his mother. JoEtta was gruff and rough but a good person.

Whatever the connection, Heath didn't answer. The car went silent again except for the endless drip of rain from the overhanging trees.

"Heath?"

He didn't move.

She touched him. "Heath."

He didn't respond.

"Come on, pal, stay with me. I don't like it when you take naps. It's not fair. You can't nap if I can't."

Heart in her throat, she grabbed his wrist, felt for a pulse. A thready beat pulsated against her fingertips.

"Heath, wake up. Talk to me."

He didn't.

Help needed to get here and it needed to get here now.

Chapter Two

Cassie pulled out her cell phone and tried again to reach her brother. She had one single bar of service but maybe that was enough. When Austin didn't answer, she punched in 911 once more. Before the call could connect, she heard the wail of a siren.

She almost melted in relief. *Thank You, Lord.*

"They're here, Heath." She patted his shoulder. "You'll be okay now. Hang tight. I'm going up to the road to direct them down to you."

She didn't know if the handsome stranger heard her or not, but she shoved the door open and raced up the steep incline, heedless of the brambles that were every bit as relentless on the ascent as they were coming down. Her breath came in short gasps as she tried to hurry.

She saw Austin's truck first and though light rain peppered her skin, she rushed toward her parked car and flipped on the headlights. Austin wheeled in next to her and leaped out of the truck.

"You okay?" Her tall, cowboy brother was a born protector.

"Soaked. Cold but all right. The guy in the SUV isn't doing so hot, though."

"You look like a drowned rat." Austin reached back inside the truck and pulled out a jacket, handing it to her. "Put this on."

Grateful for the warmth, she slid her arms into his oversize fleece.

About that time, the Whisper Falls's volunteer fire and rescue truck arrived. The crew varied, but tonight was not the usual group of volunteers. As the siren died away, Mayor Rusty Fairchild, a fresh-faced Opie look-alike hopped out of the cab in a warm-looking yellow slicker and rain boots, accompanied by Evangeline Perryman and paramedic Creed Carter.

The police chief pulled in right behind the rescue truck. Suddenly the dark night was bright with vehicle lights and people carrying brilliant halogen spotlights.

With a sense of profound relief, Cassie had never been so glad to see human beings in her life. People she knew and trusted. Good people, who made up in love and commitment what they lacked in fancy equipment.

"Where's the patient?" Creed Carter asked. She was especially glad to see Creed. The husband of her close friend Haley the chopper pilot was medic trained in the military and often ran medi-flights out of the mountains. He was cool as ice water in an emergency and always seemed to know what to do.

"Down there." She pointed her flashlight. "His leg is trapped. Not sure how bad, and I think he has a head injury. He was talking but—"

"Trapped?" Creed whirled toward Evangeline, a large, rawboned hill woman who lived with a pig. Literally. Cassie should know, she painted the pig's toenails for special occasions. "We'll need the ram."

The crew grabbed a tackle box of gear, a length of hose, and something that looked like a small generator and followed Cassie through the damaged brush and trees to the accident site.

In seconds the crew, along with Austin and JoEtta, swarmed the still-running SUV. Cassie realized she was shaking all over, an adrenaline flush, she supposed, in addition to the cold and wet. She wanted to climb back into the car with Heath and make sure he was all right but there didn't appear to be room. Evangeline was in the front seat, taking vital signs while Creed shined a penlight at Heath's pupils.

She wasn't needed now, though she'd developed an odd kind of bond with the stranger and was reluctant to leave. So she stood a few feet away, shivering, and watched as the rescuers did their work.

A boom of thunder shook the earth. Rain started to fall again, peppering her and the rescuers.

"Go to the car," Austin called, looking up from his spot next to Creed. The two men, both strong and fit, were wedging some sort of long, metal tool between the door post and the dash.

She wasn't leaving. Not until she knew Heath would be all right. They were in this thing together. And she owed him a pedicure. "Is he okay?"

"He's still with us."

That was something anyway.

"Did you call Moreburg for an ambulance?" The town of Whisper Falls had no hospital and had to depend on a nearby town or Creed Carter's helicopter for medical transport. She doubted he could fly in this storm.

"'Course I did." The police chief pushed away from the SUV where she'd been shining her light on the impact site and clumped to Cassie's side, gear rattling. Over fifty and gruff as a Rottweiler, JoEtta Farnsworth was a career police officer with more quirks than this road had curves. Dressed in her usual leather vest and brown boots, tonight she was minus the aviator goggles and helmet she normally wore on her scooter patrols through Whisper Falls. Instead, she'd wisely worn a flat-brimmed hat. "They may be a while."

"Creed can't fly in this weather."

"Nope. Don't worry, we've handled emergencies up here before. Problem though, we've got our hands full in town, too."

"What's going on?"

"Tornado touched down on the east edge."

"A tornado? Oh, no!" Remembering the violent thunderstorm, Cassie shouldn't have been surprised. "Is anyone hurt?"

"Got people out checking. State police will be along as soon as they can to help out. Mostly looks like trees and power lines down, but we won't know for a while, it being dark and all, and you never can tell for sure until daylight."

"Was there damage to any of the businesses?" Her shop was smack in the middle of the main street area.

JoEtta gave her a long look. "Don't know yet, missy. We're doing the best we can, and then this feller has to run his car off in a ravine."

"I'm sure he did it to annoy you, Chief."

JoEtta snorted. "I figure you're right. What happened here? Did you witness the accident?"

"I saw him lose control, saw his taillights spin away, but in the dark, I didn't see him leave the roadway." She shivered and huddled closer inside the jacket. Austin was right. Drowned rat.

"He was lucky you came along." The chief peered at the SUV, thinking. "Speeding?"

"I don't think so. The rain was a deluge and visibility was terrible. I think he probably didn't see the sharp curve until he was in it."

"Likely you're right. He wouldn't be the first." Rain trickled off her hat brim. "I didn't want to get in the way while they were doing the extraction but I stuck my head in. I didn't notice any alcohol or drug smells, did you?"

"No, nothing like that." The only smell she recalled was the cologne-scented air freshener dangling from his mirror. "He has a bump on his head." Suddenly remembering that important detail, she yelled, "Creed, check the left side of his head near the temple."

"Got it."

"Was he coherent enough to give his name? Any info about what he was doing out here? Anything at all to help with this investigation?"

In all the excitement, Cassie had forgotten. "He said he was on his way to Whisper Falls to see you. I thought he might be a relative."

"Me?" The chief's head spun to the accident and without another word, she stomped toward the SUV and the rough whine of a gas-powered generator. Metal screeched, a high-pitched sound worse than a fork on a plate, as the hydraulic ram slowly pushed the dash away from Heath's body.

Cassie clenched her back teeth against the noise, fighting a queasy fear about the man's leg. Praying the rescue wouldn't damage him more, she trotted to catch up with the police woman. "His name is Heath Monroe. Do you know him?"

"Heath Monroe is my new assistant chief," JoEtta barked, "*if* he hasn't gone and killed himself."

"Bust me out of here, Doc." Heath punched the end icon on his cell phone as the doctor, lab coat flaring out at the sides, breezed into the hospital room. Already this morning, Heath had touched base with Chief Farnsworth and run some digital errands, but being stuck in a Fayetteville hospital felt as confining as a Guatemalan jail cell. To his regret, he'd spent some time there, as well.

"In a hurry to get somewhere?" The doctor tapped a screen on his smartphone and stared at it while they talked. Heath wondered if he was playing fantasy football or reading Heath's medical reports.

"Yeah, I am." He was always in a hurry. Criminals didn't take days off.

Dr. Amil, a short, pleasant-looking physician with white at the temples, stashed the phone in his jacket and unwound a stethoscope from his neck, stuck the ends in his ears and pressed the cold end to Heath's chest. While he listened to whatever doctors listen for, he asked, "How's the head?"

"Terrific," Heath lied. The sucker throbbed with a dull ache and every time he sat up in this humiliating backless gown, he saw spots and felt nauseated. He'd had concussions before. He'd live.

"Any nausea or vomiting?"

Heath huffed. He wanted to roll his eyes but it hurt too much. "I'm all right, Doc. I've had worse. Bust me out of here. I have work to do."

As calm as if his patient wasn't fidgeting like a six-year-old in church, the doctor removed a penlight from his coat pocket and shined it in Heath's eyes. "Pupils reactive, equal." He straightened. "CAT scan was clear, no bleeding. You were lucky. Let's look at that ankle."

With a beleaguered sigh, Heath yanked the sheet from his left leg. He was more than lucky. As in all his other close calls, Somebody bigger than him was on duty. "Leg's just bruised, Doc. Slap a wrap on it and cut me loose."

Dr. Amil didn't seem in any hurry to comply. "Just because no bones are broken, doesn't mean you can get around on this leg, Mr. Monroe. The ligaments and tendons have been sorely stretched as you can tell by the deep purple bruising around the ankle and foot. PT will be up in a while to fit you with a boot."

Heath audibly groaned. "Please tell me this is a cowboy boot, custom made, fine cowhide. Otherwise, I'm good with a brace."

The physician chuckled in a flash of white teeth against a swarthy face. "Mr. Monroe, you're a stubborn man."

"I've been told that. I won't wear a boot, Doc. Sorry. Don't bother sending one up. Too bulky. Too restrictive. Bring me a wrap or a brace or something simple and I'll get out of your hair."

Dr. Amil studied him for a moment, hand to his chin,

assessing. Heath always wondered what went on the mind of someone brilliant enough to be a doctor. Even Sam, his best friend from childhood, now an A-1 cardio-thoracic surgeon in Houston, was sometimes on a different wavelength than the rest of the world.

"You'll regret the decision unless you stay off this leg for a while. Two weeks at least with gradual weight bearing and activity."

"Understood."

"Your injuries are mostly minor, nothing rest won't cure. X-rays and CAT scan are clear, blood work is within normal limits. No need to keep you here any longer, especially since you have made up your mind to leave us." He offered a small smile. "But you *must* take it easy and give your body time to heal."

"Got it. Time heals all wounds." Which wasn't exactly true. Time hadn't healed some of Heath's deepest wounds. He'd come to grips with them and moved on, but healed? Not happening.

Troubled by his unusually morose thoughts and figuring he was more concussed than he wanted to admit, Heath squirmed, searching for a more comfortable position. In a hospital bed, he seemed to be constantly sliding downhill. The movement shot pain through his rib cage and ankle and set his head awhirl. Running off the road on his way to Whisper Falls had proven very inconvenient. "My new boss is coming to pick me up. Am I good to go when she gets here?"

He'd made a commitment and he planned to keep it even if he was twenty-four hours late and a little banged up.

"As soon as your paperwork is ready, but as I said, take life easy for a few days. No strenuous activity, no heavy lifting or sports. Avoid alcohol, sleep a lot, and you probably shouldn't make any important decisions for a few days. The nurse will give you a treatment sheet to take with you. It includes problems to look for. If any symptoms worsen, give us a call."

"Got it." He wasn't going to follow through, but he understood the message. Even though the hospital's overnight hospitality had been superb, he'd had all of it he could endure.

The minute the doctor exited the small room, Heath hobbled out of bed to get dressed. His head spun, making him lean against the wall until the fog cleared. With wry humor, he wondered if his eyes had crossed. To check, he leaned into the mirror for a look. His beard was scraggly. He rubbed a hand over it, wincing at how sore a man could be from a minor accident. After finding a plastic bag containing his clothes, he limped to the shower, eager to get rid of the humiliating gown. In the mirror, he gazed with fascination at the discoloration on his chest and shoulder. No wonder he was sore. The black eye was pretty entertaining, too.

Sore or not, he couldn't let this unexpected detour deter him from the job he'd been hired to do. He fumbled in the pocket of his jeans for the badge he'd carried every day since he was twelve years old. Running his fingertips over the now-dulled finish and the distinctive Lone Star in the center, he thought of the man who'd given his life to uphold everything this badge stood for. Heath was determined not to let him down.

By the time Chief Farnsworth crashed through the door like a battering ram, Heath had showered and dressed and was sitting in the regulation high-backed uncomfortable chair in the corner of the unit, completely exhausted and furious to be so. The shower had helped clear his head but it hadn't done much for his aching body.

"Heath Monroe, you're a heap of trouble. You better live up to your reputation."

He'd been warned that Chief Farnsworth was tough and blunt. "I plan to."

She stomped to his chair side and speared him with a long appraisal. "You look like you hit a tree."

"Feel like it, too."

"Ha! What's the doc say?"

"I'm free to go."

"You'll need a few days of R and R."

"No, I'm good to go."

The chief hackled up like a mad cat. "Don't argue with me, Monroe. You might be DEA, but I'm the officer in charge."

"Former DEA, Chief, but you're right. It's your town. I'm grateful you took me on." The slower pace of Whisper Falls was exactly what he wanted, at least for a while. They'd agreed to a six-month trial period, and after that, who knew?

"Feel lucky to get a man like you. Though I have to admit I wonder why you'd want to come to a boring, rural town to play second fiddle to someone like me. Frankly, I wondered if you'd show up."

"I'm a man of my word." He took a slow, easy inhale, testing the bruised ribs, proud to hold back a wince. "Boring and quiet sounds good right now."

"So you said. Burned out. Worn down."

Those might not have been his exact words but close enough. "Something like that."

"Well, you've come to the right place. We don't have

much crime, though the rise in tourism has caused a few issues. There was a time I could handle everything myself with a couple of part-timers and the occasional auxiliary for special occasions, but lately…Well, I'm not getting any younger. Having a full-time, experienced assistant chief will take a load off." She spun a small, straight-backed chair close to his and plopped down. "Now. About you and this accident. You'll need a few days to get familiar with Whisper Falls and the surrounding area. Might as well use that as healing time. When you start prowling around town on duty, you'll need to be in top shape."

Heath figured his definition of top shape and the chief's were two different things. "How's my SUV?"

"I had it hauled in to Tommy's Busted Knuckle after we got you shipped up here last night. You'll have to talk to Tommy." She rubbed at her nose, sharp eyes still assessing him. "Cassie Blackwell saved your hide, son. We'd never have found you down in that hole if she hadn't seen you go off the road."

Cassie Blackwell. That was the name he'd been trying to remember all morning. "I owe her."

"Sure do. She's a good girl, our Cassie. You'll be seeing her around."

He hoped so. Even with a crack on the skull, he remembered Cassie. Silky voice, dark wet hair and huge eyes. Pretty. Really pretty. He wouldn't mind seeing Cassie Blackwell again. "She offered me a pedicure."

"What?" Chief looked at him as if he was still addled.

He shook his head, thinking he was still too fuzzy to make sense. "Nothing. Something funny she said to me last night. I think she was trying to keep me awake."

"That's Cassie. She can talk a blue streak."

He remembered that much. She'd talked on and on when all he'd wanted to do was sleep. He thought she may have told him her life story and that of every person in Whisper Falls—which could come in handy in his job, if he could remember.

"Where's that nurse?" The chief glared at the door, willing it to open. "We got to get moving."

Heath's head was pounding again. He really wished the chief wouldn't talk so loud.

She pointed at him. "Sit tight, Monroe. I'll go see if I can bail you out. The blasted rain finally let up, but we got us a mess in Whisper Falls, and the sooner we get back, the better."

He waited until the blustering chief charged out of the room. Then he took out his cell phone and dialed 411. Heath Monroe was a man who paid his debts. And he owed Cassie Blackwell.

Chapter Three

The morning was clear and sunny, a perfect spring day when daffodils burst from the damp earth to nod their golden heads and the wind is so still a stranger wouldn't believe how wild the sky had been last night. That is, until they arrived in downtown Whisper Falls and saw the mess.

Limbs and trash, asphalt shingles from someone's roof, trash cans and lids, and a smattering of kids' plastic toys were scattered down the streets and against business doors. The residential areas looked far worse. Cassie had even seen a doghouse hanging in a tree. She hoped the dog hadn't been in it.

Along with every other businessperson in town, Cassie had hit the streets at daylight to assess the damage. From the looks of things, nothing was completely destroyed, but they'd have plenty of cleanup to keep them busy for days.

She wiped the back of her wrist across her forehead, tired and oddly disheartened. She should be thankful, all things considered. Her shop was intact, her family and friends were safe, and even the stranger in the accident was reported to be in good condition.

She hadn't slept much last night, given the late hour she'd gotten home and the whirl of excitement that had gone on before. Heath Monroe had played around the edges of her mind even while she'd slept. She'd awakened after a reenactment of that long period when she'd been alone with him inside the crashed vehicle. She'd been afraid for him.

All night, she'd fought the temptation to call Chief Farnsworth for an update but had waited until this morning. The chief had her hands full with the aftermath of an F1 tornado and if Cassie knew JoEtta Farnsworth, the chief had slept less than anyone.

"Thank God the tornado was a little one," she muttered as she bagged trash and listened to the whine of chain saws. Her brother, Austin, Davis Turner and a group of other men manned the saws, clearing broken trees and limbs whereever needed.

"I'm thankful we didn't take a direct hit." This from Evelyn Parsons, the town's matriarch. The older woman, whose salt-and-pepper hair was kinked tight as corkscrews in the damp morning air, had literally put Whisper Falls on the map. She wouldn't take it lightly if the town was blown away after all her efforts to revive it. Miss Evelyn had turned a rumor into a tourist attraction. People came from all over to pray under the waterfall outside of town, hopeful that the rumor was true, that God really did answer prayers murmured there. In the opinion of Miss Evelyn and most of Whisper Falls, everyone benefited from the story and it never hurt to pray. The comment made Cassie feel a little better about her own pilgrimage, though she would be embarrassed if anyone knew. "Uncle Digger said the worst damage is east of town. There aren't many houses or people out that way."

"A few but they're scattered all over the hills."

Darrell's cousin lived east of town, though he was far up in the hills and back in the woods. She should probably call the man but he hadn't been too friendly after Darrell's death, as if he blamed her somehow for the loss. Truthfully, he'd never seemed to like her and they hadn't spoken since the funeral.

"Not likely any of them took a hit. The tornado dissipated not long after it moved over the town."

"True. I'm sure they're fine." Cassie peeled a soggy magazine from the side of a building and tossed it into the bag. "I have appointments this morning. Should we open for business?"

"Absolutely!" Miss Evelyn said. "This cleanup will take days, and that's why we pay city workers and have a strong corps of volunteers. The sooner we get back to normal, the better."

At eight, Cassie headed to the salon for a quick shower and change before her first appointment at eight-thirty. By ten o'clock the small salon was packed with customers and gossipers. Everyone knew there were two places in Whisper Falls to get all the latest news: Cassie's Tress and Tan Salon and the Iron Horse Snack Shop down at the train depot, run by none other than Miss Evelyn and Uncle Digger Parsons. Cassie figured both businesses were hopping today.

Midmorning, the newly engaged Lana Ross stopped by in her quest for newspaper stories. Wearing her usual cowboy boots and bling jeans, the former country singer looked petite and pretty, her dark brown hair curving softly against her shoulders.

"Mr. Kendle wants photos for tomorrow's edition," she said. "But I wanted to be sure everyone in here was all right before I start snapping."

That was so like Lana. After a rough start to life and a failed singing career in Nashville, she'd come home to Whisper Falls and met and fallen in love with widower Davis Turner. Cassie was happy for them. After all they'd both been through, they deserved happiness. And so did their children, a trio of adorable matchmakers.

"We're all okay," Louise said. A gamine-faced woman with a shock of striped mahogany hair she wore in a short rock star emo cut, Louise was a master stylist and a creative manicurist. No one in town did nails like Louise. At the moment, she was painting filler into Ruby Faye Loggins's acrylics. "What about you and Davis?"

"Nothing damaged except Paige's trampoline. It's hanging on the back fence with the net ripped off. But boy, was the weather scary for a while."

"I heard there was some damage out by the airport. Has anyone talked to Creed or Haley?" This from Ruby Faye.

"I did," Lana said. "Creed's helicopter is all right. A couple of pieces of sheet metal blew off and broke out a window on one of the small planes parked outside though."

"That's too bad."

"At least everyone seems to be safe so far," Lana said. "But I heard Cassie had quite an adventure last night."

Like satellite dishes seeking a signal, all heads rotated toward Cassie. As sweet as her customers were, they also liked the excitement generated by a tornado or a car accident or even a big storm. The buzz of fascinated energy was like electricity this morning. Frankly, it made her tired.

"Tell us, Cassie," Ruby Faye insisted, her eyes wide and eager for more stories to share at the bait shop she and her husband owned.

Before Cassie could open her mouth, volunteer firefighter Evangeline Perryman beat her to it, giving a recap of the rescue.

"He's good-looking, too, girls. My, my, my. He made my heart flutter." She clapped a hand against her generous chest.

"That was your angina, Evangeline." This wry statement came from Ruby Faye at the manicure station.

While the others chuckled, Evangeline insisted, "He was a hunk, wasn't he, Cassie? Dark and mysterious and tight muscles. Tell them. He was a hunk."

"Well, okay, he was pretty cute." Understatement of the year. Heath was, as Evangeline insisted, a hunk.

"Did you get his name? JoEtta said he was coming to work for her."

"Heath Monroe."

"Is he single? I have a single daughter, you know, and boy, would I love to marry that girl off."

Cassie wasn't about to go there. Heath's single status was his business. If the ladies of Whisper Falls wanted to stalk the poor man, she wasn't getting involved. She was having enough problems not thinking about him as it was. Eventually she would see him again. Would he remember her? And why should she care one way or the other?

Her thoughts went back to that moment last night when the rescue team had carefully lifted Heath from the car. He'd tried to stand on his own, insisting he was all right. His eyes had found her and in that instance, they'd made some sort of sizzling connection—right before he passed out.

"Cassie? Cassie?"

Cassie came out of her reverie to see the whole shop staring at her once more. She looked down at the head she was shampooing. How long had she been standing here in a fog?

"Oh, sorry, I was just—thinking. Did you say something?"

Evangeline slapped a beefy hand on her thigh and chortled. "I think Cassie's daydreaming about our new police officer."

"Don't be silly." Even if it was true.

Cassie wrapped a towel around Fiona's well-shampooed head and righted the style chair just as the shop door opened. She finished the towel dry and reached for her tools.

"Flowers?" Louise squeaked, a hopeful sound that lifted on the end. "For who?"

Louise was happily married with a toddler but her husband, sweet as he was, was not Mr. Romantic. Louise longed for him to send her flowers or whisk her away on a picnic. Even though she dropped hints on a regular basis, he never had.

Conversation in the beauty shop ceased as the satellite heads rotated toward the florist hidden behind the vase of colorful tulips and gerbera daisies. Lan Ying, the tiny Asian owner of Lan's Flowers and Gifts, set the clear glass vase on Cassie's workstation.

"For Cassie," she announced with a sly grin, black eyes snapping with interest and humor.

"Me?" Cassie paused to stare in amazement, hairbrush in one hand and the silent blow dryer in the other. Fiona didn't seem to mind that Cassie was no longer working on her new style. She, too, stared in bug-eyed interest at the bouquet.

"Why, Cassie dear," Fiona said, "I think you must have an admirer."

Cassie laughed. "No chance."

She never received flowers. Well, unless you counted the ones her mom and dad sent for special occasions. Maybe that was it. She'd forgotten some important date. "Let me see the card."

She put the brush and dryer down with a clatter that sounded outrageously loud in the too-quiet room, and reached inside the sunny mix of yellows, pinks and purples.

"These are beautiful, Lan. You've outdone yourself," she said as she pulled the card from inside the tiny envelope. Her pulsed ricocheted. *Oh. My. Goodness. He didn't.* Her face was hot as a flatiron.

"Who sent them, Cassie? Don't keep us in suspense."

"I can tell by her expression that it's a man," Evangeline smacked with no small satisfaction. "I told you so. Either Heath Monroe is a very grateful man, or Cassie has a beau."

Heath was still half out of his head. That could be the only explanation for this uncharacteristic behavior. He worked alone. He didn't get too involved or too close. His business—his former business—didn't allow it.

He didn't like crowds, either, and judging from the noise coming from inside, there was a big one.

Heath ran a hand over his brown button-down and hobbled toward the glass door. The salon was housed in an attractive old building with an upper-story balcony painted in a cheery red and trimmed in white. The glass front door proclaimed Tress and Tan Salon.

He had never been in a beauty shop in his life. But he was a man who paid his debts. Get in, get it done, get out. If he didn't fall over first. The chief was already badgering him about R and R. Probably because of that little dizzy spell he'd experienced in her office.

His ankle felt the size of an elephant and shot pain up his leg with every step. After dumping his gear at the furnished garage apartment, he'd collapsed on the couch for a couple of hours but upon awakening the familiar drive to be up and moving had taken over.

All right, Monroe, admit it. He was curious about Cassie Blackwell, curious to know if she'd gotten the flowers, and since he was going to be living in this town, at least for a while, he wanted to make nice with the locals.

Might as well open the glass door and go inside. He'd entered worse, scarier and far more dangerous places. A chorus of female laughter rang out. With a wry shake of his head, Heath thought, *Maybe.*

He pulled open the door and stepped inside. The first thing he noticed was the sudden reduction in conversation. The second thing was the smell. Really good shampoo. The kind that compelled a man to bury his nose in a woman's hair.

His well-trained eyes scoped out the place in seconds. Three workstations but only two were manned.

Or womaned, as it were. Zebra-striped chairs, a mish-mash of hair fixing doodads and a gaggle of gawking females. And that smell. That overriding, delicious scent of all things female.

He cleared his throat. "You got the flowers."

Cassie Blackwell stood at one of the workstations. She'd turned toward the door when it had opened and now stood as if paralyzed, the mirror behind her reflecting the straight, choppy cut of her black, black hair.

Gorgeous. Last night, he'd thought she was pretty but his head had been too messed up to know anything for certain. Today, there was no doubt. His drippy-wet, shivering heroine from last night was a knockout.

"Why aren't you in the hospital?" she asked and he took note of the biggest green eyes he'd ever seen. Green, like his. Cool.

"They don't keep slackers."

Every woman in the room clucked and then a cacophony started that made his head ache worse.

"You're hurt."

"Look at his eye. Quite a shiner."

"Are you the new police officer?"

He replied to the last. "Yes, ma'am. Heath Monroe."

For some reason, this brought another round of clucking accompanied by sly looks at Cassie.

He felt a little weird being the object of all this attention. Weird but amused. In his particular role as an agent, he'd been required to keep a low profile. He'd have to get used to being out in the open.

"Nice to meet you, ladies," he said, forcing a smile that made his bruised eye hurt.

His comment was met with a round of introductions which he figured was a good thing. Getting to know the people in town would be as important to this job as it had been in covert operations.

But even as he carried on polite conversations with the women, cataloguing which one's husband ran the bait shop and which was a retired schoolteacher, and who was at the scene last night, it was Cassie his gaze kept coming back to. Medium height, she looked taller in bright red high heels that matched her equally red lipstick. If he put his arms around her, she'd hit him about chin-high in sock feet. The wayward thought startled him. He didn't know this woman, other than she'd been kind enough to help an injured stranger. Why was he stirred by the thought of Cassie, the hairdresser, in cozy little socks?

"Thank you for the flowers," she said in that same silky voice that had invaded his concussed dreams. "They're beautiful, but you really didn't need to go to all that trouble."

"If you hadn't come along..." He let the thought ride. No use going there. They both knew. "Glad you like them."

Before he could make the expected quick exit, the door behind him opened. He couldn't help himself. Years of watching his back had him turning to the side as yet another female entered the building. This one was pretty in the way of women who spend a lot of time and money on their looks. Dressed to kill in a pencil-slim skirt and stiletto heels, she was a well-groomed blonde, blue-eyed and thinner than he liked his women. Not that he'd focused much on women in the past decade. He liked the female gender—a lot—but in his line of work, personal relationships had taken a backseat. About the time things started to progress, he'd be shipped off to some dark corner of the earth. Which was just as well. He had a job to do and a vow to keep.

Automatically, he touched his pocket and felt for the badge resting against his thigh, a reminder of his life's mission and why he'd never settled down.

"Louise, I broke a nail," the newcomer announced in a voice that said a broken fingernail was a state of emergency. She held up an index finger and pouted. "Can you fix it for me right quick? Pretty please?"

The wild-haired Louise nodded. The manicurist reminded him of those wide-eyed dolls whose heads were bigger than their bodies. "Sure thing, Michelle. Give me a couple of minutes to finish Ruby Fay."

"I have an appointment at the bank in a few—" The woman's voice trailed off when she spotted Heath. "Oh, my gracious, I am so sorry for interruptin'." She stuck out the hand with the broken nail. "I'm Michelle Jessup. You must be our new police officer."

Might as well get used to it. In a small town news carried far and fast.

"This is Heath Monroe, Michelle," Cassie said, taking up the tools of her trade again. "And you guessed right. He's our new assistant chief."

"My goodness gracious, Heath, honey, you are all beat up. Oh, this is terrible. Not a good welcome to our little burg at all." She pressed long-nailed fingers to her chest in an affected pose. Most of the people Heath had encountered so far in Whisper Falls spoke with a stronger-than-Texas accent but this woman's suddenly thickened to Southern syrup. "I heard about that scary accident you had. What a blessing our little Cassie came along in the nick of time."

Heath shot an amused look at "our little Cassie," who

lifted one eyebrow but didn't speak. Heath didn't like to judge a person on first impressions, but Michelle was making a strong one.

"Very lucky. I could have been stuck down there for days before anyone found me."

"Well, isn't she just heroic?" Michelle gushed, moving into Heath's space with a flirty smile. "Your poor eye. It must hurt like crazy." She was close enough that he could smell her perfume, an exotic blend of flowers and spice. "My daddy owns Jessup's Pharmacy right down the street. If you need anything at all, you tell Daddy I sent you, and he'll fix you right up."

"I appreciate the offer. Thanks." He eased a step back.

"You are so welcome," Michelle said brightly, letting the last word trail off in a long, slow drawl. "Glad to help in any way I can. We take care of our people around here."

"We sure do," Louise muttered. "Especially our handsome new law-enforcement personnel."

A snicker ran around the edges of the room, but if Michelle noticed, she didn't let on. Heath practiced his poker face.

"I heard about your SUV being all smashed up. I am so sorry. If it can't be fixed and you have to have a new one, you come right on over to the bank and see me. As the chief loan officer in Whisper Falls, I will take *good* care of you."

A man would have to be blind, deaf and brain-dead not to get the message, though the woman couldn't know Heath was immune. He'd been propositioned by some of the best, usually when he was about to haul them to jail.

"Good to know. Appreciate it. Everyone here has been very helpful."

"Oh, Heath, you are so welcome." She tilted her head and hunched one shoulder in a pretty pose, flashing him a dazzling smile.

"Michelle, I'm ready for you." Louise patted the tabletop and motioned toward the chair. "Come on over. You don't want to be late for that appointment."

The flirtatious woman turned her back and walked toward the manicurist, hips swaying. Heath purposely glanced away, catching Cassie's eye. If he wasn't mistaken, she'd found the exchange as over-the-top as he had. Big green eyes dancing above some woman's haircut, she fawned and mouthed, "Oh, Heath."

Heath felt his nostrils flare as he fought back a laugh. Time to hit the road. He lifted a hand in farewell. "See you later."

Cassie tilted her head and smiled. "Thanks again for the flowers."

Their gazes held for several more seconds while he recalled the feel of her soft hands scanning his face and his hair. A zing of energy sizzled through him like last night's lightning.

Puzzling over the unexpected reaction to his rescuer, Heath limped out into the sunlight, the noise of female conversation trailing him. Once the coast was clear, he paused. Hands on his hips, he looked up into the sunny blue sky and laughed.

He wasn't sure what he'd signed up for, but Whisper Falls might turn out to be a lot more interesting than he'd ever expected.

Chapter Four

Thunderstorms had brewed up every afternoon for the entire week Heath had lived in Whisper Falls. The ground was a mud bog, delaying tornado cleanup. With the chief as his guide, he had spent the days cruising the town in their one and only police vehicle, getting acquainted. The citizens welcomed him with warmth and curiosity, commiserating over his wrecked SUV, his black eye and the ankle that refused to stop swelling like an overheated helium balloon.

Late Thursday morning, he propped said foot on a padded chair next to the scarred desk in what was now his official office—a closet-size cubicle beside the courthouse jail. A window looked out on the courthouse lawn, a pretty space with a Vietnam memorial marker, a statue of the town's founder and lots of springtime green. On the adjoining streetcars tooled past with slow irregularity. Easy Street was well named. Life was definitely slower here than anywhere else he'd been in a while. Not counting a tiny Mexican village that had once been his base for a very long three months.

He reached down and loosened the boot lace from

around the yellow-and-purple ankle. Didn't hurt as much today, but the tautly stretched tissues were uncomfortable and he couldn't shake the limp. His head was clearer, though, thank the Father. Damage could have been a lot worse if not for Cassie Blackwell, though he wondered about the inordinate amount of time he'd spent thinking about the woman who'd saved his hide on a rain-slicked mountain road. So far, he'd resisted another trip to her sweet-smelling, female-fixing salon—a male's purgatory—but he wouldn't mind seeing Cassie again.

"Already laying down on the job, Monroe?" With her usual rowdy entrance, Chief Farnsworth slammed into this office. No knock. No warning. Just bam! "Wimping out over a measly dab of ankle pain?"

Heath gave her a lazy smile. "That's me. Any excuse not to work."

"Figures. You Feds are all the same. All blow and no go."

"And all you small-town Southern cops are corrupt." He crossed his arms over his chest. "Where'd you hide the body, Chief?"

Farnsworth barked a laugh. She was a straight-up law enforcer and Heath liked her. Didn't mind working for her, either. He'd never chaffed at having a woman superior officer. Watching his mother raise three boys alone had taught him the value, strength and leadership of the female gender.

She leaned a hand on his desk. "One of us needs to do a safety walk through the school and look for security weaknesses this afternoon. You up to the task?"

Heath pushed back from the desk. He never figured himself as a desk man and didn't plan to be much longer. Paperwork gave him colic. "Has someone made a threat?"

"No. Don't plan to have any, either, but if they come, we want our kids protected."

"You got that right. I don't mind the trip, a good excuse to get acquainted with school personnel." And hang with the kids. He missed his rambunctious nephews and that one fluffy-haired niece who could wrangle anything out of him with a dimpled smile.

"Sure you're up to it? Requires some walking around the campus."

Heath laced his boot, ignoring the throb and the question. "Want to call the superintendent? Or should I?"

"I'll call, give him fair warning. His name is Gary Cummings. Reserved, suit-type feller but sharp as bear teeth."

"Got it." He dropped his foot to the floor and winced. Annoying. "I need to stop by the garage and check on my truck. That all right with you?"

"Fine. I'm headed up to talk with Judge Watson. The county DA is here today to go over some charges. Why don't you cruise through town and make sure the citizens are behaving themselves?"

Heath huffed softly. "Is there any doubt? The place is quieter than a tomb." *Quiet* seemed too mild a word. He-could-hear-his-hair-grow quiet.

"Just you wait, mister. Storm's got 'em busy, but summer's coming. Things heat up."

He'd believe it when he saw it.

Eager to be doing anything other than sitting behind the desk, Heath was out the door and in the cruiser as fast as his bad ankle would take him. He liked Whisper Falls and had longed for peace and quiet. Be careful what you pray for, he supposed. In his former job, he'd rarely had a quiet day and the lack of action was making him a little crazy.

He cruised the streets first, eyes alert for anything out of the ordinary. So far this week, he and the chief had rousted a truant teenager, ticketed Bert Flaherty for doing forty in a twenty, responded to a possible dog theft and three domestics. Beyond that were the basic patrols, civic responsibilities and a handful of false alarms. He was still trying to figure out why Chief Farnsworth needed an assistant.

At the end of Easy Street, he pulled into Tommy's Busted Knuckle Garage to check on his ride.

Tommy, a long, skinny man with brassy shoulder-length hair and a wooly reddish beard met him in the bay. "How's the leg?"

"Good. What's the verdict on my SUV?"

Tommy scratched his beard. "Insurance adjuster was here this morning. Sorry to tell you, Heath, but she's a goner."

Heath grimaced. He'd been afraid of that. "I'm going to have to get a new one?"

"Looks that way."

He had a sudden vision of limping into the bank to ask Melissa Jessup for a loan, of having her pout over his poor little eye and his poor little ankle and his poor little broken car. Hiding a smile, he thought that might not be a bad thing. A man could use some feminine sympathy now and then.

Tommy clapped him on the shoulder and shook his shaggy head. "A rotten shame, a nice set of wheels like that, but I can't put her back the way she was."

He'd been fond of that SUV.

A rumble of thunder sounded in the distance. The men turned their heads toward the sound. Were they due for another storm this afternoon?

"Thanks anyway, Tommy. It was good of you to go out in the boonies and haul it up out of that ravine."

"Ah, no big deal. Just glad it was the truck that bit the dust instead of you."

"Can't argue that."

As he left the garage and started down Easy Street, he spotted a jaywalker. Not that he was going to ticket anyone for the infraction, but this jaywalker caught his attention. Glossy black hair that swung against her shoulders as she bopped along, a hot pink and zebra-printed smock over black pants and a pair of black high-heeled ankle-breakers.

His boredom vanished faster than chips at a dip tasting contest.

He whipped the car into a U-turn and parked at an angle in front of Evie's Sweets and Eats. He pressed the window button and watched the smoked glass slide away just as Cassie stepped up on the curb.

"'Morning," he said.

She pivoted toward him with a smile. "Hi. Except it's nearly noon."

"Yeah." He grinned.

"How are you?"

Better now.

"Healing." He touched the bruise over his left cheekbone. "How's it look?"

"Awful." But her smile softened the word. "Maybe you should run by the bank and get Melissa to feel sorry for you."

"I've been thinking about that."

"You have?"

"My vehicle is a goner. Gotta buy a new one."

"Oh, that's too bad." She stepped off the curb to stand by his car window. A flirty breeze ruffled her heavy bangs and he was pretty sure he smelled that fancy shampoo again.

Jockeying for a better view, Heath leaned an elbow on the window opening and tilted his face. Cassie had something that appealed to him. A kind of chic wholesomeness mixed with Southern friendly and a dash of real pretty. "Think I should get a loan from Melissa?"

Cassie grinned. "She's good at her job, if you can deal with the fact that she thinks you're the hottest thing to hit Whisper Falls since Pudge Loggins's turkey fryer caught fire and burned down his garage."

He hiked an eyebrow, amused and flattered and knowing very well what she meant. "Does she now?"

This time Cassie laughed, her scarlet mouth wide beneath dancing green irises. "Haven't you noticed the number of times she's been to the courthouse this week?"

He hadn't. Man, he must be losing his radar. He hitched his chin toward the bakery. "Were you going in there?"

"Lunch. Want to come? Evie makes good sandwiches from her own homemade bread. Fresh baked this morning."

"Best invitation I've had all day." Since he'd been here actually. The school didn't expect him for another hour, so he radioed his location to dispatch and exited the car. The ankle screamed at the first step, causing an involuntary hiss that infuriated Heath.

Cassie paused, watching him. "You're still in pain."

"No, I'm fine."

She made a disbelieving noise in the back of her throat. "You remind me so much of my brother."

"Must be a great guy."

She took the statement as the joke he'd intended. "The best. You should meet him."

"I'd like that."

"Come to church Sunday and you will."

Heath reached for the antique door handle. The scroll on the amber glass was equally antique as was the rounded arch transom above the door shaded by a red fringed awning.

"If I'm not on duty, I might do that." He needed a church, not that he'd ever had time to attend much, but he believed, and church was important in a small town.

With his ankle throbbing, he somehow held the door open for Cassie and limped inside a small business that smelled better than Grandma Monroe's kitchen on Thanksgiving. Though he wouldn't be sharing that information with Grandma. The smells of fresh breads and fruit Danish mingled with a showcase of pies and homemade candies.

"A cop's dream," he muttered, only half joking.

A middle-aged woman—Evie, he supposed—who obviously enjoyed her own baking, created their orders while maintaining a stream of small talk with Cassie. When she put his sandwich in front of him along with baked chips and a glass of tea, she said, "This one's on the house, Mr. Monroe, and dessert of your choice. Welcome to Whisper Falls."

"I can't let you do that."

"You don't have a choice. Go sit down and eat." She smiled. "And enjoy."

"Don't argue with her, Heath. Trust me, she'll get her money back from you." Cassie took the lunch tray before he could and led the way to a table. There were only three and all had a sidewalk view.

"Chief called me a wimp today. I'm starting to feel like one."

"How bad is your leg? I mean really. No bluffing. Any other injuries besides that?"

"Just the ankle. Sprained. And a couple of bruises here and there." Bruises that ripped the air out of his lungs. "Annoying. But I still have all ten toes." He bit into the thick, fragrant sandwich.

"I'm relieved to hear it. When do you want your mani-pedi?"

Heath choked, grabbed for the tea glass and managed to swallow. "My what?"

The thought of Cassie touching him again gave him a funny tingle. A nice tingle, come to think of it. Did she have any idea the thoughts that go through a man's head at the most inappropriate times?

"You don't remember our conversation?" she asked. "Is the concussion still bothering you?"

"Slight headache if I get tired. Nothing to worry about."

"Are you following up with Dr. Ron? He's a really good doctor." She pinched a piece of lettuce from her plate, holding it between finger and thumb. "And the only one in town."

"Next week."

"He's terrific. You'll like him." She nibbled the lettuce and then bit into the sandwich packed with vegetables and turkey. Between bites, she chattered about plans for a community storm cleanup, the Easter sunrise service at the Baptist Church—which she deemed "not to be missed" though Easter was several weeks past—and filled him in on the small, useful details of Whisper Falls.

"Some of this sounds familiar," he said after a long, cool drink of sweet tea. "Did you tell me this in the car?"

"I thought you didn't remember."

He never said that. He remembered bits and pieces. Like her silky voice and dogged efforts to keep him awake. "It's starting to come back to me."

"I've talked enough about Whisper Falls anyway. No use repeating myself again. Tell me about you. You're from Texas, not married, no kids. Any other family back in Texas?"

"Two brothers and a terrific mom."

"No sisters? Your poor mother."

"She had her hands full."

"I imagine so! Tell me about the brothers. Older or younger? What do they do?"

"Holt and Heston. Both younger. Both in law enforcement. Sort of. Holt is a private investigator. Heston's a street cop."

She tilted her head in a cute way that bunched her hair on her shoulder. He spotted a small sparkly earring. "Did they follow big brother's path or is law enforcement in the genes?"

"In the genes, I guess. My dad was a cop." His hand went to his pocket, to Dad's badge. "A great cop. He died in the line of duty."

Her perky expression fell. "That's awful, Heath. I'm sorry."

"Long time ago. Now we Monroe boys do our best to keep the bad guys off the streets." He faked a grin. Time to move this conversation to softer ground. "Tell me about you. Besides making the women of Whisper Falls beautiful, what do you do?"

She returned his grin, though hers said she knew he was changing the subject and empathized. She was a nice woman.

As he chewed his ham and provolone, Heath recognized that he was sharply drawn to Cassie Blackwell, to her bright mouth and alabaster skin. His reaction puzzled him. She was friendly to the max, but didn't flirt, yet Heath found her astonishingly attractive. Pulse-bumping attractive. Not that he worried about it much. He was accustomed to fast, brief relationships that went nowhere. Whether from duty or boredom, his interest in Cassie would burn out like the rest.

Cassie dipped the paintbrush into a tray filled with baby-blue color while her sister-in-law, Annalisa, worked her way around the small bedroom with a roll of masking tape and a straight edge, making sure every vertical stripe on the nursery wall was perfect.

A slight breeze drifted in the open window, a natural ventilation source, though Cassie had set a box fan in the doorway to help extract the paint fumes. The fan also kept the pack of dogs, particularly her apricot poodle, out of the way—much to Tootsie's annoyance. Even now, the spoiled mutt lay in the hallway, gazing in with a wounded expression.

Cassie had offered to paint the room alone, but Annalisa had insisted on helping. After all, this was her baby, her project, but working together was fun. Cassie was grateful to her sister-in-law for allowing her to be part of transforming the old guest room into an adorable nursery for her brother's baby. It was something she'd never get to do otherwise. Like her marriage, the dream of babies had died with her husband.

"The walls are looking gorgeous, Cassie." Annalisa sat back on her heels, blond ponytail dangling, to admire their handiwork. Latte-brown already covered the upper half of the nursery and now they were striping the bottom in latte and blue. White chair rail divided the upper from the lower, and white enamel trimmed the windows, doors and the bottom of the wall. "Everything looks so crisp and clean. I can't wait to put up the moon and star decor. Won't it be pretty?"

Cassie rolled her tired neck and smiled softly at her beautiful sister-in-law and dear friend. "No prettier than the stars in your eyes."

"Your brother—" Annalisa pushed a stray lock of hair behind her ear and sighed, one of those romantic, madly-in-love sounds that said more than words. "Who could imagine I'd end up on a ranch with a cowboy where I'm so happy I pinch myself every day to be sure it's real? I really love him, Cassie. More now than ever."

Annalisa's devotion to Austin never failed to warm Cassie. Her brother had been through a terrible time with his emotionally disturbed first wife, and she'd despaired of ever seeing him embrace life and love again. But a lost and abused woman in the woods and a whispered prayer had changed him.

"You make him happy, too, Annalisa."

"I know. That's the beauty of true love. We're both

blessed, but I think I am most of all." She rubbed a palm over her basketball belly. "Finding Austin was the best thing that ever happened to me. And having our little cowboy pretty soon is a wonderful bonus."

Annalisa was one of those pregnant women who glowed. Her skin was clearer, her blue eyes brighter, and other than an intermittent battle with her blood pressure, she was full of energy. The ranch house had never been this clean! Not that housework was ever Cassie's gig. She'd rather have her toenails removed. Annalisa, on the other hand, thrived on making a house a home.

"Only a few more weeks and I'll be an aunt." Something odd twisted in her chest.

"Aunt Cassie." Annalisa cocked her head. "I like that."

"Me, too." The odd pulling came again, heavy and uncomfortable. She was delighted to be an aunt. Wanted to be aunt. Couldn't wait to hold her precious nephew.

If Darrell had lived they would have had a baby by now. Maybe two.

She turned back to the wall, carefully adding another stripe.

"You're better at that than I am."

Cassie snorted. "Painting stripes on walls is easier than painting designs on fingernails."

"I guess it would be." Annalisa went to the window and took a deep breath as she gazed out on the forest and mountain vista beyond the pasture land. Cassie was glad to see her go for some fresh air. "Everything is gorgeous and green this year."

"Thanks to the rain. It's been a couple of years since we had good spring rains." Cassie went back for more paint. "I was starting to think I'd brought Texas drought with me to the Ozarks."

"The thunderstorms make me nervous. I'll be glad when they stop." Annalisa turned from the window, tummy leading.

"Me, too. The town has a lot of cleanup to do, and wild wind and rain every evening isn't helping."

"How was your lunch with the new policeman?"

Cassie lowered the paintbrush. "How did you know about that?"

"This is Whisper Falls, Cassie. Every single woman in town has her eye on Heath Monroe, and when he has lunch with one of them, it's big news." She put a hand to her back and arched, stretching, an action that made her belly huge.

"I don't have my eye on Heath. Or anyone else." Cassie carefully placed the brush across the top of the paint can. Plastic drop cloth crinkled as she pivoted on her old, paint-splattered canvas shoes.

Annalisa ambled to her paint tray. "Nothing wrong with being interested, Cassie. He's single, seems nice and needs to make friends."

"We ran into each other by accident. He's new in town and you know me, the welcome committee. I invited him to church to meet you and Austin."

Eyes on the paint, Annalisa dipped her brush and dragged the bristles along the tray top. "Aren't you the least bit interested?"

Was she? "I like him, if that's what you mean. He has a wicked sense of humor."

She liked his strength, too, and the way he downplayed his injuries when he could easily have taken advantage of the chief and done nothing for a few weeks.

"Did you know his dad was a cop, too, and he died in the line of duty?"

"How sad for him." Annalisa lay the brush down to massage her belly with both hands.

Cassie wondered if the baby was moving. Wondered what it would feel like to have a baby growing inside. "I thought so, too."

"What's he doing here, in Whisper Falls? I mean, why here? Does he have family nearby?"

"I didn't ask."

"That's not like you."

"Don't worry, Michelle Jessup will find out for you."

"Probably so. She was in the Iron Horse this afternoon."

Oh, good grief. "Was that how you found out about our lunch?"

"She saw you and Heath come out of Evie's together." Resting on her knees beside the paint tray, Annalisa flashed a grin. "She thought you looked very cozy. The two of you were laughing."

Cassie frowned. "What's wrong with laughing?"

"You know Michelle. She was buzzing about our poor injured and oh-so-handsome policeman." Annalisa put her splayed fingers against her chest in an imitation of the banker and drawled. "She sincerely hoped poor, lonely Heath didn't let Whisper Falls's man-hungry females eat him up."

Cassie rolled her eyes. "Poor Heath is right. I like Michelle, but sometimes her daddy's-perfect-darling brattiness shows through the polished veneer. She can be a tad pushy."

"Doesn't hurt that Heath is very easy to look at." Annalisa hunched her shoulders and grinned impishly, blue eyes widening. "Don't tell Austin I said that."

"Tell Austin what?" At the male voice, both women looked toward the door. After a pat to the poodle's head, Austin stepped over the box fan.

"Nothing important, darling. Girl talk."

Cassie reached for a rag to wipe paint from her fingers, amused. "She's throwing you over for the new cop in town."

"Grrr." Austin's upper lip curled. "And here I thought I might like the guy. Now I have to beat him to a pulp."

Knowing he teased, Cassie tossed the paint rag at him. It bounced off his chest. "Down, tiger. She's all yours."

"Yes, I am." Annalisa waddled over and lifted her face toward his. The cowboy was considerably taller and broader than his leggy wife and his darkness contrasted with her fair hair. They were a beautiful couple. If Cassie didn't love them both to pieces, she'd be jealous.

"Nobody can take your place," Annalisa said, moving close until her belly bumped his. As Cassie looked on, Austin cupped the mound that held his child. With an aching tenderness, the pair shared a long, loving look before Austin bent his head and kissed his wife.

Cassie glanced away, busying herself with the cleanup. She loved them. She was glad for their happiness. But lately...

After comfortably sharing a home with her brother and sister-in-law for nearly two years, she was beginning to feel like a fifth wheel.

Chapter Five

"Ankle's still giving you trouble. Take time off and see a specialist."

"It's fine. I'm healing." Through sheer force of will, Heath refused to limp the four feet from the doorway to Chief Farnsworth's desk.

"Don't con me, Monroe. I saw you coming across the parking lot. You limp like a dog with a wooden leg."

"It's only been a couple of weeks. I'm all right. Now, what's this deal we're going to at noon?" He didn't care a bit where they were going but a change of topic was in order. His ankle was not a big deal. His job was.

"City planning committee. They want to meet you, for one thing. For another, they want our input on security for the new park they're hoping to build out near the waterfall." Chief went to the coffeepot. "Want some?"

Creed raised a hand. "I'm good. Thanks."

"Creed Carter called this morning." The gurgle of coffee sounded against the ceramic cup. "He flies scenic tours over the Ozarks. You met him at the accident scene."

A misty memory of that night floated somewhere

in the back of his mind. "Saw him at church yesterday, too. Nice guy."

He'd seen a number of other people—including Austin Blackwell and his very pregnant wife—thanks to Cassie with her big warm smile and easy welcome. His eyes had zoned in on her the moment he'd limped through the double doors into the foyer and seen her chatting with Miss Evelyn Parsons. Then she'd invited him to sit with her and her brother, an offer he couldn't refuse. He'd liked the service all right, but mostly he'd liked seeing Cassie again.

"Are you paying attention, Monroe?"

"Sure thing, Chief. You said Creed spotted something out of the ordinary on a chopper tour this morning."

"Huh. Don't know how you do that. Zone out and still get the drift of my conversation."

"Skills, Chief." He shot her an ornery grin. "Must be the Fed in me."

The federal-versus-local jibes had become a regular part of their conversation. She was usually one up. Now they were even, though he had no doubt she'd zing him again real soon.

"Ha!" She dumped a little tub of creamer into her coffee and tossed the container in the trash. The can was starting to overflow. "I think we should check out the scene. Even though no one has said a word about any home losses from the tornado, we don't always get the complete news from the outlying areas."

"Did Creed get coordinates? We'll need to check to see if the area has been occupied. I'd hate to think someone was under a pile of debris for this long."

"You and me both. I'm going to take a run out there. Think you can handle things here?"

He'd much rather take a drive to the country. "Got it. Let me know if you need assist."

Forty-five minutes later, Chief Farnsworth was on the phone. "Monroe, better get out here."

"What's going on? What did you find?"

"We'll talk when you get here. Alert dispatch and head this way."

He'd no more than hung up when it hit him. Chief Farnsworth had taken the cruiser. He didn't have a vehicle.

The chief was laughing at him as Heath rattled to a stop alongside a mobile home—or what appeared to have been a mobile home. A pile of sheet metal, furniture and debris was scattered in an irregular pattern beneath a stand of broken trees.

Heath slammed out of the dented, rusty old truck and strode with the smallest limp possible toward his guffawing boss.

"Forgot about the vehicle issue. That's what happens when you work alone too long." She adjusted her sunglasses, a pair of goggles straight out of the Amelia Earhart era. "Where did you get that old truck?"

"Tommy at the Busted Knuckle. I rented it from him."

"Resourceful."

"You'll get a bill for it."

Her bark of a laugh caused a pair of cardinals to take flight. "You need your own truck. City pays mileage and upkeep. Take off tomorrow and get one."

"Works for me." His eyes had been taking in the

scene all during the chitchat time. "Looks like the tornado hit here. Either that or a meth explosion."

"Funny you'd say that. Come over here by the A/C unit and see what you think of this."

Following her lead, Heath picked his way across the mounds of trash, thankful no dead body had been discovered in the ruins. Trash, papers, clothes, food containers were spread everywhere, even into the nearby trees. Appliances and furniture had been ruined either by the storm or the elements.

"What do you make of these?" With a snap, the chief donned rubber gloves and went to her haunches, indicating a ripped trash bag and its contents.

An adrenaline chill prickled Heath's skin. "That looks familiar."

"Thought it might." She tossed him a pair of gloves. "Let's bag it up and take it in for analysis, but I'd bet my badge we'll get a positive hit for drugs."

"Cocaine." Carefully, he pushed the debris aside with the toe of his boot. "An unusual amount of baking soda to keep on hand, wouldn't you say?"

"Think they were cooking crack?"

Her reply surprised him only a little. Remote areas were often the heart of illegal drug operations simply because they were hard to police. Even though Whisper Falls seemed Mayberry perfect, Chief had probably run into her share of druggies.

"Looks that way," he replied. "If we poke around, we'll probably find other paraphernalia—unless they took it with them."

"I guess you've seen plenty enough to know."

Grimly, Heath lifted one of the bags, noting the telltale markings. Drug cartels marked their packages, though he didn't recognize this particular brand. "Way too many."

"So the fellows that lived out here were likely dealers." Chief used a stick to carefully rummage for more evidence. An investigator never knew when a dirty needle might catch her off guard.

"Or smugglers who brought in the powdered cocaine, cooked it into crack and then moved it to their army of dealers." He leaned close and sniffed. Too much rain had eradicated the smell. "Do you know who lived here?"

"Man name of Louis Carmichael. Kept to himself, none too friendly, didn't come into town much."

"Appears he had a reason for keeping a low profile."

"This is more your area of expertise than mine," the chief said. "Tell me what you think."

"Let's go through the debris and see what else we find. I want to know who brought it in, where it came from, where it was headed. If they were packaging and selling from here or distributing elsewhere. Lots to consider." Heath pushed to his feet.

"You'll take the lead on this." It wasn't a question.

Heath parked his fists on his hip bones. The badge in his pocket was like a flaming thing, a warm and ever-present reminder. He'd wanted a break from the war on drugs, but he had a commitment, too. He'd take the lead, all right, and he'd track down the slimeballs who'd killed his father. Maybe not the exact person, but all who dealt in the drug trade were guilty. And he was the man to bring them to justice.

The next morning Heath stopped in at Evie's Sweets and Eats for a coffee and Danish before his trek to the

Fayetteville car dealership. Cassie was right. Evie was quickly earning back the cost of her welcome lunch. Add Evie's homemade bread to the bonus of seeing Cassie here on several occasions and he was becoming a regular.

As he pulled open the door, Heath glanced across the street toward the Tress and Tan. Cassie's shiny green Nissan wasn't in the usual spot.

With a curious frown, he went inside. Where was she? Sick? He'd never known her to run late. The salon lights came on by eight-thirty every morning and didn't shut off until after six. He knew. Just as he knew the routine of every other business in town. Knowing was his job.

"'Morning, Heath," Evie called, her full face pink with exertion, as she lifted trays of fragrant pastry into the display cases. "May I help you?"

He cast another frown toward the salon. "Has Cassie been in yet? Her car isn't there."

"Cassie?" Evie ran a dry cloth along the front of a windowed display. "This is Wednesday. She's never there on Wednesday or Sunday. Her days off. You asking for a reason?"

"No. No. Just curious. She's always so…punctual."

"Punctual." Evie smiled and tossed the polish cloth onto the counter behind her. "That she is. Now what can I do for you, Heath?"

"Fortify me for a day of truck hunting. I'm headed to Fayetteville. Coffee to go and a couple of those cherry Danish."

"I saw you driving Tommy's old beater."

"Nice of him to rent it to me."

"Skinflint should have loaned that old dog to you."

She poured an extra large serving of coffee, capped it, and pushed the disposable cup toward him. "Who's going with you?"

"Nobody but me."

Her eyebrows shot halfway to her widow's peak. "How are you going to get two vehicles back to Whisper Falls?"

With the fragrant scent of good coffee tickling his nose, Heath stared at the woman for two beats. She was right. He needed an extra driver.

The concussion must have been worse than he'd thought.

The phone call from Heath Monroe had been unexpected but when she'd heard his plight, she knew the request had nothing to do with her in particular. He didn't know many people in town. She was available. He needed a favor—someone to drive. That's what friends were for.

And frankly, the call had come at the best possible time. She'd been cornered at the post office listening to Mr. Pierce rant about politics and the cost of living. Not that she didn't hear this particular topic on a regular basis at the shop, but there she got paid to listen. And Mr. Pierce had a way of loudly spitting his opinions for all to hear.

Eager to be anywhere else, using Heath as an excuse worked like a charm. Mr. Pierce patted her arm, gave her a piece of Juicy Fruit and told her to have a good day. Thank goodness.

Fifteen minutes later, Heath, clunking along in Tommy Ringwald's loaner truck, picked her up outside the salon. He popped out of the truck, limped around the front and opened the passenger door, waiting for her to get in.

"You sure you want to ride with me?" he asked, expression slightly amused.

No one had opened her door since her wedding day. She was kind of flattered. "You're not going to run off in another ditch, are you?"

"Not today." He flashed a dangerous grin and slammed the door. Cassie's stomach jumped and the reaction didn't have a thing to do with the metallic sound of a rusty old door.

Perplexed, she adjusted her skirt, tugging the red hem to her knees while Heath circled the front of the truck. He was still limping and she couldn't help thinking the injury was worse than he'd said. She also thought he looked good in navy slacks and a light blue polo. Really good. Fit, trim. Nice.

Oh, that troublesome stomach. She needed a Tums.

Heath slid onto the bench seat and started the truck. The movement whipped the spring air and released the slightly oily scent of Tommy's mechanic bay and Heath's dark woodsy aftershave. The combination was heady and manly and a huge change from the usual froufrou scents at the beauty salon.

"Did you see Dr. Ron this week?" she asked.

"I did. He said I'm fit as a fiddle and should stop slacking before the town council fires me."

"You lie." She softened the phrase with a slight smile.

"And you smell good, so we're even." He put the truck in gear and headed out of town.

She sniffed her wrist. Funny how all she could smell was him. "Distracters don't work with me. I have a brother. What did Dr. Ron really say?"

"You're a hard woman."

"Dr. Ron said that about me?"

And then they both laughed.

Heath drove like a man who'd spent plenty of time behind the wheel. Relaxed but focused, one wrist loosely draped over the steering wheel while holding the bottom with the opposite hand. He wore the watch she remembered from the accident. The glow-in-the-dark military piece.

"I'd put in a CD but this truck doesn't have a player," he said.

"Too bad. I guess you'll have to sing. What?" she asked when he looked appalled. "Don't you want to keep me entertained on this long, boring trip?"

"I want you to survive this long, boring trip."

"Okay, then, I guess you'll have to talk."

So they did and the trip wasn't long or boring at all.

Cassie Blackwell missed her calling. She should have gone into interrogations. Except Heath didn't exactly feel interrogated. He felt relaxed and he'd laughed more today in their journey from dealership to dealership than he had since the last time he'd been home with the family. She was witty and sharp and kept him on his toes. Interesting, too, with very astute input on car buying.

Now, after an entertaining lunch at Olive Garden in which Cassie had shared a crazy story about climbing behind the waterfall to pray, he had narrowed his vehicle choices to two SUVs. Same make and model, different colors and options.

"This one is really nice, Heath." Cassie drew in a deep breath as she rubbed her hand over the tan leather seats. "I love the smell of new cars."

He liked it, too. Buttery soft leather was a no brainer. Since he'd been old enough to pay his own way, all his vehicles had contained leather seats. Now, he went for the luxury. Heated and cooled seats, memory positions—not that anyone else was going to be driving his truck. Pricey but worth it.

"What do you think? Red or black? Both are loaded with all the options I want." They had just returned from a second test drive of the sparkling new black SUV. Cassie sat in the passenger seat, checking out all the options while the salesman rode along in back.

"If you're driving it for work, the red will stand out more."

"Which could be a bad thing."

"Spoken like a sneaky cop."

"I think I'll go with the black." He spoke to the salesman that hung on to every word like a hungry puppy. Scratch that. Like a hungry shark. "Knock off seven grand and include title and tax and you've got a deal."

The salesman—Jack—looked pained. "I could go three, but seven…"

"Five." Heath clapped him on the shoulder. "Come on, Jack. Cut me a deal. The lady's tired of looking." He didn't know if that was true or not. Fact was, she was perky as ever, and he wasn't all that fired up to end their day. He was, however, tired of bartering with salesmen.

Jack scribbled frantically on a notepad. Finally, he looked up. "I think we can do that. Come on inside the office and we'll start the paperwork."

Heath shot Cassie a triumphant wink. She gave him a thumbs-up and a sassy grin. Yes, sir, today was going his way.

With Cassie's high heels clicking on the concrete lot

and his blood pumping with excitement over the new set of wheels, Heath followed the salesman inside the showroom and into a small office.

They were halfway through the paperwork, slowed by an enthusiastic conversation between the salesman and Cassie about whether men should color their hair or not, when Heath's cell phone vibrated.

He glanced at the number. "I better get this. It's Chief Farnsworth. Will you excuse me a minute?"

He rose from the plush chair. Police business shouldn't be discussed in public and he could think of no other reason why the chief would be calling. "I'll take this outside."

"Go ahead." Cassie waved him away with a smile that settled over him warm and sweet. Barely focused on the call, he said hello and walked out under the awning.

"You about done lollygagging in Fayetteville?" Chief Farnsworth asked with her usual bluster and without a word of greeting.

He turned his back on the showroom window and the distraction inside to stare out over a sea of shining new cars and trucks. Traffic zipped past on the four-lane running in front of the dealership.

"Finishing up the paperwork now. What's going on?"

"Ran into some information I thought might interest you."

"About?"

"The reports came back on the packaging we found. Cocaine, all right. I'm thinking the place may have been a destination for smuggled cocaine and a cooking house for crack which would end up on the streets of Arkansas."

"Figures. Anything on Louis Carmichael?"

"Yep. Nice rap sheet. Mostly piddly misdemeanors but he's been on the radar since he was a teenager."

"Any leads on where he is now?"

"No. Disappeared like smoke, but he'll turn up. Bad eggs always do." She cleared her throat. "Heard something else of interest too when I was poking around. Don't know if it's connected or a case of bad timing, but his cousin, a fella name of Darrell Chapman, may have stayed there for a short time. And now he's dead."

Heath wrinkled his forehead in thought. Where had he heard that name? The concussion no longer banged like a ten-year-old drummer, but Heath was still muzzy on some things. "Darrell Chapman? The name sounds vaguely familiar."

"It might. You had lunch with his widow the other day."

"Cassie?"

Heath spun to gaze through the showroom window at the black-haired woman chatting away with the car salesman. A knot thickened in his throat.

Was sweet, friendly, *attractive* Cassie Blackwell involved in drug trafficking?

Chapter Six

For Cassie, the day with Heath had been a blast and if she received more than usual amount of teasing at the salon afterward, she didn't care. She was into friendships, not romance. Take the mayor, for instance. Good friend. They had dinner often, went to events together, but they were nothing but friends. Same with every man before and since Darrell. Friendships lasted longer than romance. And in her case, even marriage.

Driving home in the new SUV, with Heath tailing along in Tommy's clunker, had been fun, as well. She'd never felt as swanky as she had in that fancy new vehicle with all the bells and whistles. They'd had a great day together. So, Cassie was not the least bit surprised when Heath arrived on her doorstep the next evening.

"Hey," she'd said when she opened the door.

"Hi. Am I intruding?"

"Of course not. Come in."

"Sorry I didn't call first."

"Friends are welcome anytime. We aren't formal."

He stepped inside the living room where Annalisa and Austin sat cozied up on the couch, going through a baby name book for the umpteenth time. When they spotted Heath, Austin and Annalisa exchanged speculative glances. Cassie wanted to thump their love-struck heads.

After he'd exchanged greetings with the others, Heath turned to Cassie and said, "Mind if we take a walk? I'd like to talk to you about something."

"Let me change my shoes." She hurried into the bedroom and put on sneakers, curious to know what he wanted to discuss. Was he going to ask her out? Her goofy stomach fluttered at the thought, and she didn't understand why. Heath was her friend. Like Mayor Fairchild, they could hang out together. No big deal. But the more she thought about the upcoming conversation, the more nervous her belly.

From the living room, she heard the rumble of male voices as the men talked weather and Heath's new vehicle. When she returned, the living room was empty. She looked outside to see her brother with his head under the hood of Heath's sparkling new Expedition. The butterflies settled down. Heath was showing off his ride.

Laughing, she jogged out to them. "Nice wheels, huh?"

"Amazing." Bent at the waist, her brother turned his head toward Heath. "You have GPS?"

"Yep."

"Satellite radio?"

"Your sister said it was essential." He flashed her a grin. "And the engine has power like you wouldn't believe."

"Man." Austin straightened. "Towing package?"

"Yep. That, too. Want to take her for a spin?" Heath dug in his pocket and dangled the keys.

"You sure?"

"I wouldn't have offered otherwise. Go ahead. Enjoy."

"Thanks." Austin's expression was as excited as a kid on Christmas. "Come on, darlin'," he said to Annalisa. "Let's test drive this baby."

Annalisa cocked her head, a twinkle in her blue eyes. "Does this mean we're buying an SUV?"

Austin grinned and patted her tummy. "You never know. Babies need plenty of room."

"Well, since you put it that way..." Annalisa waddled toward the passenger door.

With tenderness, her brother assisted his pregnant wife into the vehicle, waved and drove away.

"That was nice of you."

Heath shrugged. "It's a guy thing. No big deal. Now, about that walk?"

The butterflies returned and brought their cousins. "Have you seen Whisper Falls yet?"

"No, but you told me about it yesterday. The place where people pray."

"Among other things." She still felt a little foolish about her own trek behind the falls. She wasn't sure why she'd done it. A person could pray anywhere, and the death-defying climb hadn't done her a bit of good. "It's a gorgeous area for picnics and swimming, hiking, too. Let's walk that direction. Even if we don't make it all the way, you'll hear the water and smell the river. These woods are beautiful."

Spring had exploded into full bloom with tiny yellow and white flowers carpeting the ground. Birds dipped from earth to tree and fence post, courting. The evening was cool, but not cold, and the sky a blue-gray with building clouds in the southwest.

"More rain tonight," Heath said.

"Probably. The ground is a little soggy in spots. Watch your step."

They crossed the backyard and walked through the pasture leading out of the small valley that cradled the ranch and up into the mountain. The grade was a long, easy incline she'd ridden or walked many times, particularly in the days after Darrell's death when she'd needed to be alone, to cry and ask the questions God never answered. She'd never understand some things in life, but she'd learned that God's love was there to guide her through any storm.

"Are those Austin's cattle?" Heath asked, pointing to a large herd of black Angus.

"Yes, and his horses, too. Except for the buttermilk-colored one. She's mine. Do you ride?"

"City boy, remember?"

"Oh, that's right. Bless your heart." And then she laughed. "Sorry, didn't mean that in a derogatory manner."

"No offense taken. I rode a pony at the fair when I was a kid. One of those that goes around in a circle. Does that count?"

"Everybody has to start somewhere." She laughed again. She had done that a lot the last two days.

They walked along in silence for a ways. Heath stopped once to pick a cluster of bright pink flowers—phlox, she thought, but wasn't sure. Her friend, Haley would know. Flowers were her passion.

"For enduring yesterday's car hunt," he said, presenting them to her.

"Nice." Cassie sniffed the small blooms. "I really

didn't mind. It was actually fun." Which said so much about her social life.

"For me, too. You're good company." He wiped a hand down the leg of his jeans and looked off toward the mountains. She could see he had something on his mind and didn't know how to start, so she decided to help him.

"All right, now. Let's get down to business. What did you want to discuss? An appointment for that mani-pedi? Walk-ins are welcome at Tress and Tan."

She gave him an impish look, surprised when he didn't respond to the tease. His sense of humor was one of the things she liked about him. "Why so serious?"

"Just wondering about some things."

"Like what?"

His eyes found hers and held. She tried to read their green depths but came up empty.

"Your marriage, for one. Chief told me your husband died on your honeymoon. I'm sorry."

The topic surprised her a little. Surprised and jabbed. She hadn't seen that one coming. She turned aside and gazed into the deep green forest. The woods seemed silent and empty but she knew they teemed with life. "Me, too, but thank you. Losing him so soon was horrible. We just didn't have enough time, but when we met, I saw forever in his eyes. It probably sounds silly and overly romantic but I knew he was the one."

"Just like that, huh? Bam! Love at first sight?"

"Exactly." She smiled a little, remembering. "He walked into the Iron Horse snack shop and ordered a Sprite and a bag of Cheetos. I was sitting at the bar talking to Uncle Digger when he noticed me and ordered another Sprite and a bag of Cheetos, sending them down to me. He grinned and raised his paper cup in a toast." She sighed. "And I was a goner."

As she'd intended, Heath chuckled. "Sprite and Cheetos are the way to a woman's heart."

"To mine anyway. There was something so easy and carefree about Darrell. I don't know how to explain love, but I adored him and he adored me. He did so many little things that made me feel loved."

"How long had you been together?"

"Four weeks and six days."

Heath stopped in his tracks. "Four weeks?"

She'd expected his shock. Her friends and family had been even more stunned. "Darrell had only been in town a short time to visit his cousin when we met. But those few weeks was all I needed to fall in love. Austin thought I was crazy, but when he saw how happy Darrell and I were together, he gave his blessing."

"So you got married."

"Eloped. Well, sort of. We went to the courthouse in Whisper Falls and Judge Olsen married us."

"Where was the honeymoon?"

"Mexico. I'd never been, but Darrell loved Mexico and wanted to show it to me. The water is so clear you can see the fish, and the beach is glorious."

"I'll have to agree. Beautiful place."

"You've been there?"

He picked up a rock, gave it a fling. It clattered in the distance. "Cancun is spectacular. Snorkeling there is the best."

"Darrell took me snorkeling and I loved looking at the pretty fish. He preferred to scuba dive. I wasn't ready for that. He dove. I snorkeled and played on the beach."

"Is that what happened to him? An accident while diving?"

Cassie pressed her lips together. The sun had gone behind a cloud and the air was cooler. She crossed her arms against the chill. "Apparently."

"Weren't you with him?"

"I should have been." Though she'd learned not to feel guilty or responsible, she did have regret. "We'd had the best day together on the water, and Darrell wanted to go out one more time. I was tired and wanted to stay at the hotel, so he ordered room service for me and a massage. So sweet and thoughtful." She smiled sadly at the memory. "When night came and he didn't return, I knew something had happened. Darrell wouldn't have purposely worried me."

Though she was over the terrible screaming grief, that long Mexican night and the next gorgeous sunny morning were indelibly imprinted on her memory. In a foreign country, she hadn't known where to turn. She'd contacted the hotel security who were no help at all, saying that her husband was probably drunk somewhere or having a fling. Not her Darrell, not her brand-new husband.

"When did they find him?"

"Later that afternoon. He'd washed up on a remote beach. Drowned." She shook her head. "I never understood that. He was such a great swimmer and in terrific shape."

"Do you mind if I ask what Darrell did for a living?"

She pivoted toward him, suddenly aware of a tension in his words that hadn't been there before. Suddenly wondering why Heath was asking so many questions. "Why?"

"Just wondering." He shrugged, a look that spoke of nonchalance, but Cassie had a feeling he wasn't casual at all. There was something going on here that had nothing to do with romantic interest in her or simple curiosity about her late husband.

She studied Heath's poker face for several long quiet seconds before saying, "He was in sales."

Heath's green gaze slid away from hers. He reached in his pocket with one hand. "Did he say what kind of sales?"

"Pharmaceutical. He told me before we married that he would have to travel a lot in his work. He was the sweetest man. He wanted to be sure I could handle the alone time." She kicked at a rock with the toe of her shoe. "I never got a chance to find out."

"I really am sorry, Cassie."

His sympathy defused her defensiveness. Maybe she was imagining things. Friends could ask friends about anything. Right?

"I'm okay now. He's been gone nearly three years and life goes on. Anyway, that's what my big brother tells me."

"A loss like that never goes away. The pain dulls, you move on, but you don't forget."

Of course, Heath would understand. He'd been there with his father. Knowing they shared a similar heartache made her feel close to him—in a friendship kind of way. "You were only a little boy. Losing your dad must have impacted your entire life."

"I guess you could say that." He cupped a palm beneath her elbow as they started up an incline that led toward the river.

"You should be able to hear the waterfall from atop

this rise," she said. "There's the Blackberry River below. See it? Like a silver ribbon through the green trees? The water flows down from the falls and winds through this valley past the edge of town."

They stood atop a ridge with the river below and the forest to their left. Beyond was a wildness of woods and sky and stunning spring landscape, green and blooming. Dogwoods, he thought. "The view's nice from up here."

"It's glorious." She stretched her arms wide. "The word *nice* is too puny."

"I stand corrected." He gave her a lopsided smile she found charming. Even though a strange heaviness nagged in the pit of her stomach, she found a lot of things about Heath charming.

"Want to climb the rest of the way up to Whisper Falls? We still have another mile to go."

"No, this is far enough." He drew in a deep breath and looked up into the sky. The sun was starting to ease toward the western horizon, a giant orange ball against a graying sky. "Listen, Cassie, I need to ask you something important. You may not like it."

The knot in her belly tightened and grew hot. She'd been right. There was more to Heath's questions than friendly conversation.

Though his face gave nothing away, his voice and posture were tense, watchful.

"Okaaay. You're kind of making me nervous. What is it?"

"All right, here's my question. Straight out." He thrust both hands in his pockets as if he didn't trust them. "Did you ever get the feeling Darrell wasn't what he seemed? Did you wonder if he kept secrets from you?"

"No! He wouldn't."

"Are you positive?"

Maybe a few times, but they were still in the early days of getting to know each other. "Why would you ask such a thing? What is going on, Heath? Do you know something about Darrell that I don't?"

"I'm not going to jump to conclusions. This is a fact-finding mission." His hands went deeper into his pockets. His jaw was tight and hard.

"You're investigating Darrell?" Her voice rose in agitation. Her fingers tightened on the cluster of flowers. "That's crazy. He was a wonderful man."

"Did you know his cousin, Louis?"

"We met a few times. He didn't seem to like me much. Why? What does any of this have to do with anything?"

Her knees had started to shake and she wanted to sit down. No, she wanted to run back to the house and tell Heath to take his weird questions somewhere else. What had happened to the charming, funny man of yesterday?

"Louis's trailer blew away in the tornado."

Alarm raced along her nerve endings and prickled the nape of her neck. She was becoming more confused by the minute. "Is he okay?"

"We don't know. He wasn't there. We were hoping you might know where he would go after losing his home."

"We? Heath, is this official police business?"

"Do you know Louis's whereabouts, Cassie?"

"No, I don't. When Darrell died, he seemed angry, as if I was to blame. We haven't spoken since the funeral."

"Did you know anything about Louis's business interests?"

"No." She crossed her arms over her racing heart, crushing the scent from the tiny blooms. "Heath, I don't understand all these questions. What's going on? Please, I thought we were friends. Tell me what this is about."

"We *are* friends, Cassie, and I owe you. I don't like asking all these questions, but they're important and you're the only lead I have." He stepped toward her, the sun gilding his dark hair, and tugged at her arms. "We have reason to believe Louis may have been involved in the drug trade."

"No," she breathed.

"Did you ever see or hear anything that made you suspicious?"

She shook her head. "I went to his trailer with Darrell only once and it was so junky and cluttered, I didn't want to be there. Louis didn't want me there, either. He was upset with Darrell for some reason and they went off by themselves to talk. When we left, Darrell was in a bad mood."

"Could Darrell have been working with Louis?"

"Absolutely not!" she said hotly.

"Okay, okay." Heath raised both hands in surrender. "No more questions. You're killing that poor flower."

Cassie uncrossed her arms and stared at the pink phlox. She felt as wadded and bruised as it looked. "Darrell was a good man, Heath."

"I hope so, Cassie." Heath's warm hand closed over hers. "For your sake, I hope so."

Chapter Seven

All night and into the next morning, Heath's brain whirled with the information he'd gotten from Cassie. He didn't want to believe she was involved in anything illicit, but she wouldn't be the first good citizen who'd gotten caught up in the money generated by the illegal-drug industry. Yet he couldn't just toss away the fact that she'd been there for him when he'd needed someone. Not once, but twice. And he liked her. A lot.

He also knew the danger of getting emotionally involved during an investigation, especially with his only lead. The job came first. Dad deserved that much from him, regardless of his interest in a pretty woman. There were plenty of pretty women. He had only one dad.

Ruminating his next move in the investigation, he drove the gleaming black Expedition up and down the streets of Whisper Falls, stopping now and then to talk or to investigate the out-of-ordinary. Folks were friendly and interested in the new vehicle and the new police officer. Good folks, mostly, though he knew from experience even the most peaceful towns harbored a dark element.

He'd come to Whisper Falls in need of that peace and quiet and already he'd encountered the darkness.

He should have expected as much. Ferreting out darkness seemed to be his calling.

Removing Dad's badge from his pocket, he placed it on the dash where he could see it. His father had taught him to seek the truth because the truth would set him free. Today he felt as if seeking the truth bound him tighter than any ropes or chains ever could.

Cassie was involved, one way or the other. The question was how did he find out which?

He stopped at the courthouse to meet with the chief. As he entered the side door, he greeted Verletta, the day-shift dispatcher who handed him the thick stack of today's mail. At fifty-something, Verletta wore her blond hair to her shoulders and a pair of red plastic glasses perched on her nose. She knew the job and the town and everybody's ancestry clear back to the war of aggression and thought nothing of calling up Heath or the chief, for that matter, with the message, "You'd better get on down there." She made him smile but he always went because, for all her unorthodox methods and raspy-voiced commands, Verletta was rarely wrong. As usual, this morning she had a fountain Coke the size of a pitcher within easy reach—to keep the whistle clear, as she put it.

Mail tucked under his arm, Heath went on through to the chief's office and found her rummaging through a file drawer as if she wanted to rip someone's head off. He hoped it wasn't his. He tossed the packet of mail on her desk and said, "You look annoyed."

"I *am* annoyed. Been up since three this morning.

Didn't Verletta tell you? A couple of idiots busted into one of the senior units."

Heath tensed. "Why didn't you call me?"

"You're still recovering. I handled it."

"I'm recovered. Stop coddling me." He fisted his hands on his hips, as annoyed as she looked. "Did you catch the perps?"

"Caught them, wanted to knock their heads, but turned them over to the parents. That's why I'm mad. Those kids have been in trouble before and their parents always make excuses and bail them out."

"A night in jail might scare some better behavior into them."

"My thoughts, too, but being juveniles the law is lenient."

"They won't be juvies forever. The seniors all right?"

"Scared. Shaken. Mr. Abernathy had a heart spell which meant Dr. Ron had an early-morning call, too. He'll be all right." She barked her laugh. "Both of them."

"Anything else I need to know about?"

"Check the log. Anytime there's a break-in, the elders get spooked and we get calls." She slammed the file cabinet. The sound ricocheted off the walls.

Heath had a feeling the chief was wishing she could slam some heads instead of metal drawers. He understood. He'd been there, but a good cop did his job and left the rest to the courts, as hard as that often was. "I'll spend some extra time at the complex today. Park the truck, walk around, say hello."

"Good plan. Knock on a few doors and introduce yourself. Make them feel safe again." She tossed a manila folder onto her desk. "Could Cassie Blackwell shine any light on the Carmichael investigation?"

"How did you know I talked to Cassie?"

"Had coffee at the Iron Horse. Annalisa told Digger who told me that you and Cassie took a long, romantic walk."

Small town grapevine. Heath snorted. "Any idea how long Darrell Chapman was in the area before he and Cassie hooked up?"

"Not really, but it bears checking. Don't know when he came to visit his cousin, either, but he hadn't been around long. If he was, he stayed in the woods. You're thinking the deceased was involved?"

"Maybe. Probably. Either that or he showed up innocently and learned something that got him killed."

The chief's eyebrows went up. "His death was ruled an accident."

"Yeah. In Mexico where it's simpler and cleaner to say a tourist had an accident."

"You're the expert." Heath could see the wheels turning in a very sharp, if somewhat eccentric mind. All cops were a different breed. Some were just more different than others. "What do you think happened down in Mexico?"

"I'm mulling a few theories." And didn't like any of them. "How long have you known Cassie?"

The roller chair clattered on the tile as Chief Farnsworth yanked it back from the desk to settle in. "She moved here with her brother, Austin, about six or seven years ago, as I recollect."

"So, how well do you know her?"

The chief began to rifle through the mail, tossing unopened junk in the too-full trash can. Did she ever empty that thing?

"Her granddaddy owned the piece of property where

the ranch is now. I knew him. Good people. I have a hard time believing James Blackwell's granddaughter is involved with drug dealers, if that's what you're getting at. If her husband was running drugs, she may not have known."

"Maybe. But we have a job to find out."

"Suspicious sort, aren't you?"

"Pretty much." Came with the territory.

The chief paused from the wild sorting event to laser him with a long, intent look. "Word of caution, Monroe. Cassie is well-liked in this town. I wouldn't let word get around that you think she's involved in drug trafficking unless you have some very solid evidence. In the meantime, step lightly."

"I plan to." He believed in the scripture: "wise as serpents and gentle as doves." At least the wise part. He was working on the gentle. "Why don't you take a breather, get some rest. My leg's good today. I can handle the rest of the shift while you catch up on sleep from last night."

"Don't put me out to pasture, Monroe. Between me and the handful of part-timers, I've been policing this town nearly as long as you've been alive." She tossed him an envelope. "Take your paycheck and get busy earning the next one."

Pulling to the curb outside the bank, Heath's gaze drifted down the street to the Tress and Tan. A mature woman, snazzily dressed and carrying a bright yellow handbag, entered the building. He wondered if she was there to see Cassie.

Inside the bank, he handed over his first official paycheck for deposit into his brand-new account. While he waited for the receipt and some petty cash for his wallet, he leaned an elbow on the slick counter and scoped out the space. Did JoEtta have a blueprint of the bank on file in case of robbery? As the chief claimed, he was a suspicious sort, seeing crime before it happened.

Two other tellers were busy with customers, a farmer in overalls, a young mother with a toddler hanging on to her leg. A scattering of desks was inhabited by equally busy employees typing away on computers or rummaging through paperwork. Through the glass-enclosed offices, he located the bank officials, including Michelle Jessup. His gaze lingered for a moment longer than he'd intended. The blonde was elegant and high-end in a straight mustard-colored dress and black jacket with pearls at her throat, wrist and ears. She must have felt his stare because she glanced up. Immediately, she rose from her desk and came out to greet him.

"Why, Heath, what a nice start to the morning. How is that awful leg injury?" She was much lower key here in the bank than she'd been in the salon. More professional friendly than over-the-top flirtatious. He kind of liked the change.

"Healing. Thanks." As soon as he said it, his ankle shot pain up to his knee just to spite him.

"What brings you in this morning? A loan for that gorgeous new SUV?"

"I have that covered already, but I appreciate the offer." A man whose lifestyle was too busy to spend much money and who'd had an expense account for the rest could save a lot over the years.

"Well, shoot. I could have fixed you up."

He imagined she could have. "Maybe next time."

Michelle beamed at him with a bright, beautiful

smile that probably cost more than he'd made in his first year of work. Someone had told him, Verletta he thought, that Michelle was the only child of the pharmacist and the only granddaughter of a well-to-do family. She was accustomed to money and attention.

"If you have a few minutes, come on in my office for coffee. We'll talk. I want to be sure our bank is treating you well." She winked. "Don't want to lose you."

The teller returned at the moment to count out his change. Turning slightly, not wanting to be rude to either woman, Heath stuck his hand out toward the teller.

"Can't today. I'm on duty."

Behind him, the teller counted out his cash. He only half listened because Michelle's long-fingered hand touched his elbow. "Rain check?"

Why not? He was new in town. She was attractive and they were both available, although he had a feeling she might be more available than he was. Still, she was interested, and he had nothing to go home to but a big-screen television and his own thoughts. "A rain check sounds good."

As he walked out into the overcast day, he sent another look toward the Tress and Tan, a reminder of the investigation he'd only begun. Michelle might be a pleasant distraction but Cassie needed to be his focus. He didn't like having to play her, but an agent did what he had to do. If Cassie was involved in a trafficking scheme, the subterfuge would be worth the effort. He wondered what she was doing for lunch....

Cassie sat across the table from Heath, still questioning why she'd agreed to this last-minute lunch invitation. She wanted to be angry with him after last night.

He'd accused Darrell, the sweetest man ever, of being a criminal. But that was impossible, and she wanted to make Heath understand as much. The length of time she'd known Darrell didn't matter. He'd adored her. He had treated her like a queen, like a gorgeous woman instead of a buddy who gave free haircuts.

"What do you recommend?" Heath asked, tapping the menu with a knuckle. "I've never eaten here before."

"Everything tastes good. Home cooked and fresh. I like the cheeseburger and cottage fries but I'm a junk food lover."

"Kindred spirits, then. A cheeseburger sounds good."

Kindred spirits? She didn't think so, though she had to admit she'd liked him until last night. Today, he was cool as a cucumber mask, behaving as if he hadn't insulted her late husband's memory, as if they were the best of friends. Strange, confusing man.

"You're quiet today." He pushed the one sheet, plastic-covered menu to the end of the table.

"I don't hear that very often." She held his gaze, not smiling, laced fingers in a death grip. It was unusual for Cassie not to smile at everyone, but today Heath was a bug under inspection. Until he got off Darrell's back, he was on her bad side. A people person, she didn't often have one of those, but Heath Monroe had found it.

He must have read her tension because he leaned forward and placed a hand atop her clasped ones— and surprised the daylights out of her. They were less than a yard apart. Mere inches, really. Completely disconcerting.

Cassie could see a razor nick beneath Heath's soul patch, a little swatch of whiskers beneath his bottom lip. Very faint lines had begun to form across his forehead and around his eyes. All together, they gave him a slight bad-boy look.

"Mad at me?"

"A little," she admitted, though if she was *really* mad, she should move her hands from beneath his warm, strong grasp and stop staring at his mouth and eyes. She was mad. She really was. But she didn't move.

"I'm sorry if I upset you. I didn't want to. Forgive me?"

Well, since he put it that way. To withhold forgiveness was wrong. "If you won't talk about Darrell anymore."

Very green eyes—eyes as dark and mysterious as jade—rested on her face. Sitting this close to a man who held both her hands and her gaze with a burning intensity should have felt threatening, or at the least uncomfortable. Instead, her breath grew a little shorter and her toes tingled.

The waiter chose that opportune moment to return with their order. Flustered at being seen holding hands with the new assistant police chief, a man she didn't want to like, Cassie jerked her hands away. Heath sat back against the red vinyl booth, a soft, quizzical expression on his face.

What in the world had just happened? Her neck was hot. Her pulsed raced as if an electric current ran from him straight into her heart. She sat back, too, and took a deep breath, filling her lungs with fresh-food smells instead of Heath Monroe. Cassie Blackwell did not get flustered over a man. Ever. Time to get this lunch back on her terms.

"To friends," she said, lifting her burger after the waiter had left.

He raised his sandwich in a toast. "Friends sounds good."

Cassie bit into the juicy hamburger, mollified by his easy manner. Whatever had sparked in her had obviously not affected Heath. Which was good, right?

"How's the ankle?"

"Practically healed. Only aches if I'm up too long. The doc cut me loose." He took a sip of Coke, grabbed a fry. "So, fill me in on all the gossip. What do the experts at Tress and Tan say is going on in Whisper Falls that a peace officer should know about?"

"Jed Thompson and Marty Bates broke into the Abernathys' apartment this morning. That's the big news of the day. The little twerps."

He titled his sandwich toward her. "Already know about that one."

"Oh, I guess you would. I hope they get in big trouble for scaring Mr. Abernathy like that. Karen Littlejohn— she works at the Quick Stop on the corner by the senior complex—said Doctor Ron was called out and all the seniors were scared and upset."

"They are. I spent some time with them this morning, did a walk-through of the yards, even went inside if they asked me. Met Creed Carter's granny. Nice lady but I think she could hold her own against a burglar with that cane of hers."

"Did she share her peanut candy?"

"How did you know?"

"That's Granny Carter. She'll make you some biscuits and gravy, too, if you hang around long enough."

"Do I hear the voice of experience?"

"Mmm-hmm," she said as she finished chewing a bite and swallowed. "I'm sure the residents feel better for having you check things out. It was thoughtful of you."

"Just doing my job."

She didn't care if it was his duty. Taking time to ease worries was a good thing to do and she liked him better for it. "Did you hear that Miss Evelyn and the city council set this Saturday as community spring cleaning?"

"Missed that. Tell me about it."

So she did, and as she talked and ate, two things guaranteed to relax her, the tension left her shoulders. Never one to hold a grudge, Cassie enjoyed people too much to remain angry. She knew Darrell was not a criminal, and that was all that mattered.

"Can you do me a favor?"

Inside his apartment that evening, Heath flopped onto his couch, cell phone to his ear, talking to his brother in Houston.

"What now?" Holt asked in a wry voice. "You need money?"

Heath snorted. "Doesn't everybody? You want to give me a million or two?"

"The check's in the mail, like always." Holt chuckled at the familiar joke. "What's up?"

Heath propped one hand behind his head and pictured his younger brother. Taller than Heath at six-three, and rangy like a major-league pitcher, the dark-haired, dark-eyed Holt was a martial arts black belt who could take a man down faster than a bullet. Heath should know. He'd been the guinea pig too many times. Holt looked like everybody's best friend, but beneath the amiable smile was one tough PI.

"Family first. How are Krissy and the kids?"

"Good. Ashley's had a cold and is a grump."

Heath's heart squeezed. Ashley was his four-year-old niece. He'd walk on fire for that dimpled darling. For all of them if push came to shove.

"Give her a hug from Uncle Heath and tell her I love her. The boys, too."

"Will do. Now what's this favor you want?"

"I need you to take a trip to Mexico."

"Mexico? Why do I have a feeling this isn't a vacation?"

"You could make it one. Take Krissy and the kids."

"Am I paying for this little getaway?"

"If it's a vacation you are."

"No vacation then. Spill. What's in Mexico?"

"I'm not sure anything is but I'm working an investigation into possible drug trafficking out of there."

Holt whistled softly. "Bad place for that, son. *Bad* place."

"Don't I know it?" He'd been up to his eyeballs in trouble in Mexico more than once.

"So here's the deal. Whisper Falls had a tornado the night I came in."

"I remember. Ran you off in a ditch. How's the bum ankle?"

"Good." He'd downplayed the accident for the sake of his mother, not wanting her to feel the need to fly to Arkansas. All Holt knew about was a sprained ankle. It wasn't the first time he'd kept an injury to himself. "After the storm, someone reported damage in the rural areas. That's when we stumbled onto a demolished trailer, paraphernalia and a missing home owner."

"In Whisper Falls? The rural town you described as

a quiet little place in the mountains where you could chill for a while?"

"It is. But you know me and drugs. We have this on-going war. If they're around, I find them." Or maybe they found him. Either way, the battle raged.

"Still carrying Dad's badge?"

"Always."

There was a hum of quiet between the brothers that filled in the gaps. No words were needed. They both knew why Heath did what he did. Their father was the reason all of them were in law enforcement.

Finally, Holt broke the silence. "What's the connection with Mexico?"

"The evidence reeks of Mexican cartel. Cocaine. Probably smuggled up from Colombia and repackaged for the U.S. Add to that the troubling issue of a man who lived or stayed briefly in that house. Name of Darrell Chapman. He and his new bride honeymooned in Mexico and he turns up dead on a pretty Mexican beach."

Holt made a low noise in the back of his throat. "I'm starting to smell something."

"Yeah, something stinks, all right. But other than the evidence found in the trailer, all of this is circumstantial. The man could have been an innocent bystander with no knowledge of his cousin's side business. And he could have very well drowned as the death certificate claims."

"Or the honeymoon could have been a setup, a meeting place, a drop-off or pickup. Then our Darrell boy could have made someone unhappy and gotten himself whacked."

"That's what I need to know. Will you check it out for me?" Heath thought of his lunch with Cassie and his conscience twinged a little but the job came first. For her sake he hoped Darrell was clean as Ozark spring water.

"Why not turn the case over to your pals at the DEA and let them handle it?"

"I can't. Not yet. It's personal." His own words caught Heath by surprise.

Holt held on through a beat of awareness. "A woman?"

"Maybe," he admitted as much to himself as to his brother. If Darrell was dirty he wanted justice done, but he didn't want Cassie hurt in the process. He wasn't sure why she was any more important than any other case he'd been involved with, but she was.

"Don't tell me it's the widow."

"All right, I won't. Got a pencil? I'll give you the details."

"Who said I was going?"

Heath just laughed.

Chapter Eight

Heath's suspicions had bugged her for days. Even though the new assistant chief had kept his word and said nothing more about Darrell, the question of her husband's innocence hung between them on every occasion. And there had been a lot of those since the hamburger outing.

As if he was trying to make up for the wound he'd inflicted, Heath turned up frequently to take her to lunch, to help with the storm clean-up, and last night he'd even stopped by at closing time with a pizza.

Figuratively speaking, a girl could fall in love with a man who enjoyed a thick crust supreme with double cheese and Canadian bacon as much as she did. Though the ladies at the salon tried to fan the flames of romance, Cassie simply rolled her eyes and carried on. Given her track record with men, they should know a friendship when they spotted one. Darrell was her one and only, but being nice to the new people in town came naturally. It was who she was—even if the newcomer was especially handsome and charming and male.

Still, Cassie was strangely disquieted that she could

like Heath at all. That she could get an extra buzz of energy when he cruised past in his big, fancy Expedition or popped into the shop to say hello. And that on this Saturday evening after a long day on her feet, she would be eager to leave the relaxed comfort of her PJs and crochet hook. But she was.

"You look amazing." Annalisa waddled in from her evening walk, moving slower by the day. Her newly full face glowed with the effort. One hand rubbed round and round on her large belly; Tootsie, the apricot poodle, trotted alongside, a willing but unlikely protector.

"Thank you." Cassie glanced down at her attire. Nothing fancy. Jeans and bright blue top with strappy heels. The usual. Except for the chiffon scarf and blingy bracelet she'd added. And the spritz of perfume. "You look miserable tonight."

Annalisa groaned as she stretched her back. "I feel miserable, too. Junior here is taking up space I don't have."

"A few more weeks and you can breathe again."

"Yes, thank the good Lord." With affection and pride, the pretty blonde patted the top of her belly. "Is Heath coming over?"

"Should be here any minute. We're going to the concert in the park. He's unofficially on duty, as always, and needed a friend to hang out with."

Her sister-in-law smiled a Mona Lisa smile that suggested more than friendship was in the air.

"Don't start," Cassie said, pointing a freshly done nail. "I get enough grief at the salon."

"Then why not admit you like him for more than a friend?"

"Friendship is all I have to offer."

"Love can come more than once in a lifetime, sweetie."

"Not for me." She'd been numb so long she wouldn't know love if it dyed its hair chartreuse and rode shotgun in her Nissan.

"He's a terrific guy. Everyone seems to like him and he goes to church, too." Annalisa pointed a puffy finger. "You should give him a chance."

Cassie had never told either Austin or Annalisa about Heath's insinuations, of how he'd insulted Darrell's good name. She didn't want anyone to think less of her late husband and a stain on his reputation was sure to happen if word got around. The sting had faded but she hadn't forgotten what Heath had done. She couldn't. "Friends, Annalisa. That's all."

Her sister-in-law eased her swollen body into a chair, holding the padded arm as she went down with a groaning sigh. "Look at the size of my feet!"

"Whoa, honey! You have to get those puppies elevated."

At the word *puppies,* Tootsie trotted to her side and looked up with bright, eager eyes.

"Not you, darling." Cassie smooched at the dog as she pushed the ottoman into place and gently lifted Annalisa's feet. "Is your blood pressure up again?"

"A little."

Cassie gnawed the side of her cheek. From working with women all day, she knew high blood pressure could spell danger during pregnancy. "Have you called your doctor?"

"Yes, Mommy. This morning."

"Let me nag. That's my one and only nephew you have in there. Can I get you anything?"

"No, but you're sweet to offer. Austin will be in soon

and he will rub my back. It's killing me today for some reason." To prove the point, she arched and squirmed trying to get comfortable. "Your brother gives the best back rubs."

A mix of sympathy and envy stirred in Cassie. As much as she delighted in her brother's happiness and the coming child, they were a constant reminder of what she had missed.

Even though Annalisa had asked for nothing, Cassie went into the kitchen, poured a glass of filtered water and carried it to her sister-in-law. Tootsie trotted merrily along, tags jingling.

Life had certainly changed since her brother had married. The once-quiet ranch was lively with family preparations, baby talk, dreams and plans for the future. There had never been any question about her continuing to live at the ranch after their wedding, no hint that she was in the way, but sometimes she wondered. Newlyweds with a baby on the way needed their space.

But where would she go? This was home.

She went to the window, uncharacteristically discontent. A shiny black SUV wound down the long driveway.

"There's Heath," she said. "I have to grab my purse."

"He better not expect me to get out of this chair."

With a snicker, Cassie whipped her phone from her back pocket. "I'll text him a pregnant woman alert."

Annalisa's hands rested on her belly. "You do that."

Cassie hurried down the hall, grabbed her purse and the file folder she'd prepared. By the time she reached the front porch, Heath was out of his vehicle and halfway to the house. The limp that had slowed him down for weeks had disappeared, replaced by a confident stride. No swagger, no over-the-top machismo. Just confidence and strength. No wonder he was a great cop and the folks of Whisper Falls had taken him in like a native. He had an air about him that made people feel safe and protected.

"I got your text. Is everything all right with Annalisa?" he asked as they met on the grassy lawn.

"She's been like this for a week. Being nearly eight months pregnant is wearing her down." When he took her elbow, she let him guide her to the passenger side of the truck, enjoying the mannerly attention of a non-related male.

"Up you go. You look really nice."

"So do you. Green is your color." The Kelly-green shirt turned his eyes to emeralds.

"I'll blend into the grass in the park. Do-wrongs won't see me coming."

"About the only do-wrongs you'll find at a May concert in the Whisper Falls park will be teenagers making out behind the trees."

He pumped his eyebrows, his gaze dropping to her mouth. "We may have to do a stakeout."

Cassie was certain her face turned as red as her lips. The idea of kissing Heath, of the feel of his scant mustache against her mouth exploded in her head. Unable to shake the thought, she did the only thing she could. She rolled her eyes. Heath laughed. There was something about that short, intense laugh of his that sent pinpricks of pleasure dancing over her skin.

The laugh. The man. The thought of kissing him. What was wrong with her?

She tightened her grip on the file folder.

Heath saw the movement and hitched his chin toward

her lap. "Whatcha got there? Words to *Rocky Top* so we can sing along?

Cassie opened the file, letting his joke slide. Any self-respecting fan knew the words to the famous bluegrass song.

Might as well get this over with. "This is a file on Darrell."

He jerked, spun his focus toward her, eyes wide and surprised. "You kept a file on your husband?"

"No, silly. I made one." She tapped the folder. "This has our honeymoon itinerary, phone records, hotel reservations, even the bill for the flowers he sent me the day of his death. Every record I could find or print off the computer. After you accused him of being a criminal—"

"I didn't accuse him, Cassie. Asking questions is not an accusation."

Why didn't that make her feel any better? "Then let's say you insinuated. Whatever term you want to use, you raised questions that I want answered."

"I thought you didn't want to discuss this again."

"I didn't at first but the more I think about what you said, the more it bothers me. Darrell was not a criminal. I want to help you prove that."

Heath refocused on the country lane. His square jaw worked. Nostrils flared. Finally, he gave her a quick, hard glance and said, "What if you're wrong?"

She'd thought about that, had lain awake more than one night pondering her late husband's activities, wondering if she'd been the biggest fool on earth. The questions nagged at her like an ingrown toenail, cutting into every good memory she'd treasured up to this point. Closure had become a necessity. "Louis may have been involved in bad things. That wouldn't surprise me at all. I can't believe it of Darrell."

"All right. Tell you what. If I can prove him innocent, I will. But I'll need your cooperation. Everything you know."

"These records are all I have. What else can I do?"

"Witnesses often don't know what they know. You see or hear something, some anomaly that doesn't quite fit but you blow it off thinking it's nothing."

"I guess that's possible," she said doubtfully.

"Oh, it's possible. Even likely. Trust me on that."

What choice did she have? She'd already betrayed Darrell by digging through his computer files with a suspicious eye.

"Tell me everything you know, every detail you remember, especially about the trip to Mexico."

"I did that already."

"You gave me the short version. I want the long one. Times when you weren't with Darrell. Where did he go? Who did he meet and do business with? How did he act before and after? Did anything seem out of place? Were you ever worried or suspicious? Did he ever say anything, get a strange phone call, a note he didn't let you see, anything that didn't fit?"

Cassie's gut clenched into a knot. Now she understood how people felt during an interrogation. It wasn't fun.

"Nothing."

"If you think of anything, write it down, text me, call me." Heath hammered away with rapid-fire questions, asking things she'd never considered. Cassie dug deep, searching for any clue, though nothing she told him seemed that important.

By the time she reached the park, Cassie was no longer excited about a bluegrass concert.

Heath felt like a jerk even though he shouldn't have. Extracting this kind of information from Cassie had been his intent from the start, his reason for making excuses to see her every day. Now he wasn't so sure. Part of him wanted to forget the investigation and have a good time with a woman he liked. Yet the badge in his pocket burned with the flame of justice.

The Whisper Falls Municipal Park sat at the west end of town where Easy Street became the highway leading out of town. To park, a car simply pulled off the road and found a spot. Sometimes that spot happened to be in someone's yard but as long as there was no Keep Off sign, people parked where they wanted to. It was a system that had served since the town's founding and unless progress paid for paved parking, the system would continue.

Heath found an empty, grassy space next to the funeral home—which was kitty-cornered from the park—and pulled in. He killed the vehicle and turned toward his date. A relationship that had begun as a means of obtaining information had become more. He wasn't ready to put a name to his feelings, but Cassie meant something.

"Have I put a damper on the evening with my questions?" he asked softly.

"It doesn't matter."

"Sure it does." He gently took the folder from her and slid it under the front seat. From the bandstand, a fiddle played high and sweet. "Let's put this away, try to forget about the case for a while and enjoy ourselves. The music is calling."

"Okay." But she looked so serious now.

"Hey." He tilted her chin with his thumb and stared into a pair of sorrowful irises of pale green that stayed in his mind even when he wasn't with her. Like the rest of her. Cajoling, he said, "I'll buy you a pizza. Extra large."

A hint of amusement flickered. "All to myself?"

He stroked his knuckle along her jawbone. Her alabaster skin, beautiful with her very black hair, was every bit as soft as he'd expected. Like sun-warmed rose petals. Without knowing it, he'd let her creep into his subconscious. "Only if you want to see an officer of the law salivate in public."

Her nostrils flared, the makings of a laugh, and he knew he'd won when her red lips bowed. "When do we get this pizza?"

Heath took his hand away. Brushing Cassie's skin interfered with his reasoning—and a lawman had to be alert. "Whenever you say."

"Pizza Pan stays open until midnight on Saturday night."

His mouth curved. "Concert first. Pizza later?"

"You're on, big boy." She raised her hand for a high five. He slapped her smaller palm and gave her hand a quick squeeze. A secret promise that he'd do his best to protect her, all the while hoping he didn't have to break her heart in the process.

They exited the SUV and sauntered across the freshly mowed grass into the park. Popcorn scented the air. The band was in full throttle, banjoes dueling while a stand-up bass thumped out a rhythm. Hard to stay in a dark mood with that kind of energy vibrating the airwaves.

Heath gazed around, scoping out the environment. "Good crowd."

"The weather is perfect, and Whisper Falls is known for good bluegrass events."

He catalogued the spots he considered problem areas, though he was here only as backup in case something hinky went down. No one expected that in Whisper Falls. Except him. He always expected trouble. Maybe that's why it found him so often.

The band kicked into the next number. A lively, sawing fiddle took center stage.

"Name that tune," he said.

"'Orange Blossom Special.'"

"Impressive. Are you a fan?"

She smiled. "I've been to these concerts before."

"Cheater." He snagged her hand and when she didn't pull away led them through the milling crowd. Cassie was a people magnet and stopped frequently to greet customers and friends and church members, drawing him in. For a man who'd been rootless since college, belonging to a town was different but nice. He liked the town, enjoyed the friendly Southern people.

All during the exchanges, Heath remained alert in his role as security. When a pair of teenagers hooked up in a fight, he left Cassie with friends and hurried toward the rumble. The small circle of onlookers saw him coming and the fighters broke apart, breathing heavily. One kid had a nosebleed.

Heath stepped between them. In a calm, firm voice, he settled the issue, took the nosebleed to a makeshift first aid station and contacted parents. By the time he'd taken care of business, Cassie wasn't where he'd left her. He pulled out his cell phone and flipped through the contacts for her name. Before he could complete the call, the blonde and beautiful Michelle Jessup approached him.

"I saw what you did, Heath. So brave."

He fought an eye roll. "They're just kids."

"Still, kids today…" She shook her long hair as if she thought all of today's teenagers were one step away from mass murder.

"Well." Offering a polite head bob, Heath started to leave. "Good to see you."

She stopped him with a hand on his arm. "I would sure love a nice cold drink. And after the concert, dinner perhaps? I know the coziest little place down in Moreburg that serves thick, rare steaks and double baked potatoes."

A couple of weeks ago, he would have said yes. Something had changed, something that troubled him.

"I'm here with someone," he said, glad it was true. Michelle was beautiful and the type of woman he would have dated a year ago, but he simply wasn't interested. Not anymore.

"Oh." She pouted, an adorable pout that had doubtless worked on men all of her life. "What about our rain check?"

He removed her hand from his arm and gave the fingers a squeeze. His cell phone rang and, glad for the interruption, he said, "Excuse me," and pushed the talk button.

"Heath?" Cassie's voice sounded breathless. "I can't find you. I have to leave."

"I'm at the first aid station." His hand tensed on the smartphone. "What's wrong?"

"Can you take me home? I need to go to the hospital."

"The hospital?" Adrenaline surged into his bloodstream. With an apologetic glance, he turned his back on Michelle. Frantically, he searched the crowd for Cassie's familiar black hair and bright blue shirt. "Are your hurt? Sick? Talk to me."

"Annalisa is in labor."

"Meet me at the SUV."

She hadn't expected Heath to come with her, but, after making sure the auxiliary officers had everything under control, he'd insisted on heading straight to Fayetteville to the hospital. In his Expedition.

When they'd arrived at Regional Medical Center and started across the parking lot, Cassie paused. "You don't have to go inside."

"Want me to leave?"

"No, I'm glad you came." The admission surprised her. "But I don't want you to feel obligated, either. Driving me this distance was above and beyond the call of duty."

They paused at the crosswalk to let a car pass. The hospital was large and busy. One ambulance was pulling away as another came in. People entered and exited, some in street clothes, others in medical scrubs with security name badges on their chests.

"This isn't duty, Cassie. I'm here because I want to be. If you'll let me, I'd like to stay."

When Heath reached for her hand, Cassie was glad for the contact. Her fingers were cold against his hard warmth. Secure. Safe. "I'd be glad for the company."

"Look at you," he chided softly. "You're all shaky. Good thing I didn't let you drive yourself. You wouldn't want to end up in a ditch on a dark, lonely stretch of road."

The reminder of their first meeting brought a fleeting smile, but worry nagged too much to joke. "Annalisa is only eight months along. Do you think the baby is all right?"

His eyebrows raised. "Like I'm an expert?"

She huffed a short laugh that had absolutely no effect on her jitters. "Me, either. All I know about childbirth is what I've learned standing over women's hair. The stories are terrifying."

"Fifty hours of hard labor with no anesthesia and only a rusty bullet to bite down on?"

"Close enough."

"I've been with my brothers a couple of times when their kids were born." He stood to one side and let her enter the building first. "Everything went fine, but they were basket cases."

As Cassie stepped into the entry, cool air from overhead vents prickled the skin on her arms. She rubbed at them, belly jumping with nerves for her family.

"That's why I'm here. Austin will need me, even if he doesn't realize it yet. He is so in love with Annalisa, if anything should go wrong, he'll crumble."

"Did he say anything was wrong?" Heath punched the elevator button. A pair of passing nurses gave him the once-over before exchanging grins, though he seemed oblivious.

"No, his call was brief. He said she was admitted and in labor and he was waiting on the OB-GYN to arrive."

"Then say a prayer, and don't borrow trouble."

"Right." Heath wasn't a man who talked a lot about his faith but she knew he believed. Prayer and faith was the right direction, no matter what the problem.

"That's exactly what I'll do." It was what she'd already done all the way to Fayetteville, but until Annalisa and baby were declared fit, she'd keep on praying.

They rode the elevator to the designated birthing floor, finding Austin without having to ask at the desk. The big, good-looking cowboy was standing outside a room talking to a doctor clad in green scrubs.

"He looks worried." She grabbed for Heath's hand, aware that she'd repeatedly clung to him today. Right now she wasn't even going to question the reasons. He was here and he made her feel better. Enough said.

"He's a first-time father. Of course he's worried. Midnight feedings, kindergarten, buying a car when the kid's sixteen, prom night, paying for college, and then there's the rehearsal dinner at the wedding." Heath raised his free hand in exclamation. "A man could go nuts."

He was joking to ease her tension and Cassie loved him for it. "You're pretty handy in a scary situation, you know that, Officer?"

"That's me. Sworn to protect and serve."

He was a lot more than that, but she didn't say so. They approached Austin who saw them coming.

Her brother looked at her with a beleaguered expression and said in a haggard voice, "I'm glad you're here, sis. We're in trouble."

Chapter Nine

Cassie went into action. Like the natural caregiver she was, she slid in next to her brother's side and put her arm around his back. "What's going on?"

Austin dropped an arm over her shoulder, gripping it with a calloused hand. "They can't stop her labor, and it's too early."

Cassie gazed toward the physician who looked hardly old enough to be out of college. He was a big guy, fresh-faced, blond and blue-eyed with peach fuzz for whiskers. "Are Annalisa and the baby in danger?"

"We're keeping a close watch. Baby is small but appears big enough to be viable."

She hated words like *viable*. This was a baby boy, a person, her nephew. Viable sounded so…so…medical. "What about Annalisa? Is her blood pressure the problem?"

"So far so good. We're monitoring everything and at this point, letting nature take its course. Should anything change, we have staff on hand ready to act."

"So the baby is going to be born tonight?"

"Looks that way."

A zing of fear-tinged exhilaration shot through Cassie. Tonight she'd meet her brother's son. Her nephew. The first grandchild in their family.

"How much longer?"

The doctor's smile was sympathetic. "A while. She's in the early stages."

"Can we stay with her?"

"Absolutely. She'll need you. Especially you, Austin. Give Annalisa plenty of support and encouragement, and try not to worry too much."

Easy for him to say.

"I'll be in the hospital. Let the nurses know if you need anything. Okay?" The young doctor offered a re-assuring smile.

"Will do." Austin held out his hand. "Thanks, Doc."

Cassie could feel the slight tremble in her brother's body as she moved away from his side. Austin was cowboy tough but Annalisa was his Achilles' heel. She'd brought him out of his reclusive shell, helped him find his way back to the Lord and had given him all the love missing in his first marriage. He was mush with her. Cassie had always found that sweet and endearing, a clue to the deep, caring man that was her brother. Tonight, it worried her. If anything should happen to another wife—

She cast the ugly thought into her mental trash can. They were all praying. Annalisa would be fine. So would baby boy.

As the doctor walked briskly away, Austin offered his hand to Heath. "Good of you to come with her, Heath. Thanks."

"Glad to." Heath shot a teasing grin at Cassie. "I'm not a big bluegrass fan anyway."

"She dragged you to that, huh?"

Cassie gave Heath a soft punch on the arm. "You love it, and you know you do. Both of you."

Austin's mouth lifted at the corners, but his eyes didn't smile. As much as they wanted to distract him, he was too worried about his family. "Ready to go in the room? I don't like to leave her alone. I only came out to talk to the doc in private."

"Were you afraid of what he might say?"

"Yeah." He ran his fingers through his hair. "I hate this. I hate seeing her scared and in pain. I want to punch something."

"Hang in, Austin." Heath clapped him on the shoulder. "I've stood beside my brothers in your shoes. They both vow that the end result is worth it."

"She wants this baby so bad." He looked sheepish. "Me, too."

"And you'll have him, safe and sound. Stop worrying," Cassie said. "Did you call Mom and Dad?"

"They're trying to get a flight out, but you know how that goes. Can't get here until tomorrow. Dad said they might drive, but that's at least six hours without sleeping first. With Dad's bad back, I told him to wait until tomorrow when they're fresh."

"Good idea. The baby will be here by then and they can spoil him while you and Annalisa rest."

"Yeah. Let's hope. Unless—"

"Hey, stop that. No 'unless' to it." Cassie leaned her face close to his, willing him to be positive. His first marriage had left him doubting the goodness in life. Annalisa, and his newfound faith, had done a lot to change that but tonight fear gripped him. "Everything is going to be okay. You hear me? You've put your life in God's hands. He's got your back."

"She's right, Austin," Heath said. "Baby will be here by morning, and you'll forget about this anxiety."

Austin drew a deep breath through his nose and nodded. "I'm counting on that."

"Come on, then." Heath clapped him on the shoulder again. "Let's go say hello to your beautiful wife. And I'll tell you about the time my brother fainted in the delivery room. No joke. Big, tough street cop. Bam! Out like a light."

Cassie watched in admiration as the new Whisper Falls police officer soothed her brother with his wit and charm and calm demeanor. Her heart turned over in her chest. The man had a way about him.

They entered the birthing unit where Annalisa was connected to several monitors and an IV. The machines ticked and beeped in a regular rhythm, and the filtering system pumped out the smell of cool, ionized air and clean sheets. Annalisa's eyes were closed but the moment the door swished, she opened them and turned her head. "Austin." She reached a hand over the metal bars.

Her brother was at his wife's side instantly to kiss her forehead and murmur something Cassie couldn't hear.

"What did the doctor tell you?" Annalisa's face was shiny with moisture. Anxiety and discomfort wrinkled her forehead.

Austin smoothed the lines with his fingertips. "The doctor says everything's fine. We're fixin' to have a baby, sweetheart."

"Oh, Austin." Then a contraction must have started because she closed her eyes, face tight, and began to take slow, deep breaths the way she'd learned in the countless videos they'd all watched.

Austin counted, encouraging her, talking in the sweetest manner. Cassie's insides squeezed at her brother's tender love for his wife.

Thank You, Lord, for bringing her into his life. Keep them in Your loving hands tonight. Give them the beautiful, healthy baby they want so much.

She glanced at Heath who was watching them, too, a curious light in his eyes. To her surprise, she was holding his hand again. She didn't know when that had happened, but the connection brought comfort.

When the contraction ended, Annalisa opened her eyes, spotting Cassie and Heath. "Hey, you two. Stop hiding by the door. Come in here and make me laugh."

"Tell us if we're in the way or when you need privacy," Cassie said. "We can hang out in the lobby."

"Stay. At least for now. When things heat up, I may not want anyone around to hear me blasting Austin for causing this."

"Hey!" Austin pretended insult.

She squeezed his forearm. "You know I'm kidding. I wouldn't change places with any woman in the world right now no matter what. We've waited a long time for our little prince to come. All I want is for him to be strong and healthy."

"Me, too, babe, but I have a feeling it's going to be a long night for you."

And it was. For hours, between nurse and doctor visits, the four of them played card games and told stories until Annalisa became too uncomfortable to participate. By midnight, the patient was tiring fast. To give the couple some time and privacy in these last hours,

Cassie and Heath found an open snack bar. Only one other person occupied a table.

"Sorry about your pizza," Heath said as they sat down at the empty table with machine sandwiches and cold drinks.

"Oh, you're not getting out of it that easy, mister. You still owe me a pizza."

"Good."

"Good? Why would you say that?"

"Because you'll have to go out with me again."

Cassie's heart jumped. She stared at him across her chilly ham and cheese. "Go out? As in a date?"

"Got a problem with that?"

Did she? Darrell floated into her consciousness along with Heath's accusation that her late husband was dirty. How could she possibly date him? But she already was, in a manner of speaking. She looked forward to seeing him. Wanted to talk to him, be with him, hear his opinion. Was she betraying Darrell's memory?

Oblivious to the churning doubts in her head, Heath said, "Someday I want to take you out for a real meal."

Okay, safe ground. She tried to look aghast. "As in healthy stuff? Don't you dare!"

They both laughed, breaking the tension. He was joking, being his usual easy self. But a real date with Heath Monroe sounded…nice. She wanted to dress up and go somewhere swanky on the arm of this man.

And she was starting to scare herself.

"I'm getting tired," she said, blinking away the grit in her eyes. Fatigue was the only excuse for her bizarre attraction to Heath tonight.

"All things considered, why wouldn't you be? Work all day, support your expecting brother all night."

"Don't forget I have to entertain you, as well."

"Am I work?"

More than he could ever know. "You've been great, Heath. I don't know what…" She let the words drift off, not wanting to say too much. Her emotions were a tangled mess she hadn't sorted out. Inside, a war raged between honoring Darrell and falling for Heath.

The thought brought her up short. Falling for him? No, no, she was just tired and emotional.

She laid aside the tasteless white-bread sandwich, surprised to find her food nearly eaten. She'd been hungrier than she'd realized. "I'm done."

"You look done," Heath said in a wry voice. "Done in. Come on." Heath scooped up their trash and deposited it before pulling out her chair. "You can lie down in the waiting room and catch a nap. I'll keep watch over brother and wife."

She could get used to his Texas manners. "What about you?"

"Lawmen don't need sleep."

"Ah, yes, the guardian. Protector of women and children and old ladies crossing the street."

"Don't forget puppies and kitties." His cute smile wrapped around her like a warm wind.

She definitely needed rest.

Curled up on a sofa in the waiting area, Cassie dreamed muddled dreams of Darrell and Heath and a crying baby on a Mexican beach. She woke with a start, pulse banging. The dreams weren't particularly frightening but something was wrong. Something she couldn't quite remember.

"Cassie." Heath's mellow voice sounded urgent. "Are you awake?"

"I am now." Sitting up, she pushed at her hair, aware of how she must look. One glimpse of Heath and she forgot all about her disheveled appearance. "What's wrong?"

"There's a problem with the baby. The doctor's talking to Austin and Annalisa now."

"A problem? Oh, dear God." Adrenaline shot through her veins stronger than a triple espresso. Panicked, she grabbled for Heath's hand, clinging. "What is it? Is he—"

"His heart rate is too low. They're talking about a C-section."

"Okay. Okay. A C-section. That's no big deal these days. Right?" She took a deep breath, trying to get her bearings. "I can't think yet. I was dreaming…"

"It's okay. Sorry to awaken you like that."

Cassie put her fingertips on her forehead. She was usually calm and alert in emergencies. Must be the strange, misty dream. "What time is it?"

"Three in the morning." He glanced toward the double doors and stood. "Here's Austin now."

Cassie ran to her brother. "Is she all right? What's happening?"

"I only have a minute. We're doing a C-section. I have to gown up."

"They're letting you go in?" Heath sounded as surprised as she was.

"Yes." Her brother's face was taut and pale with fear. "I won't let her go through this without me."

Tears welled in Cassie's eyes. "I love you, Austin."

"Love you, too. Pray for us." Then he was gone,

striding in his long, cowboy stride toward his wife and son and a medical emergency.

Heath alternately prayed and reassured Cassie, trying to ease her worry with a conversation about outrageous baby names such as Pickle and Hashtag. To her credit, she'd come back with some doozies. Karaoke, for one, had made him snort.

She was a gamer, trying to remain upbeat, but her gaze drifted to the doorway over and over again. She loved her brother the way he loved his, and that counted big-time with him. Family was everything. Though he'd never been in her situation, he could empathize.

When a nurse in surgical attire pushed through the doorway, they both leaped to their feet.

"Annalisa?" The anxiety in Cassie's voice hurt him. Like Austin earlier, he wanted to punch something. Or better yet tuck her close to his chest and hold her. His suspect's widow was messing with his head.

The nurse smiled. "She did great. So did Daddy. Baby will be in the nursery in a few minutes."

"He's all right?" Cassie was squeezing Heath's hand so hard, his fingers were numb, and he didn't even care.

"Five pounds and four ounces of healthy outrage." She smiled again. "Wait until you hear that cry."

"He's all right. Heath, they're both okay." Before he knew what she was about, Cassie flung herself against his chest.

What else could a man do? He wrapped his arms around her and held her exactly the way he'd imagined.

Cassie didn't know what had come over her but being in Heath's embrace was amazing. She was a little embarrassed by her behavior, but by the time she'd regained her wits and backed away, pulse thudding like shoes in a clothes dryer, word came that the newborn was in the nursery. She dragged Heath out of the waiting room and rushed down the hall to the wide glass panes. She'd worry about the hug later.

A row of tiny swaddled babies lined the nursery. Inside, near the back, Austin stood beside a nurse peering into an Isolette. The cowboy's big hands were inside the crib, tending his son while the nurse looked on, her mouth moving. When Cassie and Heath approached the window, her brother looked up. The smile he gave them was one of relief and joy and not a little pride.

Cassie grinned hard enough to break her jaw and pointed to the baby and then to herself, indicating her desire to see him. With endearing awkwardness, her brother lifted his naked son in his huge hands and turned him toward the window. A wrinkled face puckered into an annoyed cry. The tiny arms and legs jerked inward.

"Oh, my goodness." Cassie pressed closer to the pane, snapping photos with her cell phone. "He's beautiful. Look at him, Heath. He's wonderful. So tiny and tough and precious."

"Your brother is a blessed man."

"Blessed," Cassie murmured, thinking Heath used exactly the right word. With uncharacteristic neediness, she battled the urge to lean her head on the lawman's sturdy, dependable shoulder. He was as close as a whisper, his side touching hers, his warmth seeping through her skin. If he turned his head, they'd be nose to nose. Mouth to mouth.

Something powerful turned over in her chest.

Bewildered, she refocused on her nephew and watched Austin minister to his son's needs and then slip out of the nursery and head toward Annalisa's room. Cassie and Heath remained at the window, watching the infant sleep. Now swaddled in a blue print blanket, baby boy Blackwell wore a stretchy blue stocking cap. Precious beyond words.

The heaviest emotion engulfed Cassie. A powerful yearning for more than a successful salon and a lot of great friends. An undeniable pull stretched from her to Heath. She pressed against the cool nursery window, stunned by the tsunami of emotions brought on by one baby's birth. She closed her eyes, drifted, aware of the man at her side, of the baby in the nursery, of the empty places in her heart.

"Cassie." Heath's voice was quiet.

"Hmm?" She was, she realized with a start, about to fall asleep against the cool window pane.

"You're tired. I should get you home."

Tired? She was out on her feet. She must be to keep having these aberrant thoughts about her life. About Heath. Tomorrow, after a long sleep, she'd be back to her old self and feel differently.

"Home sounds wonderful. I am exhausted and you must be, too, but let's see Annalisa for a second first, okay?"

"Whatever you want."

"I don't even think that's possible."

He tilted his head. "Excuse me?"

She wanted a baby of her own. She wanted him. "Nothing. I'm getting delirious. We should go."

She started to walk away but Heath caught her arm and pulled her back. "Is something wrong?"

Everything. Nothing.

Stunned at her crazy thoughts, Cassie shook her head. "I'm too tired to think. I want to see my sister-in-law, and I want to go home and sleep for a week."

He studied her for a long moment as if he could see through her head and read her mind.

"I think I can arrange that." The corners of his mouth curled. "Except for the week of sleep which sounds pretty good to me, too. Good, but impossible with our work schedules."

Cassie raised her cell phone for one more snap of the sleeping infant. "I'm totally in love."

The words, softly spoken, took on a new meaning with Heath at her side. She swallowed down the stark, hungry yearning. She could love her nephew. She could love her family. But romantic love was not part of the deal. Not with a man who believed the worst about Darrell.

The sky was beginning to lighten by the time Heath drove the last quarter mile down Cassie's driveway. She'd dozed off several times during the trip but jerked awake as frustrated as a wet cat to have fallen asleep.

"You need me to keep you alert," she claimed. "I'm too tired to drag you out of a ditch tonight."

He didn't tell her he'd trained his body to sleep when it could and stay alert the rest of the time. He'd worked plenty of night shifts and twenty-four-hour days. Instead, he'd laughed at her and called her sleepy head. What he'd really meant was sleeping beauty. More than once, he'd glanced at her dozing profile, propped against the passenger window, and wondered what was happening between them. There was more than an investigation going on here. The trouble was he didn't know how to get around the fact that he'd started dating her to extract information. There was nothing wrong with subterfuge in the line of duty, and yet he felt compromised, conflicted…and as low as a snake's belly.

He rubbed a hand down his face and turned the A/C vent up a notch to keep alert.

He cared for her and it was eating him alive. The man in him wanted to come straight out and tell her the whole story. The agent in him held back.

He still didn't know if she'd been involved with her husband in drug trafficking. He didn't want to believe the worst, but that was his heart talking.

She was loyal, he'd grant her that. Either loyal or culpable and covering her tracks.

He hissed through his teeth, frustrated.

He hated thinking this way. Hated that he'd become so jaded about other human beings that he had trouble sorting the good guys from the bad.

Cassie was dedicated to clearing Darrell and to her memories of one of the shortest marriages on record. He hoped that was all, because a man like him understood that kind of loyalty. Understanding didn't make the truth of the situation any clearer.

"Hey, lazy," he said softly as he put the vehicle into park. When she didn't move, he unbuckled his seat belt and leaned across to touch her shoulder. "Want me to carry you inside?"

Eyes closed, she nodded. "Mmm."

He'd been teasing, but the notion kick-started his heart. Why not? What would it hurt? Relief-fueled exhaustion had knocked her out cold.

Heath eased out of the driver's seat and went around

to lift her into his arms. Austin's ranch dogs—the lab and the shepherd—ambled up, tails wagging as they sniffed his pants leg. He gave each a friendly pat before scooping up his passenger.

Cassie was thinner than he'd realized and easy to carry. When she snuggled against him like a child, his thudding pulse served as a reminder. This was not his little niece dozing after he'd taken her to a Disney movie. This was a woman who did crazy things to his head. A woman who might be involved in drug trafficking. His job was to find out what she knew, no matter the means and no matter how she moved him.

And he'd never disliked his vocation as much as he did this moment.

At the house, he lowered her to the porch swing, bracing the wooden structure with his shoulder and leg to stop the sway. "Sorry, Sleeping Beauty. I don't have a key to your house."

"What?" Muzzy headed, she opened her eyes and glanced around, her voice thick and confused. "How did I get here? Are we home?"

"Home."

He sat down beside her and pulled her sleep-lazed body close to his side. For support, he told himself, until she was fully awake. Feminine, soft, she smelled of sunshine and salon shampoo and something quint-essentially Cassie. "The sun will be up soon. Want to wait for it?"

"Mmm. Sounds beautiful." She gave a great, heaving sigh and settled deeper against him.

Something tenderized inside him, a mallet driving out the hardened spots. He stroked the side of Cassie's face, smoothed her hair and waited for the sunrise.

* * *

Cassie awakened with a smile. Someone was touching her hair. Someone warm and gentle and male. Or maybe she was dreaming again, though the moment felt real. If only he would kiss her, the way he used to do. The way she hadn't been kissed in a very long time.

She put her arms around his neck and lifted her face. "Kiss me," she whispered.

His body went still. In the breaking dawn she couldn't read his face, but she heard the sharp intake of breath. "Are you sure?"

The pleasant rumble of his voice made her pulse dance.

"Mmm. Very."

Wide hands caressed her face with the greatest care and then slid into her hair before he touched his lips to hers. The kiss was tentative, questioning as though he held himself in check. As sweet and tempting as a hot fudge sundae. Cassie burrowed in, kissing him back. The kiss lengthened and one became two. So nice. So wonderful. Her chest filled with a beautiful pleasure. For a brief moment—too brief—his arms tightened and then he released her and pulled away.

"The sun is rising over the mountains," he said softly.

Cassie roused herself from the languor, increasingly aware of her surroundings. A warm flush eased up the back of her neck. What in the world had come over her? She'd kissed Heath. And she'd liked it.

"I'm sorry," she said, and pushed to her feet. Her whole body felt weak and heavy.

"Don't be. The sunrise is beautiful."

He'd intentionally misunderstood. Though he was right, of course. The May sun peeked lemon-yellow above a layered sea of gold and coral that drifted above the deep green of the woods. In seconds, brilliant light spoked the sky illuminating a scatter of dark clouds from the inside out. It was a poet's sky, a dreamer's morning. She thought of her songwriter friend, Lana, and hoped she was awake and watching.

As for Cassie, her fatigue was too great, and her brain was cloudier than the heavens. "Gorgeous, but I'm too tired to enjoy it."

"Go on, then. Get some rest," Heath said gently, placing one last kiss on her forehead. "Aunt Cassie."

The new term brought a smile as Heath dropped his hands and turned, stepping off the porch.

She wanted to call him back and explain, but what would she say? *I was sleepy. I kissed you by mistake.* Because in her heart of hearts, she was afraid that wasn't true.

Bemused, bewildered and yearning, Cassie closed the door to the empty, silent house. She didn't go to bed. Not yet. She went to the window and pulled aside the curtain. She watched as the dome light flared inside Heath's SUV, a flash of shadowy light. Her throat filled at that one last glance of Heath's face before he started the SUV and drove away.

Tootsie tapped in from the hallway and rubbed against her legs. Cassie scooped her up and held the fuzzy little poodle against her cheek before letting her out to do her business.

She was overtired. That was all. She wouldn't have kissed him otherwise. Would she?

Disloyalty tugged at her.

Darrell was gone. Heath was alive and real and she might be falling for him, as impossible as that seemed.

"Lord, this is crazy. I'm worn down. Overemotional. The new baby and all." She sucked in her bottom lip. "Oh, Jesus, I always wanted a baby."

Tears prickled her eyes. She was definitely exhausted. Things would seem different after a few hours' sleep.

Chapter Ten

He was losing his edge. And he knew better. Heath had seen it happen too many times. A cop fell for the wrong woman and she took him down.

But try as he might, he couldn't keep Cassie out of his head. The snap of green eyes, the slash of bright red lips curved in a mischievous grin, the sweet and sassy depth of personality. A man who claimed Cassie as his woman would know a partner and friend, as well as a love. And oh, how she loved. He'd seen her with her family, her customers, her friends, her church. He knew her loyalty to her husband's memory. Cassie loved them all with a passion as warm as an Ozark summer.

After sleeping most of Sunday away, Heath had given in to the urge and called her. He'd asked about the baby, kept it light, and never mentioned the devastating kiss. Neither had Cassie.

He'd phoned his mother, too, and then made two more calls to hassle Holt and Heston awhile. Granted, Heath was restless, troubled by circumstances of his own creation.

Now, late Monday morning, he drove the streets

of Whisper Falls, combing the residential areas for an eighty-seven-year-old Alzheimer's patient who'd wandered away from his daughter's home.

On the dash, his father's badge glinted in the bright sunlight, an ever-present reminder of his calling. Yet he couldn't believe Cassie was involved with Louis Carmichael's drug business. Or maybe he didn't *want* to believe it. That was the trouble with relationships. They skewed a man's focus.

As he turned a corner onto Oak Street, he spotted an elderly man sitting beneath a tree across the street from the school. Children played on the playground, their voices carrying to him like a cheerful wind. Heath's chest tightened, both with relief at having found the man and at the poignancy of his location. That Elmer would come here, near a school, made perfect sense. The old gentleman had been a science teacher for many years.

After a confirmation glance at the photo on the seat beside him, Heath radioed the news to cancel the silver alert and whipped in next to the curb and got out, approaching the man.

"Elmer, are you okay?" Heath knelt on one knee next to the thin, withered old man. His clothes were smudged with dirt as if he'd fallen, and he smelled of arthritis rub. Compassion thickened Heath's throat. Someday, he or his loved ones might be in this position. "Sharon is worried about you."

"Sharon?" Elmer asked in a frightened voice. "What is this place? Everything looks different."

"Don't worry, sir. I'm a police officer. I'll take you home."

"That's nice of you, son." Though his rheumy eyes were clouded, Elmer's entire body sagged in helpless, hopeless relief. "Marjorie made a carrot cake this morning and I'm hungry. My wife is a fine, fine cook."

"Yes, sir." Heath helped the elderly man to his feet, keeping the sadness from his expression. Marjorie, he knew from the daughter's information, was his long-dead wife. "Let's get you home."

Within fifteen minutes, he'd returned Elmer to a greatly relieved daughter, feeling good about the outcome, but pity for the situation. Elmer was fortunate to have a loving daughter to care for him. Her role couldn't be easy.

Who would be there for him if Alzheimer's came calling someday?

As he sat inside his truck on a tree-lined street aching for a confused old man, his mind returned to the bone he'd been gnawing for days. Cassie Blackwell and her husband.

Holt had no news to share yet. Too early. He had a case to finish before he could leave for Mexico. Even then, a private investigator might not discover anything that wasn't already known. Nonetheless, Heath's instincts were strong and they told him something was hinky. The question was, did Cassie know? Was her professed cooperation and the file full of information a ruse? His instincts said no. But maybe his emotions were getting in the way again.

He never should have started this crazy thing with her. If she knew of his suspicions, that he'd begun seeing her as means to gather evidence, she'd hate him. In a way, that might be the best thing. Kick him to the curb and get it over with before more damage was done.

But Saturday had meant something special. In those moments when they'd watched the newborn boy together, he'd discovered a hole in his life, the missing link, so to speak. Family. Oh, he had Mom and the brothers and their terrific broods, but no one of his own. No one to make plans with. No one to dream dreams and build a life and have kids. No one to take care of him when he was old and frail.

He was thirty-six years old and he'd never wanted any of that. All he'd ever cared about was taking out the bad guy, honoring Dad's memory, making the world a better place. He wasn't even sure he wanted it now, but those stunning minutes at the hospital and again on Cassie's front porch when she'd kissed him had Heath wondering if perhaps he was missing something important.

"Lord, I don't ask for much, but I could use some guidance."

Maybe he should turn the investigation over to the DEA and forget about it. No, too soon. Too little evidence, and in his arrogance, he wanted to solve the case for himself while protecting Cassie. The effort seemed on the verge of backfiring in his face.

Better call Holt again tonight and see if his brother could jumpstart things from Texas.

His radio crackled and he took a call from dispatch. A domestic dispute. Not his favorite call, but he radioed back and headed that direction.

"Isn't he the cutest baby ever?" Cassie stood above Tara Wilkin's head, painting highlights into her shoulder-length brown hair. Tara held a dozen photographs of Austin's new baby.

"A darling for certain. What did they name him?"

"Levi Austin. Annalisa insisted on naming him after his daddy, and I just love it."

"Adorable and very cowboy."

"Austin says Levi will be a bull rider. Annalisa says no way her baby is getting on a bull." Cassie smiled, remembering the cute argument the pair had had at the hospital.

"I think Annalisa will win that one," Tara said. "I can't imagine letting my son on a two-thousand-pound bull."

"Me, either!" Not that she had a son.

"Tell her who took you to the hospital and stayed until the baby arrived." This from Louise whose rust-red hair looked electric-plug wild today.

"It's not a big deal, Louise. I didn't have my car."

"You could have gotten it."

"I was in a hurry."

"So apparently was your handsome hero in uniform who remained by your side *all* night."

A titter of excitement swept through the shop, a wave of speculation.

"Wait a minute," Cassie insisted, pointing the paint brush. "That sounds bad, but it wasn't. We were at the hospital all night waiting for the baby to arrive. Nothing happened."

Well, not exactly nothing, but not the kind of thing they were tittering about.

"Why is your face turning red?"

"It is not!" She spun toward the mirror. Sure enough, her cheeks glowed like a traffic light. "Y'all are embarrassing me. Heath and I are pals."

"Fiddlesticks," Miss Evelyn said, her fingertips deep in a soaking bowl. "Uncle Digger said the pair of you were giggling like teenagers at the Iron Horse the other day. Looked cozy and romantic over Cokes and fries."

Cassie groaned. She and Heath had been laughing about one of his dumbest criminal stories. He had a gazillion and they made her laugh like a loon. There was nothing romantic about it. Except when he'd touched her hair and told her she smelled good.

"You've been a widow long enough, Cassie," Tara said. "And if I had a hot-looking officer of the law in pursuit of me, I'd slam on my brakes and let him catch me."

The shop ladies howled with laughter. All Cassie wanted to do was slink away.

Louise lifted Miss Evelyn's hand from the soak solution. "I'm here with you all day, Cassie, sugar. I know how you light up when Heath Monroe comes through that door. At least admit you like him for more than a friend. That old 'pals' story is getting stale."

"I do not light up."

"Do, too. Now, confess. We're your friends. We have a duty to know."

Cassie rolled her eyes. "If I do, will all of you stop badgering me?"

"No. We'll want details."

Another chorus of laughter. This time, Cassie clamped her mouth shut and concentrated on Tara's hair. Okay, so they were right. She had a thing for the new assistant police chief and it didn't feel a bit like friendship. Saturday night, or rather Sunday morning at sunrise, had pretty much sealed her fate. The frozen places had started to thaw. The numbness was giving way to feeling, something she'd never expected to happen. But her friends didn't understand the dilemma, didn't realize how risky and terrifying it was to step out of her comfort zone and cross the lines of friendship. The thought of giving her heart, maybe to lose it again, was scarier than climbing Whisper Falls during an ice storm. She didn't, however, say that to her friends.

After work Cassie walked out of the salon without so much as a glance toward the courthouse. She didn't look on the streets for Heath's big black Expedition, either.

She drove to Resthaven, a tidy, cedar-lined cemetery situated on the eastern edge of town. Her little Nissan probably knew the way by itself, she'd driven here so many times over the last three years. The gates never closed and the place was usually deserted and blessedly peaceful, especially at night with the stars overhead. Cassie knew because she had spent a few nights beside Darrell's gravesite in those early, pain-filled days.

A hearty wind whipped her hair as she approached the red granite headstone carved with Darrell's name. The wind carried the scent of cedar and newly mowed grass across the bright flowers and silent graves.

At the gravesite next to Darrell's, a small American flag *whap-whapped* in the breeze. At the foot, a bronze WWII marker proclaimed the dead to be a veteran like many others buried here in this peaceful vale. To her knowledge Darrell had never served, but she wasn't positive. They'd had so little time together. There were too many things she didn't know about her late husband. Would never know now. She'd never even met his family—if he'd had one other than Louis Carmichael.

She stroked her hand across the bumpy name carved in sun-warmed granite. "Why didn't I know more about your life? Was it because everything happened so fast? Or did you have secrets?"

Shame was an instant and sharp rebuke. She didn't want to believe the love of her life could have been involved in criminal activity, and yet Heath had made her doubt. She was ashamed of that. Ashamed of lost loyalty.

As she'd done dozens of times, she sat down on the cool grass and leaned against the headstone. In times past, she'd wept for all that had been lost. Today, she contemplated…and prayed.

A cardinal fluttered to the ground, a flash of color, like her favorite red lipstick. Darrell had bought it for her. He'd loved her in red, his favorite color.

"I still wear it," she told him, though only the cardinal heard.

Something niggled in the back of her mind. A faint memory she couldn't quite bring to the fore.

She had the sudden urge to drive out to Louis's trailer house. Darrell had lived there until the wedding. Some of his things were likely left behind in the rubble, though Louis had claimed the opposite and refused to let her look. She didn't know why the cousin had disliked her so much. But according to Heath, Louis had left, apparently before the storm, and hadn't been heard from since.

Maybe she'd find something her beloved had left behind, something to reassure her that Darrell had been the man she'd believed him to be.

The winding road grew narrower and less traveled with each passing mile as Cassie guided her car deep into the lush Ozark woods. Clouds of redbud trees lined

the roadsides, sprinkling their lavender-red blossoms on
her windshield. The only person on the remote ribbon
of dirt, Cassie rolled down her window and breathed
in the spring. A sweet, floral scent, higher pitched than
peach but every bit as luscious, filled the interior of the
car. Dogwood, perhaps?

When she approached a fork from which one way
ambled off to the left like a cow path, Cassie knew the
trailer site was near. Though she'd been to Louis's mobile home only once, she remembered the way because
she and Darrell had lingered at this fork, had gotten
out of the car and walked a ways holding hands, a romantic stroll.

Today she didn't stop the car, but the memory
swamped her for a moment and moistened her eyes.
Those had been good days, happy moments when the
future seemed impossibly rosy. And indeed, it had been
impossible. Only she hadn't known it then.

With a regretful sigh, she blinked away the moisture
and followed the winding trail deeper into the trees until
it dead-ended at the wreckage of a mobile home. She
supposed she should have come sooner, when Heath
had first told her about the tornado damage, but she'd
been afraid of Louis.

The thought gave her pause as she stopped at the end
of the rough-cut driveway. Louis had made her nervous,
but until now, she'd never acknowledged the fear. He'd
never been nice to her and had accused Darrell of selling out when they'd married. She still didn't understand
what he'd meant by that.

As Cassie exited the car, an eerie silence hung over
the abandoned place. It was as if the trees had eyes and
knew the secrets hidden among the rubble. The trailer

had been in bad shape before the storm, but now only sheet metal and the remains of Louis's life—and Darrell's—covered a long swath of ground. Even the well house had collapsed. The tank was gone, too, but not ripped away by the storm. The remaining pipes were too neatly cut.

Someone had taken the tank, probably to recycle or use it as their own. Hill families were often poor enough to scavenge, and she wondered what else had disappeared at the hands of looters.

The yellow police tape still surrounded a small area at the center, though a piece of tape would not deter treasure seekers. The wind in her hair, she gazed thoughtfully toward the place where Chief Farnsworth had found evidence that Darrell and Louis sold drugs. She still couldn't believe Darrell had known what his cousin was doing. When she'd been here that one time, she'd seen nothing out of the ordinary, other than a man who clearly did not want her there.

Careful to be on the lookout for copperheads and shards of glass and metal, Cassie moved through the debris. Here, the ground remained soggy from the heavy spring rains and repeated thunderstorms. They'd had more than their share this spring, so much that anything worth salvaging from Louis's trailer was likely ruined.

A cottontail bolted out from beneath a stuffed, upturned chair. Cassie yelped, throwing her hands out to the sides in alarm. The rabbit, as startled as she, rocketed into the overgrown grass and weeds. Cassie laughed at her skittishness, though several minutes passed before her pulse returned to normal.

She wasn't exactly afraid to be here, but the place gave her the creeps just as its owner had done.

"Why did I bother?" she muttered as she looked around and toed the rubble. There was nothing here. Nothing left that mattered. Heath and Chief Farnsworth would have removed anything of value, wouldn't they? Or was that not in the line of police work?

She stepped over a downed tree, disheartened and yet not ready to give up the search for some small bit of encouragement. A shiny object caught her eye, probably a gum wrapper or pop tab, but she walked toward it, wishing she'd changed her shoes before making this trip. Her heels stabbed holes in the soft ground. Given her respectful fear of snakes, she used a stick to push aside wet leaves and paper. A small gold-colored lid appeared. Cassie stared in bewildered surprise. Discovering the lid was as unsettling as finding a snake. She picked it up, growing more and more puzzled, for indeed she recognized the tube-shaped object…because it was hers.

"What is this doing here?" She turned the familiar tube over in her hands. This was the top to one of her lipsticks. She must have dropped it that one time Darrell had brought her here and argued with Louis.

She turned the lid over in her palm. Sun glinted off the metal. It was only a lipstick cover. There was nothing sinister about that, and yet she had the weirdest disquiet. Thanks to Heath's insinuations, she was tilting at windmills, imagining misdeed where none existed.

More focused now, she poked at the decaying leaves, turning them up along with bits of paper, broken shingles, and miscellaneous trash in search of the remaining lipstick case. With effort, she muscled a busted chest onto its side, spilling the contents from the drawers. Why hadn't Louis salvaged any of his belongings before he'd left? Or had he left before the storm struck? Did he even know his house was in ruins? Where was he? Where would he have gone? Did he know the police wanted to question him?

Frustrated, she wished she'd known more about Darrell and his family. He'd always been vague. He was from out west and his parents were dead. That's all he'd ever said.

She pilfered through the chest, aware of the invasion of privacy. Cassie didn't care. If Darrell had left anything behind, it belonged to her, not Louis. If she could only find one little hint to prove Darrell was not involved in Louis's illegal activities.

A troubling thought appeared like a gnat in her ear, insisting on attention. She let it in, turning it over for examination. Why had Darrell come to a tiny rural community in the Ozarks in the first place? Was his cousin the only reason? He certainly hadn't come to claim a job opportunity as Heath had done. But hadn't she likewise wondered why a man of Heath's training would give up a federal agent position to play second banana in a small town police department?

Most of the chest held nothing but clothing items, most likely the reason Chief Farnsworth and Heath had left the chest and its contents behind. In the bottom drawer, beneath a T-shirt, she spied a small, folded piece of paper. Cassie opened the page…and her knees went weak.

"I love you," the note read in Darrell's tidy print. "Forever and always. You are the best thing that ever happened to me. Tonight is too far away."

Below the sweet words, her handwriting responded,

"You are my breath, my every heartbeat. I can't believe I finally found you. Thank you for loving me."

Sinking to the side of the rickety, broken chest, weak as water, Cassie recalled the evening, after a busy day's work, when she'd found the note on her windshield beneath a wiper blade. Joy had burst inside her to be completely loved, to be the beloved focus of this one, wonderful man. That evening, she'd returned the note hidden inside a candy bar she'd slipped into his pocket. It was the first of many "secret" love notes they'd written to each other.

"But you kept the first one," she whispered, not caring that moisture once again clouded her vision.

Regardless of what else he'd done, Darrell Chapman had loved her. Of that one thing she was convinced.

When the wave of bittersweet memory passed, Cassie continued her search though she had no idea what she was after other than a lipstick tube which had no meaning. Seeing more papers stuck beneath a rumpled pile of rags, she pulled them out and began sorting through. Clearly this had been Darrell's dresser, or at least his drawer. Notes, old bills and even a few maps of Mexico. Not unusual, given Darrell's love for the country's perfect diving beaches. She had so little left that had belonged to him. Though the papers were of no value to anyone else, these were things Cassie wanted to keep.

She smoothed one of the maps open on her lap, recalling the day they'd discussed their honeymoon and he'd showed her where they would go, exciting her with stories of Mexico's beauty, of the sea and the fish, the beach and the sun.

Her finger went to the spot he'd circled in red. Playa

Del Carmen. Awash in memory of those three perfect days, she hardly looked up when a big black SUV, glinting in the fading sun, rumbled down the driveway.

Heath's boots crunched on debris as he exited the Expedition, his attention on the woman sitting amidst the chaos, a handful of papers in her lap.

"Hi," he said, not wanting to startle her though she'd surely heard his approach.

She lifted her face then and his stomach dipped, that roller coaster drop he was starting to equate with each initial glance of Cassie. Memory of Saturday night, of the sweet companionship, the shared birth, and those troublesome kisses gripped him. His gaze, that misbehaving reaction, shot to her mouth before he could bring it under control.

"What are you doing out here?" Was that a blush on her cheekbones? Was she remembering, too?

"I was about to ask you the same thing." He stepped over a dirty, soggy pillow to reach her. Tears glistened on her lashes. He reached out, touched her cheek with only the tips of his fingers. Her skin was warm and moist. "Have you been crying?"

Her hand followed his, expression puzzled. "Have I?"

"Something's wrong. Tell me." His chest filled with the painful need to make things better and the sharp realization that by being himself, who he was called to be, who he *must* be, Heath could only make things worse for her. Wanting to hold her more than he should, Heath perched a hip on the sideways chest, found it sturdy enough, and settled next to her. They connected shoulder to knee, though not enough when he really wanted her in his arms. "What's upset you? Did you remember something?"

"If you mean pertinent to your case against Darrell, no. But I *was* remembering."

Ah, yes, of course. Remembering her late husband, that impossible competitor. Darrell had lived here. Maybe they'd even met here and spent time together in this place.

Then, the agent in him took charge and dropped an ugly suspicion into his brain. Why was Cassie here now? Had she driven to the trailer in an attempt to hide evidence he and Chief Farnsworth might have missed? He started to ask but didn't, not sure he wanted the answers. Not today with Saturday night as fresh in his mind as the scent of dogwood blossoms from the nearby woods. "You look sad. Am I intruding?"

"I'm okay. Just trying to sort through my thoughts. How did you know I was here?"

"A guess. I saw you drive out of town earlier but you never came back. Chief said you visited the cemetery often but you weren't there."

"I was there earlier. Then I got this wild idea to come here."

"What for?"

"I wanted to find something to make you understand. I needed to look."

A breath of fragrant breeze lifted a lock of her hair and set it dancing. Heath smoothed it down again. He loved her hair, sleek and black and as shiny as his new truck.

"And did you find anything?" He leaned over her shoulder, caught the scent of her hair salon and wished he wasn't suspicious of her coming here. He also wished they were two people who'd met outside of his job, away from the deceit and danger of the drug world that would not let him go. A map was spread on her lap and some-one had made notations, circled places along the water's edge.

She shrugged. "A few clothes and papers that belonged to Darrell. They were in this chest. I guess you didn't take them as evidence because they weren't important."

"Chief searched the chest." She'd not mentioned anything of importance. "I see you found a map."

"Yes. A map of Mexico."

Heath's instincts went on police alert. "Darrell's or Louis's?"

She angled her face in his direction. Her clear green eyes were flecked with yellow, like pots of gold hidden in spring grass. He wanted to take her in his arms and forget all about the investigation, but the map could be important. The chief must have missed it somehow during her search, a fact that would infuriate her. But at one point, they'd experienced a cloudburst that had sent them running for their vehicles. It was the only reason he could imagine for the chief's misstep. She would never have intentionally disregarded anything related to Mexico.

"Darrell's. He showed it to me before our honeymoon." She tapped a spot. "See? Where he circled the city?"

He saw more than that on the map and wondered if she knew. Frustrated to have missed this piece of evidence, he suppressed the desire to snatch the map from her fingers.

"I found some other things, too," Cassie went on, her voice soft. "A note he sent me. It's kind of personal."

"You don't have to show it to me." Truth was he didn't want to see it. He didn't want to read another's man personal notes to this woman.

"I'd like for you to see it. Then maybe you'll believe what I do, that Darrell would never have done anything to hurt me."

"I never said he would have."

"You implied that our trip to Mexico was more than a honeymoon."

He had, and he still believed his assumption was correct. Cassie knew it, too. He could see the hurt lurking in those fascinating eyes and was sorry. Sorry she'd married Darrell. Sorry he'd gotten personally involved with a suspect's widow. Sorry if this turned out to be more heartache for both of them.

"All right. What do you have?"

Heath hoped she had proof of her husband's innocence...and hers. It would make his sleep much more restful.

Cassie handed him an ordinary sheet of paper, and the cop in him immediately wondered if the document contained useable prints. He'd found no Darrell Chapman in the database but fingerprints might resolve that.

"Go ahead. Read it."

He skimmed what was essentially a love note between the two of them, nothing useful in an investigation, but painfully romantic to read. "I'm not sure how this proves anything, Cassie."

"Don't you see? Darrell loved me. I was his everything."

"And he was yours," he said. What was happening that he was jealous of a dead man?

Cassie said nothing, but continued to stare at him, willing him to accept what evidence denied. He couldn't.

"Anything else?" he asked quietly and saw her disappointment. It was there in the drop of her shoulders, the downward curve of her enchanting red mouth, the cool retreat in her eyes. He'd dashed her hope, a terrible thing to do.

"Just this." Her reply was despondent as she turned a palm up and parted her fingers. A bronze/gold tube flashed in the sunlight.

Heath's radar started to whirr. Proceeding with caution, careful not to touch the tube, he said, "What's this about?"

"A lid to my lipstick. I found it over there." She pointed to a pile of rubble similar to dozens of other piles. "I must have left it here the one time Darrell brought me out to meet Louis."

"Do you have one missing?"

"I'm not sure." She frowned, pursed her lips. Ah, those distracting lips. "Not that I recall but I have several of this brand."

"Would you object to my keeping it for a while, along with the maps?"

Cassie recoiled, closing her fingers around the tube. "Why?"

"Police business." *Fingerprints, drug residue, to study what I see on that map.* "In an investigation, we like to look at everything."

"These are personal, Heath. There is nothing to investigate. Chief Farnsworth would have taken them if they were pertinent."

"Will you trust me on this, Cassie?" He held out an upturned palm. "I promise to get them back to you as soon as possible."

She hesitated so long he thought he might have to demand them, something he didn't want to do. He was walking a tightrope in this case already, that fine line between caring for Cassie and his code of ethics. In fifteen years in law enforcement, he'd never been this personally involved with a potential suspect, never been this close to walking away from what he believed in, what he'd lived for since he was twelve years old.

His father's badge burned against his thigh, a symbol of dedication and honor. Was Heath Monroe about to become a bad cop, because of a woman?

"Cassie," he urged. "Please."

She gnawed at her lip, eyes worried. "I'll get them back?"

"You will."

She placed the map, the tube, and the letter in his hand. "I'm trusting you."

"I know." And that was the crux of the matter. He was secretly investigating her. And she trusted him.

Chapter Eleven

⌒

Cassie was in a strange mood when she left the tornado site, but Heath had offered to buy pizza and she couldn't pass that up. Torn between loyalty to Darrell and attraction to Heath, she was in turmoil. Not that she still clung to Darrell's memory like some wan heroine in a Southern novel who grows old and dies still mourning her loss, but that she felt a certain responsibility to preserve her late husband's good name.

"I'm in no hurry to go home," she told Heath inside the oregano-scented Pizza Pan. "Austin and Annalisa need some time alone with the new baby. I'm sure they'd prefer I make myself scarce for a while."

She needed the distraction, as well. Too often of late, her sleep was disturbed by spinning thoughts and jackrabbit memories she couldn't quite pin down.

A video game played by a pimply teen whirred and clanged and flashed lights as he racked up points destroying space invaders. The greasy smell of cheese—her favorite smell in the universe next to the salon—permeated the vinyl booth.

"Did they tell you that?"

"No, they wouldn't. But I'm trying to be sensitive." She smiled. "They haven't had much time alone since they married, thanks to *moi.*"

"When did they come home from the hospital?"

"Last night." She fiddled with the plastic straw poked through a lid into the ice and Coke. "I've been thinking of getting an apartment."

"Yeah? Why?"

"Oh, you know." She fluttered her fingers. "They're a family now, and I'm in the way." Well, didn't that sound pathetic and whiney?

"Have you talked to your brother about this?"

"Of course not, silly. He'd deny it, and it's just a feeling I've had lately."

He picked up one of her fingers and rubbed the back of it. The connection soothed, as he'd intended. Heath was good at that. Soothing. "Why not wait it out, spend some time with your new nephew first? See how things go in the next few weeks or months."

"Maybe." She wasn't sure of anything lately. She, a confident businesswoman, one of the movers and shakers in Whisper Falls, had lost her self-assurance.

She looked at the strong, steady, masculine finger fiddling with her turquoise nail. Did Heath have something to do with this restlessness? She was afraid of that answer, afraid he did, afraid he had tilted her world. Like Louis's trailer, tipped on its side and shaken, her neat, tidy life was flying apart since the night she'd followed an SUV down a ravine and met Heath Monroe.

"If you ever decide to go apartment hunting…" He let the offer ride.

"Maybe I should do that. Check out my options."

"It might make you feel better, not that I think Annalisa and Austin are trying to dump you." He pushed his Coke to the side. "I mean, come on. Why would they? Built-in babysitter."

She laughed, his intention, no doubt. "Babysitter. Doting aunt. I gladly play both rolls. But I *would* like to look at apartments and small houses and see what's available. Darrell and I visited some places on the bluff but he was leaning toward a trailer in the country like Louis's."

"You never rented an apartment together?"

"Whirlwind romances don't have time for that, Heath. Darrell said something would work out when we returned from Mexico." She pulled the straw from the cup, sucked the end of it. "In a sad way, he was right."

"The chief set me up with my apartment, but I think there are a couple of others on the same street. Small but nice. Not too hard on the wallet."

"Really?" She perked up. Maybe the change was what she needed. "I want to see them."

"Then let's do it. Tomorrow after work?" He lifted one eyebrow. "And after we could grab chili dogs and cheese fries."

With a laugh, Cassie put a hand to her chest. "You sweet talker. I'm in!"

By the time she arrived at the ranch, the sun had disappeared, the porch light was on and the two faithful dogs didn't bother to get off the porch to sniff and circle. Like a set of furry bookends, one lay at each side of the door, long tails thumping the wood floor.

"Vicious beasts," she said, slowing to pat each head before letting herself inside.

Heath had kissed her good-night again. And she'd let him. Had wanted him to. She could still feel that whisper soft brush of skin against her mouth, the tickle of his facial hair. Gentle and sweet and a tad of dark passion he restrained so beautifully.

Other than Tootsie, the poodle, the living room was empty, but a high-pitched wail of angry infant came from down the hall. Tootsie raised up on Cassie's leg, shiny button eyes beseeching.

Cassie scooped her up. "Unless you and I can find another home, you'll have to get used to it, Toots. Babies cry."

Boy, did this one ever cry.

Cassie followed the sound down the hall to the nursery she and Annalisa had prepared. The room was both pretty and masculine in the palest brown and baby blue. "Master Levi is not a happy boy. What did you do to him?"

She was kidding, but Annalisa wasn't in the mood for jokes.

"Nothing. I don't know." Her usually perfect hair was disheveled and there was a major milk stain on her robe. "Why is he crying so much?"

"Don't look at me. I can fix his hair." *And yours,* but she wasn't about to say that tonight. "After that I'm lost."

"Me, too." Annalisa's gorgeous blue eyes were vexed and worried. The puffiness in her face had subsided but the fatigue had not.

"Let me do something. I don't know what *he* needs, but *you* need to rest. Where is my pig-hearted brother?" She would tear a strip off him for leaving Annalisa alone. The woman had just experienced childbirth and surgery!

"He went into town."

"Town! What for?" Cassie was indignant. How dare he?

Annalisa offered a wan smile. "You look as if you'll wring his neck."

"I will. I can't believe he'd leave you this way. Where did he go? The feed store? The jerk. You've had surgery. You need help." She rushed to her sister-in-law's side and took the baby. Levi felt as light as a hairbrush. But softer and more flexible. Scary flexible, like a bundle of warm towels.

"Don't be mad at Austin." Annalisa smiled a little, sheepish as she shuffled toward the padded rocker. The expensive handmade rocker Austin had bought from an Ozark wood craftsman. "He went to the store for me. I craved mint chocolate-chip ice cream."

That took the fire out of Cassie's smokestack. "Oh. Well, in that case, I'll let him live another day." She pulled Levi Austin close to her chest and cooed, "There now, my little man. Let Aunt Cassie fix it."

The baby squinched his eyes tight and screamed. That was a seriously red face.

"Is it time for him to eat?" she asked over the wail.

"Just fed him."

"Tummy ache?"

"I don't know how to tell."

"Me, neither." Cassie had run the gamut of her baby knowledge but she understood women and Annalisa was pale and wobbly. "You look like you're about to pass out. Go to bed. I can handle him until Austin gets back."

"Are you sure?"

"Go."

"Call me if you get tired of dealing with him."

"Go."

Like an old lady, a slightly bent Annalisa held to her incision and shuffled across the hall to the room she shared with Austin. She left the door open, an action Cassie found endearing. Annalisa's mother instinct was strong. No matter how weak and tired, she'd be back in an instant if Cassie didn't find a way to soothe her baby.

Rocking and cooing and saying completely stupid things to a crying baby who couldn't have cared less, Cassie walked back and forth across the floor. This was the way things would be if she had a child. The way of a new mother, anxious to do the right thing and not knowing what that was. Feeling her way in the dark, hoping for the best, trusting God to get her through.

At the moment, that was the story of Cassie's life. As if the tornado had swept through Whisper Falls and torn away the protective cocoon she'd been hiding in for three years. Maybe longer.

She shifted the baby to her shoulder and patted his back, careful to support his downy bobble head. With his sweet breath warm on her neck, she hummed "Blessed Assurance"—something she needed more of—and slowly, slowly Levi's cries shuddered to a halt.

"Thank You, Lord," Cassie murmured, nearly limp with gratitude and relief.

She patted and hummed a while longer then placed the tiny boy in his crib. This time he didn't stir. Standing above him, watching him sleep, a powerful love gripped Cassie.

When Austin returned ten minutes later, Cassie left her brother in charge of his wife and son and took her bowl of ice cream to her bedroom. She hadn't told Austin about the trip to Louis's trailer. He wouldn't approve. He thought she should let go of the past and move on.

Perhaps she would have if Heath hadn't come along. But Darrell had been an important part of her life and now their short life together stood in question. Before she could move forward, she needed to close the door on the past. She simply had to know if her love and life with Darrell had been real.

Setting the red ceramic bowl on her dresser, she thought of the old chest and the things she'd found at the tornado site. She was still puzzled as to Heath's reason for wanting the map and the lipstick lid, but she trusted him to return them. She felt good admitting that. She trusted Heath. Trusted him with Darrell's belongings, trusted him to do the right thing. Maybe she even trusted him with her heart.

She paused to examine the notion. Found it good and right and tucked it away inside. Someday soon, she would be ready, though she could scarcely believe a man like Heath would want her for anything more than a pal. But he did. Every action seemed to court her, to woo her, to draw her to him.

She'd had little time to look through the items she'd found this afternoon, but now she could. She spread the handful of documents on her bed, driven by a bittersweet eagerness to sort through them. One at time she opened the envelopes, read the enclosures. Mostly they included the normal, everyday bills of living with several pieces of advertisement, as if someone, probably Darrell, had tossed random mail into the drawer for later perusal. A glossy brochure for scuba equipment and reef diving. Another for condos on the beach. Another for Buenos Aires. The latter made her frown. Darrell had never mentioned Buenos Aires.

"Meet Dias. Cavern 2. 8." She read aloud from a slip of paper stuck inside one of their honeymoon brochures.

Cassie frowned at the words, pulse tripping in her throat. The writing was Darrell's. But who was Dias? She put aside the note to rifle through the others in hopes of a clue. She came across a reminder to rent a boat at a certain place and another with directions to a dive shop. The latter notation soothed her. Dias was likely another scuba enthusiast Darrell wanted to connect with in Mexico. No big deal. Nothing nefarious. No need to tell Heath.

Or should she? Weren't these items more proof that her honeymoon was exactly as it should have been?

A little voice niggled at her brain. *What if they're something else?*

They weren't. That's all there was to it.

She should tell Heath. Show him.

The photos of crystal white sand and impossible blues of the Mexican seas gleamed under the overhead light like a beacon pointing the way.

For a long time, she sifted through the mementos, regretting without grief, mulling without resolution. Then, she slid them into a drawer beneath a stack of colorful scarves, and left them there.

"There you are, you lazy Fed. Where have you been?"

Heath had just ambled into the police station, past Verletta at the dispatch desk, past the administrative assistant who made both his and the chief's life easier, and into the cluttered office of his boss.

"It's six in the morning, Chief. I've been asleep for the last six hours." More like four, but who was counting? Last night, he'd been restless enough to clean his apartment and shoot a few emails to his brothers and mom. He'd even done some research on Mexican drug trafficking routes. Imagine that. The map he'd gotten from Cassie had rung a bell. He hadn't completely connected the dots to Darrell Chapman, but he had a good start now that he'd seen the map. "What's up?"

JoEtta shoved a cup of black coffee into his hands. "Had a call this morning. Some bigwig in another time zone without sense enough to look at the clock."

"Must have been a Fed," Heath drawled. Then he sipped the scalding brew, grimaced, and went back for another sip.

The chief smirked. "How did you know?"

He hoisted the coffee in a salute. She'd given him the mug with the "I see guilty people" logo. "Saw that dig coming. Who called?"

"Somebody trying to lure you away from Whisper Falls. Asked permission to contact you. As if my disapproval would stop him." She yanked another mug from the single shelf beneath the coffee cart.

"Why, Chief," he said, in the slowest Texas drawl he could muster. "I'm starting to think you like having my sorry federal agent hide hanging around."

She sniffed, shot him a narrow glare. "Don't break your arm patting yourself on the back. You're helpful at times. When you're not lollygagging over that hairstylist."

Heath's smile tightened. That hairdresser *was* taking a lot of his time. If not for the troubling matter of her late husband…"

"Well?" Chief demanded, a hand on her hip showing her typical impatience.

Heath flinched. He'd been thinking of Cassie again

and had lost the train of conversation. As cover, he took another sip of coffee. The chief could sear the hair off a bald eagle with this stuff. "Well, what?"

"Do you, or do you not, want to talk to that bigwig Fed?"

"No need."

"No? Not interested in hogging all the glory anymore?" The constant jabs at his former DEA status didn't bother Heath. The chief knew the truth. She'd bowed to his knowledge and asked for his take on situations a number of times. She respected who he was. Correction, who he'd been. The joking around was just the way they related.

"Citations for extreme bravery clutter up my walls. Fame and fortune fades." He gave her an ornery grin. "Besides, somebody's got to keep these backwoods police chiefs in line."

JoEtta guffawed, jostling coffee onto the floor. She rubbed at the splatters with her boot toe. "So, you like us here in Whisper Falls, do you?"

"Something like that." He did. That much was true. Yet he remained troubled by the vow to his father's memory, worried he wasn't doing enough. Small town life was sweet, but it didn't offer many opportunities to bag the really bad guys. All the more reason to push harder on the Carmichael case.

"Don't tell me you haven't thought about going back to the agency." Flexibility had been part of their deal, a six-month trial period for both parties.

"Oh, I've thought about it." He took a chair, studied his coffee. "There are...situations." And he wasn't sure if the situations kept him here or gave him reasons to leave.

Chief Farnsworth circled the desk and plopped down, equipment and chair rollers clanking. "Cassie Blackwell?"

Feeling the acid burn in his gut, Heath set the coffee atop a file cabinet. He'd never even come close to having an ulcer. No use starting now.

He drew in a slow breath and let it out every bit as slowly. "Yes. Cassie."

The chief tilted back in her chair, crafty eyes studying him for two beats. "She doesn't have anything to do with this drug business, Heath."

The chief never used his given name. It made him feel young, vulnerable. He much preferred her bluster.

"Maybe. I hope not. She seems like a nice girl." *Nice girl. Yeah. Sure. Congratulations, Monroe, you slid that one out as if Cassie was nothing more than an acquaintance on the street. As if you didn't have crazy thoughts about her. Talk about compromised.*

"But you'll keep digging."

"Have to." He turned to retrieve his coffee.

"Your daddy was a good cop, too."

The statement turned him around, frowning. Had they discussed his father?

"Mace Walters told me." Those shrewd eyes narrowed, seeing more than he liked to show.

"Mace talks too much." Mace. Old friend and easy reference. But no use getting riled. His father's career was public record. Anyone could do an internet search and find the information in a matter of minutes. Heath sipped at his coffee, hiding the turmoil that spewed to the surface at the mention of his father.

"I needed to know who I was hiring. A family of law

dogs, so to speak. Commendable. None of my brats followed in my renowned footsteps."

He could see that bothered her but knew better than to commiserate. She'd spit in his eye. He also knew she'd thrown in the latter intentionally, a way of showing him that she, too, had a cross to bear.

"Dad died in the line of duty, a drug raid gone bad."

Lips tight, she nodded. "A sorry shame, too. So you became a DEA agent."

"Somebody's got to do it." He gave up on the coffee and set the mug aside for good. "But today I'm satisfied to be Whisper Falls's assistant chief."

"Sure about that? You're seeing an awful lot of Cassie lately. What if the investigation into her husband goes south on you? How will you feel about Whisper Falls if that happens?"

"It already has gone south. All the way to Mexico."

But the chief already knew that, just as she knew he'd hired Holt to dig around across the border. "I could take over from here. Call in the city boys. Leave you out of the equation."

He was touched. In her inimitable manner, JoEtta was offering him a way out of the sticky situation.

"Too late, Chief. Cassie knows I started this investigation. Now, I have to finish it."

Chapter Twelve

A storm was brewing. Another of the Ozarks' magnificent displays of terrible beauty and supreme power. Like God, Cassie thought as she darted out the back door of the salon and through the fat splattering drops of rain. Laughing, she leaped through the SUV door held open by Heath Monroe.

The inside of his vehicle was redolent of Drakkar Noir, the scent clips in his air conditioner. The fragrance, combined with rain, reminded her of the stormy night they'd met.

"You should try out for the Olympics. Great sprint." He grinned at her as she settled in, hooked her seat belt and pushed damp hair from her eyes.

"Yes, and in heels." She lifted a foot toward him. "First place in ninth-grade track. 50-meter dash."

"In those shoes? Impressive."

Cassie snorted a laugh. The crazy sense of humor was one of the things she liked most about Heath.

A stray lock of damp hair stuck to her cheek. Heath noticed and looped it behind her ear. With a wink, he said, "Missed one."

Cassie's belly jittered. A silly reaction, she thought, but the brush of his fingers against her cheek set off romantic fireworks inside of her. She was tempted to lean over the console and kiss him hello, right on that cute chin patch. Maybe even above. She refrained, of course. She didn't want him getting the wrong idea, although at this point in their relationship she couldn't say what that was. She liked him. He liked her. They enjoyed spending time together. Just as she had done with Rusty. No, not true. Being with Heath was different, and she was wise enough to admit it.

"I'm not sure house hunting tonight is such a great idea," she said when the wayward thoughts subsided. "Tracking mud and rain into someone's rental won't make a great impression."

Considering, he sat with one arm over the steering wheel, his body shifted slightly toward her. She liked the way he could appear intense and relaxed at the same time. Focused, confident, but natural. As a special agent, she supposed he'd always been on guard.

"We can try another day," he said. "Are you still game for dinner or want me to take you back to your car?"

They'd met in the parking lot next to the salon. No point in going home only to have Heath drive all the way out to the ranch.

"And give up chili dogs and cheese fries? No way!"

"Compromise, then. My weather app says we're in for a nasty night. Let's skip house hunting and go straight for the junk food."

"I love the way you think." Oh, yes. She could love a lot of things about Heath Monroe.

"It's the training." He tapped his temple. "Astute mind. Keen senses. Always ready."

"For chili dogs?"

"Always."

They both laughed, and Cassie leaned back against the plush leather and relaxed. Today had been trying at the shop. A customer wasn't happy with a color and demanded a free redo, though both Cassie and Louise had warned her the new color wouldn't work with her skin. Then Michelle Jessup had come in and shot daggers and snide remarks toward Cassie, making the other customers uncomfortable. Then there was the matter of the mementos she hadn't mentioned to Heath.

Heath's tires splashed through puddles on the way to Johnson's Drive-In, the only fast-food joint in Whisper Falls. At least at the moment. Miss Evelyn was making noises about letting in a burger franchise, though many of the town's businesspeople, Cassie included, wanted to keep Whisper Falls more personal with local merchants only.

On the drive to Johnson's, Cassie talked nonstop about the day's events, especially the irritation with a jealous Michelle—which made Heath laugh, the rat. When she finally ran dry, she pried into his workday.

"Slow," was all he said. He was about as forthcoming as her brother.

Exasperated, she said, "You had to do something besides sit around and look cute."

"Except for the fender benders, rain keeps everyone pretty low-key." He pulled under the awning at Johnson's and left the motor running as he shifted in her direction. "Was that a compliment?"

She just smiled. Of course she thought he was cute.

Gorgeous was a better word. She wasn't blind. "Order the chili dogs before I starve."

He rolled down his window, pushed the button and in minutes a carhop delivered chili-scented paper bags. When the girl left, Heath asked, "Eat here or my place?"

"Are you going to show me your etchings?"

"I would if I knew what they were, but since I don't, how about if we kick back and watch something exciting? Like the weather."

"You're a wild man." Her stomach growled, making them both snicker. "Let's go before I pass out."

"I know CPR." His tone and expression were deadpan, but she saw the twinkle in those emerald eyes.

She gave him a mock glare. "Drive, Monroe, drive."

With rain drowning the windshield and warm, moist heat fogging the glass, Heath drove the few blocks through a quiet residential area to his apartment.

Like two escapees from Looney Tunes, they dashed from the car to the house, laughing through the downpour. Cassie squealed more than laughed. The rain was cold!

Dancing on one foot and then the other, she waited in the rain while Heath fumbled with the key and unlocked the door. She rushed inside and stopped on a furry brown rug. "I'll drip on your carpet."

"Let me get you a towel. Hang on."

While he was gone, she slipped off her shoes and looked around. An efficiency apartment, the living room bled into the dining-kitchen. Apparently a bed and bath was off to the left, though from here she couldn't see anything except a doorway. The small living space was tidy other than the scatter of mail on the coffee table and a shirt hanging over the back of an ordinary brown recliner.

She trailed her fingers over the shirt. He'd worn this one yesterday. An olive-green that accented his eyes and darkened his thick eyelashes.

"I haven't had a chance to do much to the place," Heath said as he returned and handed her a fluffy towel.

Cassie stepped away from the chair, hoping he hadn't seen her touching his shirt. What was wrong with her to do such a thing? Oh, but she knew. She was almost certain she knew.

The truth was, she was making excuses to be with him. Any excuse. House hunting, the weather, chili dogs, whatever it took. With Heath, her world brightened and centered. She hadn't felt centered in a long time. Maybe never. It was scary, too, to contemplate letting her heart go again, but she was afraid it might be too late to stop.

Yet his investigation of Darrell was like a sticker in the sole of her foot, and one she couldn't remove. Heath was an honorable man with a job to do. She couldn't ask less of him than to do his best. But her heart was caught somewhere in the middle.

"Thanks." She blotted her face and arms and dabbed at her skirt and hair. "I'm damp but not too drippy." She shivered.

"Are you cold? I could lend you a shirt."

That was way too tempting. "I'm good. Thanks. Did the chili dogs survive the mad dash?"

"Only one way to find out." He grabbed the brown bag and headed toward the table, a round, black pedestal style with two lattice-backed chairs, small and cozy. "Do we need plates?"

"Nope. I believe in avoiding dishwashing if at all possible." She opened his cabinets as if she belonged there and found two glasses. "Water?"

"Cokes in the fridge if you want one. Or if you're cold, I can make coffee."

"Water's fine with me. Maybe coffee later."

"Great. Let's chow."

He pulled out a chair and waited until she was seated. Did he have any idea how endearing that was? Of course he did. Heath Monroe was no dummy. He knew how to please a woman, and it pleased her to know he wanted to.

"I like the way you do that. Your mama taught you very nice manners."

"My dad was a gentleman. I remember that much clearly." He took the chair opposite her, making barely a scrape as he scooted in. "Mom insisted we boys follow his example."

She slid the hot dog boat from the waxy wrapper and leaned down for a whiff of spice. "Man, I love that smell."

"Taste is even better." He chomped a bite of his. She watched him, liked the way he chewed with complete masculine abandon.

"Tell me more about your dad. He sounds like a great guy."

"He was. The best dad, the best cop."

"You were how old?"

"Twelve."

"You probably have a lot of good memories."

"Yeah. Never enough, of course. My brothers were younger than me, eight and ten, so their memories are fewer. I'm sorry about that. Dad was an amazing man.

Mom says I remember him bigger than life. She's probably right."

"Tell me something you remember about him."

"You don't want to get me talking about Dad. I could go on all night."

"Yes, I do. Please."

He set his chili dog on the table and pinched up a fry, pointing it at her. "Picture this. Houston in August, over a hundred degrees and so humid the air felt like soup. Dad came home from work. He had to be tired, but he'd bought us boys a Slip 'n Slide. Remember those?"

She nodded, but said nothing, letting him talk, enjoying the manly rumble of his voice, the easy drawl of south Texas.

"Instead of leaving us boys to play by ourselves, he played with us. He even sweet-talked Mom into playing, too. There we were, all five of us, screaming, laughing, soaking wet. Muddy and grassy, too, because we could never manage to stay on the slide." A smile tipped the corners of his mouth. "We played until dark that night."

Cassie smiled a little, too, touched that such a simple event lingered in his mind. Love and time and family all rolled together had that power. "It's a good memory."

"I don't know why that stands out, other than the fact that Dad was my hero." He scarfed another bite of chili dog, his eyes happy as he chewed and swallowed. "I saw him save a boy's life one spring. I must have been about ten at the time. Houston's prone to floods—you probably know that—and it had rained for days. The storm drains ran full and rapid the way they do after a big rain. A neighbor kid and I were playing, goofing off, being dumb, when he decided to take a swim in the flooded ditch."

"Oh, no."

"Yeah. One minute he was standing on the bank and the next he was gone. The current whipped him downstream that fast. I ran home to Dad, scared witless. I'll never forget his reaction. He went to one knee, grabbed me by the shoulder. Like this." His spread fingers pinched his left shoulder. "My legs were shaking, but all of a sudden I knew everything would be all right. Dad would take care of it." Heath dropped his hand to the table. "He told Mom to call 911. Then he grabbed a rope from the garage and ran."

"You followed him?"

"I had to. Bret was my pal. I felt responsible."

Responsible. She could see that. The boy had followed the man to adulthood. "How did your dad get him out?"

"He jumped in." Heath shook his head. "Every bit of training warns against it, but he couldn't reach Bret, not even with a long limb."

"That was incredibly brave."

"That was my dad. He tied the rope around his waist and had me tie the other end to the closest tree, a skinny thing I was afraid would snap under the strain. I think that's the first time in my life I prayed out loud."

"Was the kid okay?"

"Yes. Thank God. By the time rescue arrived, Dad had him out of the ditch." He huffed softly. "Bret never wanted to play in water much after that."

"Your dad saved his life."

"I'd always thought of my father as a hero, but that day, everyone in the neighborhood recognized it, too."

"If the situation arose, you'd do the same thing."

He twitched one shoulder. "I like to think I would."

He would. She knew it as surely as she knew this chili dog was spicy and warm. She took another bite, savoring the thick chili and the cheesy fries. Heath quickly dispatched his food and reached for one of her French fries.

"You steal my fries, you'll owe me."

He snatched the potato and popped it into his mouth. "Name your price."

"Oooh, that's a dangerous offer, Mr. Assistant Chief." She nibbled the end of a fry, pretending to contemplate. "Let's see. I could ask for the Taj Mahal. Or the crown jewels of Britain. But instead, I think you should make dessert." She popped in the fry.

"You think I can't cook."

"It might have crossed my mind."

"Then you, Miss Hair Salon Entrepreneur, would be wrong. I make great brownies."

"Now it's my turn to be impressed. A man who can cook."

"I bought a mix." When she lifted an eyebrow, he shrugged. "I like brownies. Mom showed me how to fancy them up. They're awesome."

Cassie shoved the remaining bite of chili dog into her mouth and rose from the table. "Come on, then, show me your stuff."

The next ten minutes were pure fun. While rain pattered against the roof, inside the cozy apartment Cassie and Heath made brownies. They bumped hips, snitched dabs of batter with their fingers and flirted outrageously. Cassie couldn't remember anything being as much fun in a long while. Which told how pitiful her frozen life had been.

"Chocolate chips? That's the secret?" she asked,

snitching one to sample, when he dumped a quarter cupful into the batter.

"One of the secrets. More to come after they're baked."

Cassie watched in fascination—and more than a little attraction—as the strong cop whipped up the brownies and stuck them in the oven. Once the timer was set, Heath grabbed the partial bag of chocolate chips and led the way into the living room.

"Man, listen to that rain." The spring and early summer had been turbulent and didn't appear to be letting up.

"The rain doesn't worry me. Listen to that thunder." Heath fished out his cell phone and studied the screen. "Severe thunderstorm."

"Are we under a tornado watch?"

Cassie crossed to the window and opened the drapes. With the living room light behind her, she could see little more than the silvery puddles beneath the street lamp. She reached for the switch and turned off the overhead, plunging the living room into shadows and highlighting the storm outside.

"Doesn't look that way." He moved next to her so that they were both peering outside, faces close to the pane. Their breath made circular fog on the chilled window.

"I guess I'm weird, but I like thunderstorms if there's no threat of tornadoes," Cassie said.

"Yeah?" He swiveled his head toward her. "Me, too."

Thunder rattled the windows. Cassie jumped.

Heath's hand touched her waist, steadied her. "Easy."

Before she could think up a reason why she shouldn't, Cassie leaned into him, let her head rest against his shoulder. He responded by pulling her against his chest, her back to his front, cuddling her, his arms draped loosely around her waist, his breath soft in her ear.

"You smell good," he said. "This is nice."

Nice didn't begin to cover the tide of emotion. Though a storm raged outside and the trees whipped and swayed, Cassie felt safe and secure in the cradle of Heath's arms.

"I smell brownies," she said, mostly to calm her raging pulse.

He nuzzled the back of her neck and gave a small laugh. "A man's dream scents. Pretty woman and brownies."

She shivered. Goose bumps formed. She liked the tickle of his whiskers against her skin. "Don't forget chili dogs and pizza."

"Hmm. Those, too." He nibbled her earlobe. "Delicious."

Cassie closed her eyes, enjoying the moment. He rocked her side to side, his chin atop her head. In silence, they watched the storm and snuggled. No more, no less, but altogether romantic.

Pea-size hail pinged the grass, bounced off the driveway. Thunder rolled and echoed like kettle drums in a long, wide canyon.

"Someday let's watch a storm from above Whisper Falls," he said.

"I'd love that. Someday." The word tormented her. Would there be a someday with Heath Monroe? Did she want there to be? The answer was yes and it scared her. With Darrell, falling in love had been easy and uncomplicated. Not with Heath.

He sighed, a heavy gust that let her know he was

thinking heavy thoughts. His heartbeat, strong against her back, increased.

"What are you thinking about?"

"You," he said.

She didn't know where to go with that so she remained quiet, but her heartbeat also responded, thumping harder against her ribs.

His lips touched the hair above her ear. In a soft murmur, a whisper really, he said, "Something good is happening between us, Cassie. Do you feel it, too?"

She nodded, tightened her fingers against his. "Yes."

She felt it, but was it the right thing for either of them?

"Good," he said, "because I don't play games. You may as well know. I'm falling in love with you."

More powerful than nature's storm, the words shook her, thrilled her, sent her soaring. Hadn't they been moving toward this moment for weeks? Every time they were together, they'd gotten closer.

But he was Darrell's accuser. How could she let herself love him?

Yet she did. The strength of that emotion, growing deeper every day, rocked her world, thawed a frozen heart, filled the empty places within.

"Oh, Heath," she managed with a troubled sigh.

He must have recognized the confusion in the sound, for he slowly turned her body until they were facing. There, in the pale shadows, he cupped her face. "What is it? I moved too fast? You don't feel the same?"

A surprising clot of tears thickened her throat. "But I do."

"You do?"

Torn between wanting to throw her arms around

him and the truth of who he was and what he believed, Cassie nodded.

He gathered her up close, his gorgeous face relieved and pleased. "I thought you were going to show me the door."

"Can't," she whispered, flirting. "It's your house."

"True." He bent his head and kissed her.

Thunder rumbled. Lightning flashed. A storm raged, both outside and in.

She was falling in love with the man who thought her late husband was a criminal. Even as she reveled in his embrace, Cassie's head whirled with guilt.

What about his investigation? What about the papers she was afraid to show him? How would they ever move forward with this between them?

Chapter Thirteen

It was after midnight when the storm subsided and conditions were safe enough for Cassie to go home. Heath followed her halfway, just to be sure she was okay and because he wasn't quite ready to let her go. They stopped on a country road, and he kissed her in the rain. They both chuckled as water dripped down their faces and into their mouths. She tasted cool as the rain, warm as the brownies they'd shared, and Heath had never experienced a more romantic moment. He loved her. He *loved* her. He couldn't quite take in the revelation, something he'd never expected to happen, something he'd never wanted.

But now he did.

Tonight had been special. He'd not intended to say the words. Not yet. But they'd popped out like uncovered popcorn too full of fire and energy to keep them in. Blame the storm. Blame the night. Blame the chili dogs.

Man, he felt good.

Back at his apartment, Heath collapsed on the bed fully dressed and stacked his hands behind his head to assess the situation.

At his choice of words, he grinned into the darkness. *Assess the situation.* Even in love, he couldn't stop thinking like a special agent.

Cassie had liked his brownies with the melted chocolate chip and marshmallow topping. She'd even fed him a few gooey bites that forced him to touch his tongue to her skin. Bothered no small amount, he'd put a stop to that by nipping the end of her finger and making her laugh. Oh, he'd liked the feel of her fingers against his mouth. Too much. So he'd backed away to keep from reacting like a caveman.

He glanced at the clock. He really should get some sleep, but energy buzzed through him with the force of a hornet swarm.

Maybe they should have discussed the investigation into her late husband's ventures. And maybe he should have kept his emotions to himself until he'd cleared Cassie from suspicion—until he knew the truth about Darrell Chapman.

He tossed onto his side, tormented. He loved her. He believed her. But an experienced agent shouldn't. Not until the evidence cleared her.

Even if it did, and he prayed it would, how would she feel if he found her husband guilty?

Restless, his sweet evening spoiled by intruding thoughts, he took Dad's badge from the nightstand and held it while he prayed.

He'd done a lot of that lately. Praying—pleading— for a happy resolution to the case.

He must have fallen asleep because he woke to the sound of his cell phone vibrating against the wooden nightstand. He rolled toward it, felt the jab of Dad's badge against his side.

"Hullo." He cleared his throat.

"Hey, big brother. Were you asleep?"

Heath growled low in his throat. "Jerk."

The reaction delighted Holt. "Wake up. It's nearly 4:00 a.m., you sluggard."

Heath scrubbed a hand over his face, groggy and not a little grumpy. "You pull the wings off butterflies, too, don't you?"

"Stop grousing. I have an update for you on that Mexico drug operation."

Heath came fully awake, dropped his feet to the floor and clicked on the lamp. "Let me find a pen. I want notes."

"Too rum-dum to remember?"

Heath didn't bother to answer. His brother had a predilection for very early mornings and took mischievous delight in tormenting those who didn't. Heath put the phone down while he yanked open the small drawer in the bedside table and rummaged around, coming out with pad and pencil.

"All right," he said. "Whatcha got?"

"Enough, and more on the way, I hope. I'm still poking around but this should get your juices running. Louis Carmichael was a small-time dealer who wanted to play with the big dogs. He'd made two trips to Mexico by himself the year before sending Darrell."

"So Darrell was his mule." Heath's heart sank. Instinct had warned him. He'd hoped it was wrong.

"Looks that way. I have some other feelers out, some people I'm trying to find, but everything points in that direction."

"What about Carmichael? Any news on where he's hiding?"

"None. No sign of him here in this part of Mexico. Chances are he's in the States, laying low."

"Or dead like his cousin."

"A distinct possibility. If the two cousins decided to play games with the cartel, they were bound to lose."

"If he's alive, we need to find him. I want to know what he knows."

"I'm on it, Heath. Got some people digging in the human garbage dumps. We'll find him."

"Anything on Darrell's death? Was it an accident?"

"I have it from a pretty good informant that it was a takeout. And I ain't talking about Chinese food."

"Man." Heath grabbed the top of his hair and squeezed. "Then the honeymoon was a setup, an intentional trip to traffic drugs?"

"According to this same informant—who wasn't cheap, by the way—people are terrified of the cartel down here. Darrell was supposed to meet with a guy named Alejandro to make a money transfer. Nobody seems to know if that meeting occurred or not."

"But our boy Darrell turns up dead on the beach."

"Yes. Still in scuba gear."

"Why didn't they dump him at sea?"

"That would rouse too many questions, bro. If a scuba diving tourist has an accident, that's easy to explain. The official police report claims he dived too deep, got narced on nitrogen, drowned high and happy and washed ashore with the tide."

"Rapture of the deep." Heath understood the diving term. Nitrogen narcosis from diving too deep too fast could cause a diver to act irrationally, even to become intoxicated to the point he removed his regulator and drowned. "I don't believe it. Someone yanked his regulator or held him under."

"Most likely. But the other makes a great story to tell the grieving widow and the good old U.S. of A."

A deep groan escaped Heath at the mention of Darrell's widow. How would he tell her that Darrell was likely murdered in a drug deal gone bad? A drug deal her husband was directly involved in?

"Any indication that the widow was involved?" He held his breath and prayed.

"None. Can't completely rule her out, but the informant was surprised to hear she was in Mexico. Didn't know Darrell was married. Another says he didn't want her to know about the drug operation. If Chapman used the honeymoon as a cover—and I think he did—your girl Cassie was almost certainly an innocent victim."

Relief shifted through Heath. Cassie was innocent. Thank God. At least this was positive news.

"You still have the hots for her?"

Heath let a beat go by. Hots? He wished it was that simple. Hots went away with distance and time. What he felt for Cassie wouldn't go anywhere. "I'm falling for her, Holt."

"No way. Hard-hearted Heath falling in love? The straight arrow agent losing his heart to a suspect?"

"Knock it off."

Another hum of silence before Holt spoke again. This time his tone was understanding. "This is serious, isn't it?"

"Yeah. I think so."

"About time."

"You don't get it, do you, Holt? I'm about to implicate her husband in the international drug trade. Do you think she's going to throw herself into my arms and declare undying love when she hears that news?"

"I hear you. Sorry, bro." The brotherly commiseration helped a little. "What are you going to do?"

"What I have to do." What he always did. He grappled for Dad's badge and ran his fingers over the raised words. "My job."

After sharing with Holt the data he'd found on the map, Heath pushed the end button and headed for the shower and the longest workday in recent memory.

All day, Heath was in the worst mood of his life and pretty much everyone in his wake knew it, particularly the two juvies he'd caught destroying public property. Grimly, he figured they'd never do that again.

Cassie had phoned at noon, asking to meet at Evie's for lunch but he'd used work as an excuse. He wasn't ready to face her, especially in a public place. As much as he hoped Holt could come up with more information, the evidence was already strong enough to turn over to his pals in the DEA.

By seven o'clock his excuses were gone. He got in the Expedition and pointed it toward Whisper Falls and the Blackwell Ranch.

Cassie touched her bare toe to the porch and set the swing in motion. The cool wood felt good against her feet, achy after a day of standing in heels. Austin called her crazy for wearing them but trendy shoes made her happy, confident. Foot cramps were a small price to pay.

With crochet in hand, she listened to the domestic sounds inside the house. Austin banging pans in the kitchen as he helped with the dishes. Annalisa's happy voice sharing every moment of baby Levi's day as if he was the only baby who'd ever spit up half his milk or wet a diaper.

The sweetness of it brought a prickle of tears. Cassie dashed at them with her crochet—a stocking cap, one of many she'd agreed to make for the church's Siberian orphan project. Funny how she disliked cooking or cleaning but crochet was fun. Cooking had been fun, too. With Heath.

Hoss and Jet, Austin's ranch dogs, ambled up from somewhere, grinning. "What have you two been up to? You look guilty."

The dogs flopped at her feet so that with every swing, her toes grazed Jet's back. The graying black Lab groaned with pleasure at the contact.

Beyond the ranch, beyond the brilliant green pasture land dotted with black cows, the ancient mountains formed a purple fortress. Evening sun splintered through the trees, cast patches of gold against the green grass on the yard. Along the porch edge, a black-and-yellow bumblebee buzzed sentinel above a purple coneflower. Last night's storm had washed the air, leaving it sweet and piercing.

Last night. She sighed.

Last night with Heath had been beautiful. She'd never expected to feel this way again, to have hope for the future with such a fine man. Not that their relationship had gone that far, but he loved her. Hands resting on the soft black yarn, she closed her eyes, reveled in the feeling of being loved and let it fill her.

For better or worse, she should have trusted him with the papers she'd found at the trailer. For better or worse. Like the marriage vows she'd taken with Darrell.

Tomorrow. She'd take the papers into town tomorrow.

Satisfied with the decision, she picked up the needle and yarn and began to chain stitch. Both dogs lifted their heads and looked toward the road, a sign that company was coming.

When a big black SUV turned into the drive and headed her way, Hoss and Jet ambled off the porch, tails fanning the air. Happiness swamped Cassie. If she'd had a tail she would have wagged it, too.

Heath.

She put the yarn aside and tripped barefoot across the soft grass to greet him, smiling broadly as she went. As Heath stepped out of the Expedition, she tiptoed up and kissed him. For brief seconds, his hands came up to grip her arms and he held her to him. Then he stepped back and removed his sunglasses.

Cassie's welcoming glow slipped away. "Something's wrong."

He hooked his sunglasses in the neck of his shirt. "We need to talk. Alone. Can we walk?"

A warning bell went off in her head. The last time they'd walked the ranch, he'd accused Darrell of dealing drugs. "Is this about Darrell?"

His shoulders—those broad, strong, responsible shoulders—sagged. "Yes."

He didn't want to tell her but he would. As much as she wanted him to let it go, forget his suspicions, law enforcement was too deeply ingrained in his nature. "Let me get my shoes and tell Austin where I'm going."

She hurried into the house and when she returned, Heath leaned against the front of his vehicle, staring into the woods, jaw hard as the mountains. He'd replaced his sunglasses.

He pushed off the truck and fell into step with Cassie

and the two dogs, saying nothing. Cassie's heart rose into her throat, thudded frantically there. She didn't want to have this conversation. Not after last night. Not now. Now that she loved him.

She reached out to the side, slid her hand into his, heard his slow exhale.

The dogs darted into the woods, noses down. Cassie and Heath walked a hundred yards before either spoke again.

"You may as well get it over with," she said. "What did you learn?"

"I never wanted to hurt you. I hope you believe that. I wanted to be wrong."

The sunny day dimmed, her heart chilled. "What are you saying?" She could see he struggled with whatever was on his mind, dreaded her reaction, and Lord help her, she couldn't promise him anything. "Tell me."

He looked off through the valley gouged deep by an ancient glacier. "I'm sorry, Cassie. I wish I didn't have to tell you this, but Darrell smuggled drugs and money in and out of Mexico for his cousin Louis. We don't know yet how long they'd been working together. At least three trips. Likely more."

She loosened her grip on his fingers, pulled away. "You're wrong. I told you that before. Maybe Louis did those things but not Darrell."

"There are witnesses, Cass, and evidence. That map you found with the notes and circles? Places he'd been? Most are common trafficking routes and the others are hot spots of drug use. We're checking them out, but I'm confident we'll discover either Darrell or Louis made drops and pickups at each of those destinations. Or planned to."

She was already shaking her head. "Those were places he'd scuba dived. He told me about them. Showed me pictures."

"I'd like to see those pictures if you don't mind."

"What if I do mind?" Her heart hammered in her throat as she thought of the documents in her bedroom. She'd wanted to believe they were innocent just as she'd wanted to believe Darrell was innocent.

Heath stopped in the trail near a lush tangle of blackberry vines and Indian Paintbrush. His expression looked as bereft as she felt. With hands out toward her, he said, "Don't do this, Cassie. Don't make this harder. The evidence is clear. He used diving as a cover for his business."

Her stomach rolled, cramped. She folded her arms over her middle. "Always?"

Heath's gaze skittered away. "We don't know."

He was holding something back, but she was afraid to ask, afraid she didn't want to know. She'd been so sure Darrell was innocent. She'd trusted him. But she trusted Heath, too.

"You keep saying we. Who is we? You and Chief Farnsworth? Your friends in the DEA? Who are you getting this information from?"

"My brother, Holt, at the moment. I told you about him. He's a private investigator. A good one. He went down to Mexico."

Her gaze flew up to his, disbelieving. "At your request?"

"Yes. At my request."

He claimed to love her, but he'd sent someone to Mexico to destroy her memories. To break her heart.

"He found proof?"

"Witnesses. Strong evidence." He took both her hands and oh, how she wanted to erase this moment and return to last night. "Holt's work is solid, Cassie. He's not wrong about this. He has a few names and addresses, meeting places. And he's confident there's more to discover."

She tugged her hands away, crossed her arms over her chest and held on tightly lest she fly into a million pieces. She had names and places, too. Now she realized what they meant. Her husband had been a criminal.

"The lipstick lid I found," she started, suddenly too aware of how important every detail had become.

"No drug residue, if that's what you're asking, though I thought there might be."

"Drug dealers use women's cosmetics to smuggle drugs?"

"They use anything they think will work."

Anything? She steeled herself against the thought pushing at the back of her brain. As much as it hurt, she had to know. "Our honeymoon?"

Heath went still, wary. "What about it?"

"You know what I'm asking." The truth would make you free. Wasn't that what Heath liked to say? And what the Bible promised? Then why did she feel as if her world was falling apart? As if last night's storm had ripped away her shelter and destroyed her.

"Tell me, Heath."

He glanced away and then back to her, arms limp at his sides. She saw compassion in his expression and knew the answer before he spoke.

"A reliable informant claims Darrell was smuggling money on that trip. He apparently tried a double cross.

We're unclear on the exact details, but the cartel frowns on that kind of thing. I'm really sorry, Cassie."

"They killed him?" Her voice trembled. She could barely whisper the words.

"We're almost certain."

Cassie closed her eyes against the regret in his, against the sharp pain that stabbed through the center of her soul. Her stomach cramped like a virus.

Oh, Darrell. I loved you. I believed in you. In us.

But Darrell had lied to her. Her marriage had been a sham, a cover for drug trafficking.

Grief and shame flooded her. She'd been a fool, a needy, lonely woman caught up in a whirlwind romance by a handsome, smiling drug dealer who'd used her to cover his crime. Had he ever loved her at all? Or had their quick marriage been more about his need to cover a crime than about his love for her?

When she opened her eyes Heath had stepped closer, his expression worried. She wanted to accuse him of lying, but why would he? Heath had no agenda other than truth. A truth he'd do anything to learn.

If she hadn't been reeling, wounded, devastated, she would have pitied him. "Coming out here to tell me couldn't have been easy."

"No."

Last night he'd claimed to love her. And she loved him. Even now, with her past shattered at her feet like the storm-damaged trailer, she yearned toward Heath, wanted him to hold her as he'd done last night, to comfort her.

"Could I ask you one more thing?"

"What's that?"

"Was our relationship—you and me—" She started

and stopped, floundering for the words, wanting reassurance while fearing the worst, her mouth dry as bleached bone. "Were you only with me because of this investigation? Is that why you asked me out?"

"No!" He spun away, spun back, face desolate. "At first."

"I see." The ache rose into her temples, pounding there with cruel efficiency. Two men she'd love. Two men had used her for their own means. Maybe she was the kind of woman no man could ever truly love.

"Cassie," he said. "It's not like you think. Let me explain."

"You lied to me."

"I didn't." He reached for her. "I was doing my job."

At what cost?

Palms pushed out, she resisted, shaking her head, frantic she'd burst into tears if he touched her. She bit down on the inside of her lip, holding on to her control. "Well, there you go, then. You've done your job. Now I think you should leave."

His arms fell to his sides, jade eyes searching hers. "Let me walk you back to the house."

"I'll be fine." She'd hurt and survived before. She could do it again. Oh, but this was different. This pain—double betrayal from the men she'd loved—ripped like a saw blade.

"I don't want to leave you—"

You already have. "Go, Heath. Please, do me that courtesy."

"We have to talk. I'll call you—"

"No. I need to be alone. I need time." Two lifetimes at least.

He fisted both hands on his hips, nostrils flaring.

Emotion swam in his eyes. Confusion, anger, sorrow. "Is this what you want? The way you want it to end?"

Her head jerked up. "Nothing is the way I want, Heath. It simply is."

Before she could make a more complete fool of herself, Cassie turned her back, called her dogs and sprinted up Blackberry Mountain, leaving Heath Monroe behind.

Chapter Fourteen

For a solid week, Heath, aching and angry, used every spare moment to research the case of Darrell Chapman and Louis Carmichael, praying, hoping, dreaming that he'd find something better to share with Cassie. He'd broken her heart, watched her crumble before his very eyes and then walk away from their budding love.

She'd hated him for the truth. But he'd had no choice. Truth was truth.

Then why did he ache and yearn? Why did he lie awake at night longing for a way to make things right with her again?

Some part of him hoped to clear Darrell and play the hero, bringing Cassie good news instead of bad. Instead, the more he learned, the more convinced he became that two small-time operators had gotten in over their heads. If he could only find Carmichael for questioning, he'd be happy.

No, that wasn't true. He wouldn't be happy. He'd devastated the woman he loved and that was a hard pill to swallow. She'd broken him, too, the moment she'd turned her back and left him. He loved her. Wasn't that enough? But he knew the answer and it stung like a burn. She'd loved Darrell's memory more than a future with the agent who'd discovered the truth.

Still, he couldn't let go. He'd called her every day, not knowing what he'd say but needing to hear her voice. She refused to answer. Twice he'd seen her. In a small town like Whisper Falls, running into each other was inevitable, but she'd ignored him. Turned and walked the other way as if he was invisible.

There was no denying how much that hurt.

But his father's death had taught him that the price of justice was sometimes high.

As he turned the corner of Oak and Fairdale near the park, he spotted a car with a missing taillight and executed a traffic stop. He still felt strange performing routine police work such as this, but he pulled to the curb behind the car and scanned the Ford's interior before stepping out of his vehicle. Thinking tactically had saved his life on more than one occasion.

Fortunately, today he was in no danger. The taillight belonged to Haley Carter, Cassie's artist friend.

Allowing a smile, Heath approached the window Haley had rolled down. "Morning, Haley. Did you know you have a taillight out?"

The pretty auburn-haired woman turned her head toward the back as if she could see her fender. "Do I?"

"Yes, ma'am."

She screwed up her face in a grimace. "Does that mean I'm getting a ticket?"

"No ticket. Just get the light fixed. Wouldn't want an accident with that cutie in the back." He bent low to look in at Haley's little girl. "Somebody's catching a nap."

Haley laughed, a wind chime sound. "Anytime she's fussy, I take her for a ride."

"And that puts her out like a light?" The little one's head was flopped to one side, her bow mouth lax, long lashes stroking her pink cheeks.

"Every single time. Just wait. When you have kids, you'll do the same thing."

When he had kids. Like that was going to happen.

"Yeah," he said, but his heart wasn't in it.

"Listen," Haley said, squinting up into the sun. "I've been meaning to ask Cassie, but since you stopped me, I'll ask you. Creed and I would love it if you two would drop by for a visit sometime. We could have a cookout."

Heath was thankful for sunglasses.

"Appreciate the invitation." Not going to happen but it was nice of her to ask. He tapped the top of the car with the flat of his palm. "You get that taillight fixed today. Okay?"

"Promise. I'll run out to the heliport right now and have Creed do it."

"Sounds like a plan. You have a good day now."

"Don't forget to ask Cassie," she said right before her window closed.

Heath watched her pull away and then headed back to his truck, stomach churning. Friends considered Cassie and him a couple. So had he. But given his line of work, perhaps this way was better.

The fact that she didn't want to see him made sense. By doing his job, he'd hurt her and he hated that. He'd shattered her illusions about Darrell. He'd destroyed her fantasy of their perfect love, but knowing why she hated him didn't make it any easier to let her go. They were just beginning. Now they were done.

His radio crackled and he answered. "Monroe."

"Heath, Pudge has a problem down at the bait shop. A couple of rowdies trying to fight." There was nothing stiff or fancy about Whisper Falls dispatching. She simply stated what needed to be done.

"I'll head over there now."

"Oh, and Heath? That DEA guy called again. Says he wants to sweeten the pot, whatever that means."

"Got it. Thanks, Verletta."

In less than three minutes, Heath was inside the fishy-smelling bait shop and in five more, two men, both drunk, were handcuffed and in the backseat of his SUV. After booking them into the jail to sleep it off, he headed into his office to do the paperwork and make that call.

"Agent Jefferson. Heath Monroe."

"Monroe, good to hear from you." Heath's old boss had a voice straight off the streets of Philly where he'd grown up. "You know why I'm calling. Are you ready to come back to work for us yet?"

Heath rubbed at the whisker patch on his chin, contemplating. The timing was perfect. Maybe the phone call was God's way of nudging him along. "I've been thinking about it. What do you have in mind?"

The line buzz said he'd surprised Jefferson with the easy admission. But why not go back to a job he loved and was good at? Nothing for him here in Whisper Falls anymore.

"I've got a promotion with your name on it and a nice pay bump. I can also offer you a choice of location. How does that sound?"

"Sounds promising."

"Don't play with me, Monroe. Give it to me straight.

You're one of my best agents. You don't belong in a tiny place like Whisper Falls. You've too much expertise and we need you. They don't."

His old boss was only partly right. Fancy lot of good his expertise had done him in Whisper Falls. The only time he'd used it, it had cost him the only woman who'd ever made him think about forever.

Heath kicked back in his roller chair and surveyed the small office he shared with the part-timers. His jacket hung on a peg. A photo of his nephews and niece was propped on his desk and a colored picture Ashley sent him was thumb-tacked to the bulletin board. He'd started to settle in. "How soon do you need to know?"

"Today, tomorrow, next week. The sooner the better." Jefferson cleared his throat. "I'll start the paperwork." He chuckled. "You'll come back. It's in your blood."

After Heath rang off, he sat at his desk staring at a different kind of paperwork and thinking. Drug enforcement was his career, his life, his commitment to justice in memory of his father. As his former boss had reminded him, he was good at it.

He opened the photo gallery on his phone and scrolled through. Half the shots were of Cassie, of something they'd done, somewhere they'd been. Simple snapshots with her dogs, with baby Levi, with brownie batter on her nose.

A searing pain cut through him, hot and expanding inside his chest until he wondered if he'd erupt like a volcano. He loved her. But that was over. Her silence was signal enough, and belaboring the point would only hurt them both more.

He closed the app.

Whisper Falls was a fine town. He liked the people

and if he were ever to settle anywhere permanently, Whisper Falls could be the place.

He pulled Dad's badge from his pocket and placed it on the desk, a reminder of his vow, of his calling. The war on drugs needed him more than Whisper Falls.

Cassie heard the rumor from Michelle Jessup who'd delivered the news like a cat with a belly full of cream. Heath was leaving. She'd been so shocked at the news she'd spilled a bottle of shampoo in Mable Harmon's lap and all over the floor. Cleaning up had taken forever and Michelle had sauntered out of the salon as pleased as could be.

Cassie supposed she shouldn't be surprised that a man of Heath's background and training would grow bored with the slow, small-town pace. Still, some foolish, broken part of her yearned to see him. He didn't know, couldn't know that she watched the street for his black Expedition and ached each time he parked in front of Evie's Sweets and Eats. She was being ridiculous, all things considered. They were as over as last year's replacement TV shows.

"Earth to Cassie. Earth to Cassie. I'm busy over here." Louise raised a bottle of nail polish above the hands of a customer. "Answer that phone, please."

"Oh. Sorry." Cassie grabbed for the landline. "Tress and Tan Salon. Cassie speaking."

With the receiver cradled between her neck and shoulder, she went through the motions of handling the caller, though her heart wasn't in the conversation. Her heart wasn't in much of anything these days.

She hung up the phone and finished folding a load of clean-scented towels while Louise completed Betsy

Loggins's manicure. When the woman left and the shop was empty, Cassie's friend and partner stormed around her workstation.

"Want to talk about it? Or should I say him?"

"Nothing to talk about."

"Oh, please. Spare me. Think I don't know the signs? You've been distracted and quiet for a week. Heath doesn't come around anymore. You don't dance out the door to meet him at five every evening. You're not—" she threw her hands out to the sides "—sparkling."

"We broke it off." Cassie concentrated on making a perfect square of the hand towel.

"So what? Don't let a little spat and your silly pride stand in the way. Kiss and make up. You love him."

"Just leave it alone, Louise." Cassie turned away to put the stack of towels on a shelf. "I know you mean well, but Heath and I can't work out. He's leaving."

Louise marched around in front of her. "Who said?"

One hand trailing the terry towels, Cassie admitted, "Michelle popped in with the news this morning. You were over at Evie's chowing on cherry Danish."

"Michelle wants him. She lied to throw you off the scent. You should ask him yourself."

"Maybe I will." And maybe she was looking for another lame excuse to talk to him. Was she so pathetic that a man could betray her and she still wanted him? Her head was tangled with crazy thoughts and uncertainties. She didn't know anything anymore. "I think I'll take an early lunch. Carly canceled."

Louise slumped into a pitiful expression and whined, "Again? Her nails, too?"

"Sorry."

Louise rolled her kohl-rimmed eyes. "Nothing like waiting until the last minute."

"She always does." Grabbing her wallet, Cassie exited the shop and walked across to Evie's shop, eager to avoid more discussion of Heath Monroe. If he left town, she could forget him, and maybe he'd take his evidence and accusations with him and no one would ever know what a fool Cassie Blackwell had been.

Inside Evie's Sweets and Eats, she strode to the counter, pointy heels tip-tapping, to order a chicken salad wrap and baked chips. The place was busy, the few tables crammed with customers, so she had to wait. Normally, she'd use the time for conversation with other businesspeople and friends who frequented Evie's, but today she didn't feel like talking to anyone.

When her food came, she took the items and turned to leave, thinking a walk in the park might do her good. Before she reached the door, the knob turned and Heath stepped inside.

Heath looked up, saw Cassie standing inside the door and felt his world stop. He slowly removed his sunglasses, drinking her in like a man in a long drought. When he reached her eyes, his chest contracted. Escape was written all over her face.

Hurt, wary, unsmiling, he said, "Cassie."

"Heath."

She looked good. Beautiful.

As if they were both on freeze frame neither moved. Heath's pulse bounced against his collar.

"How are you?" he asked and then softer, "Are you okay?"

"I'm fine. Thank you." So stiff and formal, as if he'd

never said "I love you." As if he hadn't held her and kissed her. "Yourself?"

He leaned closer, touched her elbow. "I tried to call you."

She edged her arm away, clenched it to her side. "I've been busy."

Too busy to care? Too busy to listen, to understand that he'd meant her no harm, but he'd had to do his job?

"I heard you might be leaving Whisper Falls."

His mouth went grim. A man had no privacy in this town. A decision not yet made and already the rumor mill had him gone. "Word gets around fast."

"So it's true?"

"I'm considering." *Unless you want me to stay.*

"Is it your old job? The DEA?"

"My boss called me again this morning."

"He must want you back badly."

He'd told her about the other calls but this one was different. "He offered a promotion, choice of locations, more money." Though Heath had never been about the money.

"Where will you go?"

"Wherever I choose." He told her the options, the job description, made the opportunity sound impressive mostly to convince himself that he wanted to travel again. But not to Mexico. Never again to Mexico.

When he finished the explanation, she beamed a bright smile that should have warmed him but left him cold instead. "You'll take it, then, and you'll be the best. The job sounds perfect for you."

"I suppose." *Will you miss me? Will you be sad I'm gone or will you sweep us away like castaway curls from your salon floor?*

His radio crackled. He wanted to rip the device from his belt and throw it out the door. "Excuse me while I check this call."

"I need to get back to the shop. Good luck on the new job."

"Cassie," he started and then didn't know what to say. He didn't want her to go. He wanted to tell her, but there was so much inside and all of it useless at this point. He was who he was. He couldn't change even if he wanted to. Full of regret and longing, he simply said, "Take care of yourself. Be happy. I want you to be happy."

Her bright smile wavered but she found it again.

"You, too. I mean that, Heath. I wish you every good thing. I'll pray for you." Her fingertips grazed his shirt sleeve. "I'll always pray for you."

Before he could delay her any longer, she slipped past him and out the door.

Cassie couldn't do this anymore. Her face was about to crack. She couldn't go on smiling and pretending all was well when she was crumbling inside.

Heath was leaving. Anything they might have had would go with him. Nothing she could say or do would stop him anyway. She was the gullible fool who'd married a drug dealer, and he was the DEA agent with the powerful sense of right and wrong. He must think she was stupidest woman on the planet, a woman whose new husband hadn't loved her enough to protect her from himself—if, indeed, Darrell had ever loved her at all.

For the rest of the afternoon she went through the motions of styling hair and friendly chitchat, none of which she remembered. All she could think of was the conversation with Heath. Like a revolving door, his words circled back again and again. He wanted her to be happy. How in the world did he think that was possible?

When the day finally ended, she got in her car and drove home to the ranch. Austin and Annalisa had taken the baby in for his checkup and hadn't yet returned, for which she was thankful. She didn't want to talk to another person. She didn't want anyone else to ask what was wrong.

Other than the faithful dogs, Cassie was blessedly alone. Restless, hurting, needing to think and pray, she changed clothes and saddled her horse for a long, private ride in the woods.

As the buckskin plodded up the trail, past the place where she'd learned the truth about her pseudo-marriage, the sun warmed her back and shone glossy on the horse's cream-colored neck. In the west, thunderheads built, huge and white and fluffy like a giant's cotton balls.

She passed a vivid orange butterfly weed, alive with thirsty monarchs. Black-eyed Susans lined the pathway, nodding their sunny faces toward her in greeting or perhaps in sympathy. June, the month of brides, was beautiful in the Ozarks. Normally, the natural beauty refreshed her. Today she simply prayed for peace.

Letting the horse take the lead, Cassie rode for a while without direction. When she heard the gush and roar of Whisper Falls, she realized this had been her destination all along.

She'd prayed here months ago to feel alive again. And look what that had brought her.

Dismounting, she tied the horse near a stand of grass at the base of the pool and started the ascent to that secret, spiritual place behind the foaming cascade of water.

Spray coated the rocks and dampened her face and hands. She was halfway up when the tears came, hot against the cold spray. God had answered her original prayer. The numbness was gone. She could feel again, but she had discovered the hard way that feeling hurt too much.

Too burdened and heavy to continue, she abandoned the climb and came instead to sit on the gray limestone rocks beside the pool at the base of the waterfall. Lacy ferns formed a canopy overhead. Knees drawn up under her chin, Cassie stared into the mirrored pool and prayed. She prayed to understand God's will and direction. She prayed for Heath, for his job and his future wherever his pursuit of justice might take him because she loved him. Most of all she prayed for God to tell her where to go from here. She couldn't trust her own judgment about men, not after the double fiascos.

Losing Darrell had been sharp and cruel and fast. Losing Heath was a slow, burning agony.

She couldn't return to business as usual. For so long after Darrell's death, she'd convinced herself that she was destined to be alone, the sister, the friend, the best salon operator in the Ozarks. No matter how much she enjoyed her work and her brother's family, her life felt empty and meaningless without love. Not love for love's sake. Without Heath.

But Heath was leaving. For all his sweet words and passionate kisses, like Darrell, he hadn't loved her. He'd needed her for an investigation, and love had been his weapon.

At the harsh reality of that bitter, bitter truth, Cassie put her face on her knees and grieved.

Chapter Fifteen

Heath hadn't accumulated much in his short few months in Whisper Falls. As usual, moving on should be easy.

He perched his hands on his hips and surveyed the little apartment. Not much to pack. A few boxes. His clothes and personal effects. His computer and TV. A man couldn't get along without his big TV. All of his belongings would fit in the back of the SUV. One trip and he'd be gone for good, never to look back.

He sank into the old brown chair and rubbed his palms over his face. Who was he kidding? He'd be looking back at Whisper Falls for years, maybe forever. A man didn't fall in love every day of the week and then forget about it.

He thought about driving out to Cassie's house. Maybe if they talked one more time, maybe things would work out.

Heath chuffed, a sharp sound in the silent apartment. "Who are you kidding?"

Nothing could work out with Cassie. He'd blown that chance. Even if he could go back and change what happened, he wouldn't. Oh, he might handle a few things differently, but Chapman and Carmichael were dirty and deserved justice. That was the Monroe way and he was duty bound. He couldn't expect Cassie to understand. Nor could he expect her to forget that he was the man responsible for sullying her husband's name.

A knock sounded at his door. Heath spun toward the entry, hope leaping in his chest, powerful and out of control. "Cassie."

He flipped the locks and yanked the door inward.

A dark, lanky man leaned against the door frame, grinning his ornery grin.

"Holt?" The pulse in Heath's throat began to slow as hope turned to curiosity. "What are you doing here?"

"Can't a man visit his big brother?"

"I'll be in Houston next week. You could see me then. Is something wrong? Is Mom all right?"

"Relax. The family's fine." His brother pushed away from the door to look toward the distant landscape. "Always wanted to see an Ozark summer. I thought I'd take the scenic drive."

Granted, Whisper Falls was a spectacular jewel in summer with birds and butterflies, flowers and trees a riot of color and life, but he didn't believe Holt for a second. "If that's true, where are Krissy and the kids?"

"Dropped them off in Texarkana to see her folks. She sends her love."

"So you came alone."

"Yep."

A thought that had been circling around Heath's brain popped to the front. "Mom sent you."

Holt's slow, wide smile eased up his cheeks. "Looks like my cover's made, but don't be blaming Mom. We might have talked but I brought myself. You gonna let me in?"

"Oh, sure." Surprised at himself for keeping his brother at the door, Heath stood to the side and let him enter.

"Small but nice." Holt did a quick survey, his PI gaze missing nothing. "Great TV. You get cable up here?"

"Satellite."

"HD?"

Heath smirked. "This is the Ozarks, not Timbuktu."

Holt barked a laugh and slapped his hand atop the TV. "Man, it's good to see you."

"Same here." Heath couldn't help smiling at his younger sibling. As a kid Holt had been as hyper as a terrier. The man was full of focused energy. "You're looking tan."

"Mexican beaches are great. Especially on your money." Holt smirked, a brotherly gotcha as he circled the room in his long, loose stride. "You're already packing?"

"Collecting boxes. I'll pack next week. You want a Coke or something?"

"Thanks. I'm parched." Holt folded his long body into the brown recliner and accepted the Coke Heath offered. "What's the hurry? A few weeks ago, you were loving on this quiet Ozark outpost."

"Things change." Heath flopped onto the couch. He was glad to see his brother again whatever the reasons. Phone calls were great, but in person rocked the house. He missed his family.

"The Mexican problem have anything to do with this sudden change?"

Heath dragged in a breath, exhaling on a gusty sigh. "Yeah. It does."

"Figured as much. Mom said you were pretty messed up about something and being the brilliant strategic thinker I am, I put two and two together and came up with the widow you're in love with."

Heath sat upright. "I never said I was in love with her."

"Yes, you did. You are. For the first time I can remember, you talked about a woman the way I talked about Krissy before I let her snag me. The way I still do." Holt tilted his Coke can like a finger point. "Stop trying to blow smoke at a master investigator, and give it to me straight. What's going on down here? Why are you jumping ship? How does the widow fit into all this? I told you she was clean and getting cleaner with each piece of the puzzle. So what's the problem, bro? Grab your lady and do-si-do."

Heath leaned back against the couch and stared up at the ceiling fan stirring the air in lazy swipes. Holt would keep pecking at him until he knew everything just the way he kept pecking at an investigation until all the parts fell into place.

"All right, here's the deal." His shoulders slumped. He, a decisive, life-and-death kind of guy couldn't run his own business anymore. "I messed up. I started seeing Cassie—Darrell Chapman's widow—for the wrong reasons. Mostly."

"What exactly does that mean?"

"I took her out at first to discover what she knew about her husband's operation."

His brother made a humming sound. "Dude, you are in a world of hurt."

"Yeah, well, thanks. That helps a lot."

Holt lifted both palms. "Just saying."

"At the time I thought she might be implicated in the drug ring. I liked her, enjoyed her company, but in the beginning I was all about the investigation."

"You let her think it was more?"

"Basically."

"Oh, son." Holt dragged out the word with a shake of his head. "Bad move. You're lucky to still be breathing."

Holt didn't know Cassie. She didn't fight. She retreated. Fighting might have felt better. Clear the air, let it rip.

"My plan was fatally flawed from the beginning. Instead of thinking small town, I acted like an undercover agent. Infiltrate, get to know her, pry out some information and move on. A normal investigation, exactly the kind I've done for years."

"You dated suspects?"

"No, I didn't date suspects!" The idea made him mad. Did his brother really think he was that low? When it was necessary, he befriended suspects and got to know them. He didn't date them. "Never."

"Until now. Until Cassie." Holt hummed again, his restless foot making slow circles. "You may have thought you were out to collect evidence, but the heart knew something you didn't."

"Tell me about it. I was blindsided. One day, I'm praying she reveals something in the case and the next I'm praying she's innocent and wondering how to get out of this mess without breaking her heart or mine."

Holt was nodding, his sharp, analytical mind filling in the blanks. "Then I call from Mexico with a break in the case. As the case unravels so does your romance. You get the bad guys, you lose the girl."

"Something like that." Heath studied the side of his condensing Coke can, recalling the look of shock and betrayal on Cassie's face. "Cassie didn't take the news well."

"You told her? That you'd dated her as part of the investigation?"

"Unintentionally." When Holt only stared as if he thought his older brother was an idiot, Heath shrugged. "She asked."

"Then she threw you out."

"Basically." Threw him out, turned her back, handed him his heart on the side of a summer-blessed hill.

He took a long, burning pull on his Coke.

"So you decided to quit your job and hit the road again. Forget about the woman."

"The DEA is what I know. What I'm good at. I apparently don't do so well with small towns and personal relationships. What other choice did I have?"

"You can dig in your heels and make this thing work. Call the lady up. Go see her."

"Won't happen. She hates me, not only because I dated her for the wrong reasons but for proving her husband was a do-wrong. She thought he was a superhero, a Romeo who doted on her." Heath tapped his chest with one finger. "I'm the guy who shattered her fairy-tale illusions. You think she's going to forgive that?"

"Have you told her how you feel, and that you hate what happened? That you wish you could change it?"

"She knows."

"Does she? Let me give you a piece of advice, bro. Women need words." When Heath stared at him with hopeless eyes, Holt clumped the soda can on the coffee table. "You know what I think?"

"No," Heath answered wryly. "But I'm pretty sure you're going to tell me."

"And you'd be right." Holt sniffed. "You're afraid of commitment. You love this girl, and you're afraid."

A quick jolt of anger had Heath leaning forward, fists clenched. "Don't be a moron. My middle name is commitment. To justice. To the drug war. To Dad's memory. My record stands for commitment. You know that better than anyone."

A tiny smile tilted the corners of Holt's mouth. "Stirred you up a little, didn't I?"

"Yeah." More than a little.

His brother tilted back in a long, easy stretch and crossed his legs. Only his dark eyes, brown points of radar, revealed his intensity. No wonder Holt was a good PI. He'd come on affable and relaxed while prying every bit of information from a source. And then, bam! Like a mouse trap, he sprang.

"The family had a meeting, Heath."

"About me?" Heath touched a hand to his chest, surprised again. "A meeting?"

Holt nodded. "Heston and Mom wanted to come along on my little scenic drive. I told them I'd handle this first round. But if they need to come down and talk to you, I can give them a call."

"What is this? Some kind of intervention?" He felt a little horrified by the thought. He was the man of the family, not some troubled teen or struggling alcoholic.

"Take it how you want. We're worried. All your adult life, you've been married to your job, taking the worst assignments in the most dangerous, darkest places."

"Nothing wrong with that. Somebody's got to do it."

"Other agents get married, buy a house, settle down. Not you. You've never even owned a dog. Man, there is something sick about that."

"Lots of people don't own dogs."

"You like dogs. You're the kid who slept with a flea-bitten mutt until you left for college."

"Addie didn't have fleas."

"No, she had puppies and you wanted to keep them all."

True. He missed having a dog and had enjoyed hanging out with Cassie's friendly, furry trio. "Dogs need lots of attention. I wasn't around that much to take care of one."

"My point exactly. When you left the agency and moved to Whisper Falls, Mom was overjoyed. Finally, her eldest was growing roots. When she learned you were dating someone special—" Holt raised his hands in a hallelujah.

"Courtesy of my big-mouthed brother, I suppose."

"Of course." Holt showed his teeth. "Here's the deal in a nutshell, Heath. You've allowed Dad's death to take over your life. It's time to let it go."

The statement rocked Heath. Let it go? Abandon his vow to honor his father in exchange for personal happiness? "I can't. Dad was my hero. He deserves justice."

"We've given him justice, Heath. All of us boys are doing our part to fight crime. All of us honor him every day of our lives. You're the only one who's taken the responsibility too far."

"Not possible."

"Yes, it is. Dad was first and foremost a family man.

He loved us, Heath. He wanted the world for his boys and Mom."

"Yes." Heath rubbed a hand over his whiskers. "Yes, he did. He was the best."

"Do you think you're the only son who loved him that much?"

The question struck him in the chest like a bullet. "No, of course not."

"Do you think Heston and I don't do enough? That we don't do our part to honor Dad's memory and legacy?"

"I don't think that at all."

"Good, because I'd have to take you down and spit in your ear if you even suggested such a thing."

The silly statement lightened the mood. Heath grunted, remembering some of the ornery things brothers did to each other.

"Dad would be proud of you both."

"I believe he would. Being an honest member of law enforcement *and* a good family man is the way I honor our dad. Do you hear what I'm saying, Heath?"

"Maybe I do." Heath nodded, the light slowly dawning. "Yes, I think I do."

All these years he'd subjugated the personal side of his life in pursuit of justice for his father. He'd believed with all his heart that Dad would have expected that much from the oldest son. But Holt was right. Dad wouldn't have wanted that. Dad was a man first, a cop second. Somewhere along the line, Heath had turned the priorities around.

"Tell me one thing, bro," Holt said softly. "Do you really want to leave Whisper Falls?"

"No." There was the truth. A truth that would, indeed, set him free. The weight he'd carried for weeks, perhaps years, lifted from his shoulders. "I was happy here until—"

Holt pushed up from the chair to clamp a long, hard hand on Heath's shoulder. With understanding in his voice, he said, "Maybe you should give that lady of yours a call."

Hope plummeted. Truth or not, Cassie and he were over. "She won't answer."

"Then go see her. Talk to her. Make her listen. At least try."

That faint hope glimmered back to life. He didn't know if Cassie would ever forgive him for being the man who used her to bring down her husband, but he was going to find out.

Bent over the changing table, Cassie fastened the tabs of Levi's tiny diaper. Fresh from his bath, the little man smelled sweet and clean and his translucent skin gleamed under the overhead light. Even after his scary start, her nephew was thriving enough that Austin and Annalisa had left him with Aunt Cassie to have their first date night since the birth.

"Aunt Cassie loves that idea," she said as she swaddled him in the soft, blue blanket and then picked him up. She inhaled the fragrance of him, thankful to God that he was healthy and strong. "You're a handsome boy. Just like your daddy. What?" She pretended to listen. "Oh, if you insist. I'll give your pretty mama some credit, too."

Tootsie, the poodle, lifted her head from the floor and cocked an ear.

Cassie grinned, both at the poodle and her own silliness. At only a few weeks old, Levi still looked more like a wrinkled old man than either of his parents, but someday, he'd be a lady-killer.

"You're going to be a gentleman, too. Not like some men I could name." Men who would lie and use women. Men who put their own agendas before the women they claimed to love.

The bitter root she'd been fighting dug a little deeper. She'd prayed for God to take away the anger and hurt, and she wanted to understand. She'd even talked to her close friend Haley about the situation. Sweet Haley had sympathized but advised her to look at things from Heath's point of view. Then she'd told her to get in there and fight for the man she loved.

"Heath's point of view? Really?" She had no idea what that was, but if he cared for her, he wouldn't be leaving town. He wouldn't have misled her.

And Cassie had no fight left in her.

Levi started to fuss and Cassie carried him to the rocker. With a toe to the floor, she set them in motion, snuggling the soft bundle to her chest. "Better to focus on you than men. Even if you will be a man someday."

As if he understood, Levi squinted midnight-blue eyes at her for a full five seconds before they crossed. Cassie smiled. He was so adorable, her nephew. She loved being an aunt, was thankful to have this opportunity to love a child. Grateful because she was done with men. Levi was as close as she'd get to having children. "So I'd better enjoy you, little mister." She kissed him on the tiny nose.

The house was quiet. No TV. No music player. Tootsie curled on the rug beside the changing table, chin on her paws, listening with drowsy eyes. Cassie enjoyed the house like this, when she could hear the air vibrate and the baby's breaths.

She rocked the infant, letting her mind drift to the pretty artwork on one wall—a night scene of the moon and stars above a silver lake lapping against an empty, peaceful shore. Though she didn't want to go there in her memories, she recalled the last full night of Darrell's life as they'd strolled a moonlit beach, hand in hand. He'd been especially quiet and when she'd questioned, he'd blamed fatigue.

Something tickled at the edge of her memory, some featherlike itch of disquiet. Nothing Darrell had said but a feeling she'd experienced when they'd met another couple on the beach. A tight string of tension had vibrated in the balmy, ocean-scented air, though the conversation had been casual, an impromptu meeting of two couples on a Mexican beach.

In the aftermath of tragedy, Cassie had forgotten the encounter, but now she realized something had been off-kilter. The woman had complimented her brightly flowered skirt, a gift Darrell had purchased in the hotel souvenir shop. Nothing unusual about that. The odd thing had been the man's comment. What had he said?

Something about the price of roses had gone up.

The woman had laughed and said, "Oh, but you'll still buy them, won't he, Darrell? No matter the cost."

Darrell had said something in return, but his laugh had been dry and forced. And his hand against hers had been sweaty. She'd not thought much of it at the time. A brief moment on a beach with strangers.

Later, Cassie had asked about the couple and Darrell had denied knowing them, saying they must have overheard her call him by name. She'd believed the easy explanation.

But now, in the light of what she knew, Cassie didn't think so. Darrell, she was convinced, had known the pair. The exchange about roses rang a strange, unsettling bell that echoed in her head. There was something. *Something.*

She gently placed Levi in his crib and hurried to her bedroom and the box containing photos and mementoes of a husband she had never really known. Darrell had lied to her, betrayed her, pretended to be someone he wasn't. It was time for her to stop protecting him. She'd come to accept that, as painful as it was. Somewhere in this box could be the answer.

She removed the items she'd copied for Heath and rifled through them, studying each one with a fresh eye. Photos, receipts, notes. Frustrated, she dumped the remaining items onto the bed. A colorful pair of maracas, whimsical, useless keepsakes like the jumping beans and a plastic drinking cup emblazoned with the hotel's logo. Souvenirs of a honeymoon that began in joy and ended in despair.

She gave the maracas a shake then put them aside to once more search through the bits and pieces of paper— the hotel bill, receipts.

She turned over a receipt, and there it was, though she'd looked at the page many times without seeing what was there. A small, handwritten notation on the delivery confirmation for a dozen roses, signed by Darrell. The air whooshed out of her lungs as she read, "The price of roses has gone up." And then a number to contact for more information.

She'd thought her new husband so wonderfully generous to order flowers for her every day. Now, she dug through the box for the other receipts, despising her suspicions. Hands shaking, she found another cryptic reference to roses and money and one with the words, "Delivery by Dias tomorrow night at 8. Room 2."

They hadn't stayed in room two.

Now she understood the note she'd found at the tornado site. Darrell had somehow used his gift of roses as a means to pass messages to drug contacts.

What a naive fool she'd been.

Heath was right. But like Darrell, Heath had used her for his purposes. She was doubly foolish and doubly humiliated.

At three rapid barks from outside, she shoved the receipts into her pocket. Though too early for Austin and Annalisa to return, she couldn't chance them seeing her tears. They'd never understand without the explanation she wasn't ready to give.

Tootsie shot off the bed, a furry cannonball, and ran for the door, yapping. Levi awakened, startled and began to cry. Dashing at her moist eyes, Cassie hurried to the nursery and picked him up.

"Shh. Shh," she murmured, gratified when his cries ceased the moment she snuggled him to her chest and went toward the barking dogs.

A shiny black SUV pulled into the drive. Her heart leapt, stuttered, hurt. Her legs felt like water.

"Heath." Quickly, she tamped back the glad reaction. He wasn't hers. He didn't love her. He was probably bringing her more bad news about the investigation.

Oh, Heath. You were right. And I don't want you to leave. But he would. She wasn't enough to keep him here.

Resolved to be strong, to give him the evidence and

let him go without tears, Cassie stepped out on the porch and asked, "What are you doing here?"

Halfway to the porch, Heath froze in his tracks. Hers wasn't the greeting he'd hoped for. Yet there Cassie stood holding a baby and looking so motherly and beautiful, his whole being strained toward her. She was what he wanted—no, needed—in his life more than anything. This woman, a future together. The family they could make.

Holt was right. After God, a family and a woman to love kept a man grounded and filled. Heath had been running on empty for a long time.

On the drive from town he'd planned his speech, but now, with Cassie staring holes through him, the carefully arranged words abandoned him.

He started toward her, watched her mist-green eyes go from hurt resistance to bewilderment and then to resignation. Cradling the baby in the crook of her left arm, she reached into her pocket, withdrew a rumpled stack of paper and thrust it at him.

"You'll want to follow up on these, especially the phone number. I think Dias was Darrell's contact." Her voice was stiff and cool. She swallowed, revealing her stress. "Maybe his murderer."

She'd remembered something. He could see it in her eyes, the despair of knowing the truth. But he hadn't come about the case. At the moment, he didn't care about anything but her.

Almost rudely, he pushed her hand aside. "Later. I'm not here about the investigation."

"No?" She stepped back in surprise, wary as a doe. "Really? I thought that's all that mattered to you."

"The case can wait. This can't. I can't."

"Then why are you here? To say your goodbyes? Because I don't need that, Heath."

Her lips trembled and he despaired, knowing he caused her pain.

But a woman needed the words. Wasn't that what Holt advised?

"What if I'm the one who needs something?" He took a step toward her. She backed away.

"I can't help you anymore. Take the information and leave." She thrust the papers toward him again.

Really frustrated now, he stalked her until she backed into the wall of the house and further escape was impossible. "I need you, Cassie. You and only you. Forget the investigation, forget everything else."

Her mouth opened. Her lips trembled as her stoic expression began to melt like candle wax. She spun away. Her shoulders arched, heaved, and Heath berated himself. Was she crying?

"Cassie, don't. Please." He touched her shoulder. She stiffened but her body quaked.

From the corral, a horse whinnied, tail swishing at flies. Flashy pink flowers sprawled along the porch railing. Butterflies dipped and curtsied in the evening sun, supping the sweet-scented nectar. A man with his training missed none of the details, but he only had eyes for the woman.

He took her elbow and gently turned her to face him. "Cassie."

She shook her head and made a feeble attempt to pull away. "The baby."

"Can we go inside and talk? About us."

Her expression was stark and wounded, like a kicked puppy. "There is no us."

Heath's heart plummeted. Holt was wrong. Cassie wouldn't have him back. She wouldn't forgive him.

As if he felt the adult tension, the baby began to wail, a high-pitched, red-faced squall that split the air. Both of the big dogs winced and disappeared around the corner of the house.

Without a word, Cassie went inside the house and left Heath standing alone. He felt like an idiot for coming, but better an idiot than never to know.

Jaw tight, he pounded on the door and then without permission, opened it and walked into the living room. He smelled pizza and would have smiled if the situation wasn't breaking his heart. His Cassie loved pizza. But she was nowhere in sight.

He raised his voice above the baby's cry. "I'm not leaving until you talk to me."

From down the hall, toward the nursery she'd proudly shown him, the baby quieted. A large sunburst clock above the fireplace ticked. The peach-colored poodle padded in to sniff his pants leg and then disappear into the nursery.

He'd already made a fool of himself. "Why stop now?" he murmured.

If Cassie wasn't going to come out, he'd go to her. With nothing more to lose but his pride, Heath strode to the open nursery.

"We're going to talk."

Cassie, leaned in to settle her nephew, turned her head. Her silky black hair swept across her cheeks. "Don't, Heath. This is hard enough without..."

"Without what? Without telling you that I made a

terrible mistake? That I love you and if I could change what happened, the way it happened, I would? That I'd do anything to make things right?"

Slowly, she straightened, and Heath knew he finally had her attention.

"You do? You would?"

"I would. My entire adult life has been about my work and bringing honor to my dad. I was wrong about that, too. Life is so much more. Family and home and the right woman to love." When she didn't move, he said, "If you want me to grovel, I will."

"No." Then more emphatically, "No. Never."

But she didn't help him, either. "Then what will it take to win you back? What do you want? Name your price, Cassie, and it's yours."

She took a step toward him, reddened eyes swimming with emotion. "All I ever wanted was for you to love me. Truly love me."

"I do. I should have told you everything from the beginning, but I didn't know I'd love you this way. I've never felt like this about a woman before. Forgive me, Cassie. Let me be the man you need, the one you love."

"I don't know what's true anymore." She closed her eyes and put a hand to her forehead. A frown formed there, furrowing her brow. "I was wrong about Darrell and then about you. How do I know this time is right?"

He closed the gap until they stood a breath apart, not touching, but with everything in him, Heath longed to hold her and make up for all the hurt he'd caused. He longed to smooth away her frown with a kiss and make her smile again.

He tapped the place on his left chest. "Listen to your heart. You know. Hear my voice, see this man ready to go to his knees to gain your trust again." To prove his worth, he did exactly that. He went to his knees in front of her, took her hand and said, "I love you. After what you've been through, you'll say it's too soon and I promise not to rush you, but I know you're the one for me. I want to marry you, Cassie."

A gasp escaped her parted lips. "You do?"

"With all my heart. Say you love me, too, or tell me to hit the road. Your choice."

She stared at him for such a long moment that his stomach tumbled. In slow motion, she followed him down to her knees. The frown fled and wonder filled her expression.

"You're right." She touched the place over her heart. "I do know. In here." A beautiful smile lit her face. "I wish things had been different, but I can't hold a grudge. I love you, Heath. And I say yes."

A flood of joy and relief and thanksgiving rushed through him greater than any adrenaline thrill.

With a tenderness he didn't know possible, he cupped the face of his love and joined his lips to her soft, trembling ones. When she moved into his embrace and held him tight, he owned the world.

Epilogue

Two years later

On a Sunday afternoon in late spring, the skies filled with dark clouds and rain drenched the tulips as thunder echoed through the hillsides. The Blackberry River gushed over Whisper Falls and like a silver, curling ribbon circled past the town of the same name.

The people gathered in the fellowship hall of New Life Christian Church were accustomed to stormy springs and so they'd come anyway to share in the day's festivities.

Despite the damp outdoors, the interior of the hall was cozy, if humid, and thick with the scent of barbecued ribs from the newest restaurant in their growing town, Tony's Pig Stand. Haley's whimsical fairy vases centered each pink-clothed table with flowers from her garden. Annalisa and Lana had outdone themselves on the baby table. A pink and dark chocolate cake surrounded by chocolate-covered strawberries sat in the middle of tablecloth caught up with a bow. Above the table a printed banner proclaimed, "It's a girl!"

Children dashed through the building in a game of tag regardless of their mothers' efforts to calm them. Voices chattered and laughter boomed in harmony with the thunder.

Cassie felt as if she was living in a dream as her friends and customers and family milled around the large hall in celebration of the child she'd never expected to have. They'd invited everyone they knew, and she was gratified for Heath's sake that the men had come, too.

"The guys will probably end up at the game tables in back," she said, smiling up at her husband of eighteen months.

"Not till they get their fill of these ribs." Heath pumped his eyebrows. "Gotta make up for not giving them a big wedding when we got married."

"True." They'd waited six months before exchanging vows. Heath claimed they were the longest six months of his life, but they'd gotten to know each other better and had time to fall deeper in love. When the day came, they'd promised "until death do us part" with a lifetime of conviction. The wedding had been small and spiritual with only family and closest friends in attendance, but this baby shower was huge!

"Do you think we ordered enough ribs and potato salad?"

"If we didn't, you can always call the Pizza Pan and order out thick pan pepperoni. You still have them on speed dial, don't you?"

Cassie grinned. "Don't torture me. I'm trying to eat healthy."

Heath placed a hand on her belly. At six months

along, the baby wasn't yet huge but was more than the speed bump of a couple months ago.

"Proud of you." He kissed her on the cheek. He knew she'd become an unlikely champion of healthy eating and exercise and had even given up her highest heels for the sake of their unborn child. "Now, I'd better mingle with the guys or they'll call me a sissy."

She laughed and gave him a push. "Go. I want to talk babies with the girls anyway."

She went to the clutch of friends stacking baby gifts and keeping track of who brought what. Haley, Annalisa, Lana Davis and Louise directed the party, and all she had to do was enjoy.

"You'll have a ton of thank-you notes to send."

"Lucky me." And she meant that. Her life was blessed. Many friends and a wonderful family.

"Is that Heath's brother he's talking to?" Haley asked.

Cassie turned to look. "That one is Heston. Holt is with his mom, the dark-haired lady talking to my parents. They're with Miss Evelyn and Uncle Digger. See them over there?"

"Gorgeous men," Haley said.

Cassie bumped her shoulder. "You have a gorgeous man, too."

"Don't I know it? Look at how handsome he looks juggling the baby in one arm with Rose on his back."

"He's a good dad. How does Rose feel about having a brother?" Creed and Haley had a new baby boy, adopted two months ago.

"At four, she likes to play the big-sister role. But she might be a little jealous. We're working on that." Her auburn-haired friend gazed at her husband and children with such love, Cassie teared up. But then, everything made her tear up since she'd gotten pregnant.

She'd even cried when Lana had sung the national anthem at Pumpkin Fest last fall, her first clue that she was expecting a baby.

She sniffed and dabbed at her eyes with the balls of her hands. "I am the happiest woman in the world."

"Oh, honey." Lana gave her a quick hug. The tough girl had turned to a sugar cookie since her marriage to Davis Turner. She still wrote articles for the newspaper but her songwriting had found success in Nashville and she made frequent trips there for business. Cassie knew she grieved for the twin sister who'd never come home. They were still praying and believing that someday she would. "I'm happy for you."

"When are you and Davis going to have a baby?"

Since having Levi, now a toddler cowboy, Annalisa wanted all her friends to have a baby.

Lana blushed at Annalisa's question and reflexively touched her stomach. Four pairs of eyes followed the gesture.

"Are you pregnant, too?" Cassie asked.

"Shh. Don't say anything." Lana, unable to hide the grin, put a finger to her lips. "We're not ready to announce yet, and today is your day. But yes, I am."

The four women squealed and Cassie grabbed her friend in a hug, her belly bumping into Lana. "This only makes today more precious."

Lana fanned her flaming face with both hands. "I can't believe it. Sydney and Paige are twelve and Nathan's ten. Davis and I thought we might not have any more, but God had different ideas. I really, really wanted a baby, and Davis is over the moon." She laughed. "And a little shell-shocked."

"This is wonderful. I'll save all my baby things for you," Haley said. "Cassie can save hers, too. That way, whether you have a boy or a girl, you're covered."

"Speaking of baby things," Lana said, obviously to take the attention from her thrilling announcement. "Let's open presents!"

And so they did. Though they couldn't corral the gleeful children who were running on a sugar high from the cupcakes, the men and woman gathered around the mile-high gift table. The men, with good-natured machismo, rolled their eyes at the frilly, lacy clothes and needled their assistant police chief about the overdose of pink.

"The only thing keeping them inside is the storm," Cassie joked.

Standing behind her, Heath leaned down to whisper, "And the fact that I carry a gun."

Cassie giggled. From that wonderful day at the ranch, he'd never looked back. JoEtta had been thrilled at Heath's decision to remain on the force, and he'd become a terrific assistant police chief, a role he seemed to relish.

Cassie knew he'd rather be on the golf course today or at home watching baseball. The fact that he was at a baby shower, with her, made her love him more. This was, as he'd told her, his baby, too, and he didn't plan to miss a moment.

By the time the baby shower ended and people drifted away, amidst good wishes and promises of cookouts and dinners and haircuts, the storm outside had passed.

"You're tired, babe. We'll load the truck. You take it easy." Heath hoisted a new car seat while his brothers and their wives each gathered up boxes and bags.

Cassie paid him no mind. If her husband had his way, she'd stay in the recliner for nine months and knit. Her hunky man was a doting husband. "I'll bring the light stuff."

Arms loaded with diapers, she followed her husband out into the rain-washed evening. A glow gilded the cool, fresh atmosphere.

"There you go," Heath's brother Holt, whom she'd come to adore for his easy, teasing manner, slammed the truck's back door. "Everything is loaded."

"You guys go on," Cassie said. "I want to make one more pass through the hall and make sure everything is restored to order."

Heath's mother took Cassie by the shoulders and kissed her cheek. "We'll meet you at the house. You look beautiful, dear."

Those pesky tears sprang to Cassie's eyes. She laughed to cover her embarrassment. "Thank you, Kate, for everything, especially for your son."

Kate gazed fondly at Heath who had circled around the car to chat with his brothers and Austin. "You're good for him, Cassie. He's happy now. Finally."

"He's made me happy, too. I can't begin to explain."

"You don't have to." Kate patted her arm. "See you at the house."

With a slam of car doors and engines, the last of the shower guests drove away, leaving Cassie and Heath alone. Cassie hugged herself, heart full, as her husband came toward her.

"I have something for you, but I wanted to give it to

you when we're alone. With our families at the house, this may be our only moment today."

"Another present?"

"No, not exactly a gift, but closure." He tugged her hands free and held them, facing her. "Louis Carmichael was arrested last week in Arizona, trying to cross the border. Holt knew what this meant to us, Cassie, so he flew down there and spoke with Carmichael. Don't ask me how, but my brother has a way of getting people to talk."

"For which I will ever be thankful," Cassie said, knowing Holt was responsible for their reunion.

"Yes, well, Carmichael spilled some interesting beans. He blamed Darrell for ruining a good operation because of some woman."

"Me?"

"Apparently Darrell wanted out of the operation after he met you. Carmichael insisted he finish what he started or he'd tell you everything."

"And that last trip cost Darrell his life."

"Carmichael says he tried a double cross. Not smart and he paid for it. The man wasn't perfect, but he loved you, Cassie. You can stop kicking yourself for being fooled by him. He cared for you."

She laid her head on his shoulder and considered this latest revelation. Everything that had happened brought them to this moment. "He still used our honeymoon as a cover."

"Perhaps he did. But it's over now. You can be at peace with that part of your past."

"Yes." She'd long ago moved beyond the heartache and shame but Heath's news brought her peace and a much needed sense of closure. Carmichael was in jail and Darrell was not quite the villain she'd thought. She leaned back a little to meet her husband's gaze. "Thank you for telling me."

"My pleasure." He kissed her ear and sighed softly. "We've weathered some storms, haven't we, sweetheart?"

"Yes, we have. And we've come through stronger because of them."

She thought back to that stormy night when they'd met on a rain-slicked county road. To the tornado that ripped past town and opened up the can of worms left by Darrell and Louis. To the storm within from the hurt and heartache and confusion in the aftermath. Now, today, on the day of their baby shower another storm had rattled the windows and shook the skies. And as Heath said, they'd weathered them all.

"Look," he said, pointing over her shoulder.

Cassie spun in his arms, as much as a pregnant woman can spin, to see a glorious rainbow arching above the little town of Whisper Falls.

"God's promise," she breathed, awed. "So beautiful."

"It reminds me of us." Heath slipped his arms around her from the back, his hands resting on their baby. "Life brings storms but there's always a rainbow. You're my rainbow, Cassie."

She leaned back against her man, resting in his strength and reveling in his love. Indeed, she thought as she looked at the glorious bow of color against the blue sky, they'd faced their share of storms, but the aftermath had been the most beautiful rainbow of all. A never-ending rainbow called love.

* * * * *

WE HOPE YOU ENJOYED THIS

LOVE INSPIRED®

BOOK.

If you were **inspired** by this

uplifting, **heartwarming** romance,

be sure to look for all six Love

Inspired® books every month.

www.LoveInspired.com

"What's your name?"

The woman's eyes widened and her hand shook so that she could barely hold the mug of tea without spilling it. She set it carefully on the coffee table. "I don't—I don't know my name."

"How can you not know your own name?" Caleb asked. "Do you know where you live?"

"Nein."

"What were you doing out there?"

"Out where?"

"Where was your coat and your *kapp?*"

"Caleb, now's not the time to interrogate the poor girl." His *mamm* stood and moved beside her on the couch. She picked up the small book of poetry. "You were carrying this, when Caleb found you. Do you remember it?"

"I don't. This was mine?"

"Found it in the snow," Caleb said. "Right beside where you collapsed."

"So it must be mine."

Caleb noticed that the woman's hands trembled as she opened the cover and stared down at the first page. With one finger, she traced the handwriting there.

"Rachel. I think my name is Rachel."

Rachel let her fingers brush over the word again and again. Rachel. Yes, that was her name. She was sure of it. She remembered writing it in the front of the book—she'd used a pen that her *mamm* had given her. She could almost picture herself, somewhere else. She could almost see her mother.

"My *mamm* gave me the pen and the book…for my birthday, I think. I wrote my name—wrote it right here."

"Your *mamm*. So you remember her?"

"Praise be to *Gotte*," Caleb's *dat* said, a smile spreading across his face.

"Is there someone we can call? If you remember the name of your bishop…" Caleb had sat down in the rocker his mother had vacated and was staring at her intensely.

They all were.

She closed her eyes, hoping to feel the memory again. She tried to see the room or the house or the people, but the memory had receded as quickly as it had come, leaving her with a pulsing headache.

She struggled to keep the feelings of panic at bay. Her heart was hammering, and her hands were shaking, and she could barely make sense of the questions they were pelting at her.

Who were these people?

Where was she?

Who was she?

She needed to remember what had happened.

She needed to go home.

Don't miss
Amish Christmas Memories *by Vannetta Chapman,*
available December 2018 wherever
Love Inspired® *books and ebooks are sold.*

www.LoveInspired.com

LIEXP1118